*"Come, kiss me, Haley Bennett..."*
*Sheik Zayn murmured. "I'm*
*starving for the taste of you...."*

She was losing it, Haley thought, and would continue to do so if she kept looking into those enigmatic eyes. How compelling they were, how beautiful. She sat up straight on the bed, her feet tucked beneath her, and placed her hands tentatively on his broad shoulders. "Will you be satisfied with one kiss of welcome from your prisoner?"

His brow rose. "Does one simple kiss frighten you?"

Haley slid her palms along the smooth, bare skin of his shoulders. "It could...." she said deliberately. She moistened her lips and looked at his mouth. Very slowly she closed the gap that separated them. She bent her head and took the soft edge of his ear between her teeth.

Then she bit him.

"I want *out* of here!" she growled.

Dear Reader,

Holiday greetings from all of us at Silhouette Books to all of you. And along with my best wishes, I wanted to give you a present, so I put together six of the best books ever as your holiday surprise. Emilie Richards starts things off with *Woman Without a Name*. I don't want to give away a single one of the fabulous twists and turns packed into this book, but I *can* say this: You've come to expect incredible emotion, riveting characters and compelling storytelling from this award-winning writer, and this book will not disappoint a single one of your high expectations.

And in keeping with the season, here's the next of our HOLIDAY HONEYMOONS, a miniseries shared with Desire and written by Carole Buck and Merline Lovelace. *A Bride for Saint Nick* is Carole's first Intimate Moments novel, but you'll join me in wishing for many more once you've read this tale of a man who thinks he has no hope of love, only to discover—just in time for Christmas—that a wife and a ready-made family are his for the asking.

As for the rest of the month, what could be better than new books from Sally Tyler Hayes and Anita Meyer, along with the contemporary debuts of historical authors Elizabeth Mayne and Cheryl St.John? So sit back, pick up a book and start to enjoy the holiday season. And don't forget to come back next month for some Happy New Year reading right here at Silhouette Intimate Moments, where the best is always waiting to be unwrapped.

Yours,

*Leslie Wainger*

Leslie Wainger
Senior Editor and Editorial Coordinator

Please address questions and book requests to:
Silhouette Reader Service
U.S.: 3010 Walden Ave., P.O. Box 1325, Buffalo, NY 14269
Canadian: P.O. Box 609, Fort Erie, Ont. L2A 5X3

# THE SHEIK AND THE VIXEN

## ELIZABETH MAYNE

*Silhouette*®

INTIMATE™ MOMENTS®

Published by Silhouette Books

**America's Publisher of Contemporary Romance**

SILHOUETTE BOOKS

ISBN 0-373-07755-6

THE SHEIK AND THE VIXEN

## ELIZABETH MAYNE

is a native San Antonian, who knew by the age of eleven how to spin a good yarn, according to every teacher she ever faced. She's spent the last twenty years making up for all her transgressions on the opposite side of the teacher's desk, and the last five working exclusively with troubled children. She particularly loves an ethnic hero and married one of her own eighteen years ago. But it wasn't until their youngest, a daughter, was two years old that life calmed down enough for this writer to fulfill the dream she'd always had of becoming a novelist. Since then, she has published four Harlequin Historical novels. *The Sheik and the Vixen* is her first contemporary for Silhouette.

To D. Andrew and John Jr.
Love, Kaye

# *Chapter 1*

"Lordy, if that don't look like the backside of Terralingua Canyon I'll eat my hat."

Haley Bennett cocked her ear to the voice in her headset and peered at the barren, rocky earth thousands of feet below. "Roger, Dad. Looks like West Texas, all right. Can't say when I've seen more dust, unless it's that time you made the whole family go camping. Didn't Mom threaten you with divorce to get us back to civilization?"

"Kid, you ain't old enough to remember that!"

"Wanna bet?" Haley Bennett laughed as her father cleared gravel from his throat and sputtered.

"What I'm saying is, there ain't that much difference between land here and back home in West Texas. Dry, Lord a'mighty, there ain't a drop of water from Pecos to El Paso. Wouldn't want to make an unplanned landing in either place."

"I read that loud and clear. There's the pipeline."

"That's our landmark then, we follow it all the way to little ol' Coo-way-tee International." The depth of his Texas drawl made Haley chuckle. "I reckon we'll be at the Persian Gulf in a quarter hour."

Haley yawned as her eyes traveled across the state-of-the-art console, noting fuel status, engine pressure, air temperature and altimeter readings. Locked onto autopilot, she didn't have much to keep the tedium at bay.

"Don't you go getting sleepy on me, baby-girl." Her father's drawl came again through her high-tech headset.

Haley knew how to shake off a sleepy spell and break the monotony of flying on autopilot. Take manual control. She nosed into the golden dawn and flew the Vixen 2000-2 in a roundabout figure eight, under, over and around the plodding, straight-as-an-arrow course of her father's Vixen. "Who's sleepy?" she challenged. "Wanna race upside down to the gulf?"

"Settle down, Haley-girl. I don't want a single bolt, rivet or widget rattled out of place in either of these two ladies."

"The crystal wouldn't dare rattle in the galley!" Haley teased. It wouldn't, either, not with the velveteen-covered foam casings she'd designed within each cubby. The only way any breakage would occur on a Bennett Vixen was if it was deliberate.

Grinning over the force of G's pressing her against the molded seat, Haley flew a wide elliptical orbit around her father's identical jet. A rush of adrenaline to her brain obliterated the last trace of boredom.

"Don't you hate turning these babies over to someone else, Pop?" she asked in a fond, whimsical voice.

"Hate it? Naw. What would I do with a flying boardroom? I do all my arguing at the kitchen table."

"Well, I mind. I could use a toy like this."

"Toy?" Jim snorted. "It's time you stopped playing with toys and giving me ulcers and settled down to give me grandkids instead. Cut it out, Haley. Girl! You just made me spill my coffee."

Haley executed two barrel rolls in quick succession, talking while the horizon tilted and spun. "Don't look to me for grandkids. I just got started playing the field."

"Hmmph! At twenty-four you're old enough to have exhausted the field."

"Why, you devil!" Haley didn't try to keep the laugh out of her voice. "I'm as innocent as the day I was born!"

"You just pull back on that throttle, sugar bear. We've come all the way from Texas with no mistakes. There won't be time to spruce up when we land. The minute your godfather, Uncle Jack cracks the door, there'll be a hundred of those sheiks swarming over both these ladies, going over them with a fine-tooth comb."

"I know, I know," Haley grumbled good-naturedly. She came even with her father's jet, surrendering the lead.

The planes would get all the attention. Not even Miss America stood a chance of being noticed with a lady like Haley's Vixen 2000 gleaming on the tarmac. When it came to her father's clients and their craving for fast, sleek machines to fly through the air in splendor and ease, Haley fully understood a mere woman's second-place rating. It didn't do any good to get jealous, either.

There was a time when she'd thought being extraordinarily tall and having corn-silk hair that hung inches past her waist ought to have gained her some notice. That was before she'd realized that men who hungered for jet speed and open skies, who pitted their wits against the bonds of earth, craved women second, third, and in some cases, not at all. She suffered from the same fever. It was a rare man indeed who could entice her into giving up those spare precious hours of flight time so necessary to keep her skills equal to the requirements of her licenses.

It took only a couple of sorties into the world of aviation to learn that jet pilots were as arrogant as she was. Cocky, spoiled and self-confident, Haley Bennett was a different class of female entirely, an aviator—and a darn good one—not to mention she was Jim Bennett's youngest brat.

That she'd inherited her traits from the man flying the lead plane made her doubly proud. But those same traits made it doubly hard to find a soul mate who could fit into her world.

Haley's trouble was, she'd never settle for a man who didn't have the same passion for flying that she had. It was the Bennett curse. She had resigned herself to the curse at sixteen, when she'd earned her first solo license and her boyfriend of the moment had puked in her Piper Cub.

A lot of soap and water had washed out on the tarmac in the eight years since. The test of true love inevitably was a zip around South Texas skyways. Guys who turned green in air pockets, rainstorms or barrel rolls just couldn't cut it in Haley Jane's book.

To make matters worse, like her brothers and sisters, Haley could dismantle and put back together any engine that man had thus far devised. Mechanical ability flowed in their bloodlines, even though their mother didn't know a ratchet from a spanner.

Easing off the throttle, Haley said, "Seeing as how we're almost there, I'll slap on my serious face. What's the first order of business when we land?"

"Selling Vixens!" Jim affirmed. "It's my intention to write up another twenty of these babies before I sack out and let you fly me home in the goose."

"That old rattletrap." Haley scoffed at the company's albatross, an ancient DC-7. She squinted at the golden light reflected off the desert. "I should be so lucky somebody ditched the goose in the middle of this desert."

"Ha, you know better. Jack keeps it gassed up and raring to go just for you."

"I'm not going anywhere until I've had twelve hours' sleep, two steaks and a quart of beer," Haley insisted. "And a shower and a change of clothes."

"You'll be crying for a featherbed next. You're getting soft, Haley-girl." Jim's chuckle was warm, mellow. He was right proud of his youngest daughter and her flawless blueprint designs. She made precision and accuracy of flight design seem carefree to the point of accidental.

His Haley Jane was a perfectionist—a stubborn, muleheaded, aggravating female genius, to boot. Jim Bennett had to search sometimes to find anything to complain about. Then Haley would crop up and do somethin' impulsive, somethin' so all-fired irrational—a hundred percent female—that every one of his gaskets could blow. Like this trip.

James Matthew Bennett, Jr., Jim's eldest son, the heir-apparent of Bennett Enterprises was supposed to be flying the Vixen 2000-2 to Kuwait. But that was before Matt, the thirty-three-year-old, levelheaded right-hand man to Bennett Industries' volatile redheaded CEO, had been goaded into a tennis match the day before yesterday by his squirt of a baby sister. In the throes of Texas's midmorning heat, Matt had gone after a serve of Haley's that any idiot could have seen was going out-of-bounds. Lounging in the peanut gallery on the back patio overlooking the tennis court, Jim Bennett had watched in horror as his eldest son's leg had snapped right out from underneath him.

Though he knew better, Jim swore that Haley had made the wide serve on purpose. She had to have greased the soles of Matt's tennis shoes, because the argument over who was going to fly the second Vixen jet to Sheik Wali Haj Haaris had begun the minute the blueprints came off of Haley's computer-assisted drawing board.

When the first of the immensely rich sheik's pretty babies had come out of the hangars for inspections and test flights, the argument between the Bennett siblings had escalated to outright war.

Only three members of the family-operated corporation held the licenses necessary to fly this class of aircraft, Jim, Matthew and baby Haley. No one dared suggest he stay home and let the youngsters take the planes, but Haley had had the audacity to demand she go along, period.

A couple of weeks ago, Jim had agreed to allow his talented daughter to come along as his copilot. It was capitulation to her outright manipulation. He knew it, damned if he didn't, but it seemed the only way to end the in-house fighting. It was pretty hard to intimidate Haley. Jim didn't have a good handle on it and poor Matt had never mastered the skill, ever. The girl had been running circles around Bennett men since the day she was born.

"You know," he said, "I still want a straight answer to why it was so all-fired important that you got to deliver these planes yourself, Haley."

"Call it a vendetta," Haley responded with a chuckle. "A strike back at purdah. Dad, these planes are my design, and mine alone. Nobody but me touched a single one of the designs that overrich oil prince fell in love with. He's paying you enough money to float a couple of third-world nations for a year, just to have a fleet of them. One for each and every one of his spoiled, male chauvinist sons."

"Is that what got your back up, girl?"

"Something like that. Those sheiks are all a bunch of preening peacocks. Every last one of them!" Haley said contemptuously.

"I still don't get it," he said bluntly.

"I'm talking about *your* sheik's sons, Dad. He's got twenty, according to the last count."

"So? He can afford it, can't he?"

"Yeah? So could you. Do you realize that all of Sheik Haaris's sons were educated at Oxford, Harvard and Yale?"

"So what?"

"None of his daughters have been."

"What's your point, Haley?"

"The Vixen's my baby! Call it pride in craftsmanship. Call it one-upmanship. Call it stupidity of the first degree. I want just one conservative Muslim sheik to have to face up to the fact that a woman can do as fine a job as a man. That's why I'm flying this plane today."

"Sugar bear, we're in the business of modifying airplanes. That's what we do for a living. It ain't our job to judge the people who buy our planes. That ain't the way I've raised you to be."

"I'm not judging anyone, Dad. All I want is to see the look on Prince Wali Haj's face when you introduce H. J. Bennett to him. I won't say a word, either. I'll just stick out my hand and smile for the cameras."

"Hell's bells, you'll start an incident with that sassy mouth of yours. I'm telling you right now, Haley, I'm leaving Kuwait with Sheik Haaris's commission for the other twenty planes in my back-order book. You start thinking about something else and you'll wind up sitting out the whole negotiation in the back office. I mean it!"

Haley laughed. "Look at it this way. Maybe some desert prince will offer you twenty horses for my sassy mouth."

"They do, and I'll take the offer so fast your little blond head will spin," Jim bantered right back. Haley's laughter over the radio was music to his heart.

"Admit it, Pop. It won't hurt our business for these plane-mad people to know you've got a whole passel of kids just as gifted as you are, males . . . and females."

"Hmmph," he grunted. That sort of flattery tripping off Haley's tongue usually made Jim Bennett as malleable as putty to his youngest daughter's whim. As if he didn't know when he was being manipulated! "You'll mind your p's and q's when we land in Kuwait, just the same."

"Of course I will," Haley assured him in a perfectly bland professional voice. "Business is business."

"Damn straight," Jim concurred.

"Well, lookie there, Pop, we've got company at nine o'clock," Haley announced.

"Been there for the last hour, chatterbox. It's a hawk reserve out of Riyadh. They're on maneuvers this week."

"Well, I'll be. That must mean we've kissed the desert goodbye."

"Yup. Kuwait's dead ahead. Better get our ears on."

"I've got static on my radio. Leave the short range on, okay? I love your heavy breathing."

While her father laughed, Haley looked at the distant gray bird in the golden sky. Clearly, it was a hawk, a military patrol. She left her radio open as her dad made contact. A cultured English voice asked her to identify herself, and she did.

They both logged into Kuwait International's multilayered holding pattern, circling the busy Mideast airport. In this exercise, as always, her father took the lead. The boss of the company had the rank to land first.

"Tell Jack to get steaks out of the freezer as soon as you land," she told him. "I'm starving to death up here."

"Will do. We're the only orange-and-white hangar. Keep a sharp eye for it when you taxi round. See you on the ground, sugar bear," Jim promised.

Haley waited for her landing instructions as she cruised over brown land and slick green water just south of the crescent of Al Kuwait Bay. "Kuwait control, this is Bennett Vixen 2000-2. It sure is crowded up here. Are weekday mornings always like this?"

"Roger, Vixen 2000-2, every day is like this," a controller responded in English. "Stick to the southern dogleg at twenty-five hundred feet." Haley scanned the crowded airways. Above her, six commercial 747 liners and a Concorde circled monotonously. At twenty-five hundred feet, she counted no less than twelve jets similar to the Vixen. Her radar screens informed her of a whole lot more circling below. Getting clearance to land was going to take a while.

It was coming up to 8:00 a.m. Kuwait time. Haley yawned deeply. Her last stint in bed was more than forty hours ago. The Vixen's generous cockpit now felt cramped and crowded, too confining for words. Twelve hours at the wheel, solo, covering eight thousand miles, hadn't seemed so daunting when they took off yesterday from San Antonio.

Her time in holding lengthened to tedium.

A glance at her watch showed it nearing 11:00 p.m. back home. Bedtime and she was feeling jet lag. Her neck hurt from sitting so long. Another yawn made her breathe deeply and blink. She knew her dad had to be feeling worse than she. He was thirty-plus years her senior.

Both of them ought to have had their heads examined for not bringing copilots. They had had trouble with last-minute visas. Some days her dad could call the State Department and get everything he wanted, including a red carpet waiting on the tarmac. Then there were days like yesterday, when nothing went right and everything that could go wrong did.

Their original flight plan had been lovely little hops. San Antonio to Lisbon, Lisbon to Baghdad with an overnight stop to get some shut-eye and a couple of hot meals.

Haley had an itch to see Baghdad and shop at the bazaar that was like no other bazaar in the world. She'd tapped out her savings account to do just that.

That opportunity went down the tubes when permission to travel Iraqi commercial airspace was abruptly canceled. No explanation was given. It had forced a complete change of flight plans. The only alternate route they could get over any so-called friendly Arab country had been from the Saudis, long-standing clients of her dad.

It paid to have connections. It took twice as long and twice as much fuel to fly around Africa as to cut across it. Jim Bennett wasted nothing, including precious fuel.

Haley chuckled, rephrasing that characteristic affectionately to penny-pinching tightwad. As if any man who commissioned planes like the Bennett Vixen-2000 could ever be considered a tightwad. There was not a single component of this plane that was cheaply made. Nothing had been scrimped on, from the hand-rubbed hardwood veneers to the imported leather of each seat. The plane was compact, yes, designed to transport ten adults maximum, but in such luxury as some people would never dream.

The power-packed jet engine was her brother Thomas's venue. What he could do with a fuel mix and a little tinkering defied explanation. Consequently, she and her dad had struck out yesterday afternoon on a six-thousand-mile nonstop flight, intending to do it in fourteen hours maximum.

The jets could hold Mach one indefinitely. They could maneuver like a fox outrunning hounds. In the next moment, a clumsy military transport lumbered across Haley's airspace. She buzzed out of his way with a quick twist of her wrist, which brought her dangerously close to two prop-wing commercial flights on the dogleg return over Al Kuwait Bay.

"Hey!" Haley shouted in her headset. "Who's minding the store?"

"Roger, Bennett 2000-2. Maintain assigned flight path and altitude."

"I'm not the one in the wrong lane, guy, and while I've got you on the horn, be advised I'll be riding on fumes if this merry-go-round continues much longer. Any chance of an earlier berth, over?"

"Roger, Vixen 2000-2, we copy. Advise of exact fuel status and range."

Haley stated the factual data. She wasn't critical, having a solid range of four hundred miles, but each loop in the endless landing chain ate up seventy-five.

"Copy that, Bennett Vixen 2000-2, proceed to seven hundred feet. Hold for next approach on runway six."

"Roger, thanks, control." Haley relaxed and looked forward to walking, relishing the prospect of ground underfoot. Idling, she glanced out the window and watched as her father's Vixen scooted down runway six, landing as prettily as a white-wing dove touches the earth.

Haley banked and lost sight of the runway. She concentrated on enjoying the turn, the sheer maneuverability of the Vixen, the flying. She put down her landing gear and smiled approvingly at the natural drag it added to her speed. The last arm of the steep turn west swung her into the runway's apron, approaching the city of Kuwait in a forty-degree tilt over hazy, blue water and gray smoke.

Smoke?

Haley blinked. *Must have been fog.* There hadn't been any mention of fog from the tower. Her right wing hid the city. Runway six rushed at the Vixen's pointy nose.

Another yawn pulled Haley's cheeks. How good it would feel to stand, stretch, feel the hot, hot desert air on her refrigerated skin. The runway rapidly grew wider. She lowered the Vixen's tail so her rear wheels would be first to touch the tarmac.

A plume of smoke rose in the middle of the long runway. Static crackled in Haley's ear. A shriek followed. The controller screamed, "Bennett Air, Vixen 2000-2! Abort landing! Return to twenty-five hundred feet. Repeat! Abort landing runway six! Vixen, do you copy?"

Haley's yawn died midstretch. One hand hauled the wheel back. The other shot to her ear, to adjust the volume on her shrieking headset. "Control! This is Bennett Air Vixen 2000-2, copy! Aborting approach to runway six. What the hell is going on down there? Oh, my God!"

The terminal erupted like Mount Saint Helens. Glass and concrete exploded, sending a plume of black smoke and flames over planes parked at the terminal gates. The control tower shattered. Her headset emitted another deafening shriek, then went dead.

Her other ear heard *boom, boom, boom* sounds. Haley yanked up the Vixen's nose and cut a diagonal over the flaming end of the terminal. Huge sheets of glass fell to the ground and shattered. At two hundred feet, she tacked a sharp tight corner and came back full circle. She didn't care what was in the air around her. She had to know who, what had crashed.

"Dad!" She switched to the radio channel they'd communicated on throughout the journey. "Dad, can you hear me? Daddy! Answer me! Are you all right?"

"Haley!" Her dad's voice crackled over a static-charged speaker on the Vixen's console. "There're rockets and bombs flying everywhere. Don't land that plane. You hear me, girl? Get the hell out of here! Go home!"

# *Chapter 2*

Haley's low, panicked retreat over the city revealed a nightmare down below. Every quadrant of Kuwait City spit tongues of smoke, concrete dust and flames into the sky.

Haley's hand remained on the radio while she searched the crowded sky above her. Without controllers issuing constant instructions, the skyway became a massive spaghetti bowl of confusion. Every pilot realized exactly what Haley did. It was every man for himself. The radio channels jammed just as the traffic lanes did.

Heading toward open water, Haley sped past plazas filled with army tanks. Transports spewed armed commandos onto the city's streets. The public beach swarmed with helicopters, hovering above troop carriers disgorging soldiers by the hundreds. It was an invasion!

Haley was low enough to see machine-gun-toting Rambos turn their muzzles skyward and fire at her blue-and-white Vixen.

Bullets ripping through the skin of the airplane accomplished what her father's message hadn't. She yanked back on the rudder and went straight up. The force of several G's slammed her against the contoured seat.

At six thousand feet she banked and turned south, circling. She checked the damage. A few clean holes in the jet's left wing was all she could find. She cut a short loop high above the city, stunned and disoriented. At this altitude, Kuwait City looked like a refinery inferno Red Adair wouldn't be able to touch.

An ugly green ocher Soviet-made MiG fighter at ten o'clock lorded over the sky. Stunned, Haley gaped at the wicked-looking plane, trying to decipher its insignia fast. "What is going on here?"

Her radio suddenly came back to life. "Attention!" shouted a guttural voice. "All civilian aircraft in the vicinity of Kuwait International Airport . . . You are violating Iraqi airspace."

Haley double-checked her map-finder program, steady on one computer screen. Her instruments couldn't lie.

"No, I'm not. I'm in Kuwait airspace!" she yelled at the MiG, taking the announcement personally. "And I have permission to be here. Back off, buddy."

"Attention, all commercial and private planes!" The voice droned on, oblivious to Haley's chatter. The MiG kept coming straight at her. "Kuwait International is closed. All civilian flights must leave the area. Kuwait International is closed. Those flights needing to refuel may identify themselves now. State your needs and escort to Basra will be provided."

Haley didn't need to think twice to know she'd get no response from control at Kuwait International. Not when the tower had exploded before her eyes. Her hand trembled as she pushed in the code for emergency assistance at the nearest civilian airport.

"Attention, Dhahran, this is Bennett Vixen 2000-2. Soviet jet number 79-523-1. Mayday! I am a civilian plane cleared for landing at Kuwait International. My fuel range is critical. Dhahran, there's something going on in Kuwait that isn't funny!"

Haley read the MiG's identifying numbers for the benefit of her onboard recorders. There was jamming on all frequencies. Maybe no one anywhere would hear her.

Anger took away her fear. It was positively uncivil to use MiGs against unarmed private planes.

Haley banked again. She hit full throttle and passed over the burning city at Mach one. She wasn't about to let a Soviet MiG force her to fly God knew where! The pilot wouldn't dare fire his missiles at her. That was too unthinkable.

The warning, being repeated in other languages, hogged precious radio space. Haley repeated her urgent Mayday. Response came immediately.

"Vixen 2000-2. Iraqi pilots have orders to open fire. For your own protection, turn to a heading of zero-five-seven North."

"Iraq?" Haley blinked. She glared at the MiG. It was big, ugly and very menacing, and yes, it did have a flag painted on its camouflaged tail. "Damn! Control, identify yourself. Provide coordinates indicating point of origin. State your authority to interfere with radio channels reserved for commercial flights."

"Attention, all planes in vicinity of Kuwait International..." The blasted voice returned to the same dull, uninformative message given before. Frantically, Haley tried to remember what she knew about Mideast politics and who sided with whom. "Where the hell is Basra?"

Haley turned to her radio as her only lifeline, opening access to every frequency at once. "Attention, Controller. Give coordinates of point of origin. Vixen 2000-2 over Kuwait airspace. I need clearance to make emergency landing at Kuwait International. What is source of hostility? Pull off your military planes. Hello, America! Is anybody out there patrolling the gulf? Help me! Mayday!"

It was a wild shot, a stab in the dark, but one never knew who was riding the skies. Maybe there were a couple of American flyboys out there on the periphery who could help her—or an aircraft carrier out in the gulf.

"I repeat, *Mayday*. I am an American citizen on private business to Kuwait and my plane is out of gas! If you fire on this plane, it will be an act of war duly recorded in my transcorder. Back off, buddy boy!"

Haley punched up her radar and fixed the MiG behind her, or thought she did. There was so much stuff in the air it was hard to tell. Her computer screens looked like a video arcade gone wild. The *beep* accelerating on her tail had to be the MiG. On her second sweep over the city, the *beeps* doubled and tripled. She recognized the clutter. Ground-fired rockets.

Ignoring her panic, the voice on the airway switched languages, warning all commercial flights to leave Kuwait. Go elsewhere. A missile shot past Haley's windscreen. The danger became too, too real. Had that MiG fired at her?

"Oh, hell!" She pulled viciously on the wheel and stamped on both rudders. The Vixen cut a roll that would have made her father shout over china breaking in the galley. Two rockets shot out from the MiG while she was upside down in the top of the loop. Releasing the right rudder, holding down the left, the Vixen rolled a hundred and eighty degrees. Haley was upright, glaring into the fighter pilot's black eyes as she buzzed him so close he had to feel the heat of her afterburners on his face.

"I'll take you with me, you bastard!" Haley grimly gritted her teeth. She'd done a few crazy stunts before in planes, but never anything like that, ever! She wished a mountain would rise up and smack right into the MiG's nose.

Gulping to slow down her slamming heart, Haley sought refuge in a monstrous cloud of black smoke. She took a deep breath and read all her dials, gauges and screens. The yellow fuel light winked caution.

Emerging from the sooty cloud, she found an ominous gray bird directly over her right shoulder. She shook her head to clear it, then scanned the instrument panel and read the compass. She was flying due south at six hundred miles per hour.

One computer screen flashed a note that the border was just under two minutes ahead. The fuel-status warning gauge hummed as persistently as an annoying gnat. *Beep! Beep! Beep!*

"I know I'm out of gas!" Haley yelled at the computer console when it automatically brought up the screen advising her she was endangering the aircraft.

Tearing her gaze from the constantly changing dials and screens, she looked at the sky around her, then swallowed. "Oh, hell!"

She counted five MiGs converged in the sky ahead of her. Directly above her, the sinister shadow inched closer and closer, blocking a quick retreat back to the gulf. Her onboard radar found another plane just as big directly underneath her, coming up fast and closing.

Haley's fingers trembled as she pushed in the manual switch on the radio to open every frequency. This time, there was panic in her voice. "Mayday, Saudi, Dhahran controller, this is Bennett Air Vixen 2000-2. I am approaching Saudi airspace with hostile aircraft all around me. Five MiGs dead ahead and I don't know what all above and below me. I am a civilian pilot, American citizen."

"Vixen 2000-2. This is controller, Basra, Iraq. All air lanes over Kuwait have been closed. Turn north now, or you will be fired on. Air silence is in effect, over."

"Where the hell is Basra? I'm out of gas, damn you!" Haley shouted back. The radio was absolutely silent. It didn't even crackle.

"Emergency. Mayday, Mayday. Dhahran, can you read me? This is Bennett Air Vixen 2000-2. I repeat, I am entering Saudi airspace now! I do not have the fuel to make Dhahran! Advise of nearest landing field, immediately!"

The ugly plane over her head nudged forward, giving Haley glimpses of cone-pointed missiles under its wings. She jumped and screamed reflexively when two rockets ignited and burst free of their carriers. Terrified, she hid in the jet's shadow. She swallowed, licked her lips and stared at the rockets speeding at the MiGs guarding the Saudi border.

Her computer impersonally delivered a monotone message, "In forty-six seconds, you will enter Saudi Arabia. Have you logged a new flight plan?"

The yellow caution on the fuel gauge switched to a steady red glow. She'd hit critical petrol status.

"Great!" Haley slumped against her seat. Her hands were so sweaty she could barely hold the butterfly wheel steady. The radar screen beeped the ominous intimacy of the huge jet rising beneath her.

The five MiGs executed a textbook roll, evading the rockets. Two tore off in a blast of white exhaust to the east, one shot north over Haley's head, the other two split west. One rocket hit a heat trail and exploded. The other flew off into the empty desert.

Haley's head swiveled, visually tracking the MiGs. Their insignia marked them as Iraqi, one and all.

"So who in God's name is over and under me? Rambo?" she muttered as the Vixen shot over the border.

Before her words were out, Haley cut her speed drastically. What shot forward over her head was a needle-nosed F-15 fighter jet, judging by the configuration of its tail. The lumbering oaf skulking beneath her line of sight stuck like a leech to the Vixen's underbelly, a sinister *beep* on Haley's radar screen.

The code numbers on the F-15 were easy enough for her to read, but she had no ability to decode Arabic writing and no time to sort out flags or other icons.

Almost immediately, the fighter jet stalled, pulling up and slowing, waiting for her to catch up. This time when it came closer, it came intimidatingly close. So close that if it accidentally dropped its landing gear, the Vixen's molded windscreen would be crushed.

Horrified, Haley helplessly watched the heavily armed fighter completely cover the bright blue and white skin of the Vixen.

"Oh, God help me," Haley whispered.

To her left the intruder below came into view, maneuvering with the F-15 to form a box out of which she couldn't possibly corkscrew free. She couldn't keep her eyes on radar screens, monitors and two other planes. She could concentrate on only one thing, keeping her plane inches away from that dreadful specter above. The F-15 was so close they could kiss paints and streak one another.

*He's either suicidal,* she thought, *or the best pilot she'd ever crossed in her life.* Not even her Thunderbird-trained father would risk a maneuver like this. Haley Bennett wasn't going for it! Throttling full speed ahead, wasting precious gas, she fought containment. The F-15 shot ahead, deliberately cutting her off by putting his left wing in front of her nose.

For a split second, Haley gawked at the scorch marks of emptied rocket carriers marring the F-15's silver wings. She spied a Kuwaiti flag painted under its wing. She could clearly see the other jet was a Royal Saudi issue, *made in America, too.*

"Is this a free-for-all or what?" Haley vented her frustration. She screamed when the F-15 cut his speed and nearly dropped in her lap. His message was clear. He'd tolerate no more evasive action. "I'm out of gas, lughead!"

The acrobatics she practiced in the wide-open sky back home were useless over an endless, empty desert with gas at the critical stage.

They slowed considerably, extending her range. The Saudi jet rocked his big fat nose to one side of her and lowered from her line of sight. The Kuwaiti F-15 kept cramming down on top.

"What is the matter with you? Turn your radio on and tell me what you want! Airplanes don't entwine wings like lovers tangling arms in bed! Get off! Give me space to fly, you stupid jerk, before you kill all three of us!''

That was the most irrational speech Haley had ever screamed in her life. She meant every word of it. Her hands shook on the controls, but she didn't dare let go of them, not even to shake a fist at the horrible brute.

One wrong move, one spasmodic jerk on her part, and the Vixen's beautiful nose and molded fiberglass cockpit would be smashed by the fighter jet's solid steel wing. There wasn't even a chance that she could get to a parachute and bail out.

Haley swallowed, her throat dry and raw. ''You've made your point, Omar!''

The pilot pointed south across the Saudi desert. Silently, Haley nodded acquiescence. She gripped the wheel, heading the direction he had pointed. The too big, too damn close end of his wing tip lifted from in front of the Vixen.

Only then did Haley realize how crazy he had to be. Insane, a fanatic, an assassin . . . He was ready to die because a private jet had invaded his bloody war!

The Saudi pulled off to a companionable distance once she'd submitted to escort. Haley's neck cramped and knotted with sweat. Her heart pounded. The harsh, bright morning sun hurt her eyes. Anger contracted her throat and stung tears on her lashes. Whatever was going on, she would have an earful to say to this camel jockey when she touched the ground.

If she touched the ground.

Her shaky hands held the Vixen on a course both bully planes approved. Reading her dials and screens made her sweat even more. Even with the cutback in speed, less than a hundred miles of fuel remained in the Vixen's tank. Frantic, Haley ran a search on her computer for landing sites, cueing it to locate any private field within range. It came up with zilch. Haley began searching for any stretch of asphalt down below.

The Kuwaiti F-15 rocked its wings, signaling. Haley looked up and found herself actually staring into the pilot's eyes. He was that close. The strong sun illuminated his face, made his dark, intense eyes and black eyebrows visible, despite his mask and helmet. Now she knew how a sparrow felt when a peregrine falcon swooped in for the kill. He used hand signals. She was to go down to five hundred feet.

*Right! And crash into a sand dune.*

She shook her head no.

He very definitely pointed down and made a universal sweeping motion with his palm flat out, indicating landing.

"I'm not ditching this plane in the Summan, buddy boy," she said bitterly, and kept prompting the computer to find her civilization of any kind within fifty miles.

The logic of the electronic brain informed her that the airport at Kuwait was the most suitable, and suggested what speed she should glide at to make the distance.

"A lot of help you are!" She swore at the blue screen and looked up in time to find the damn Kuwaiti crowding the Vixen again. This time, he did more than just violate physical space. He was going to make her go to five hundred feet, or else make her crash and burn.

The Vixen didn't stand a chance against such bullying. Neither did Haley Bennett.

Five, six miles farther along, the shadows of the three planes stood out in sharp clarity on the endless sweep of rippling sand. The Vixen looked like a hatchling caught in the pull of two condors.

As she stared at her own shadow, Haley realized for the first time since this nightmare started that her plane had no markings to indicate it belonged to an American businesswoman. Its registration numbers V-2000-2 could be read universally, but the bold lettering on the glossy exterior was written in Arabic, *al-Haaris*. She had personally painted Kuwait's flag on the Vixen's proud tail. That, she realized as she looked at her fuel gauge, was a moot point.

"Hey, Omar! Are you listening?" she snapped into her headset. "I'm out of petrol!"

He crowded her into a thirty-degree turn due east.

"Great option!" Haley muttered. Again the man in the cockpit signaled with his hand, go down to three hundred feet. Haley shook her head, but she cruised to the demanded altitude.

He didn't look like a killer. Surely God couldn't be so perverse as to give eyes like that to a madman. She tried not to think of anything, just to fly the plane. It wouldn't be long before it didn't matter.

The pilot pointed ahead. Haley rubbed her tired eyes. She couldn't see anything there except glaring sand.

Then a dark blur swelled on the horizon. It became more distinct, forming into a semblance of habitation in the desert. A water tower, an oasis, a mirage, maybe. The water tower shifted shapes to become a minaret poking heavenward.

At an incredibly slow crawl, the three planes rumbled low over tents, camels and date palms. Riders on camels and horses whirled, swinging rifles across their mounts' necks, scattering flocks of sheep. Ahead, dead ahead of the Vixen's nose, a straight path of sun-bleached concrete bisected a gorgelike valley between the dunes.

Low buildings edged the gorge. As Haley flew over a hump in the sand, she saw an entire military base with plenty of runways spread across the whole width of the deep gorge.

Why a sigh of relief escaped Haley's lips just then, she didn't know. No one landed in radio silence. Yet, it was clear that was exactly what the sheiks of the airways intended for her to do. She lowered her wheels, listening to them lock in place, then banked two degrees to correct her line of approach. The Vixen dropped a hundred feet in less than a mile, easing onto the wide-open runway.

That stinking falcon stayed right with her, a hairbreadth behind as her wheels touched the concrete. Haley screamed when she realized the F-15 intended to land alongside her. "Holy Mother of God! What are you doing?"

No plane could maneuver on landing. It was straight-ahead stop or crash and flip into blazing oblivion. Planes were not equipped with side-view mirrors to know what the drunk in the next lane was doing. Turning one's head during landing was asking for trouble. Hands had an insidious way of following head direction.

Her back wheels touched at a speed of two hundred and fifty miles an hour. The Vixen's nose refused to bite concrete because of the speed and the heat rising off the ground. Haley whipped past the painted mid-runway marker and broke every landing rule she'd ever learned. She turned to look for the bigger jet.

The F-15 came down like a rearing stallion. Rear wheels smoked as the fighter jet touched rubber on terra firma. Nose up, it threatened to bite the backside out of her Vixen. If she hit her retros too hard, he'd be on her and over her.

"I'm going to kill you." Haley snapped back around, gripped the wheel so tight her nails dug into her palms. She put up flaps and the nose of the Vixen touched ground, then she switched on her retros and pressed the throttle forward, decelerating slowly, slowly, slowly. With precious little runway left, she closed her eyes, clenched her teeth and stomped on the brakes. Her whole body tensed, expecting instantaneous impact from the rear.

It didn't come. The Vixen crawled to a creep. No jolt threw Haley flying into the console. No scream of metal crushing or explosion deafened her.

Haley opened her eyes. She was alive! Her hands flew over the console with professional precision, shutting off retros, snapping on ground lights, leveling flaps, unlocking the ground steering. The Vixen rolled to a dignified stop with twenty yards of concrete left.

The Kuwaiti fighter jet remained on her tail. A lane to the right promised to take the Vixen out of harm's way.

The Saudi fighter jet had dropped much farther back. It flew low overhead, rumbling thunderously as it passed. Haley read that as an attempt to make certain she didn't take the option of flying off on her own reconnaissance again. Had her fuel gauge read anything but empty, she would have.

On empty, her only option was the taxi lane.

Kuwait 88-34601 sucked her exhaust as she taxied off the runway.

Haley didn't need a crystal ball to tell her she'd landed in a hornet's nest of strategic defense engaged in a serious, massive scramble to arms.

The mouth of every half-buried sand hangar yawned wide open, disgorging planes and helicopters hastily fitted with bombs and rockets. The scream and drone of engines revving for takeoff split the desert air. She saw an array of planes she hadn't ever seen assembled together: American Harriers, F-14's, F-15's, French Mirage and British-made Tornados. *Saudi money could buy anything,* Haley thought.

A groundsman flagged her off the crowded ramp, onto curiously marked parking. The Vixen's bright blue-and-white wings looked gaudy against the host of desert-camouflage fighter jets. The sun was off the horizon by a hand span or two, the shadows long. The groundsman urged her under a stretch of netting that wafted in the wind like seaweed on a sandbar.

Once she was parked, the groundsman chucked blocks beneath her wheels. Haley sat back and her arms went limp. The digital clock on the Vixen's dash read 8:27 a.m.

Omar the Magnificent turned off the alley and drove his damn F-15 right up in her face, nose to nose. That wasn't an accurate assessment, for the F-15 was three times the size of the Vixen. Its wicked gunner's snout pointed way over the top of her plane, thank God. Still, Haley wanted to jump out and drag the pilot from his seat, then slap, kick, stomp and beat the everlasting hell out of the man.

He looked down from his bubble-shrouded windshield and grinned at her.

"Why, you stinking, dirty son..." Haley's fear percolated to a rolling boil. Her hands moved, conditioned by years of training to switch off all systems, but her eyes never left his.

"You and me, Omar." She let the steam out. "Alone, ten paces apart, any damn weapon you choose. Right here and now in broad daylight, bare-handed, armed, I don't give a damn. You owe me satisfaction."

She doubted the arrogant bully comprehended her exact words, but she had no doubt he knew exactly what her thoughts were. And she'd be damned if she'd break the stare down with the likes of him. He hadn't cut her any slack. She refused to grant him any in return. He was no longer grinning like an idiot, either.

Her ground air was still cycling when the door of the Vixen's cockpit was wrenched open. A blast of unholy, hotter-than-Hades air shot into the cabin. A soldier reached up to jostle her out of the pilot's seat. He stopped in his tracks and shouted at someone behind him that the pilot was a woman, a blonde. *"Innaeho gaemil ash'er."*

Not even that intrusion broke the stare down between Haley and the fighter pilot. His shoulders inclined forward, as her own did. She reached for the compartment that held her documents. He released the glass shield shrouding his finely formed head and shoulders. The elongated half bubble went up in a buzz of hydraulic wizardry as he unfastened his dangling mask.

Locked in telepathic combat, his head moved in acknowledgment of the challenge given by her eyes. It was accepted. There was no expression on his face. It was unreadable, but

Haley wasn't reading his face, she was reading his soul, marking it.

A swarm of invaders rushed onto her plane from the passenger door, barking harsh, incomprehensible words, searching the plane's unoccupied quarters.

Refusing to be rattled on the ground, Haley secured the plane. As an extra precaution, she calmly coded the computer prior to shutting down all systems. The sophisticated computer that monitored each of the Vixen's functions could be accessed with one key password. The Vixen was as good as locked in a vault in Fort Knox. It could be jacked up and towed, but no one could fly it.

That lockout made it perfectly safe for Haley Bennett to leave the cockpit and step into the bedlam on the tarmac.

Before doing so, Haley carefully removed the colorful scarf at her neck and used it to secure the loose hair at her nape. The hot wind on the ground was strong. She had no intention of fighting flying hair while trying to make sense out of what was happening here, fight a language barrier and barter for a tank of gas.

Urged to disembark, she finally did so with her leather attaché case and a pocket Berlitz in Arabic.

Her spine almost refused to straighten out, she'd been sitting for so long. She was a little on the dehydrated side, and bone-tired. All thoughts of hunger and fatigue had evaporated a half hour ago over Kuwait International.

She actually welcomed the heat after so many hours in the rarefied atmosphere of the Vixen 2000-2. Ignoring the phalanx of curious Saudi soldiers, Haley turned to watch the Kuwaiti pilot descend to the ground.

Someone had the audacity to touch her hair as she was turning. The cold, quelling look Haley gave the young man made him drop his hand as if he had been burned. "Touch me again, buddy, and I'll rip your heart out."

She had no delusions that any of these men understood her threat, but they appeared to have never seen anyone like her. With some startled awe for her mode of dress, they gave her space, although not much. She turned back to the fighter-jet pilot, somehow knowing that her fate rested in his hands.

She hoped he spoke English. If she was truly lucky, he might have been trained to fly in her country.

Haley viewed military pilots as cookie-cutter men, selected by preset standards to fit into ever-decreasing cockpits. Most stood five foot ten. Swaggering, arrogant fellows that could be interchangeably mixed from plane to plane, country to country, without batting an eye. Her father and her eldest brother broke the air force's mold, standing six-four in their stocking feet.

The man who dropped to the tarmac in fatigues and dangling harness did also. He was a head taller than most of the minions swarming about him. He had a set of shoulders that a tall girl like herself would kill to have on a dance floor.

One sweep of her eyes and Haley noted the man's unshaven jaw, his shadowed eyes and the striking combination of features on a face that was unquestionably handsome. His mouth unsettled her the most. A sensuous, generous mouth that at this moment was grimly twisted above a jutting, arrogant chin.

Not one of the babbling soldiers crowding her could look her in the eye. They were drones. She swept them out of her focus, concentrating only on Mr. Arrogance as he strode toward her.

He had rank, too. As he pressed through the melee, all on the field saluted like rigid jackdaws, leaping away from Haley. She caught a glimpse of gold stars winking on the shoulders of his flight suit.

Haley stiffened territorially before the plane that had brought her into his domain. One sharp command issued from him and the men backed off, giving him maneuvering room. He stopped a few feet in front of her and stared at her face assessingly. A flicker of surprise glittered in the cool depths of his eyes, then faded behind an immutable expression. With deliberate ease, his eyes left hers and traveled insolently downward, sweeping across Haley's sleekly fitted blue-and-white flight suit. Not once did his gaze travel off her body to admire the beautiful airplane at her back.

An alarm went off in Haley's head. She saw the flush of color seep into his skin and the flare of his nostrils as if he detected the scent of her perfume. Her whole body reacted to his unexpected assessment. His territorial inspection of her attributes in such a frank and personal manner made her quiver with hard to contain rage. Never having upstaged the Vixen in her professional life, Haley stepped back.

Before his eyes returned to her face, her right arm moved, delivering a resounding slap to his shadowed cheek.

"Swine!" Her hand stung, but never had a blow been more deserved. "You could have wrecked my plane! Killed both of us attempting a tandem landing!"

He caught her wrist and jerked it to a stop between them.

"I may yet take the pleasure," he said in English. He summoned an officer emerging from the passenger compartment of the Vixen. There followed a very brief and blunt spate of Arabic, her wrist crushingly ignored for the duration of the exchange. The dialogue ended and his attention returned to Haley in full force. The pressure on her wrist intensified. "Where is Sheik Haj Haaris?" he asked.

The blister of words ran together. Not Hag-Harry, the way Haley's father drawled in his lazy Texan way. It took Haley precious seconds to decode the pilot's question. She retorted, "How the hell should I know?"

Vehemently, the man blasted her with more words, hot, scalding. His temper seemed to burn with the heat of the desert itself. A veritable litany of scorching Arabic preceded his return to English. "Do not play games with me, woman. I won't be baited, where my father's life is concerned. Where are the passengers?"

"Passengers? I have no passengers."

Haley gulped then, sensing overwhelming danger as she surrendered her vital papers to the aide flanking the pilot.

Just then, another jet took off with a burst of deafening sound. A tangled moment passed, where no voices could be discerned by anyone on the ground as the Kuwaiti pilot shouted at her. Veins stood out on his neck and throbbed on his forehead.

"You took off from Kuwait after the shelling started. Where is Sheik Wali Haaris? Did you leave him stranded in Al Kuwait International?"

Haley mustered an answer through clenched teeth. "If you expect answers, you'd better cease manhandling me."

His fine aquiline nose rose another inch or more above hers. The vise on her hand intensified. "You will answer. How did you get possession of my father's plane? Did you seduce one of my brothers into giving it to you?"

Her control snapped. "What?" Haley shouted. She yanked on her arm to remove it from his iron-fisted grip. "Listen up, Omar, I happen to be the designer of this plane. It hasn't been delivered to Sheik Haj Haaris, yet. I was on my way to Kuwait to do just that. My father is on the ground in Kuwait and there are bombs falling everywhere. I couldn't land. The control tower and the terminal blew up in my face as I approached the runway. As things stand this very minute, the Vixen is mine because it belongs to my company. As for seducing your brothers, shall I tell you exactly where the lot of you can deport yourselves?"

"What is your name?"

"Haley Bennett. What's yours, Omar?"

The young lieutenant flipped through the scant papers that Haley carried in her small briefcase—passport, wallet, credit cards and manifest. Only two other documents were part of her package, the ownership on the Vixen 2000-2 and the export release from the Feds rubber-stamping the Bennett Industries sale. "The woman's papers are in order, General Haaris. There is no Kuwait stamp entered in her passport. Perhaps she had not landed, yet."

"That's what I just told you."

"Take her out of my sight!" the Arab commanded. "See that she is confined."

"Now just a minute here!" Haley yanked on a grip she had yet to break. "You're not going to imprison me! I'm an American citizen, you barbarian!"

"You are a woman, Miss Bennett," he countered. "I have not the time to devote to your intimate challenge. There is military business afoot and my country needs my services. You and your pretty little plane will keep until I return. I assure you, I will look forward to our personal combat."

"Think so?" Haley wrenched her wrist out of his hand at last.

The pilot's eyes flickered over her once again as she spun away from him. Seeing the long swatch of blond hair that switched angrily across her hips, he riveted to a stop and barked at the young officer in Arabic.

"Transport Miss Bennett to Anaiza by helicopter at once. Tell al-Dia-Allah she is to be sequestered as to the law of Islam. No man is to see her hair unbound or uncovered again. Is that understood?"

"Yes, sir!" The lieutenant snapped a crisp salute to the Arabic command. Haley half turned, wondering what that was all about, but had no time to ask questions as a jeep full of rifle-toting soldiers screeched to a halt beside them.

The lieutenant took the wheel from the driver and Haley was jammed into the passenger's seat. Someone tossed her folded garment bag containing her toiletries and changes of clothes into the jeep before it lurched forward on grinding gears and smoking tires.

The generalissimo swaggered back to his F-15 and the crew on the ground began reloading his empty rocket casings.

Haley saw no more as the jeep sped around a revetment. Past the next embankment of sand, a squadron of helicopters shot skyward, every one of them headed north.

More jets rocketed airborne. Shielding her eyes from the lash of flying sand, she concluded the Saudis were throwing every piece of weaponry they had into the hostile sky.

The jeep squealed to a halt beside an ancient Huey helicopter. She was destined to be hustled elsewhere. As jet engines broke the sound barrier, she protested boarding another aircraft without first having access to facilities inside the terminal.

The lieutenant's response tested his command of English to the limits of his ability. "There are no facilities here for a woman. It is a great insult to every soldier present to suffer your presence among us. A woman may not show her face or her uncovered hair. This is Saudi Arabia, *gaemil.*"

# Chapter 3

Before she went off the deep end, Haley fought a valiant battle to get hold of herself, think and calm down. She was tired, frightened, jet-lagged, dehydrated and surrounded by an uncountable number of hostile armed men whose language she didn't speak. These Arabs looked at her with...well, she didn't know what their scathing, disturbing looks meant.

What she knew about Saudi Arabia she could stuff in a thimble. She'd made an overview study of Islamic art for the purpose of making eye-pleasing designs. There her inquiry had ended. Everything else she knew about the Mideast was media gleaned, via telecasts of terrorist bombings, ongoing internal wars, propaganda and coup attempts. None of which she'd ever followed. She couldn't think of any Arab she'd ever met in her twenty-four years.

Yes, Sheik Haaris had come to San Antonio and finalized his order for the Vixens, but she had not been included in those meetings. Her father and glib-tongued Matthew had handled all contractual negotiations.

In fact, when the white-robed sheik had visited the Bennett detail shop, the six women who worked on the assembly floor had been given a paid holiday. Likewise, the three Bennett sisters, also employed by their father's company, didn't go within five miles of the plant that day.

Margaret, Katie and Haley had laughed it off and chalked up the day to their father's astute maneuvers to gain Bennett Industries a highly favorable contract. Only Haley had voiced dissatisfaction with the repressive action. Some of the sting of that repression had fueled Haley's insistence on flying her Vixen to Kuwait.

Right now, she wished she'd never been handed the design problem in the first place. Her thoughts turned to worry about her father. What, dear God, could have happened to him? Had the 2000-1 exploded, caught fire or been hit by a bomb? What about her uncle Jack and the hangar, the supplies on the ground? What about the goose, the old DC-7 hunker plane?

A million more questions without answers flashed through her mind as the helicopter sped west across the desert. What were these Saudis going to do with her? Would she and her dad be held for ransom or become hostages in some stupid political game? Her dad had important clients in this part of the world, but for the life of her, she couldn't remember a single patron's name. What was she going to do?

The inability to answer any of her own questions only intensified the massive headache blooming behind her eyes. For too long in the noisy, drafty helicopter, Haley sat with her eyes closed and her fingers pressed to her forehead.

Then she jolted up straight, eyes wide as she took a look at everything that it was possible to see—the earphone-covered heads of the pilot and the navigator of the helicopter, and beyond the windscreen, the sweeping ocher-and-tan desert.

Too late, Haley realized. She should have looked for landmarks from the very start, noting directions, making contingencies for escape before she became a prisoner. Glaring at the sight unfolding before her tired eyes, she silently groaned.

The helicopter was settling onto a clearly marked helipad atop a cluster of buildings nestled on a rocky hillside. The slopes were stark and barren. She saw no other sign of civilization near this outpost on the edge of oblivion.

For all Haley knew, she was at a prison.

Four men rushed up an outer stair to meet the helicopter. All wore ankle-length robes. Two carted AK-47's. To Haley's great relief, the third seemed a gentler sort. He bowed profusely before her as he offered a long, slender hand to assist her out of the craft. The fourth scrambled into the cargo bay and snatched up her scant luggage and leather briefcase.

Ducking the sweep of rotor blades, all four escorted her down the steps into the adjacent enclosed courtyard. The bearer scuttled ahead on slippered feet, opening and closing heavily timbered doors between courts. A striped robe fluttered around his bony ankles, but Haley could concentrate on nothing but his black turban that had a silk tail hanging off the center of his back.

As they passed a series of gates, the two machine-gun-toting banditos never spoke a word. Their piercing black eyes regarded her with the same distrust she'd noted in the soldiers. The third seemed openly worried, and fired lots of questions Haley's way that she could not answer because she couldn't hear him over the roar of the helicopter's rotor as it retreated into the sky.

Haley racked her brain, summoning every smidgen of self-defense and survival lore she had gleaned from years of watching television. She expected imprisonment and had the resistance of a marshmallow to prevent it.

It threw her even more off-balance to step inside a beautiful tiled, ornately columned hall of such massive proportions she was reminded of imposing government buildings. Wide balustraded stairs rose to a cool upper level. Within minutes of walking along Persian-carpeted halls where vases overflowed with exotic greenery, the babbling man, whose English was dismal, at best, swung open a set of doors to a private chamber.

Expecting an austere cell, Haley gawked at a living area that belonged on the cover of *Architectural Digest*.

Along the way to this lavish setting, the armed banditos had faded behind the scrollwork. The scuttling porter set down her garment bag and briefcase and disappeared. The tall, rather thin man struggling so valiantly with English threw open another set of doors to reveal a bedroom of such ostentatious wealth Haley nearly swallowed her tongue.

"This . . . make you . . . comfortable . . . *lalla,* yes?" he asked haltingly.

"I stay here?" Haley blinked stupidly as he bowed three more times and made gestures with his hand, touching his head, chin and breast.

As he straightened, a smile beamed from his lean face. "Here, yes! Com...for...table, here, yes, sleep, baaathe, rest." He put his hand to his forehead, looking dismayed. "Forgive...my Anglais...please, mam'selle. Many years pass since I speak it, yes. One becomes, how you say, rus-tee, yes, rusty. That is the word. Please, be comfortable. You are tired. Rest. Bathe away the strain of your journey. A meal will be waiting for you when you emerge from the bath. Do you require a woman to serve you?"

Haley looked to the low table where her travel bag had been laid. "No, I have everything I need. Thank you."

Maybe, she thought as the man departed, drawing the outer doors shut in his wake, *maybe this is a hotel of some sort.*

She found it hard to keep that thought in mind when she dropped her weary body into a huge, tiled tub of steaming water that bubbled and swirled around her tired limbs. Never in her life had she been in a hotel equipped with such lavish amenities. She'd have gone to sleep on the spot and probably drowned if she hadn't been so hungry.

Refreshed by the bath and dressed in the smart slacks and cotton shirt she'd brought along for sight-seeing, Haley returned to the formal living room.

There, she found that the servant who had introduced himself as Ali had spread a veritable feast on a round glass-topped table large enough to seat eight.

She sat down without ceremony, slavering over frosted fruits, seasoned vegetables, marinated meats and rice dishes fit to serve a king. First, she tasted a goblet brimming with a tart apricot drink. Her stomach contracted with gratitude. Remembering her manners, Haley spread a fine linen napkin over her lap and looked up at the man. "May I ask you a question?"

"But, of course, Mademoiselle Bennett." The servant bowed obsequiously, most solemn-faced.

"Where am I?"

"This is the winter palace of Sheik Zayn Haji Haaris."

"In Saudi Arabia?"

"In Anaiza, Arabia. The desert is all the same, mam'selle."

"I do not want to assume anything incorrect here, you understand? Is your Sheik Zayn Haji Haaris the son of Sheik Wali Haj Haaris?"

"His eldest son, my lady, by his first wife, Yaella. This was her family home. The young prince has inherited it, as is custom."

Haley divined much from the Arab's simple explanation. First, and most importantly, she was likely as safe as she would ever be . . . under these strained circumstances.

Haley raised an eyebrow in mute acceptance and began to tuck into the food. She concentrated on a heavenly batch of rice and seasoned mutton. As she ate, the sharp edge of her deep hunger lessened and she thought of questions. "Ali, do you have news of what happened in Kuwait? Has the newspaper arrived? Or better, is there a broadcast in English on any television channel?"

The man gave her a puzzled look, and Haley wondered if she was taxing his scope of English by talking too rapidly. Then his expression lost its perplexed look and he said smoothly, "No, mam'selle. We do not have such things. In Riyadh you could learn world news, but here in Anaiza most of what happens in the world passes us by."

Haley knew her face showed her disappointment at that answer. "Riyadh." She echoed his accent, trying out the word on her own tongue. Her attempt sounded like a blend of vowels, lacking the hardness of consonants altogether. She ate another bite of the delicious rice, chewing thoughtfully. "How far away is Riyadh? How long will it take me to get there?"

He gave her a look that Haley could only interpret as paternal. Were he decked out in a stole over his long whitish robe, Haley would have identified him as a priest. And, in spite of her basic unease, Ali's calm and unthreatening demeanor did a great job of soothing her concerns. His words did not.

"It matters not the distance or the time of the journey to the capital, *lalla*. You may not go there."

"Why not?" Haley set her fork down. Alarm welled inside her like a flash flood. Her calm in the aftermath of the tempest, she realized, was shock. Any moment she could lose control. She swallowed the jolt of fear, determined not to let her emotions get out of hand again.

"You are Ammerikaan? Yes?"

"Yes. I am."

"You have not been to Arabia before this?"

"No. I never have. This is my first visit."

Ali spread his palms open in a gesture of universal understanding. "A woman may not travel here without her father's permission. Your father is in Al Kuwait, yes?"

"To the best of my knowledge, yes."

"Well, there you have it, mam'selle. When your father comes, you ask his permission, and should he grant it, you may travel about at your leisure."

His reasoning left her reeling.

"Do you know how I got here?" Haley asked perversely.

"Yes. Sheik Zayn delivered you to our safekeeping."

An oversimplification, if Haley had ever heard one. "Just for the record," she murmured as pleasantly as she could, "I flew my own plane into the middle of a war over Kuwait City, Ali."

"A war over Kuwait, mam'selle? I do not want to correct a guest as I know that would be most unpolite, but surely you are mistaken. That cannot be."

"I hate to be the bearer of bad tidings, but what else does one call bombs flying everywhere? An airport terminal blowing up before my eyes?"

"I do not know, mam'selle. I have worked many years for the Haj Haaris. He is most fundamental man, very upright in his beliefs. He would not allow a woman to move beyond his protection, not even a foreign woman. But, do not worry, no matter the trouble in Kuwait, you will be safe here at Anaiza."

Haley blinked twice over the servant's smooth deflection of her worries. She wanted to argue that what she'd seen and experienced had nothing to do with the fundamental beliefs of the man whose hospitality she was temporarily forced to accept. "You've missed the point," she said quite calmly. "I cannot sit here doing nothing when my father is in the middle of heaven only knows what kind of danger."

"I see." The solemn-faced Ali nodded gravely, as though he considered her words. "But, I can see that your journey has exhausted you. You must rest, yes? When Sheik Haji Haaris returns, you must speak to him of these things that trouble you. It is not within my power to answer your questions about Kuwait."

Ali busied himself with clearing the table. Haley saw it was pointless to argue. He was right about her being exhausted. The truth was, she was bordering on collapsing right where she sat. That opulent bed she'd seen in the next room beckoned to her.

Though how she was going to sleep when she had so many worries she didn't know. And his advice to save all her questions for Sheik Zayn Haaris didn't make her feel any more like resting.

In her present state, she couldn't begin to figure out how she was going to reason with that walking nightmare of chauvinism she'd slapped on the tarmac. That thought dropped red-hot acid onto the magnificent meal she'd consumed.

Haley glared at the double doors Ali closed on his way out with the rolling tray. Did she hear the click of a lock? Was she imprisoned? She shuddered, wondering if a man with an Uzi slung over his shoulder stood watch just beyond the carved rosewood. Should she get up and find out? She decided against it, and rubbed the pads of her fingers across her eyes. Even that gentle motion hurt. She'd been awake too, too long.

This, she concluded, was a situation that was going to take some maneuvering to work her way out of. Wisely, she knew she was too worn-out to deal with such complexities just now.

The shuttered bedroom was cool and dark and blessedly silent. The bed was as soft as thistledown, the pillows perfect, accepting the aching weight of her head and easing the tension in the back of her neck.

The minute she closed her eyes, she saw herself standing in front of one of the most beautifully designed planes ever to touch the sky. Before her stood the most arrogant man God had ever touched. His covetous stare was not fixed upon the Vixen. Instead, his burning, black-lashed, dark eyes bored into her soul.

She opened her eyes. "It didn't mean anything," she said to the dazzling opulence that surrounded her.

Haley turned onto her side, cradled her throbbing skull between the cool spread of her fingers. She stared at the intricate, carved screens shading the windows from the harsh sun. What am I going to do? Why did Omar have to have such a beautiful name? Zayn. She shook her head against the soft pillow in wonder. What to do, what to do?

The answer to that question and all others eluded her. Thought was a merry-go-round. Her yawns deepened and Haley dropped into a deep dreamless sleep from which she did not awaken for hours.

# Chapter 4

A young maid looked in on Haley every few hours until sundown, then slept on a small pallet at the foot of Haley's bed during the night.

Maari reported to Ali that the sheik's guest still slept at daybreak. Checking on her charge at noon, she found no difference, other than Haley's changed position. But at six that evening, when Maari was summoned to her master's presence and she reported the long sleep of the American woman, Sheik Zayn was not pleased.

"Do you want me to wake her up, master?" the little servant asked.

"No. I will check on her myself."

"As you wish." Maari returned to her duties elsewhere. Zayn Haji Haaris waved Ali aside over the dinner that had been prepared for him and he went up to the quarters given to Haley.

He paused along the way to inspect rooms that hadn't been used since his mother's death ten years ago. They were clean and orderly. Most were furnished sparingly. Seventy years had passed since any concubines had graced the winter palace. Yet the harem remained, a private secluded oasis in the midst of a massive household. Zayn thought it a great waste to have so much space allocated to a man's use and to have nothing within the rooms that gave any pleasure.

In previous centuries, eunuch guards monitored the harem, but he had no such persons in his employ. That did not mean that well-trained guards were not on the grounds. It was as unwise for any sheik to be that foolish in this day and age as it had been in his great-grandfather's time.

Zayn entered the formal reception room. He'd had it modernized several years ago, but as he spent most of his time traveling between Kuwait, London and Paris, visiting Anaiza was something of a rarity.

The pace of modern business kept him hopping, and coping with jet lag. Never, not even in his wildest dreams, had he thought he would be caught in his Air Force Reserves uniform, actually defending his country. Had he not been duty bound to return to Kuwait for the two-week reserve session, he would most likely have been vacationing in Cairo like most of his countrymen.

Fate had placed him in the airways over Kuwait, trading jokes over the radio with two Saudi cousins training on similar maneuvers. Fate had nearly given him a heart attack when the act of war was confirmed and he sighted his father's newest toy jet streaking out of Al Kuwait with an Iraqi MiG on its tail. Fate had given him an American woman who knew how to zip through the air like a lightning bolt. Fate had given him the presence of mind to send her to Anaiza.

Today, this moment, he was thankful that Allah had given him this retreat. And if Allah was merciful, every member of his family would soon be safe within Anaiza's peaceful walls.

Within the harem, cool silence greeted him. The door to the bedroom stood ajar. His leather soles made no sound on the Persian wool rug. Muted twilight filtered through the ancient rosewood screens. The slanted rays fell across the empty, rumpled covers of the bed. He cocked his head sideways, listening for movement. Hearing none, he frowned.

Stepping into the bedroom, he searched for the woman who should be there.

A single garment bag spilled its contents onto the settee at the foot of the bed. The doors of the bath were wide open, but only daylight illuminated the large room. His step quickened as he approached that door. It wasn't possible she had gone elsewhere. Maari had just assured him the woman slept, oblivious to any efforts to awaken her.

"Who's there?" a voice demanded from the bath.

Zayn touched the wall switch and flooded the room with light. Haley Bennett rose from the last step of the deep inset pool, hastily yanking a short, silken robe over her wet skin. Behind her, a smoky-mirrored wall reflected the rear view of her tantalizing pose. A twisted tangle of dripping hair slid down her back. She cocked her head, scowling and squinting.

"What do you want?"

Although he was dressed formally in traditional robe, *kuffiyah* and gold-braided *'iqual,* Zayn was still surprised the woman did not recognize him.

"We have met, Miss Bennett."

"You!" Haley's squint went to open-eyed surprise. *Lord, he's tall, and that face framed by cloth, oh my! Wouldn't Mother flip to meet him! No, wouldn't Mother die if she knew I had just stepped out of the tub and nearly been caught in the altogether!* Reining in her rambling thoughts, she hauled the edges of her robe tighter across her bosom. "Do you always invade the privacy of a guest's bath?"

Zayn almost smiled at her delayed reaction. She was unaware that her efforts to cover her front side with the inadequate silk robe worked to her disadvantage by revealing a tantalizing outline of her backside and glorious legs. Disciplining the corners of his mouth, he kept his face straight and stern as he met the blaze of her eyes.

"You are privileged, Miss Bennett. It is rare that any guest of my house is granted such personal attention."

"Well, pray don't expend yourself on my account!" Haley countered as her fumbling fingers sought the tie belt dangling at her hips. A sudden shiver made her all the more aware of how vulnerably naked she was beneath the robe. Before him!

"My servants expressed deep concern at the length of your sleep. I have merely come to assure myself that you are alive and well and have come to no harm."

A deep flush raised Haley's color. Her first thought upon wakening had been to enjoy that splendid tub again. Thank the Lord, she'd finished her bath before she'd heard her doors open without so much as a single knock. She'd only just managed to pull the robe that she had found in the bath over her wet body before the intruder appeared at the open doors.

"I am perfectly fine," she said a little stiffly, making a secure knot of the belt at her waist.

He made no effort to retreat and stood there openly admiring the curves of her bare legs. It wasn't more leg than Haley had ever shown. It just seemed strange to do so in front of a man wearing more clothing than a monk.

"Do you mind," she said pointedly.

"Certainly not. What man in his right mind objects to a personal showing of a work of art? You are an exquisitely formed woman."

Haley narrowed her eyes at the compliment. "So that's the way of it, is it? Would you like to write a testimonial to Gold's Gym in San Antonio?"

Familiar enough with American culture, Zayn was not put off by her disclaimer. "The gift of a body such as yours is the province of Allah, Miss Bennett, not a gymnasium."

"And you, sir, are laying it on thicker than corn syrup on a pancake. What are you doing here?"

"Merely satisfying my concern that you did not waken."

"Blame jet lag, stress, flying through a war zone with a mad bomber on my back. I am awake now. If you'll grant me some privacy to dress, I would like to speak with you . . . out there." Haley indicated elsewhere with a swift jerk of her head.

"As you wish. I will await you in the lounge." Zayn bowed graciously. He stepped out of the bath, drawing the doors closed.

"Whew! Talk about feeling vulnerable." Haley exhaled.

She ran to the wide vanity and fumbled on the marble countertop for the contacts she'd taken out and left soaking. She dressed hastily, exchanging the robe for her linen pants and shirt. She'd left her bra tucked in a corner pocket of her garment bag. She certainly thought it prudent not to make a mad, wet dash into the bedroom to retrieve it. She had taken enough risks in a damp robe. That man did not need any encouragement!

She worked a brush through the wet tangles of her hair, braided it and turned it into a prim coil at her neck, securely pinned.

Dressing accomplished, she opted for bare feet. That was a sign of the Texan in her. Whenever possible, Haley left off shoes. Omar waited in the lounge. She thought if she put on her boots, she might be tempted to kick him to kingdom come. Bare feet definitely stifled that urge.

Haley closed the bedroom door behind her and stepped into the spacious lounge. He had put on the lights, all of them. She had the distinct feeling that the room had shrunk while she'd been sleeping. Or was it because he was in it?

Zayn Haaris was standing, and turned to her as she entered. Haley deliberately refused to look directly at him as she circled the room. When she did move her gaze up to his too-handsome countenance, the frown of displeasure in his eyes took her back a bit.

Had she thought him stone-faced on first meeting him? A man who never gave away his feelings? Most definitely. But he felt free enough on this meeting to allow some of his feelings to show. Disapproval ran rank. She wondered why. In the bath, approval had gleamed from his dark, sensuous eyes and she was not so blind without her contacts that she hadn't seen it. More important, she had felt it! His change of mood threw her off-balance.

"Come. Sit down. We will talk." His invitation was stiffly spoken, formal.

Haley crossed the room, but stopped first at a trolley laid out with glasses, ice in a silver bucket and what not.

"I would like something to drink first."

"I have ordered tea."

"Something stronger." Haley dropped to one knee, checking behind the closed door below the serving tray. There was a can or two of pop.

"You are seeking whiskey?"

"Whiskey?" Haley rose to her feet, perplexed by what she detected as condemnation. Normally, she wouldn't take that attitude from anyone. At her age, she didn't have to. "No, I just woke up, Omar. Coffee is the first order of my day."

"Coffee," Zayn repeated. He went to the intercom and spoke briskly in Arabic, ordering coffee brought to them.

For lack of anything stronger at the moment, Haley poured water over a glass of ice and drained it. Anything to delay turning to face him. Obviously he wasn't going away until they'd had a chat. She left the empty glass on the tray and, turning, faced him.

"Well? What now, Sheik Haaris?"

"Come, sit down, please. There are numerous things we must discuss. You have nothing to fear from me. After all, our fathers are involved in business together. Correct?"

"Technically." Haley granted him that much. She refilled her glass, continuing to delay approaching a man she didn't feel quite safe approaching.

No, it went deeper than that. Something unsettled, ruffled the air between them, as if there were a throbbing air current or a pulsing undertow dragging her to him. She fought it, resisting it out of hand because she didn't know what else to do. But he was so damned attractive that she yearned to let go and be pulled into it . . . whatever *it* was.

*Don't be silly,* she muttered to herself, and cast a significant glance at him, speculating about what magnificence was hidden by all that folding linen. The flowing robe didn't fool her one bit. She'd already seen him in a flight suit, and if anyone had flaws to their body shape, a flight suit revealed them. Clearly, she wasn't the only person in the room who knew how to lift a weight bar. She was sure he did some power lifting in his spare time, too. Hastily, she snapped her thoughts back to where they belonged with a silent, mental scold for their being so unruly.

She was supposed to figure out whether or not *he* was the type who would pounce the minute she became still, and here she was wondering what would happen if she did the pouncing!

The sitting area contained no single chairs, only those ultramodern sectionals that formed groupings. Knowing she had to sit somewhere, Haley dropped onto a curving corner of the first pit grouping, scooted back and tucked her bare feet beneath her. She set her glass of water on a coaster on the low Ming coffee table and folded her arms defensively across her chest, awaiting his next maneuver.

The sheik remained standing for a moment longer, studying her. He did not like her hair twisted into that tight knot at the back of her head. He cared nothing for her modern pants or the shirt that would swallow a woman twice her size. Her firm chin rose a few degrees, and though she said nothing, he could sense her defiance. It was nearly a palpable thing. Her cocked eye-

brow and set mouth told him she would give an excellent fight
before surrendering anything she considered valuable to her. The
fullness of that same mouth implied that she was of a passionate nature and that a conquest would be sweet and fulfilling for
both of them. Half smiling at those inner deductions, he took
the couch opposite her.

Haley watched the man most carefully as he sat down. The
edges of his gilt-trimmed robe parted, revealing dark, tailor-
made trousers encasing lean, muscular thighs. She tried to keep
her gaze fixed to the not-so-neutral ground of his eyes, but it was
hard not to take a peek or two at such an utterly splendid male.

All right, she scolded herself mentally once more. She did
know a few hunks back home. Bodybuilders who used the same
gym where she worked out four times a week. Not many seemed
overly blessed with brains or sensitivity. Like as not they were
as misjudged on the surface as she was. No one expected a stat-
uesque blonde to have brains or mechanical ability.

Mostly, she knew short, Napoleonic imbeciles, middle-aged
mechanics and Einstein-like computer whizzes whose sex appeal ran in negative numbers. On the basis of that, she almost
had a right to sit here and take a very good look at a splendidly
built, exotic man whose sex appeal throbbed like a secondary
pulse beneath his skin. The trouble was, what she saw appealed
to her a great deal. Oh, yes, it did.

He could also fly jets.

They had that much in common alone.

Then, of course, because her mother was going to have to
know every single detail Haley could possibly remember, she
had to note the smooth fit of his handmade, leather shoes, the
lingering hint of an exotic, private-label after-shave, the ta-
pered length of his fingers and the immaculate, blunt cut of his
nails. After all, it wasn't every day one had a chance to meet a
real live sheik . . . the equivalent of a prince.

Zayn found her silent evaluation moderately curious. He had
been prepared for babbling histrionics. Where were her fears?
Why had she deliberately flaunted her superb body twice before his eyes and now made every effort to obscure her nipped
waist, full breasts and achingly wonderful long legs? And that
hair . . . she had ruined it, by tying it in a gross knot severely
pulled back from her face. What game did she play?

"Well," Haley said abruptly, bringing her gaze to his wide, sculpted mouth. "You did say you wanted to talk. Do you have news?"

"News. You want to know the news?"

"Yes, of course. What has happened in Kuwait? Was it a terrorist attack? Some wild faction run rampant, a revolution or a coup attempt?"

"The truth is much more abhorrent," Zayn replied. "Kuwait was taken over by a hostile neighbor with a very large army."

Haley frowned. "The whole country? Is my father safe?"

"No one in Kuwait is safe at the moment, Miss Bennett. The airport was one of the first targets of the Iraqis. And yes, the whole country has been taken. The Iraqi army holds all three borders. Other than that, I have no more specific information to give you. No one does."

What he'd said couldn't have been more stunning. Haley stared at him. She processed his words, but was unable to believe it as truth. "That's impossible, isn't it?"

"You will find no argument from me that it is the worst news I or any of my countrymen have ever heard in our lives. But as to its being impossible, then, Miss Bennett, the impossible has been done. It is done, a fait accompli. An act of aggression that is denounced by every known political entity, but impossible, no."

"Why?"

"The reasons for the invasion are unclear, but I am positive it comes down to the oil fields and the revenues they produce. Are not all acts of war based on greed and wealth?"

"I wouldn't know." Haley swallowed the dryness in her throat. "What of my father? Where is he? Did he refuel the Vixen and get out of the country? Is he here in Saudi Arabia looking for me?"

"At this precise moment, I do not know where your father is specifically. To the best of my knowledge, he was unable to leave the airport."

"Oh, God." Haley swallowed again. She pressed her fingers to her forehead, trying to think. "I never should have gone to sleep. I have to get to a phone immediately, call home and find out what my com**pany w**ants me to do. If Dad is still in Kuwait,

I can fly there and bring him home. Can you take me to the nearest international telephone?"

"No, Miss Bennett. I regret that I cannot. My time here is very limited. Currently, I must hold myself at the disposal of the emir of Kuwait for military business. You understand that we are in a state of war."

"Well, yes, I understand that," Haley agreed. "But I must get to a phone and find out if my father is safe."

"Your father is as safe as any man in Kuwait."

"What if he's being held hostage by some fanatical group?"

"All persons in Kuwait are being detained by the Iraqi military. There has been no specific clarification of the status of American citizens inside the country."

"What does that mean?"

The sheik's answer was delayed by the arrival of Ali with the coffee. Zayn Haaris served her a cup, saying warningly, "You will find our coffee much stronger than American brews."

Haley sampled the aroma first. It was strong, promising to give her system the kick start it needed. The spicy cardamom flavor was a new experience. Settling grounds wasn't. She sipped the coffee gratefully, realizing how important this one addiction was to her ability to think clearly and feel alert. It was strong enough that she didn't need her usual three cups to get her going. "That is much better," she said finally.

The sheik inclined his head, acknowledging the sigh of relief in her words. She was a very pretty woman, despite her clothes and her unflattering hairstyle. He was content to watch her guarded movements, to study her. He had no clue on her age.

"It is very good coffee." She sat back, cup and saucer in hand and focused her eyes upon the man opposite her. "Now, let's get down to specifics. I will need to return to my plane immediately. I assume you can make arrangements for me. I do not have a visa for Saudi Arabia, but I am certain the State Department and your government will understand how I came to be here."

"They will understand what I explain to them, yes. However, you cannot leave my household."

Zayn's last statement fell like a bombshell in the quiet room. Haley's jaw tightened. "Am I under arrest?"

"These are not the quarters of a person held under arrest, Miss Bennett, I assure you."

"That assures me of nothing, Sheik Haaris. You are imply-ing arrest and if not that, detention."

"It is for your own safety."

"Bull!" Haley snapped. "Call it whatever you want, you're threatening to hold me hostage."

"I repeat, these are not the quarters of a hostage or a person under arrest. Do not insult me."

"Then I am free to go."

"No. I am sorry to inform you that you are not free to go anywhere. This is Saudi Arabia, Miss Bennett. Here, women do not drive automobiles or fly airplanes." This time, it was his eyebrow that raised speculatively.

"Need I remind you that I am an American citizen?"

"Citizenship is irrelevant in the desert. Within these walls, you will continue to be treated as an honored guest. You will be safely cared for until arrangements can be made for you to leave the country."

"I'm not staying here," Haley affirmed.

"Miss Bennett—" Zayn relaxed against the firm cushions of the sofa "—you are in Saudi Arabia. Here a woman covers her head, wears a veil and goes nowhere without the escort of a male member of her family. Regrettably, there is no member of your immediate family here to take charge of you. Hence, as the son of a business associate of your absent father, the responsibility for your safety becomes mine. You simply must remain at Anaiza. The laws regarding the travel of unescorted women are strictly enforced. I do not wish for your experience in Arabia to be any more difficult than it has to be. Now, I suggest you let your hair down and try to relax."

"Let my hair...no!" Haley set her coffee cup on the saucer with a rattle. The smooth devil was doing everything he could to disarm her.

"I would prefer that we continue our discussion in an atmo-sphere less laden with mistrust."

"Oh, do you?" Haley's eyebrow went up in decided pique. She wiggled her bare toes and retorted, "Tell you what, Omar. You take off your shoes and get as relaxed as I am, and I'll consider taking down my hair."

"A sharp tongue will not gain you my assistance." Zayn studied her with growing fascination.

"Are you implying that if I resort to using my so-called feminine wiles, let my hair down and blatantly make an effort to seduce you, you will suddenly become as malleable as putty in my delicate little hands."

A twitch in the corner of the sheik's mouth told Haley he fought with smiling outright. "My dear Miss Bennett, I am implying nothing of the kind. Nor would I ever describe hands as broad and strong as yours as delicate. I do not think there is a delicate bone in your entire body. That is not to say that I would not be agreeable to seduction. You are a beautiful woman. Very tall for my usual tastes, but your hair might make up for that flaw were you to let it down where I could see and enjoy it."

Haley's jaw sagged at his quick turnaround. He was damned close to smirking.

"Look, let's just stick to the facts, okay? I need to return to my airplane. It took you ten seconds to shout an order on the tarmac and arrange my transport here. Kindly repeat the gesture. I will be out of your hair the minute I start the Vixen."

At those statements, the sheik fixed Haley with a curiously blank stare. She found that more disturbing—no—*all* of his looks caused her skin to prickle. He sipped his coffee then said mildly, "It is better that we do not flaunt convention."

"Look, I'm here out of necessity, not perversity. Surely the governments involved will understand that."

"The reasons for your presence matters not. You have no choice except to abide by the laws of the country where you are. The consequences, should you not comply with custom, would not be to your liking, I assure you. Since I may deduce from your antagonism that conforming is the last thing you will consider doing, you will remain at Anaiza. Safely out of harm's way until I can personally return you to your family in America."

Haley forced her jaw to unlock. "If absolutely necessary, I can conform to whatever custom is dictated. That doesn't mean I have to like it. However, I am telling you that I am not going back to America without my father or uncle Jack. If that means I have to go into Kuwait in a veil and a robe, fine! Keep your customs and traditions intact. I am not going home without my father or uncle."

For the first time, Haley detected a note of warmth in his too-direct gaze. A small smile creased the corner of his extravagantly chiseled, sensuous mouth.

"I admire your determination. Such courage in the face of great danger is laudable, however impractical. But I cannot allow you to do that, either. You do not fully understand the danger. I would never be able to live with my conscience if something happened to you that I could have prevented. Be assured that so long as you remain sequestered at Anaiza, you are under my protection."

"Sequestered!" Haley almost jumped to her feet screaming on that word. "Look, how do you propose I join my father and complete the business we came to the Mideast to finish?"

"Until the troubles in Kuwait have worked themselves out, no business can be conducted. It was an unnecessary complication for you to arrive as the pilot of the second plane. One that your family members must greatly regret at this very moment. I have checked into the matters regarding the Vixen airplanes my father ordered. There was no mention of a female pilot. I am aware in your country some women take such employment. But here, you do not have the same latitude. Your choices are extremely limited."

"I am completely opposed to this purdah thing. I won't stand for it. I have to join my father. We came here on business. I have a job to do, and once it is done, I am going straight back home."

"I do not wish to have this conference between us become a test of wills, Miss Bennett. You are my guest. Kuwait is in turmoil. You will remain in Anaiza."

"Just a minute, Sheik Haaris. We have one great big problem here. I don't want to stay at Anaiza. I want to leave your house immediately. If I cannot travel freely because of some touchy situation in Kuwait, I prefer going to the capital or wherever the nearest American embassy is."

"Before you—"

"Oh, no." Haley refused to be interrupted before she said all she needed to say. "I can pay my own way in this country or any country in the world. I don't need another uncle, and I am out of the market for big brothers. The two I have at home are more than plenty. And while I'm on the subject of brothers, let me tell you neither of them would dare to dictate where I can or cannot go, as you have so foolishly tried to do. I make such decisions for myself, thank you very much."

"Are you finished?" Zayn said with deplorable finesse.

Haley was just getting ready to launch another round of her liberation speech, when she remembered the Vixen and the trump card it offered.

"Not quite. One more thing, Sheik Haaris. If you keep pushing me around, I'll see to it that my company cancels the sale of twenty Vixens to yours." Haley paused for dramatic effect and to gauge his reaction. The blasted man didn't so much as blink an eye! Didn't he think she had the power to cancel the sale? Well, he was in for a big surprise. Her vote carried as much weight in the boardroom as any other member of the family-owned corporation. "Let me guess what Sheik Wali Haj Haaris would think of your interference then?"

"I have already canceled the sale," Zayn said matter-of-factly. "The plane you attempted to deliver is worthless. Not a system inside it is working as of this moment."

"Is that so?" Haley lifted her coffee cup and smiled with great satisfaction. She blew softly onto the hot brew, making ripples. "Well, that is the first piece of good news you've given me. Now there is absolutely no reason for us to continue this charade. Take me to the base, and I'll get my worthless jet and go about my business. Then I won't have to worry about a Neanderthal like you abusing the Vixen's delicate systems."

"The more sensitive the mechanism, the more valued a satisfactory response from it would be, Miss Bennett. You should restrict your opinions to fields where they might have some value."

"Aeronautical design *is* my field," Haley rejoined smugly, placing her cup and saucer on the coffee table between them. "Where I come from, I'm considered something of a whiz kid, though at my advanced age of twenty-four I consider the kid bit inappropriate. There is nothing wrong with the Vixen, I just made sure you and everyone else is locked out. Take me back to the base and I'll have the Vixen running in the blink of an eye."

"No."

"How about if I say please, nicely?"

"No."

Arrogant swine, Haley thought. Arrogant, handsome swine! Haley stood up, smoothing her hands down the sides of her pants.

"Is that your final word, Omar?"

A muscle flexed in the sheik's smoothly shaven cheek telling Haley that she'd scored a big one. All right, she admitted privately, it was a below-the-belt hit, but his tactics were unfair, as well. How many innuendos was a girl supposed to ignore? She was still smarting from the crack about how he'd value a response from a sensitive machine! Who was kidding whom? He was deliberately holding her prisoner. Judging by the heat in his chocolate-drop eyes, he was on a slow burn to a meltdown.

"I must say it has been an interesting chat," she said. "Do drop by another time. You are delightful company, Omar."

"Sit down, Miss Bennett. I have not ended my visit."

# *Chapter 5*

The force of his soft-voiced command hammered a wedge into Haley's veneer of polite civility. No man dared issue orders to her. Across the safe distance of the Ming coffee table, she prepared for the real battle.

"I beg your pardon—"

"And well you should," he interrupted smoothly. "Apology accepted."

"Ha!" Haley barked. She stomped to the door and flung it open. "You had something to say as you leave..."

She let her words dangle leadingly, and did one of her mother's favorite tricks, gestured to the opened door. It worked for Emma Bennett beautifully. This lump sat where he was, not bothering to rise, not even moving his hand to put his cup down on the table.

"I never repeat a command, Haley Bennett."

Diamonds could have fractured in his glare. Haley wasn't one to be intimidated easily, but Zayn Haaris looked more dangerous at that very moment than when he'd turned apoplectic on the airfield on discovering that his father wasn't on board her Vixen. Danger pulsed in the air, yet the man hadn't moved a muscle, not yet. Only the growing coldness in those liquid dark eyes indicated that Haley had passed over the line of what insult he would tolerate. Shrugging in mock carelessness, she eased the door shut with a soft click.

"Suit yourself," she said bravely.

Actually, that god-awful fight she'd felt brewing between herself and this arrogant man seemed imminent. Pacing restlessly, not wanting to occupy the same planet he did, she prowled the large room, circling the sofas.

Her fingers itched to slug him, to pick up any number of priceless vases and throw them at him. She needed a physical release from the knotting tensions threatening to cripple her.

She had to do something with her hands quickly—before the temptation to clobber him with a lamp overcame her.

She attacked the ice bucket, filling a glass, splashing water on the polished tray. She wiped it with a square of spotless folded linen. Then Haley circuited the entire room one more time, aware she was on the brink of making a complete fool of herself. She cast a sideways look at him. His expression was brutal; mouth tight and grim above a clenched jaw that showed no sign of relaxing anytime soon.

What had she done? What *hadn't* she done? Hell, a veritable list of never-dones seemed to float in Haley's active mind. The mere thought of going to the mat against a man of his ilk filled her with dread. She couldn't win. Why should she even bother to try?

To give in to him without questioning any of the things he'd told her was anathema. She wasn't a naive child. To continue challenging his natural authority served no further purpose, either. What should she do?

Finally, she came back to the coffee table where she'd started this minor revolt, took cup and saucer in hand and sat down on the sofa to his right. She tried very hard not to look sullen as she pointed to the pot of coffee. "May I have some more coffee, please?"

He raised his right hand and turned his palm over in a sweeping gesture that invited her to help herself, all without speaking a word.

Haley sat forward to fill her cup and held the pot aloft in a mute signal of inquiry regarding refilling his empty cup. He made the faintest acknowledgment, a flick of his eyes, no more, in the direction of his cup.

*He has the silent treatment down to a science,* Haley thought
mutinously as she returned the pot to its silver tray. All at once,
the whole setting seemed too intimate, too personal to bear...to
be sharing coffee with him. Her body throbbed with an awareness that she'd never in her life felt so strongly.

Her eyes feasted on the movements of his long-fingered hands
as he stirred the steamy liquid with a silver spoon. She lowered
her lashes as that hand raised the cup to his mouth to sip the
brew.

Still, she stole a glance under those lashes, one of those sideways looks that probably told him a great deal about how in-
tolerable she found her present position, how weak and
vulnerable she felt.

There was no uncertainty to him. His will was harder than
stone. It was she who was meant to knuckle under. And she had.

His last spoken words echoed over and over in her mind. *I
never repeat a command.* He didn't have to repeat anything
when he had the power to enforce his will by sheer mental dom-
inance. Haley ground her teeth. She was seated again. This time,
closer to him. *I'm an idiot!* she thought. The stress showed in
her behavior, not in his.

Haley flashed him a hateful look, deeply resenting his intrusion into the wonderful little world of successes she'd created for
herself. By her reckoning, they should be meeting as equals.
Then why did she feel so outclassed and inadequate? Why
couldn't she drag her eyes away from him? Resist watching lean,
tanned fingers touch an inanimate object and subdue the longing that his touch would become personal? Hell, she'd probably jump out of her skin if he did touch her!

He set his cup down without a single chink from the china.
"Are you naturally this high-strung and anxious, Miss Bennett?"

"Are you asking if I'm a type A personality? Praise-oriented,
eager to please and overactive?"

"No. I am asking if your anxiety is ruling your behavior. Can
you not relax knowing that you are safe from all harm at this
moment?"

"Am I?" Haley asked bluntly. "Am I truly safe here? Can
you answer that?"

"Yes, of course I can. Can you be specific in the danger you
perceive?"

"Well, let me put it this way, I'm not worried about bombs falling on my head and blowing me sky-high."

"I see." His eyes locked with hers.

Those black orbs pulled with the strength of an electromagnetic field. She realized the moment she shied away, she gave more ground than she'd already surrendered. She tried to recapture her advantage with words. "If that is so, then it shouldn't bother you to leave."

"You will get used to my presence better if I remain."

"Why should I? Our association is temporary. We won't meet again once this crisis is over."

"You will not insist on coming to my country when you deliver your next plane, H. J. Bennett?"

"The deal is off. You just said so and I agreed."

"What I really said is your plane does not work."

"My plane can't be pirated. There is a difference. Did you expect the latest technology? Or are you satisfied with old-fashioned starters that anyone can hijack?"

"Touché, Haley Bennett. If you are keeping score, that point I concede to you. Would you now have me assume you can make your lovely Vixen 2000-2 work?"

"Of course I can. But in light of the position you have placed me in, you can consider my assistance going no further than name, rank and serial number. I won't tell you any more than that."

"Now you border on becoming childish. Very well, play that game if you must. You removed certain papers from the plane. They were inside a leather case. Bring them to me."

"They won't help you."

"Have I asked for help? No, I have asked for the Vixen's papers."

"Suit yourself," Haley muttered under her breath.

No point was served by her withholding the Vixen's papers. During the time she'd been asleep, he had had ample opportunity to order his servants to search her belongings. She rose and went into the bedroom and saw her garment bag lying on the bench at the foot of the bed, but no briefcase. She didn't see it in the bedroom and returned to the lounge.

"Ah, there it is." She found her attaché case on a low mahogany table near the door. She took it to him and said, "Is this every woman's lot in life, stepping and fetching for you, Sheik Haaris?''

He did not rise to the bait. Instead, he took the briefcase, reached for the lamp on the table at his elbow and moved it to shine over his shoulder. He leaned forward, opened the briefcase, and moved aside his cup and the coffeepot before allowing the contents of the case to slide onto the gleaming tabletop.

Haley tucked her feet under her again and sat back with her coffee, passively watching as he searched through her things. Oddly, she felt calmer. They were on familiar ground. His scrutiny of her passport failed to ruffle her, not even when he compared the photo with her face, as if one did not belong to the other. Maybe she was one of those rare people that photographed well. She couldn't begin to guess what else he might be thinking.

"You lied about your weight," he said at long last.

"I certainly didn't," Haley countered defensively.

"You don't weigh one hundred twenty-five pounds."

"I don't weigh an ounce over that," Haley insisted.

"You do not have the curves of a woman of that weight."

Insulted again, Haley snapped, "Well, I have the bones!"

"You take offense very easily."

Haley rolled her eyes. He could stand to learn a thing or two about tact. He thumbed through the balance of her personal items, including her wallet, pausing to read her driver's license, her aviator's licenses, and to study pictures of her family and friends. He counted her cash and traveler's checks. When he'd finished his inspection, he wagged her five crisp Kuwait mille bank notes between them. "Tell me again that you were not in Kuwait? Where did you get this currency if you were not in the city?"

More than a little annoyed, Haley glared at him. "Have you ever heard of the Cullen-Frost Bank, Sheik Haaris? One can purchase any currency desired back home."

He considered her answer without comment, then returned his attention to the plane's documentation papers.

"There is no operations manual here."

"The person who creates the manual doesn't need it."

Zayn Haaris sat back, regarding Haley with hooded, inscrutable eyes. "Are you saying you are that person, Miss Bennett?"

"Got it in one!" Haley pointed one long finger his direction and smiled like a very sated cat full of canary.

He smiled and very gently shook his head. "Impossible."

It astounded Haley what a smile did to his face. The genuine smile softened his hard, masculine features, making him all the more irresistible. Haley felt as though she were sinking in quicksand. Egads, but there was a hint of a dimple in his left cheek! Recovering, she cleared her throat and told her eyes to quit playing tricks on her.

"My being the designer of the Vixen may be unacceptable by your standards," she managed to reply without any smugness, "but impossible, Sheik Haaris? No."

"Where are the operations manuals?" he said, obviously not believing she was the plane's designer.

"All of the vital documents for the planes are crated on my father's jet. He's a stickler for protocol and procedures. That means, the manuals are in Kuwait. Shall we go there and have a good read?"

"How very shortsighted of you."

"Think so?" It was Haley's turn to break into a smile. "I can't help thinking it was very farsighted of my father to insist on taking all the important junk with him. That way, he knew I'd have to tag right along beside him. The beauty of that is, you can't start the Vixen without me."

That impasse satisfied her. But she wasn't satisfied with the growing attraction she felt brewing with each clue he gave of his true personality. Every blasted aggravation worked to make him more of a challenge, more fascinating to her already charged libido. She wondered what sparks would fly if she touched him, deliberately.

She had his face mapped and memorized. His voice was permanently imprinted on her mind, as was the hard, muscular body she knew was beneath his clothing. In short, she had him fixed and read. And what she saw, she wanted.

That revelation caused a sudden lurch inside her chest. Though Haley made every effort to retain her outer calm, internally, her body seethed with ever-increasing awareness of him as a man. The attraction was dramatic and pronounced, disorienting.

Blood hammered in her temples. Each of her senses sharpened. Fingers ached to reach forward and touch. Ears tuned in to the nuance and inflection in his voice. Her nose separated the subtle differences between coffee and after-shave. Her eyes were having a field day. Only her sense of taste was unsatisfied. She would bite her tongue from now until doomsday before she'd give in to what that sense wanted her to do.

Altogether, she was being tied in knots. She rarely had time for dalliance. But, why him? she wondered. She couldn't answer that question. She want to ask why they continued to talk about the Vixen when it was no longer the real issue.

"There are ways around any lockout," he said smoothly.

"True. Can you program or reprogram a computer?"

"Now you are being impertinent."

"Touched a nerve, have I?" Haley chuckled. "Take me to the Vixen. I'll demonstrate all of its amazing features."

"You may tell me how to start it."

"Not in a million years—" Haley stopped herself from calling him Omar. She no longer felt any need to insult him. Far from it; she realized what she really wanted was his outright admiration for the beautiful machine she had created. Yet not one thing this man had said or done had shown her outright that he wanted the Vixen 2000-2. But she knew he did.

He lusted after the damn plane even though he did a magnificent job of not revealing a single emotion.

A smile creased Haley's face as she pictured him sitting in the cockpit, thwarted, frustrated, the controls in his hands and the machine valiantly unresponsive. He could only wish he had the little lady airborne. Sort of the way she was doing, sitting on his fine couch, drinking his fabulous coffee and not daring to move close enough to touch him.

"Where is the operations manual?"

"I told you. It is with my father in Al Kuwait."

Zayn Haaris frowned. These were not the answers that he wanted to hear. He gave one last search through the unimportant assortment of papers. Nothing in it would make the airplane fly. He rested his elbow on the back of the sofa, turned toward her, his hand over his mouth while he thought this out.

All at once he smiled, then laughed, deeply amused. "You wish me to believe you are the Vixen's designer?"

"Don't judge me by the color of my hair," she snapped. She didn't like the way his smile spread to his eyes, either.

"I understand. You wish to play games, to be induced into telling me where the manual is, to be forced?"

"Right, bring on the whips and chains."

"Perhaps the keys you left on the plane are not the correct keys. They open the locks and fit the ignition, but that is all."

"If you think my key will help, take it. It is in my wallet. Help yourself. You'll get nowhere."

"I will contact your company in Texas and request another manual to be sent immediately by air express."

"By all means do, Sheik Haaris. Have you had occasion to meet my brothers? Matthew runs the company in my father's absence. Tom pitches in in a pinch. Both will suggest you request my assistance to access the computers. In fact, at the moment, no one on earth other than me can start the, Vixen 2000-2. I made certain of that before I left it sitting on your Saudi tarmac. At Bennett Industries, we employ a state-of-the-art lockout. That way, no one has to worry about bandits strolling up and saying "Open sesame" and stealing one of our planes. I, too, have read the *Arabian Nights*."

"Now, you are being impudent."

"Am I?" Haley drawled, totally unaffected by his glare. Nor did she feel the slightest worry about retribution. His hands were absolutely tied. "You know, you've antagonized me, big time. You're flat out of luck, sir. I won't help you."

"You have a very peculiar way of doing business, Miss Bennett, cutting off your nose to spite your face. And it is such a pretty face, too."

"Don't waste compliments on me, please." Haley held up a warding-off hand. "I won't fall for them, believe me. I won't fall for any trick."

Zayn cocked his head to one side, grinning. "You think you're smart?"

"I think the word most people use is *brilliant,* but I've never let it go to my head."

Haley's grin was as big as Texas now, lighting up her eyes with mirth. She liked clashing swords with him, especially when she came out the victor. *For the lack of a password, Ali Baba was locked out.* She wanted to ask him how it felt to be the one without any choices. It was a fine turnaround. She wanted to laugh at the irony of it all but she couldn't. The only thing that held her back was that she didn't think he would see any humor in the analogy.

Zayn reacted naturally to the beautiful smiling woman he saw emerging from the haughty, aloof creature who had first sat down to this interview. With her exquisite blue eyes warm with laughter, Haley Bennett was utterly irresistible.

"Tell me," he said, then leaned toward her, his head only inches from her crown of golden hair. "Were I to take you to the plane, could you really start it?"

"Was I flying it when we had the pleasure of a near midair collision?"

Her eyes flashed at him, blue as the sky, lovely as a pool of cool water. He moistened his lips, aching to taste her. He deliberately baited her, wanting to see her next reaction. "That is a matter of opinion."

Her lips parted and she drew a breath inside her chest. Her breasts swelled against the white cotton and that chin of hers thrust upward at an angle to him, so defiant.

"I'm going to have to pound you if you keep this up," she told him. "Yes, I was flying the plane. Yes, I can damn sure fly it all the way back home and you won't get to keep it! So lighten up. Insult me again and see where that gets you!"

Zayn spread his arm across the sofa back behind her.

"You actually expect me to believe you did not take the plane from Al Kuwait International? Let us be serious. So there was not time for you to clear customs or have your visa stamped. It stands to reason that your father told you to leave. But you cannot expect me to believe that you flew the Vixen solo all the way from America."

"Believe what you wish. I'm here. That should prove something. Furthermore, I need a telephone. I've got to let my mother know I am alive and all right. And if you haven't got one, kindly allow me to use the radio in that blasted helicopter you keep on the roof of this mausoleum."

"Neither would do you any good. You do not speak Arabic, and Anaiza is much too far from any English-speaking monitoring devices. Nor would you be able to make contact with anyone in Kuwait. We are out of range."

"I don't like this. I'm not going to sit here twiddling my thumbs doing nothing when my father is in danger."

"There is nothing you can do but sit and wait. However, you could be more accommodating. I have a use for the Vixen. Give me your codes and I'll see that your company is issued the money it is due."

"When pigs fly!"

"Be careful what you say."

"Why must I exert more caution than you? I'd say we are equals here. Do as I ask. Release me, help me get to my father and uncle in Kuwait, pay what you owe us, then I'll tell you how to start the Vixen."

"My dear Miss Bennett, I am unable to grant any of your requests. You may not leave this house to go anywhere. Your father cannot leave Al Kuwait any more than my own father can at this very moment. Lastly, the money you demand is now being held frozen by banks worldwide because of the aggression of Saddam Hussein. All Iraqi and Kuwaiti assets have been frozen. Our oil tankers sit in American, Japanese and English ports, seized by customs agents. Kuwaiti gold and currency in foreign banks cannot be touched. Until the situation ends, you are stuck where you are. My guest, Haley Bennett."

"Your prisoner, Sheik Zayn Haji Haaris."

"You are a foolish woman to taunt me."

"I would be more foolish to accept your word regarding anything we have just discussed. My autonomy is much too important to surrender into a stranger's hands."

"You do not have a choice."

"There is always a choice."

"So, we are at a standoff."

"Oh, I would definitely say so." Haley frowned, digesting all he had stated. "Wait a minute, did you just say that all Iraqi and Kuwaiti assets have been frozen worldwide? What about automatic banking?"

"Frozen, to all intents and purposes."

"But surely, you have monies in banks elsewhere."

"And at this very moment your president is telling King Fahd that American forces must be allowed to take over the defense of Saudi Arabia."

Haley's eyes widened. "It's that big of a crisis?"

"Much bigger. It has been implied by your government that we Arabs do not have the right to set the price on oil from our wells, that we must sell oil at the price America is willing to pay. This much is at issue, yes."

"Who listens to political rhetoric?" Haley shook her head. "It has nothing to do with what takes place in the boardrooms when business is conducted. Producers sell, consumers buy. I came here to sell planes."

Zayn's eyes widened, again passing over her slender body in a manner that was just short of insulting. "First you claim to be a pilot, next the plane's designer, now you're on the sales staff. Just what is your purpose in Bennett Industries?"

"Forget the insults and the bedroom eyes. They don't work on me. You'll just waste your time. How serious is the crisis? Are we talking war, here, between Saudi Arabia and America, or what?

Again, Zayn suppressed a smile. So she wouldn't tumble easily for a searing look. She was bold enough to give tit for tat. He couldn't help admiring her bravado, misplaced or not. It added to her charm and increased his desire for her. He would offer her more explanation.

"War? I do not think so. There have been threats from Washington that we must shut down Iraqi pipelines through Jordan and Saudi Arabia. Your government's assistance in this, an Arab problem, has been refused, but should your government go through with its threats to place soldiers in Saudi Arabia, there will be grave repercussions. This is Arab land and we will not surrender it."

Haley held up her palm. "Wait a minute. This is confusing me. Which are you, Kuwaiti or Saudi?"

"Neither, I am nomad. I am Muslim. I am my father's son. I am Bedouin and my home is Summan, the Rub' al Khali, Mecca, Baghdad, Al Kuwait, Cairo, the Sinai, Jordan. No matter where I go, my heart faces Mecca and I heed the Prophet's call. I listen to what is good for my people."

"I don't want to get into a political argument," she said. "I'm ambivalent about governments. One's as good or as bad as another. All I want to know are the facts. What's happened and what needs to be done next from my standpoint. That certainly cannot be sitting here, doing nothing."

"Were I to take your statements at face value, I would still be unable to allow you to leave," Zayn replied. "There are certain strategic constraints you have unwittingly stumbled upon."

"'At face value?' What does that mean? What do you mean by 'strategic constraints'?" Haley rubbed her fingers against her forehead. Her hair must be pulled back too tight. Either that or he was giving her a migraine. "Are you referring to that military base I landed at in the desert? Surely you don't think that the American armed forces don't know about it. You can't be that naive to think I'm a spy. Good Lord, the military has satellites that can read license plates on moving automobiles. You can't keep a secret of a hidden ballistic base, not even in the desert, Sheik Haaris. And you can't think I am a spy. I was out of gas. My Mayday call was real. I can prove it."

"We have already ascertained that your call for help was necessary," he agreed. "The tanks in your jet were dangerously depleted. Had that not been verified immediately upon landing, you would never have had the opportunity to be my personal guest. Instead, you would have been a guest of Saudi Intelligence."

"How lucky can a girl get?" Testily, Haley drummed her fingers on the soft leather cushion at her side. She shot a glance around the velvet prison and wondered if she really was all that lucky to be here; restraint was restraint.

"Well," she demanded finally. "What next, Bozo?"

Zayn allowed overwhelming silence to intrude between them. Her insults mirrored her desperation. In the battle of wits, she was losing and knew it.

"You are an astute young woman, Miss Bennett. Surely you will have no difficulty figuring out what comes next."

"Oh, yeah, sure I can. You want my plane because it adds one more possible weapon to your impressive desert arsenal. Let me see, Falcons against Vixens at twenty thousand feet above the desert. Bennett Industries is not a defense contractor, Sheik Haaris. We have nothing to do with the machines of war."

"*Inshallah.*"

"I repeat, we do not make military planes. We do not make components for anything other than radar and computer equipment. What does *Inshallah* mean?"

"The will of Allah is the will of Allah," he explained. "My company has not contracted with Bennett Industries for twenty fighter jets. We have purchased twenty jets. What use we put them to is our concern after the sale. However, I will tell you this, all of my personal resources are at the disposal of my country. I will have those planes. Each and every one of them.''

"Let me guess. You're building your own personal military base out there in the desert.''

"You have an overactive imagination.''

"I have an overactive imagination, ha!'' Haley laughed aloud. "I suppose next you're going to try to convince me I didn't actually see Al Kuwait International explode. Do you think I don't care because it wasn't my hometown the rockets were leveling?''

"From your words and actions thus far, I assume you care deeply about Haley Bennett only.''

"You're a swine,'' Haley said forcefully. "My father happens to be trapped in your country. And so is my godfather, Uncle Jack. Besides that, I have two sisters, two brothers and a mother back home who must be worried sick about the three of us.''

"You make no mention of a husband, though you are well past the age when a woman should be married.''

"The day hasn't come that I'd marry just because I've passed the age of consent,'' Haley said without thinking.

His dark eyes seemed to bore right through her. Haley gulped as a wash of heat flushed her cheeks. Why couldn't she keep her mouth shut?

"A desirable woman such as you should be married.''

"Are you applying for the position?'' she demanded haughtily.

"I do not think so. I would have no patience with a woman whose bold tongue would force me to take measures to curb her defiance of my will.''

The sheik's cool response left no doubt in Haley's mind that he found her entirely unsuitable, which was quite all right in her current state of mind.

"Good,'' she responded with a proud toss of her head. "You'd be the last man on earth from whom I'd request a résumé. No woman in her right mind would willingly consent to becoming another statistic for violence.''

"Are you assuming that as an Arab I know of no other means but physical violence to assert my will?'' he asked chillingly.

"Are you implying that you know the fine art of compromise? So far in this conversation, I have seen no indication that you hold that trait in esteem."

"We have not discussed one issue that merits compromise, Miss Bennett. Thus far, you have only made impossible demands that I cannot accommodate."

"Only because you are a pigheaded, rabid male chauvinist who intends to have his own way no matter what the cost."

Zayn Haaris had the audacity to grin devilishly, inciting Haley's already fueled temper. "So much for altruism, eh?"

Too late she realized he'd baited her and she'd blundered into the trap.

"You know what?" she said hotly. "You'd better leave now. Because in another minute, I'm not going to be held accountable for the damage I do to your face."

Zayn laughed. "Yes, the whole world can see the damage you inflicted yesterday. My face is scarred for life by your lovely hand."

"I wasn't even trying then, buddy boy."

"Then by all means, try again." He sat back holding his arms wide. "I am open. Do your worst."

"Pig! Arrogant, insufferable chauvinist pig!" Haley jumped to her feet, muttering furiously, and stomped halfway across the room before coming to a halt and swiveling to face him. "Swine!"

Zayn rose just as quickly, observing her agitated behavior.

"You may have your outburst of insults, Haley Bennett. All women are creatures of their emotions and it frequently does one good to vent her temper with stomping feet and little screams. In the morning, you will give me the correct key to the Vixen and whatever codes you withhold. Do not play any more games with me. It will only distress you more when you come out the loser."

"Do you think so? Well, bigger men than you have tried to intimidate me and haven't succeeded," Haley countered. "I'm not afraid of you and I can beat you at any game you try to play."

"*Inshallah.*"

"Allah's will, huh?" Haley jerked her head up and down, revealing how aggravated she really was. "Well, sir, in the Bi-

ble it says that if a man's eye offends him, he should cut it out.
You offend me. Get out!''

"You do not wish to quote the New Testament and tell me
that if I am slapped once, I should turn my other cheek to my
enemy's hand?''

Haley's lips parted in a gasp and she turned to face him. Her
control hung by threads. ''I will never start that plane for you.
In fact, Sheik Haaris, since you won't leave, I will.''

## Chapter 6

No woman alive dared speak to Sheik Haaris in the manner this American woman did. Nor had any woman ever insulted Zayn so deeply by turning her back on him and walking out on a conversation.

Zayn deliberately followed her into the bedroom, pushed the door firmly closed and locked it before confronting her.

Haley spun around, her chest heaving. The sheik stood before the closed doors and calmly removed his checkered cloth and black-and-gold-braided headdress. He tossed both negligently onto a polished table beside the door.

"I believe when we first met your words were I 'owed you satisfaction', Haley Bennett. Come, stand before me and take the satisfaction you think you can from me."

Haley inhaled sharply. It didn't shock her that he had heard her words or remembered them. She'd said them with her radio channels wide open and meant every one. That he had the audacity to throw them back at her was diabolical. It was the equivalent of throwing a gauntlet in her face.

"I'll not grovel, if that's what you're hoping for, Sheik Haaris."

"You are afraid of retaliation?"

"I'm not afraid of anything. I can take you down any day of the week."

"Then come, my bold one. Come. Stand before me. Confront me to my face, not at a cowardly distance where the sting of your tongue whips about like a scorpion's tail. Come. Do your worst to me. I invite you."

"You command."

"Ah, I understand. You fear obedience. Do you also fear satisfaction?"

Haley bit her tongue, forcing herself not to swear. He was laughing at her! He knew exactly what he was doing, provoking her, deliberately taunting her. How the hell had he figured out that she was attracted to him? His words cut like a double-edged blade, ripping and twisting her apart.

The temptation to hoist a delicate Regency chair off the floor and clobber him was overwhelming. Trying to quell that urge, Haley crossed the room and came to stand in front of him. Outrageously, she jabbed her long forefinger into the center of his chest.

"Let me make one thing clear," she began. "I am standing here because I choose to stand here. Not because you ordered me to. Not because I am afraid of retribution. And to set the record clear, you couldn't satisfy me if you were the last man on earth, because I won't let you get near me."

Zayn almost burst out laughing. His voice was a soft caress. "You are near enough now, Haley Bennett. Shall I take what you owe me for your insults?"

"Ha!" Haley's finger stuck the target of his chest again. "I don't owe you one stinking thing. You damn near caused me to crash my airplane. You scared the hell out of me and forced me to land in *your* desert. You hold me prisoner and refuse to help me leave this country or get aid to my father. On top of that, you are damn close to implying I won't get my freedom unless I kowtow to this not-so-sly form of harassment you are practicing."

"The attraction is mutual. You are as smitten as I."

"Smitten?" Haley gasped. "How archaic a term."

She swallowed, mentally backpedaling, evading the truth, but devastated because he'd just admitted he was as attracted to her as she was to him. That couldn't be true.

"Can we please talk about something more vital?" she said. "My release from this barbaric confinement you are determined to impose. I've had enough of your gracious hospitality."

"Allah help me, but you are an ungrateful woman."

"I should be grateful to someone who endangered my life?"

"I saved your life, at the risk of my own. You were to have been shot from the sky because the Iraqis thought my father was escaping their plot. The Iraqi orders were to kill the emir, every member of his family and the political hierarchy of Kuwait."

"And that means make a target of every little private jet buzzing around the airport on August second. Right?"

Zayn's hands caught hold of her shoulders and he shook her rather fiercely. "Do not twist the facts now. Two rockets were fired at your plane. You know I speak the truth. Hussein personally ordered the executions."

"How can you expect me to believe that? That a president of a civilized country orders assassinations? We practically impeached Nixon for a petty burglary scheme. No one could get away with a crime like that."

"Saddam Hussein has, Haley Bennett, and you are in the thick of it. Were I foolish enough to allow you to streak northward in your smart little jet, you would be one more hostage to be bartered for Kuwait's gold."

"Where is your proof? You hide behind your old man's name and tell me what you want me to believe. Well, I don't believe you. For all I know, you're a maniac. You certainly act like one. You're unethical, you take outrageous risks. You're reckless. Omar the kamikaze pilot!"

"Insult me all you like, but you would not call Sheik Wali Haj Haaris an 'old man' to his face. He would cut your tongue out. My cousin and I stopped the Iraqis from firing on an unarmed plane. They would not risk shooting down a Saudi fighter to bring Kuwait's banks to heel."

"You think that excuses your caveman tactics?"

"What is it that you are so angry at? That you have not the skills to fly a plane better than I?" Zayn raised his hand to her head, touching her golden hair for the first time. She batted his arm away.

"Don't touch me."

"Stand before me without flinching like someone who is being whipped," he ordered harshly. "You have not been harmed. My hand has not struck you."

"What stinking, colossal nerve." Haley twisted away from the fingers that returned to touch her hair.

Zayn grasped a handful of buttons and fabric on her shirt with his left hand and yanked her before him. Haley gasped, and grabbed his left wrist with both her hands to dislodge the hold. His right hand dug into her hair, pulling out pins and throwing them away.

"You are a woman who has not learned what a woman is. Stand still! I am not hurting you."

"I don't want my hair taken down. I don't want you holding my blouse or breathing down my neck or shouting in my face."

"You do not know what you want, but I do!" He jerked the last pin out and ran his fingers down the long, splendid length of her braid, freeing it. "Do not ever bind your hair again in my presence."

Stunned by the vehemence in his words, Haley's mouth dropped open. Her stomach contracted and something else shook loose inside her. His fist between her breasts jerked her closer, and she put her hands against his chest to push away. Only inches separated their heads and that was mostly their difference in height.

Zayn's eyes roamed across the smooth planes of her face, lingering on the moist trembling of her mouth.

"Come, my vixen, here is the day you asked for. Here is the time and the place. Here are the weapons I choose, your lips and mine. Take the satisfaction you claim I owe you."

Horrified that he'd used her very own words to torment and taunt her, Haley dug her hands into the loose fabric of his robe, pushing to get away from him. "I wouldn't kiss you if you were the last man on earth! I was talking about shooting you, you arrogant bastard!"

"We both know the origin of your challenge! Were you a man, this would have been settled immediately after landing. When you'd picked yourself up from the ground, your jaw would have been broken, if I hadn't killed you first. I am not a man you can taunt and bait into a fiendish temper then walk away from, switching your hair across your beautiful backside. Challenge me and you pay the price."

Zayn's mouth silenced any retort she might have made. He slid one hand into her hair, then plundered her mouth in a kiss Haley thought would devour her. She couldn't breathe. She couldn't think. She didn't want to think.

Her eyes closed and she concentrated only upon the throbbing force of his mouth exploiting her own. It was what she had wanted the minute she'd laid eyes on him. This kiss, this melding. Her hands ceased their restless kneading of the fine linen clutched between her fingers and stole upward to encircle his head.

It was impossible to feel so much at one time. The rock-hard resistance of his chest, the warm firmness of his thighs, the heat of his lips spread across her own, the pressure of his teeth behind them, the grip of his hand at the back of her own head, the breadth and spread of his fingers caressing her breasts.

His head raised, his mouth leaving hers. Haley's eyes shot open and she was caught looking at the brilliant dazzle of desire shining in his eyes. It startled her so, her mouth parted to gasp in dismay.

Before her intake of breath was complete, his mouth covered hers again, this time taking sweet possession of the interior she might never have yielded were it not for the blaze of desire she'd seen. Haley struggled against her own resistance, shivering as his tongue swept inside and touched her, tormentingly teased her. She didn't want to fight it, fight him.

There was danger here, more danger than she had ever suspected, because she knew too quickly her body yearned to surrender to him. That, she could never allow to happen.

Haley renewed her struggle to thwart him, fighting to gain control over her body's headlong rush to accept his domination. Desperately, she pushed free, wrenching her mouth from his, using her hands against the hard wall of his chest to escape to arm's length.

"We must stop!"

Zayn prevented her escape by the same means he'd brought her to him, one hand fastened to the bunched material of her blouse. He allowed himself the pleasure of sweeping his fingers through the heavy, golden mass of her hair, then brought his right hand forward and cupped her cheek in his palm. Beneath the smooth surface of her skin he could feel her trembling excitement. She wanted him, that was palpably obvious.

"Why?" he asked.

Haley couldn't begin to think what he was asking. She didn't understand how clear thought could fly right out of her brain simply because of the evocative touch of a man's hand. She gripped his wrist and put his hand away from her face. "Because," she hesitantly answered, "you're making it impossible for me to think."

"What good is thinking? You are a woman. The touch of my hand upon your body is what you have wanted since the moment we laid eyes upon each other."

"Maybe so." Haley wouldn't deny what was so patently obvious. "But I won't rush into a physical relationship blindly, in the heat of the moment."

"What other way is there?" Zayn demanded. "Anything else is cold and calculated. Desire is sparked by the highly tuned emotions we are both feeling. You can't deny it."

"It's chemical." Haley swallowed, searching for any reason that made sense. "I won't fall at your feet just because I smell a rush of testosterone."

She had the oddest, strangest, most unwomanly way of speaking, Zayn decided. So blunt and sharp it made him want to shake the outspokenness from her. Where had she learned such things? Acquired the nerve to say them? He couldn't imagine what kind of a home she had come from to have a tongue so loose.

That angered him all over again because she was not the woman she should be . . . the woman her face and her luscious, giving mouth promised she could be.

Affronted by her audacious words, he caught hold of her shoulders and spun her before him, making her face the cheval mirror beside the vanity.

"Look at yourself. You are a woman, just like any other woman. You have breasts, yes, beautiful lovely breasts. Do you show them? No, you hide them in a man's shirt. And you wear pants that let you sit ungracefully and swagger when you walk. Do I strip you naked before this mirror to make you look at the body God has given you? Make you admit what sex you have?"

"You have no right to treat me like this," Haley said, all cold dignity.

"I have every right. Allah has made me the man born to tame you."

"I don't believe in such things."

"You will." His fingers slid seductively across her back and turned her against his chest. His mouth descended on hers, capturing her lips. He stilled her fighting hands and plundered the soft fullness of her mouth.

She felt shattered. Was this what she had imagined when she'd visualized fighting him? Back in the deepest recess of her mind, she knew it was. Not a fight that men engaged in where a victor emerged, no, nothing like that. This was the age-old struggle of man and woman, entwining for a different, more primal, elemental struggle.

He dragged her head back farther, one hand stroking the soft bared contours of her throat, the other clenched in the heavy mass of her hair. Haley moaned and clung to him, surrendering to the thrust of his hot, wet tongue inside her, pulsing an insidious prelude to the coming conquest. Her nipples hardened, pebbling in the firm compression of his palm and fingers passing over them. She was going out of control, the heat spreading achingly lower.

Zayn raised his head, looking deeply into the shining blue of her eyes. "Tell me that this is not what you want and I will stop."

Part of her wanted to cry off and escape. But the stronger facet of her willed her to match him kiss for kiss, touch for touch, an equal in sensual passion. In answer to his question, Haley tightened her fingers at the back of his head and pulled his mouth down to hers.

Then something else took over. Urges over which Haley had no mastery whatsoever. She wanted him, wanted him in all the ways she'd never allowed herself to want a man.

She had never met one capable of bringing out the sensual, emotional side of her nature. Zayn Haaris had broken past every barrier she kept firmly in place. She never had tantrums. She was known to be standoffish, aloof, even arrogant, but always clear-thinking and logical.

All at once her confusing thoughts made a connection she had never ever considered.

His touch wasn't a threat. Her own sleeping needs were the real threat. He was something she had to have, couldn't possibly live another moment without. The anger that flared so brightly between them was the result of an inferno of churning desire. She wanted him. He scratched the surface of her desire and she exploded.

It was no mild, ordinary passion brewing within her. The woman breaking out of the shell of unexplored sensuality was full-grown and her needs had been too long ignored. He had read her with an uncanny skill.

With him, only her sense of touch told her unerringly which direction she should go.

Haley's fingers dug into the fine razor-cut hair at the back of his head and drew his mouth down to her own. Her own kiss seemed desperate, full of need. She had not enough of him to touch, to really touch and feel the heat and resilience of his skin. A neck, a face, wrist and hand was not enough to appease her. She wanted more of him.

One of her hands scrabbled beneath the folds of his robe, passing tailored suiting to rest against the thin barrier of shirt that encased his chest. She was barely conscious of the fact that she might tear his clothes with the same disregard for further usefulness that he had for her own.

His hand descended and caught her wrist. "Slowly." The caution was delivered softly. "We have all the time in the world."

He lifted his head, and she leaned against the crook of his arm, her eyes bright and hungry.

Zayn smiled, pleased. He stroked the long, slender arch of her neck. Haley remained absolutely still as his fingers descended one by one to each of the buttons on her shirt. It pleased him deeply that she was feminine enough to dispense with the unnecessary binding of a bra. He bent his head to slowly taste the pulse beating in her throat and trailed downward on the opened vee, anticipating the heady pleasure of taking her breast within his mouth.

A knocking sound jerked Haley's head up. Her eyes sought the door that at this moment remained closed. Zayn raised his mouth only slightly from the soft white skin beneath his lips. "What is it?"

"Many pardons, my sheik," Ali's soft voice intoned behind the door. "A messenger has come from Riyadh."

"Tell him to wait."

Haley tensed in Zayn's arms. The intrusion shattered the delicate, ephemeral balance of passion. She felt her skin pebble where the bedroom's cool air touched all the places Zayn's moist mouth had warmed and sensitized. His fingers rested at the waistband of her pants. She suddenly felt naked and exposed. Worse, she felt ashamed of her own forwardness.

"It is urgent, my sheik," Ali said. "The messenger is the king's nephew."

Haley was certain that Zayn's undecipherable mutter against her throat was an Arabic curse. He bent his head lower and kissed her breast through the fabric of her shirt.

"Show him to my study. I will be there directly."

"As you require," Ali replied.

With great reluctance, Zayn straightened. A wry self-mocking smile touched the corner of his mouth. "It appears I spoke too soon. My apologies for this interruption. The affairs of state may delay what is to be, but they will never alter what is inevitable."

Zayn pulled her back into the heat of his arms and left a kiss of such wild promise on her lips that Haley barely understood his departing words. "Allah keep you this warm and giving until my return."

## Chapter 7

Zayn hadn't been out of the room for five minutes before Haley started down that long, tortuous road of self-examination. What, she asked herself, was she doing? She had to get out of Anaiza before Sheik Zayn Haji Haaris returned!

How, in the blink of an eye, could she be hopelessly in love with him? He embodied every physical trait she thought worth having in a man; tall enough that she didn't feel overgrown next to him, and darkly handsome with incredible deep, warm eyes that she got lost in. Falling in love with a desert prince made as much sense to Haley as jumping out a plane without a parachute. It was pure suicide.

Of all the dumb luck, to fly halfway around the world and land in a war zone to find her Prince Charming. It could only happen to her. What could she possibly do with a man whose idea of chivalry meant locking a woman away in a desert palace? Nothing. Absolutely nothing.

She was a career woman. She had worked hard to achieve her place at Bennett Industries. Was she going to throw away all those years of working like a dog to match the standards of excellence her father and her eldest brother set? The competition was tough in aeronautics. She hadn't any edge at the plant. No, if anything, she'd had to prove herself over and over again by being better than everyone else. Was she going to throw away her education because she finally found a six-foot-three hunk with bedroom eyes that hit all her warp-speed buttons?

Not likely.

It became even less plausible when she stopped and considered where the sheik was coming from. Forcing herself to be brutally realistic, Haley admitted that Zayn Haji Haaris could have his pick of any woman he wanted the world over. He stood light-years above her middle-class American reality. She came from family roots firmly planted in suburbia. When all the veneers were stripped away, the Bennetts were a family of tinkers. Mechanics. Good ones, yes. Specialists, definitely, but mechanics and tinkers, all the same.

Zayn Haaris was a prince. He lived in a centuries-old marble palace. He was private-school educated, nothing but the best. He could probably trace his bloodline all the way back to Alexander the Great.

So it had been an act of folly to get involved in a mad romantic fling. The fact that she was disoriented by the tumultuous events of the past forty-eight hours made her attraction feel foolish.

Determined that such impulsive behavior would not sabotage her again, Haley came to a decision. She would go to Kuwait by whatever method opportunity presented her, find her father and Uncle Jack and go home.

Morning brought a few surprises, among them the discovery of a rooftop garden adjacent to her bedroom. It was uniquely private, isolated from all the other levels of the huge house.

Bright awnings and clusters of potted palms provided shade and shelter to escape the building heat. Haley was used to heat, Texas heat. Heat that matched the temperature of this desert any day of the week.

All morning, the courtyards below bustled with activity. Haley watched the comings and goings with curious eyes.

It had been early evening when she and Zayn had parted; he to meet with the messenger from the Saudi king, she to sit alone and stew about the lingering effects of unchecked desire.

This morning found her still tied up in knots. Her brain said to run for the green hills of home. Her body ached to discover what the outcome of such unadulterated passion was. She kept her ears tuned to the sky, anticipating and dreading the return of Zayn's helicopter.

His summons to Riyadh was a blessing because she was in way over her head where he was concerned. Everything about Zayn Haaris exuded experience and sophistication. What did she know about passionate, devastatingly attractive men? From the time she was twelve years old, she'd had her nose stuck in a book or her head under a hood. All the men she knew either treated her like a kid sister or a daughter. If there had been any men that hadn't treated her that way, she hadn't noticed.

Thank goodness her mind overruled her body in this instance, because being treated like a desirable, attractive woman was a role that she couldn't instantly get accustomed to. In a foreign land, she reasoned, everything would be more exotic and appealing because it was all new to her. She simply must not allow her libido to surface again.

Last night, after Zayn's helicopter had departed, Haley discovered that she was not locked within the opulent suite of rooms. She had freedom to wander and explore the massive house.

Ali had served her a late, solitary meal after dark. Not that she found much interest in food. As for going to bed, she had slept so long, the last thing she wanted was to sleep some more. She wouldn't have minded jogging five or six miles.

She was forced to settle for a restless stroll about the grounds at midnight, which reinforced her suspicion that she did not have the freedom to exit the sheik's residence. Armed sentries manned gates that were securely barred and locked.

So the night passed, a long and dismal time because her inner clock was completely out of sync.

After the sun rose, Haley wandered through the whole complex by daylight, familiarizing herself with the layout of the rooms and the security in place during daylight. She looked for the chink in the armor and found it in the most unlikely place. The palace kitchens.

Earlier, she had paused to admire the array of vehicles the sheik kept at hand for his use. A new Range Rover, two beautiful Mercedes sedans and two rather plain, oft-used jeeps. The building itself had an alarm system and the sedans were equipped with antitheft devices. Pretending ignorance, she'd deliberately touched the hood of one Mercedes. The man polishing the Range Rover had a good laugh at what he thought was her fright and reached inside the cab to shut off the noise.

Mission accomplished, Haley retreated to the rooftop garden to consider her options for escape. She knew what cars were available, what security existed and which exit she had the best chance of breaching.

The battered jeep in the farthermost yard behind the kitchens was her best bet. The gate was ancient and rarely closed since she'd been observing. The jeep saw frequent use. Servants jumped into it to scoot into the nearby town to make whatever purchases the household needed.

Haley made particular note of the fact that any woman who left the complex did so wearing an *abba,* a black garment that obscured all features from view. None went unescorted. A bandido manning the gate with a rifle slung over his back like a third appendage drove the jeep both coming and going. That, more than anything else, brought home to Haley the truth that this was Saudi Arabia.

Maybe it was empathy for the poor women stuck in their stifling *abbas* that prompted Haley to deliberately flout custom by sunbathing on the rooftop garden topless, clad in a scandalous strip of a thong bikini. Roasting in the glorious sun at noon soothed her frayed nerves in a way little else had in the past twelve hours.

Only an occasional hawk soared overhead. That took away all the pleasure of breaking the rules. She might have enjoyed upsetting the equilibrium of one particular pilot. She was not given the opportunity to do so. No helicopter returned during her sojourn on the roof.

Shortly after noon, she retreated indoors. Though she tanned well, it was folly to risk a bad burn from too much exposure.

Ali proved to be the most resourceful man a stranded American woman could possibly have found. Haley was desperately short of clothing. He graciously offered to send a servant to market to fetch anything she desired. Haley promptly accepted the offer and made a lengthy list. The young servant, Maari, promised to fill the list as completely as possible.

Deviously, Haley was specific in her requests, asking for curious weaves and embroideries, good samples of local garments. She claimed she couldn't go home from a foreign country without presents for her mother, two sisters and two older brothers. All the while, she knew native clothing would make her less conspicuous.

That left her only one or two more crucial problems to solve on the way to independence and freedom. The first and foremost was money. She had to have Saudi money.

The next hurdle was to figure out where in the desert the base was. She knew it was north of Anaiza, north toward the Iraqi border in the Summan. She was excellent with directions, but she needed to see a map. What she really thought she needed was a trip into the sheik's study.

There were several indications that the residence had every accoutrement imaginable, including a satellite communications dish on the roof. After midday, the sheik's household shut down completely. Watching from the roof, Haley saw the guards at the gate slip inside their shaded shelter. The gardeners retreated. Even the dogs slunk under shady protuberances to escape the assaulting midday heat.

Satisfied that there was less chance to be caught now than at any other time, Haley darted inside her bedroom and hastily pulled on a simple blouse too short to tuck into her wraparound ankle-length native skirt.

The shirt was a poor fit, hugging her broad shoulders too tightly, its sleeves too short for her long arms. She pushed the sleeves up to her elbows and shrugged over the gauzy fabric. It would have to do. She couldn't waste time.

Thus robed, Haley struck off in search of the sheik's private rooms. She already knew the layout of the most obvious rooms, having thoroughly explored those during the night. She had not explored the east wing of the complex, since two sinister men had lingered near that entry door last night. Now, however, there was not a soul about.

Haley knew she'd struck pay dirt when she entered a somber, dark, formal hall. Two rows of tapestry-covered chairs faced one another across a breathtakingly intricate Persian carpet. Huge doors at the side were firmly closed to block out the midday heat. Haley scooted across the length of the room to the next set of interior doors.

No sooner did she poke her head round that door than the growl of a very large, dangerous-sounding dog made her freeze.

"Heel, Quasyr," a voice beyond the door commanded.

Haley opened her eyes wide, looking. She saw the dog, a hairy brute that gave new meaning to the word *ugly*.

"May I help you?"

The crisp English phrasing surprised the daylights out of Haley. She turned toward the voice and found herself facing a tall boy clothed in a white cassock.

"Oh, hello." Haley grinned her most disarming smile at the teenager, who looked about as angelic as an acolyte caught nipping the altar wine.

A hand signal of the boy's made the huge, growling animal lie down at his feet. He managed to clear his throat before saying very stiffly, "You may come in, Miss Bennett."

"You know who I am?" Haley straightened, spying a large relief map on the wall behind the boy. She admitted being more intrigued at that moment by the fact that the boy knew her name. "I don't believe we've met, have we?"

"Word travels fast in the desert," he said by means of explanation.

"Oh." Haley nodded. "Well, I'm off exploring. Ali did say I should make myself at home and do as I like. Did I disturb you? This is a fascinating house. May I come in and look here, too? Is the dog friendly? Is it a wolfhound? Looks Russian to me. Slavic cheekbones."

Dark eyes behind black-framed glasses seemed to study Haley with the quizzical interest of a biology student probing a specimen pinned to a lab tray. The youth tilted his head to the right.

Haley thought that gesture was a trifle familiar. Self-consciously, she tugged at the hem of her shirt and smoothed a wrinkle out of the native skirt, which was too short for her tall frame.

"You may enter," the boy finally answered.

*My, he's just a baby,* Haley realized. *A baby predator,* she amended when she saw his gleaming eyes make an outrageous sweep down her body. His eyes riveted to her unbound breasts.

*So let him look,* she thought, knowing she could stop the poor child from ogling if need be. She popped inside the large room before he could come to his senses and deny her access. Haley deliberately twitched the fold of the wraparound skirt where it closed over her knees. She needed information and didn't care what means she used to get it.

The large room was definitely an office. It opened into a conference room and several private rooms beyond. A desk squatted low on the floor and supported a computer. There was a black telephone on a credenza where the boy stood holding a fax in his hand. A fax machine!

Quadir Haaris gaped at the woman, astonished. Her unbound hair was the color of ripened wheat and hung loose and flowing down to her hips. A finely embroidered, tucked blouse rode loosely over a blue skirt the same color as her eyes. The deep scoop of the blouse's neckline exposed the golden skin of a throat as slender as a reed and the swell of rounded breasts too exquisite for words.

The trouble was, her gauzy cotton shirt was meant to be an undergarment. He swallowed, and his Adam's apple bobbed in his throat. Quadir had heard rumors about the woman his eldest brother had sequestered, but had not dreamed he would actually see her. Zayn might put out his eyes if he heard of this.

"I suppose I ought to introduce myself." Haley came face-to-face with the boy, flashing a dazzling, overbright smile. They were the same height, only he was like the puppy at his feet—still growing. "My friends call me Haley."

"There is no need. I am aware of who you are, Miss Bennett." Quadir reverted to curt formality that could not be misconstrued, ignoring the outward thrust of her hand.

Insisting, Haley kept her bright smile in place. "But I don't know you, do I?"

"I am Quadir al-Haaris, Sheik Haaris's younger brother." The boy took her hand and Haley gave his damp fingers a firm squeeze and a generous pump. Her smile became a grin.

"Well, I declare, I am charmed. Zayn didn't tell me there were more just like him hidden in these old walls. And does this ferocious beast have a name, too?"

"I call him Quasyr, Caesar." The boy's voice broke on the dog's name in English.

"Caesar, a noble name for an impressive animal. It suits him well." Haley laughed and laid on a Southern drawl as thick as she dared. "Here I thought I was alone in this big old, rambling house. Mr. Ali has done his best to entertain me, but I am so bored. Is this a library? Chance I could find a magazine on one of the shelves, or a romance? I'm dying for something to do."

As she spoke, Haley fluttered her eyelashes and strolled into the adjacent office, noting every electronic device. "Lands, is that a computer? Why, my daddy has one of them."

The boy and the massive dog padded after her. Quadir said something, but Haley hardly heard him. She was busy memorizing the layout. A Teletype machine in the corner next to an IBM computer, modem, laser printer, Xerox machine, every electronic gadget known to man. A small-screen color television was tuned to CNN. Acting like an airhead, Haley bent down over one of several computer keyboards.

"Wow, is that Arabic? I didn't know there were such things. I guess they make computers for everybody now, don't they?" Haley's vacuous Valley-girl laugh would have floored her brothers. She came to a halt before a wall of bookshelves. They were crammed full.

"Oh, my, somebody does like books. They make a room look so impressive, don't they? I'm not much for reading, but then—" she sighed "—it seems I shall go ever out of my mind waiting for Zayn to come back. I'm so lonely I could try to read a book, maybe."

There wasn't a title she could read until she came across *Man and His Symbols* by Carl Jung. The young man finally came forward, passing around her to stop at a shelf and plucked a book from it. "Perhaps this would do."

He offered a worn copy of Higgins's *Day of Judgement*.

"Oooh, rather heavy, huh?" Haley injected a note of disappointment in her voice. "You wouldn't have any Jude Devereaux, would ya?" She scanned the dust jacket before turning to the opposite wall. There, above the bank of communications equipment, were the maps.

"Say!" Haley ached for a piece of gum to complete her parody. "Ya'll wouldn't have *Rolling Stone*, would you?"

"*Rolling Stone?*" Quadir's voice slid into a third octave. His palms sweat. Her perfume floated around him like jasmine in full bloom, sweet, intoxicating and tempting. "I have a back issue or two in my room."

"I just knew it." Haley grinned. "You just look like the type to be true to rock and roll. I bet you dance good too, don't ya?"

A blush spread hotly over the boy's cheeks. Haley felt shamefully wicked for tricking him. But this was war, she reminded herself. "Would you run go get it for me? I'd be ever so thankful."

Quadir's head was swimming. He looked to his brother Zayn's empty desk and wondered if he dared risk leaving the woman alone in the office. Then he remember Quasyr.

"Quasyr will have to stay with you."

"Oh, the puppy?" Haley turned to the monstrous dog and read his measure as accurately as she had the boy's. She dropped to one knee and offered her cheek and the dog slobbered his wet tongue across her chin. "We'll get along just fine, won't we, Quasyr?"

"I'll be right back. Don't touch anything, please?"

"Why, I wouldn't dream of it." Haley grinned angelically.

Quadir rushed out of the office, taking huge gulps of air into his chest. He closed the door, shook his head and grinned like a lovesick pup. Making up his mind that if Zayn didn't keep the woman, he would, he raced for the stairs.

Haley rounded on the computer the second the door was closed. She had options. The fax, the phone, or e-mail via the computer. The screen of the color monitor was covered with a familiar home page of the internet . . . already tuned into the worldwide web. That's all she needed to phone home! The second she knelt before the low-to-the-floor console, her little finger pressed the jump key.

Her fingers flew across the keyboard typing in the e-mail address that would connect directly into the computer on her brother Tommy's desk at Bennett Air.

A glance at the clock told her it was 5:00 a.m. back home. She crossed her fingers as she nestled the receiver in the modem. Knowing Tommy's work habits, she stood a good chance he would be near his computer, tinkering on some engine part.

She watched the blue screen, rereading her message, keeping her fingers crossed, hoping for a reply.

Tommy's response came more quickly than she'd prayed.

*Haley, where the hell are you?* Relieved, Haley's fingers flew across the keyboard in answer.

*Saudi Arabia.*

*How'd you get there? Dad's somewhere in Q8. No word on when he'll get out. Bombs cont w/ sporadic ground fighting @ airport. US/Embassy advises all cits evacuate overland, via Jordan. Come home immediately, that's an order.*

*Can't. Where exactly is Dad and Vix One?*

*Dad poss. injury rt. leg, gunshot, Jack at hangar. Communic-broken. Goose gassed. Vix disabled. Have food, H2O, med sup, embas noted. Q8 under martial law. Give your quadrants . . . e-mail address?*

*Do not know quads. V-2 ok. Tell Mom, I am in no danger and will fly home w/ Dad and Jack ASAP. Time up. Love, HJB.*

Haley disconnected the call and restored the previous screen. Then she headed for the large desk and opened the middle drawer. As she thought, a handful of Saudi pocket change and a couple of banknotes were tossed into a paper-clip slot. For a second or two, she drummed her nails on the desktop, hesitating, because she wasn't a thief. But she couldn't go anywhere without money. Her mind made up, she took the large silver coins, praying they were no more valuable than American pennies and nickles. Then she took two bills, just to be on the safe side.

She completed her subterfuge just as the door opened.

Quadir rushed back into the office a little out of breath, holding a fold of newsprint in his left hand. "It's a few months old." He had taken the added precaution of putting the contraband *Rolling Stone* inside a daily paper.

Haley swiveled on the low stool with adoring eyes for the boy. "Why, you are so kind. I couldn't dare take up any more of your time."

"You have stumbled into the men's quarters. Please, allow me to escort you back to the harem."

That word *harem* caused her to draw up short. She bit on her tongue to hold back a scathing retort that would have blown her cover completely. Harem! Why, the dirty rotten scoundrel!

Reason alone kept her temper in check. She wouldn't fight a war against an innocent boy, who formally offered Haley his arm.

"Why, you are so very kind. I think I was lost, anyway." She placed her hand delicately in the crook of his arm and walked alongside him through the outer office. All the while, Haley's head swiveled, noting everything she could. *The rat had television! CNN! World news, updated on the hour! Harem! Damn your eyes, just you wait, Zayn Haaris!* She said to Quadir, "I hope I haven't caused any problems."

"None at all, I assure you," said the youth most politely. "My brother returns shortly. It is my pleasure to provide you with something to do in the meantime."

"You are such a doll!" she enthused. "So helpful and sweet. Do you work for Sheik Zayn?"

"I am a student. My brothers let me help at times."

"You mean there are more of you! Here?"

Quadir cleared his suddenly blocked throat. Did this woman have any idea of her effect upon him? Sweat trickled between his shoulder blades. His heart pounded as it only did when engaged in hard physical exercise.

"No, not here. Most of my brothers are at Hafaro."

"Where is that?"

"It is in the Summan . . . the desert."

"Family business, huh?" Haley grinned, wishing she had that gum to pop.

Once they stepped out of the east wing, they were again at the wide stairs below the balustrade that went to her quarters. Quadir stopped in the large ornate hall, venturing no farther.

"Thank you. You've been a doll." Haley reached up and pinched his cheek. "You're so cute. I bet when you're full-grown, you'll look just like Zayn."

He blushed furiously. Haley was glad she didn't burst out laughing. Keeping hard to her act, she went for the stairs, tripping along, her long skirt forgotten. She reached for it, brought up the hem to show a nice turn of well-tanned leg and waved wiggling fingertips.

"Bye now. See you at the dinner table, Quadir."

In the *harem,* Haley kicked a soft hassock and swore viciously. *The nerve of that oaf! Sticking her in his harem!*

She vented her anger quickly, then sat at the table and immediately drew a facsimile of the maps she'd seen, glad more than ever for her near-perfect sense of direction and quick mind.

Buraida was the nearest city north of Anaiza. The capital, Riyadh, was southeast. The neutral zone between Iraq, Kuwait and Saudi Arabia was north by northeast. Exactly how far the borders and the capital were in miles, she could only estimate. The one fact she was certain of was that she'd flown under a hundred miles inland from the border to an unmarked military base. Could that be this *Hafaro* the boy had mentioned?

Now, Haley had to figure out how she was going to get back there. She twirled a strand of hair round and round her finger, staring at her crude map, thinking.

There was simply no way she could leave the sheik's enclave dressed the way she was. Ali had had the brains not to provide her with that most necessary garment, an *abba*. Even if she got hold of one, Haley knew she would stand out like a sore thumb. She was too tall, too blond and too, too fair—even with a tan.

Haley dropped her chin onto her fist and stared at the intricate carved screen in front of her. Beyond it were glass windows and the rooftop garden overlooking the courtyard. She needed a disguise. And it would have to be good enough to fool everyone. Or else of the kind that would make most people look away and discount her as inconsequential, a nothing. She could not have run-of-the-mill Saudis doing double takes to look at her like that boy had just done.

The boy! The smooth-faced, beardless boy! Haley dropped her pen and ran out to the roof garden to the far corner where she could see the kitchen yard. Stretched across one corner of that enclave was a wash line with the day's laundry hanging in the hot, hot sun.

The boy!

Haley darted down the outer steps, hurrying across the inner courts. The exertion immediately affected her, causing damp sweat to pour from her body. The sun broiled everything at this time of day.

In the garage, a man leaned against a shaded wall and snored. Haley tiptoed past him, slipped into the kitchen courtyard and ducked under the wash lines. She selected pants, a heavy cotton tunic and one of those long concealing choir-type robes every Arab seemed to favor.

She might have snatched a head cloth, except all of the ones hanging reminded her of her mother's kitchen towels. Which could very well mean they were clan- or tribe-specific. She'd be better off not identifying to any specific family. She took a plain white one that could have been a cup towel or a diaper, for all she knew.

As quickly as she'd gone out, she was back in her suite with her booty. The trip had left her soaked with sweat. Hiding the garments, she stripped off her own and went into the bath to have a long, thoughtful soak.

While she lounged in the tub, she thought about the men who worked in the palace gardens. They wore turbans twisted round their heads. Oh, there were plenty of ways to disguise blond hair. And she mustn't forget water. She must collect bottles from Ali's generous drink cart in the lounge and fill them. She must be prepared, ready to leave at a moment's notice.

Thus decided on her plan of action, she would need a nap. That was her very next order of business.

# Chapter 8

Haley must have been more tired than she thought, because she fell asleep right away. When her mind came alert again, she did not want to get up at all. She yawned. She stretched. She pulled her hair out from under her shoulder. She snuggled into the soft, soft pillows and sighed. She reached for the light sheet that had slipped off her and couldn't find it. She frowned, groping about her bare knees.

"If you are looking for a cover, I refuse to allow you to have one."

Haley's eyes popped open. The sheik! He was back.

"Hello." Zayn captured her wrist and pulled her hand up to his mouth, kissing the full mound of Venus at the base of her thumb.

"What are you doing here?" Haley tugged her hand out of his grip and half sat, blinking startled eyes.

Zayn Haaris smiled for an answer, a wickedly devilish smile that melted its way into Haley's undefended heart. She immediately shook some sense back into her head.

"I asked, what are you doing here?"

"Enjoying the view." The sweep of his eyes told all.

Haley tugged down the hem of her short, silky gown, mentally groaning over her propensity for traveling ultralight. Did this man have a knack for catching her disrobed, or what?

"Well, really, Sheik Haaris, you must do something about your compulsion to invade my privacy." Haley pushed her tangled hair aside, then reached to the foot of the bed to get a cover.

"Leave it." Zayn blocked her reach with his own.

"Oh my!" Her eyes riveted to his bare chest, rippling with muscles as he moved. "What are you doing in my bed?"

Zayn stretched out, sliding his hands behind his head, the perfect pose of contentment.

"Taking up where we left off."

"We didn't leave off in bed!" Haley protested, unable to stop the sweep of heat into her cheeks.

"Indeed? There were only a few steps to be taken then."

He was so calm and confident she wanted to clobber him.

"Well, not by me, you brute. I've had a change of heart. I am not a woman of easy virtue. You and I have absolutely nothing to share with one another. Why, we wouldn't mix at all. You're…ah…Arab and I'm American. We'd never see eye to eye. I'm a career woman and you're . . . you're . . . what?"

Zayn frowned. This wasn't the greeting he'd expected. He'd spent the last twenty-four hours tied up in knots because of this woman and his desire for her. The knot inside him right this moment wasn't very pleasant, either. She'd presented an unbelievably sensuous image asleep. Haley slept like a cat, purring contentedly, waking like a tigress with an arching, limber, supple spine. He reached for her hand and she jerked away as if he were poison.

"Don't touch me!"

"I want you to come and kiss me, welcome me home."

"When pigs fly!" Haley practically jumped out of the bed. Zayn abruptly sat up.

Haley's eyes widened. She hadn't meant to speak so sharply. It was the shock of waking to find a half-naked man watching her that had her rattled. How long had he been ogling her while she slept?

"Look, I'm sorry. I didn't mean that," she said, and settled uneasily at the head of the bed. "I just woke up. You startled me. For heaven's sake, you can't pounce on a woman who hardly knows you."

"You know me," Zayn corrected. "You know everything you need to know about me."

"On the contrary, I don't know one truth. All I know is that you claim to be the son of Sheik Wali Haaris. As for proof of that, you haven't given me any."

"My, but you wake up in a devil of a cranky mood from an afternoon nap. I will address many prayers that you are not so indisposed in the mornings." Zayn decided that light, teasing banter would better allay her suspicions. "And you know that what I told you is true. I am the son of Sheik Wali Haaris and you don't need to see my passport to verify that truth."

If there was a more blatant truism, Haley wanted to know what it was. She'd only been trying to get a rise out of him. "All right, I won't argue that," she admitted. "But I think right now we had better get a few things in proper perspective."

Relaxing once again, Zayn let his eyes wander across the wild disarray of her sleep-mussed hair. It was a truly magnificent head of hair. Thick and wondrously colored by every hue of the spectrum, golds mixed with flax and warm pale honey browns. His fingers itched to touch it.

"And what would that be, my prickly one?"

"Well..." Haley weakened at the endearment. His lazy, hooded gaze sent a rush of heat along her veins. That secret smile on his lips promised a wealth of unbearable pleasures waiting in the wings. She dropped her eyes to her fiddling hands and plunged into her well-rehearsed speech, hating it, wishing she had the guts to lean across and kiss him.

"I think it's important that whatever it was that happened the other night...well, it was an accident. I'm under a lot of stress right now. We can't be going around touching one another, starting up something that would be temporary at best. I'm not into temporary flings. I couldn't handle that, and besides, I don't have to, Zayn."

There, she'd said it, said his name out loud to him. It was like forbidden music.

"What are you saying, Haley?" Zayn frowned, stung rather seriously by being rejected out of hand. "Back off, buddy boy, like you talk to pilots invading your airspace?"

"Did you have your ears on the whole time or what?" Haley grumbled.

"In my experience, a woman waits for an offer before making a blatant rejection."

"Oh, give me a break," Haley said, scowling. "Don't you think I've got enough sense to know that when a man crawls half-naked into a sleeping woman's bed, he's stating his intent."

"You gave me no indication that you would be offended when we parted. You were more than willing to be embraced and kissed."

"That's exactly my point. Things got very out of hand awful quick." Haley swallowed. "Fortunately, I've had time to get my hormones under control. It won't happen again, I assure you."

The frown on Zayn's forehead deepened. Her mixed signals were maddening. He wanted to shake her. She did not mean a single word she'd said, and they both knew it.

"You look like I'm talking Greek right now," she said dejectedly.

"If you mean, do you speak nonsense, yes, you do. What has changed? You are trying deliberately to offend me. Now cease such foolishness. I know you are glad I have returned. Now, do you welcome me home or not?"

Better judgment said not to do such a foolish thing. Staring at him, want and desire made ugly protesting noises in her heart. He pulled her to him just as strongly as iron drew to a lodestone.

"Don't you have somebody around here to give you a welcome?" she asked.

He gave her such a quelling look that Haley wanted to duck her head under the pillow. "Would I be here, asking that of you if I did?"

"Well, I don't know." Haley struggled to answer that question, hating the high color rushing up her cheeks. "That's what I'm trying to tell you. I don't know anything about you except that you're a damned attractive man."

"You know everything you need to know about me. You can feel it, right here." He reached out one hand and placed his warm fingers above her heart. "Everything that is important is in there. What you feel. What I feel. Now, come, kiss me, Haley Bennett. I starve for the taste of you."

Haley scooted across the bed on her knees and planted a sweet, welcome-home peck on his cheek. "Welcome home. I am glad you have returned, but I don't want to admit it."

Zayn caught her chin with one finger tucked underneath it. "That is not a welcome. Kiss me, Haley Bennett."

A shudder whipped down her belly, contracting deep inside her. She was losing it, Haley thought, and would continue to if she kept looking into those enigmatic eyes. How compelling they were, how liquid black and beautiful. She sat up straight, her feet tucked beneath her, and placed her hands tentatively on his broad shoulders. "Will you be satisfied with one kiss of welcome?"

His eyebrow rose.

"I shouldn't kiss you at all." She tilted her chin in a challenge. "You've been out in the world, learning what's really going on, and I've been stuck here, your prisoner."

"Yes, I can see that your shackles have rubbed your skin raw." Zayn's mirthful eyes imparted a wealth of heat.

"You must think I'm a total twit." Haley sniffed, head up, her nose high above his. "I don't like to be treated like I'm incapable of sustaining any thought weightier than what time you will return. I've been quite busy."

"Indeed?" Zayn tilted his head, inching ever so much closer to her mouth.

"Yes, and I am officially lodging a protest. Being held prisoner in your house does not constitute lady-of-the-house residency in my book. So this kiss you are asking for is given under duress."

"Does one simple kiss frighten you?"

Haley rocked her palms along the smooth, bare skin of his shoulders.

"It could," she said deliberately. She moistened her lips and looked at his mouth, firm-lipped and straight-lined. Very slowly, Haley closed the gap that separated them. She bent her head and took the soft fleshy edge of his earlobe between her teeth. Then she bit him.

"I want out of here!" she growled through the clench of her teeth.

Zayn's arm circled her waist, crushing her body against the hard contours of his. Then he rolled her over, breaking the stinging nip of her teeth. Flat on her back, Haley gasped to find herself so quickly entrapped and pinned.

"That was most definitely not a kiss of welcome, Haley Bennett." Zayn tossed a lock of unruly hair out of his eyes.

"That's right. It wasn't."

"*Inshallah*. The duty of instructing you falls to my hands. Once again, I welcome the challenge."

"Don't you dare kiss me!" Haley wiggled and tried to squirm out from underneath him.

Laughing, Zayn brought both her hands upward until they came together above her head where he could easily hold them out of his way with one hand.

"It was only the touch of your lips that I desired before, Haley. You have refused us both the solace and comfort of them. I will take my pleasures elsewhere."

Haley's breath caught in her throat.

His head dipped. His lips warmly touched the sensitive skin under her throat. Bending his head to the task, he traced a wild, hot line down between her breasts.

"Stop!" Haley howled, suddenly very much afraid. Not of him. Afraid of the shudder whipping through her body, the contracting deep in her belly. "I'll kiss you."

He raised his head and the full impact of desire running a hot race in the depth of his mysterious dark eyes doubled the ache inside her. His breath fanned across her skin, tingling the small valley between her breasts.

"You have changed your mind and would welcome my kiss now?"

Unable to muster an answer, Haley nodded.

"Then I would be delighted to oblige you, Miss Bennett," Zayn lazily replied. He released her hands to draw his fingers down and catch a fistful of that glorious hair. She turned her face to meet his, her lips parting reflexively.

"I don't know." Zayn hovered over her soft, tantalizing mouth as if he was considering his options. "You are such a devious little flirt and there are certainly a wealth of other pleasures available to me."

Haley's hands made contact with him, catching his shoulders, fingers creeping insidiously toward his neck to draw his head closer to her own. "I'm going to scream if you don't kiss me now!"

"Ah, you have no idea how much I want to hear your screams, Haley."

His lips, quirking with amusement, barely touched hers and drew back. He loved her mouth, it was the first thing about her that had attracted his attention. Full, beautifully curved, her mouth seemed fixed in a perpetual smile. Yet the lower lip was almost too full, giving her a natural, sultry pout.

It was too much. Haley moved her hands upward, securing a firmer hold upon him. His skin was tantalizing under her fingers, electrifying, his hair crisp and silky. She loved the feel of his shoulders and could only imagine the joy it would be to dance with him.

Their lips came together and Haley kissed him a softly stirring kiss, one of true welcome. It only hinted at the passion riding hard on the edges of her feelings. And to her delight, Zayn held back from taking too much too soon.

When he drew back his head, his hand stroked across her forehead and smoothed her hair away from her head.

"That was most certainly worth returning to Anaiza for," he said in a soft, very convincing voice.

She tucked in her chin, regarding him warily, uncertain if he was going to press for more. Uncertain of her limits.

Surprised that he didn't press her, Haley stared at his eyes, unable to read the reason behind the amusement glistening there. In spite of her earlier resolve to keep her distance, the man fascinated her. She had to know more about him.

"Do you ever take a woman dancing, Sheik Haaris?" Haley asked with her hands resting on the horizontal ledges of his broad shoulders. He chuckled and sat up, pulling her upward so that she wound up sitting in front of him, but not too close.

"Upon occasion I have been known to participate in purely European leisure pastimes."

"I'll bet you have," Haley said huskily, then realizing what she had said, she blushed to the roots of her hair.

His eyebrow inched higher.

She wanted to howl with frustration. He made her feel like a gauche kid straight out of high school. Why was she fighting the attraction? For the life of her, she couldn't come up with a single solid reason.

Her eyes roamed from his face to the strong column of his neck and across that wide chest swirled with dark hair. She looked back at his mouth, trembling to kiss him in a much more satisfactory manner.

"You are a devil," she said, then very slowly leaned across the distance that separated them and put her mouth to his. She kissed a corner first, tipped her tongue onto his upper lip, tracing it across to the other side.

His hand circled her waist, drawing her against the solid warmth of his body as Haley opened her mouth over his.

Only the fragile scrap of her nightgown separated their bodies. Haley sighed with deep pleasure as her body molded into the firm contours of his.

*I'm lost,* she thought as his lips bloomed flowerlike beneath hers, parting, giving her immediate access to darker and deeper temptations.

It was exquisite, tantalizing. Haley slipped her arms around his shoulders, giving as he drew her across his knees, compressing her against his hard, pronounced arousal.

She sighed when he broke the joining of their mouths and raised his head to take a deep breath. Zayn slid his hands down her hips and cupped the curves of her bottom, drawing her firmly against his throbbing shaft. She was a delicious torment, the finest he'd ever felt.

A shudder rocked her spine.

"Welcome home," Haley said quietly, a little frightened of the intensity of her feelings.

Zayn kissed her collarbone, nudging the silk strap of her skimpy gown across her skin.

Haley swallowed, achingly aware of the compression of their hips, of her bare thighs cuddling his. His thumb idly circled her breast, drawing her nipple to a taut nub that matched the other.

"Now, I am glad to be home."

With an ease that shocked her, he gripped her waist and lifted her from his lap, settling her at his side, and gripped both her hands between his own. "You have made for yourself an interesting day?"

Haley blinked, realizing he wasn't going to seduce her. "Uh . . . yes. A very interesting day."

"Exploring my house?"

"From one end to the other," Haley admitted.

"And you have found a book to read?"

Haley studied the arrogant cock of his eyebrow and understood he was telling her he knew exactly what she had been doing all day.

"One."

"Sent for clothes from the market, I see."

"A girl has to replace what she loses to crude men who insist upon ripping them off her body."

"And what will you do with four pair of identical sandals?"

"Three pair are for my mother and two sisters. One is for me."

He made a mockingly horrified expression, saying, "There are more like you at home?"

"Not exactly, sort of. We are different."

"Blondes?"

"No. I'm the only blonde in the bunch."

"Then you are more of a rare jewel than I imagined. You will come down to dinner, join my brothers and me?"

"Oh? I may do that? Violate this purdah thing?"

Zayn's mouth twitched. "It is no violation to dine with family of one's host. Besides, I was informed you had already invited yourself to the table."

"Well, yes, I guess I did. It will be my pleasure to dine with you."

Zayn said something in Arabic that Haley did not follow. He stood and took his cast-off shirt from a chair near the bed, sliding it onto his arms and shoulders. "Come and button this for me."

"No." Haley saucily tossed her hair off her shoulder. "Dangerous things happen to me when I get inside your space. Anyway, I won't be ordered to do anything."

Zayn stood with the shirt dangling open across his chest and looked at her, waiting. Then he laughed suddenly and said, "Then you must tell me what your magic word is, *lalla.*"

"*Please* will do quite nicely." Haley grinned over that small victory.

"Then, please, *lalla,* come and button my shirt. My fingers are all thumbs in your presence."

"That's a crock and we both know it. By the way, what does *'lalla'* mean?" Haley slipped off the bed, went to stand before him and started buttoning.

"Lady," Zayn said softly into the crown of her bent head.

Haley looked up. She could smell the faint scent of his after-shave and was mightily tempted to let her hand stroke that virile chest, but she restrained her libido. "You are almost irresistible."

"*Almost?*" Zayn said disdainfully. He put her hands away from him and tucked the shirt into his trousers. "We dine in twenty minutes. Ali will show you the way."

"I know the way."

"Very good. Until dinner, Miss Bennett." With an elegant, continental flair, Zayn snapped his heels together, bowed and kissed her hand.

Only when he had left did Haley allow herself to dissolve into a useless heap on the bedroom floor.

"Oh, God," she said on a sigh. "Wait till Mother hears about this."


Quadir went nowhere without his faithful dog, Caesar. At the dinner table, Haley discovered she had inadvertently maligned the huge dog by thinking it a Russian wolfhound. The great shaggy brown creature was an Irish wolfhound, a gift to Quadir from his favorite teacher at Harrow. The fifteen-year-old took great delight in tossing balls of lamb and rice, called fool, at the dog, which it snapped out of the air and swallowed in one gulp.

There was another Haaris brother at the table. He was named Issaam and he was close in age to Haley. Once it was common knowledge that she had flown one of the two Vixens from America, Issaam began asking questions about the planes. Not actually so much about the Vixen Two, but he was very interested in specific details and features of the Vixen One, which her father had flown. When he had exhausted that subject, he turned to the rest of the eighteen planes ordered by his father, the sheik.

"My understanding is the order has been canceled by mutual agreement," Haley said pleasantly, looking to the eldest for the setback that bald announcement would cause.

Zayn's eyes rested on her very steadily. Matter of fact, Haley had been assured of his constant focus on her throughout the meal. She blamed it on the tiny, bust-hugging black dress that was little more than a swatch of silk skimming armpit to armpit.

Of course, it had plenty down below where it counted. The black tube hugged her body to her hips then flared to an absolutely decadent miniskirt. Her long legs were encased in patterned silk stockings and sexy heels boosted her height to six feet. It was a "knock-em dead dress," her father said.

Zayn was too urbane to say anything about her attire. His brothers were too intimidated to do anything but drool behind their napkins.

Another ball of fool and mutton sailed into the dog's jaws. Issaam growled something that made the boy blush. He really is cute, Haley thought of the youngest Haaris.

"Do you fly?" she asked Quadir.

"No. They do not let me."

"Are there restrictions on when one can take flying lessons?"

"No," Issaam answered. He did a lot of the talking at the table. Zayn remained quiet and thoughtful at the head, watching. "But we adhere to the tenet that too much given too early ruins the man."

"I see. Good thing that doesn't apply to women. I got my first license in high school and was flying commercially by eighteen. I paid my own way through college."

"High school?" Quadir echoed, shooting an I-told-you-so look toward his eldest brother. "I will be finished with my O levels next year."

"And you will still not be flying airplanes," Zayn informed him.

"Why not?" Haley jumped in where she knew she shouldn't. It was childish of her, but she had to admit she got a rise out of challenging Zayn Haaris. "Flying is a very useful skill, especially so when distances are as great as they are in the desert. Your father must think so. Why else would he have ordered twenty planes from my company?"

That outlandish assumption made Issaam choke. Quadir gawked at her, openmouthed. Haley wondered if she'd just broken a tribal taboo by contradicting the eldest.

Zayn was nonplussed, and easily deflected the focus off his family onto hers. "Tell us more about the work your father does. How many planes can Bennett Industries remanufacture in a year?"

"Oh, that varies. Some of the refitting is very detailed. Prototypes like the Vixen take three, four months to complete. Overhauling Cubs and Cessnas take a week or so once we get them on line."

"What is so time-consuming about the Vixen?"

Haley stopped to think. "Well, actually, once the design work was finished, the refitting went ahead quite quickly. I think it was the installation of the computers that took the longest. The first plane, being a prototype, had quirks in it."

"Quirks?" Issaam frowned.

"Yes, quirks, glitches, problems to work out."

"I am not surprised," Issaam said. "That is because you have women employed in your factory. The distraction of women on the shop floor would cause many mistakes to be made."

"Excuse me," Haley corrected. "Quirks and glitches aren't gender-based. It's a computer thing."

"They are bugs in the programs, Issaam," Quadir said. Haley silently thanked the boy for rallying to the defense of women, even if he'd come to it by way of the back door.

"Statistics prove that women are less likely to have accidents in a factory setting than men," she said.

"Women belong at home with their children," Issaam declared peremptorily.

"How boring," Haley sputtered.

Quadir's head tilted to the side. A tight frown knitted on his otherwise smooth and untroubled forehead. "You would not prefer to be at home now, Miss Bennett?"

"Well, of course I would." Haley grimaced over being snared in a verbal trap. "If I were, I certainly wouldn't have had the opportunity to meet you charming gentlemen, now, would I?"

"Truly?" the boy asked. "You don't mind having risked your life?"

"No, you've got that wrong. Flying isn't as risky as driving an automobile, and everyone drives automobiles in my country. I like flying. I always have and I'm fortunate that I can do what I like to do."

"That does not make it right," Issaam countered. He certainly was coming across as a rigid conservative. "If American women would return to their homes and take care of their children, your country's crime rate would drop dramatically."

"That's a gross oversimplification of a very complex social problem," she countered. "Poverty is the major source of crime. What would you know of that? Isn't every Kuwaiti born with a guaranteed annual income in the range of sixty thousand dollars? Or is that just the men?"

Zayn cleared his throat. "This is a most unproductive discussion, especially in light of what happened in Kuwait this week. Nor is there any chance that a nation as small and insignificant as Kuwait can have any influence on American thought." He looked at his brother. "Issaam, here you have an excellent opportunity to learn firsthand why it is a young American woman has chosen a career over marriage. Obviously, with Miss Bennett's attributes, she could have any man of her choice. Yet, she has opted for a taxing and dangerous career. I, myself, am curious as to why you have never married," he asked her.

"Nobody interesting ever asked." Haley laughed.

"You can't mean that," Quadir said, making Haley feel guilty over her deliberate teasing that afternoon. "You are so beautiful, hundreds of men must have asked to marry you."

"No, they most certainly have not, and you, my charming young man, are going to devastate the ladies someday." Haley smiled at Quadir. "I'm not beautiful. I'm really very ordinary. When I was your age, I was tall and skinny as a stick. The only thing I was good for was playing point guard on the basketball team and sweeping the floor at my dad's shop."

"But you are lovely. You aren't a stick," the boy insisted.

"You missed my point, Quadir. I learned to value myself for my accomplishments—not for my appearance. I'm the same person whether I'm working on a computer, overhauling an engine or solving complex design problems mathematically. A good education does that."

"Which brings us back to computers." Quadir suddenly switched to speaking Arabic. "I told you she was smart enough to know computers. That's how she has us locked out. It's a password lockout. Of course, finding it in a random search will take time unless one of us can get her to tell us what the word is. Can you not be more helpful, Issaam?"

Haley smiled, puzzled. The switch to Arabic was so blunt and intentional that she seriously wondered if they thought her stupid. Quadir sounded so quarrelsome. Issaam regarded him with what could only be termed elder-sibling long-suffering.

She looked pointedly to the quiet man who sat with his fingers curved across his chin, listening. She decided to test a theory. "You know, I've always thought it important that every family have at least one hacker. You are very fortunate to have two, Zayn, but it will take twenty hackers to break my codes. And you still won't get the Vixen airborne. The Vixen 2000-2 will not respond to forced entry."

All three heads swiveled toward her. Bingo! Zayn's broad shoulders inclined toward her and the hint of a haunting smile curved each corner of his wonderful mouth.

"I am more than satisfied with the response I have been given up to now," he said. "I am certain my satisfaction will improve each time I apply my most persuasive hand to the Vixen's stubborn and willful disposition."

He wasn't talking jets, and his brothers were smart enough to know that. Haley's smile felt permanently glued to her face. His innuendo sunk so deep inside her, her stomach quivered. She deliberately played out a small yawn and laid her napkin on the table.

"I can't say it hasn't been lovely, gentlemen, but before the conversation degenerates further, I shall retire. Good night."

They each stood as she rose and departed. After the sound of Haley's heels had faded from the hall, Quadir helped himself to another piece of *katayif*. Returning to Arabic, he said, "I don't see what is so important about her plane."

"It isn't her plane that is so important," Zayn told him quietly. "It is the Vixen One. That plane may be the only way to get our father and your mother and sisters out of Kuwait alive."

"But the woman's father is there. Can't he fly the plane?"

"His life hangs by a thread in Allah's hands," Issaam said very somberly.

"Will he die?"

"Who can say?" Zayn snapped irritably. "I would appreciate it if both of you would return to the computers and work on this problem further this evening."

"Have you any idea how many possible passwords there are in the English language?" Quadir complained.

"Experience tells that any good code is usually the simplest and easiest to remember. In order to put limits on your search and rule out the obvious, I suggest you begin with phrases English and Arabic have in common.''

''I've been working on this for two solid days,'' the boy groaned.

''Is it important?'' Zayn asked him.

''Well, yes,'' Quadir admitted. ''But it is more likely Father has taken a car and is driving across the border, as we speak.''

''We can not know that for certain,'' Issaam countered.

''And in the meantime,'' Zayn said, ''we must allow no opportunity to ensure Father's safety to escape us. The smaller plane will be able to land on any salt flat in the desert. That might make the difference between life and death. I know you are tired, Quadir. We all are. Accomplish what you can then get some rest. We've had little of that in the past few days.''

''While you try to get the American woman to tell you the password in your own way?'' he said sullenly.

Zayn did not grace the boy's impertinent question with an answer. He retired to his study to make many necessary international calls. Shortly after midnight, the sound of his helicopter rising above the desert was heard throughout the palace.

## Chapter 9

The slap of the helicopter's rotor reverberated inside Haley's canopied bed. That was the sound she'd waited to hear since she'd retired. She threw off the covers and leaped out of bed, hurriedly donning the boy's clothing she'd lifted earlier.

She had a backup plan now. If she could not get to Hafaro where she thought her plane might be, she would head for Riyadh and the American embassy. That was the safest bet of all, but she stubbornly clung to the idea that she could get to her Vixen, then to Kuwait and join her father. If nothing else, there was the goose. Getting home would be a long, hard flight in that crate of bolts, but it could be done.

Haley dropped over the outer wall by the kitchen garden near the jeep she planned to commandeer. She made certain the guards at the main gate did not see her. Using her Swiss Army knife, she hot-wired the vehicle and adjusted the carburetor so that the engine purred more quietly. She rolled away from the palace without headlights, scattering rocks under the tires. Other than a yard dog barking at her passage, no one at the palace noticed her escape.

Within minutes, she located the main road leading to the town of Anaiza. And lo and behold, before very long she was rolling jauntily alongside a huge pipeline. The road ran parallel to it as true as the huge tubes themselves. She distinctly remembered crossing pipelines on the way to Kuwait. She was unclear about such details on the harried, tension-fraught journey away from the air base.

Everything looked different from the air, she reminded herself. The pipes were massive steel snakes mounted on concrete pylons raised above the desert floor. From the air, those same pipes had been insignificant lines severing the earth with geometric precision, just like roads and expressways. On the ground beside them, they looked more than impressive.

Their size alone gave her a different understanding of how massive Saudi Arabia's oil reserves had to be. It went beyond Haley's comprehension to figure out how many gallons flowed through those tubes on any given day—and she was a Texan, familiar with oil fields and refineries.

Now that she was on her way, Haley tried not to think about her dad too much. Tommy's cryptic communiqué had the niggling habit of returning to mind over and over again. *Dad poss. injury rt. leg, gunshot. Vix disabled.* Haley tried not to think about that, but it was hard not to when the scenery was so dull, flat and uninspiring.

Wisely, she stopped frequently.

A convoy of military trucks, jeeps and armored vehicles rumbled past while she sat at a crossroads and studied the stars, confirming her direction, wondering what she could do about a tank that was out of gas. Some of the passing soldiers waved as they lumbered on through the night. Had she had any command of Arabic, Haley would have risked asking for fuel. As it was, she was definitely happier to see them pass without stopping.

She had a drink of water from a pop bottle she'd filled in preparation for this journey and placed inside her makeshift haversack. When the convoy passed, the lonely crossroads was clear of traffic as far as she could see. It was nearing 3:00 a.m. by her watch.

Haley crawled under the jeep, opened the oil cock and drained about a quart of oil into a plastic bag. Using her knife, she scraped a glob of axle grease from the inside of one wheel, adding that to the dirty oil.

Twice earlier, she'd stopped to complete this operation, but both times the local dirt she had added to the mixture was too pale in color to be of any use. This time, Haley had found a russet clay compound, much darker and more satisfactory for her purpose. From the taste and smell of the soil, she could tell it contained clay, and definite traces of iron oxides.

Making herself comfortable on the disabled jeep, she hiked up the hems of her trousers and dabbed handfuls of the goo up her ankles. She needed color and camouflage and she needed it quick, before the sun rose at 5:00 a.m. Her hands were gooey and stained by the time her feet and exposed ankles were covered. It almost killed her to start rubbing the foul, vile-smelling concoction onto her face and neck, but it had to be done.

Since the sticky muck wasn't going to dry, really, she patted it with a liberal handful of fresh dirt straight off the ground. She risked turning on the headlights to check her work. Her hands and feet were nasty brown, filthy beyond redemption. God help her if by some quirk of fate, the desert decided to have a rainy day!

Her hair was in very tight braids, coiled securely underneath a black turban. She had used mascara to darken her lashes and eyebrows and had found sunglasses under the seat of the jeep, a bonus for sure. The dark polarized lenses would keep people from noticing the color of her eyes.

Anyone who looked at her would see a filthy youth with a very swollen face. She had a wad of black plastic stuck in her mouth, some of it pulled over to make it look as if she had missing and decayed teeth. That, she thought, was a stroke of brilliance.

For the benefit of anyone who took an interest in her, she planned to pretend she had the worst toothache ever suffered. Hurting teeth made everybody wince and look away—she hoped.

Necessity forced her to abandon the stolen jeep several kilometers shy of a set of halogen lights gleaming in the distance. The peculiarity of running out of gas next to the world's biggest supply of gurgling-in-the-tubes petroleum touched the raw side of her sense of humor, but Haley was pretty satisfied with having covered two hundred miles in five hours.

She laughed at herself as she jogged to the arc lights in the distance. The lights turned out to be a nice little town clustered at a desert oasis. She had the audacious luck of arriving just in time to catch a northbound bus.

The bus driver handed her back a passel of crumpled riyals and coins after she gave him one of the bills she'd stolen from the desk drawer in the sheik's office.

Her theory on toothache proved true on the crowded bus. She only had to moan and pretend to be in agony to turn strangers away. Of course, it helped to also look like a leper. No Saudi elected to sit by her.

The bus jostled up the road in the building morning heat with a load of passengers, live goats, chickens and crying babies. Before noon, they came to a settlement. It wasn't much of a town.

Soldiers had the road blocked, and the bus wasn't going any farther. Everyone got off. The driver ambled to a café and parked his smelly body at a rickety table to have a meal before turning the bus around and going back where he'd come from. A large crowd waited patiently for him to drink and eat before pestering to board the southbound run.

Haley concluded she had reached some sort of checkpoint. Soldiers dominated it, randomly examining the papers of those heading south, and gave directions. She eased out of the crowd and sat near the town wall on her haunches, trying to look typical. Other Arab men did the same thing, sat and chatted to their neighbors, watching the world go by.

So that's what she did, except she kept her comments to herself. She knew two Arabic words, *salaam,* and *Inshallah.* Both had universal use. When that didn't get her by, she pretended to be in pain and cried off.

There was a lot to see from the narrow wedge of shade by the wall. F-14's raced across the blue, sun-washed sky. American-made helicopters hovered low over the parched desert, scaring up dust devils in their wake. *Yup,* she thought and grinned her semitoothless, horrible grin. *Somewhere just to the north was the air base.*

Adjacent to the checkpoint stood a temporary medical station. Most of the village's activity centered in those two canvas tents.

Spurts of traffic came out of the north. None whatsoever returned. A variety of vehicles came to the barricaded road, from dust-covered Mercedeses and late-model American cars with air-conditioning, to battered trucks and crowded vans.

All had to stop and surrender their papers before being allowed to use the unguarded road Haley had just traveled. All had the look of refugees, and some needed medical attention.

Well past midday, an open truck of soldiers arrived and relieved those on duty. One group disembarked, the other packed up and headed north. Nothing escaped Haley's scrutiny. She contentedly sat and watched the show, not risking going north on foot until sundown at the earliest.

Arabs were a talkative people, it seemed. Everything was a big deal. To Haley's ignorant ears, all their conversations sounded like arguments, especially with soldiers. When a really battered city bus came to a grinding halt at the checkpoint, Haley watched with greater interest.

Built to carry fifty people comfortably, it was jammed with more than a hundred refugees. Whole families descended onto the ground, a lot of them from the Far East. Once the soldiers had looked at their papers, the people rushed to the pitiful open-air market to purchase water and round loaves of bread. The bread was pretty good. She'd eaten a loaf herself for lunch.

She would have given anything to be able to understand the chatter of the refugees. If she had seen anyone who looked European or American, however, she wouldn't have risked approaching them. It was better not to know what she was going into beforehand. She might lose her courage if she knew what lay ahead.

And she'd pretty much burned her bridges behind her by stealing the jeep and sneaking off in the middle of the night. So there was no going back to Anaiza.

Reluctant to part with more of her Saudi money for food, Haley dug into the left pocket of her stolen trousers, which was sticky with a wad of dates taken from Ali's generous trays. She allowed herself the luxury of one, and pried it from the clump and sucked it dry. She had no idea how much money she actually had, what it was worth or when and if she could get more. She had American money, traveler's checks, and her gold credit card, which wouldn't get her too far here. So she sat and sipped water from the last of the pop bottles she'd filched off the drink cart Ali had left in her room. She knew better than to risk drinking local water.

At first, the Arabs off the bus confused her. Gradually, she began to make sense out of what she was watching.

The people from the north had suffered through some kind of ordeal to get this far in the desert. Many were angry. Their young children were greatly upset, frightened and tearful. The teenagers were sullen and distrustful and volatile. Many needed to see the medics in the tents. They had bloodstains on their clothes.

The last to get off the bus was a wailing, grief-stuck old man. He was unaccompanied, and no one paid him much attention as he pulled up bundles of money from deep pockets in his robes. He waved the money in the soldiers' faces, shook it under the noses of everyone who would listen to his plaintive harangue.

Nobody wanted the money. He couldn't give it away. The old man tore the front of his ankle-length dolman apart and beat his breast, crying out his misery. Another refugee started arguing with him.

Officers came along and stopped the disturbance and sent both scurrying on their way. The hot wind caught the money and scooted it along underfoot. Still, nobody wanted the money.

Curious, Haley got up and stretched her legs. She walked with her head down so as not to attract notice and picked up a paper bill. As her eyes fastened onto a one mille bank note, she dropped to her knees on the sand. A thousand Kuwaiti dollars! She was holding a thousand-dollar bill in Kuwaiti currency. That old man had just cast to the wind two fistfuls of thousand-dollar bills!

Wait a minute! She slammed on her mental brakes and reminded herself that in Mexico one American dollar was worth nearly three thousand pesos. But Kuwait was the richest country in the world! Stunned, Haley looked around at the money blowing across the desert.

"Look at that poor boy." A Saudi medical technician pointed to the filthy boy kneeling in the dirt, grabbing every bill that fluttered past him. "He's probably never held so much money in his hands, and now it's worthless."

The doctor did not look up from the stitch he carefully knotted on the arm of an anesthetized Kuwaiti child. The boy slept in his weeping mother's arms, oblivious to the troubles around him. The gunshot wound was clean and would heal. Pausing to look outside the tent, the Saudi doctor wondered how they were going to survive this latest tragedy. He saw the boy the med tech spoke of beyond the line of patients waiting to be treated.

"What is wrong with him?" the doctor asked.

"Mouth's all swollen. Probably an abscessed tooth."

"Tell Hamil to get the boy over here. Maybe if he's not in too bad shape, he can be taken into the army. Is he a village boy?"

"Not with that robe. From the looks of the cloth, he is Wadi Rumna."

Haley was still kneeling in the dirt when the shadow of a soldier fell across her hands. She looked up through the dark sunglasses.

"Get up and come with me," the soldier said in his native language. "The doctor says he will treat your tooth."

Haley grimaced dumbly. She put her hand to her cheek.

"Don't sit there whining. Get up and get in the line." The soldier reached for her, jerking his head back toward the military vehicles. She thought he was reaching for the money and tossed it at him. Scrambling to her feet, she darted back toward the town wall.

With a *crunch, crunch, crunch* of his combat boots, the soldier caught up with her and swung her back around. His tone of voice alarmed Haley. She didn't understand a single word. "What's the matter? Are you afraid you will hurt more if the tooth is taken out?"

"*Inshallah,*" Haley mumbled around her plastic tooth device and dragged her heels as she was pulled to the tent and shoved into the line. As soon as the soldier let go of her arm, she backed off. He yanked her back, glaring fiercely.

"Stand right there, boy. That's an order. You're going to see the doctor."

Haley stood very still. The soldier wiped his hand on his fatigues after touching her. He stood there, guarding her.

She hadn't figured all this out, but she kind of thought it might mean big trouble. Swallowing, she looked inside the tent. She saw the doctor and his assistant wind a bandage around a baby's hand.

Ahead of Haley, a heavily pregnant woman held one hand against the small of her back. It was no less than a hundred and ten degrees in the glaring sun. Sweat beaded on Haley's dirty skin.

The pregnant woman had to be ready to die inside that inhumane black shroud Saudi law forced her to wear. A wave of pity and feminist outrage threatened to blow Haley's cover. But she wasn't sun-crazed completely and kept her muttering to herself. It wasn't going to do the pregnant woman one bit of good to hear an English tirade on her civil rights.

Fortunately, the bus going south was loading. Everybody who didn't live in the pitiful town or who was stuck there by royal command wanted on that bus. Off they went in a cloud of rising dust. The medical technician led the pregnant woman to the other tent and came back to Haley. "All right, let's have a look at you. Open your mouth."

Haley just stood there, not comprehending his rapid-fire Arabic. The soldier scowled at her darkly. "Open your mouth, boy. Are you hardheaded or what?"

"It really isn't necessary for you to do that," the med tech said to the soldier.

"This one is stupid, can't you tell?"

"Hamil, take a break now. You've been very helpful." The doctor stepped out of the tent, drying his hands on a towel. Ready for the next case, he looked at Haley expectantly.

Realizing that the jig was up, Haley pondered the odds of outrunning bullets, versus the ignominy of having a plastic extraction. She shrugged her shoulders and shuffled into the tent. The med tech put his hand on her shoulder and pushed her down on a steel stool.

Laid out on a standing tray were a variety of probes and scalpels. The doctor put his hand under her chin, lifted her head and probably said, "Open wide."

Haley pushed his hand away, smiled, then tucked a dirty finger in her mouth and pulled out the wad of plastic. The doctor scowled, snapped the wad out of her hand and threw it in the trash. He fussed profusely with gestures that were pretty easy to understand, demanding to see inside her mouth, anyway.

The med tech got involved at that point. When the doctor withdrew his fingers, Haley smiled her perfect, polished orthodontic grin—the most charming one she had—and shrugged endearingly. The technician said to the doctor, "He's a beggar from the city, I'll wager."

"What is your name?" the doctor demanded. He reached for Haley's dark glasses, taking them off her face. Still holding her chin, he pulled up a pocket light, then stopped, taken back by the color of her eyes.

"*Azul? Mae nae saek?*"

"*Quasyr*," Haley answered, hoping the man was asking for a name. "Al . . . Haaris."

The doctor frowned and took a cotton sponge from a bowl, dipped it in alcohol and scrubbed it across her cheek. "What is your name? Where did you come from? You are not Saudi."

Haley jerked her face away, hastily rubbed her cheek with her grimy fingers and stood up.

"Are you Kuwaiti? Iraqi?"

"He doesn't understand anything we say."

Haley shook her head, backing away from the two men. It was definitely time to go. She bowed, touched her head, her mouth and her breast muttered, "Salami, salami," then she sprinted out of the tent. She leaped over the sand embankment, determined to get away from the checkpoint. Several of the soldiers shouted. No guns fired. She ducked out of sight behind a drop in the ground and ran due north along the empty road.

She hadn't run far before she had to give up that expenditure of energy. It was too damned hot for running. That probably explained why no soldiers came after her on foot. Her lungs felt scorched.

Before she'd walked very much farther, she severely regretted the loss of her sunglasses. The sun was really harsh at this time of day. The heat, brutal. In spite of the *kuffiyah* and the turban covering her head, her brain felt as if it were on fire. She decided it was best that she stay out of sight. She kept moving north by walking on the other side of the pipeline from the road. It just went on and on and on, as far as her eyes could see.

She prayed for sunset, soon.

The palace of the Haji Haaris was looking pretty good when she collapsed under the only shade to be had, beneath the pipelines. The swatch of shade was narrow, the ground beneath the raised pipes rocky and rough. Aside from breaking the contact of skin to sun, she'd gained little benefit from the maneuver. It was definitely the wrong time of day to be at odds with the desert, she mused.

How long she crouched there feeling every pore in her skin open their floodgates, Haley didn't know. No matter how much she perspired, her skin never felt cool.

The urge to sleep was overwhelming, but it was so hot she couldn't even doze.

Just sitting there, moving only to occupy as much shade as she could while the sun tracked across the western sky, Haley began to doubt her scheme. Her biggest fear had centered on not getting caught breaking purdah. That had not happened. Neither had she anticipated getting stuck in the desert before she got to the Vixen.

Yes, she'd realized it wasn't going to be easy to travel hundreds of miles on her own in a strange country. That was the flaw in her plan. She took distance for granted. When she'd struck out on her own, it was to drive the jeep all the way to the base, or at least within walking distance of it. Three hundred miles was a snap to drive to anyone born and raised in Texas. Three hundred miles to an aviator was an hour or less. A snap.

Later, when the sun was still several hands high and the heat hadn't decreased a degree, Haley still huddled under the elongating shadow of the massive pipes. She was so thirsty she couldn't think five seconds about anything except water. Her feet hurt from blisters and burns that the sandals hadn't protected against. She wasn't sure she could get up and walk one inch farther north.

"For a smart girl, I'm pretty stupid!" she said out loud. How idiotic and foolish she had been. There was no way she was going to make it to the base where the Vixen waited for her.

Right then, she wished a whole truckload of religious police would pull up and take her into custody for dressing like a boy and wandering about without a veil. Their punishment wouldn't be anywhere near as final as the sun's. She was going to die out here.

Realizing that, Haley staggered to her feet. She leaned against a pylon, gathering what remained of her wits. She still had the dates. Now was definitely the time to eat some.

The sweet fruit stuck to the roof of her mouth and her teeth. She couldn't manufacture any saliva to wash it down. That frightened her. She knew what it meant. She was critically dehydrated. She forced herself to move, to put one foot in front of the other until she'd crossed the rocky distance to the road.

For now, she would stay on the sand-swept pavement. Some-one would come. Someone had to.

Sundown was a long time coming. When it did, it was linger-ing and very beautiful. The sand turned to scarlet. The sky glowed red, then purple and faded to cerulean blue. Far to the north, lights shimmered out of reach. But they were actual lights, man-made halogen.

Too late, she realized how impossible it was to judge dis-tances here the way she did back home. Too late, came the re-alization that the pipeline wasn't getting her where she wanted to go. If this was the road to the air base, it would have had traffic on it. There hadn't been a single vehicle since she'd struck out on it. She'd gone the wrong way from the checkpoint.

Then darkness came. The temperature dropped. Haley couldn't go on.

A Saudi patrol, three soldiers in a jeep, found her sitting in a dazed circle of her own blind footprints. Tossed into the back of the jeep, Haley greedily drank a small cup of water, then closed her eyes. Red burned through her shut eyelids. Her con-tacts felt as if they'd turned to coals. The water made her nau-seated. She'd have been a babbling idiot if she could have uttered a word.

The Saudis seemed to understand that the desert made one unable to comprehend anything. At least with the dark had come a blessed cooling of the air. But Haley was too far gone to be revived by that alone. She had no awareness of entering the military base. The next thing she knew after being picked up was collapsing in a heap on the floor of a small, too brightly lit in-firmary.

The intern was as confused about her as she was with him. He gave her biscuits to eat and small cups of water one at a time. She felt very tired, weak. Her stomach ached. Little by little, her mind came out of its sluggish inertia. She'd made it to a mili-tary base. But was it the right one?

The intern was so offended by her filth that he shuffled her off to a corner and left her alone. That was fine with Haley. Only a small portion of her mind seemed to be operating at this point. She was a feral, hostile creature intent only on self-preservation.

She huddled in the out-of-the-way corner and put off all at-tempts at communication with a closed face and tight mouth. The intern let her be, refilling the jug of water for her intermittently. Safe there, Haley tucked her head on her knees and dozed.

This was apparently acceptable. A beggar boy wasn't worth a soldier's trouble. While the intern was out eating his supper, Haley sneaked away.

There were no lights outdoors. None. It took her some time to recognize the humps in the earth as the camouflaged hangars that she'd seen days—or was it weeks—ago. Time had taken on an eerie, attenuated quality.

It was as if she were the only living soul on earth. She wandered aimlessly, lost, through the blackout, crossing runways and cluttered stretches of concrete jammed with vehicles and planes she couldn't recognize any markings on.

Row after row of parked, idle planes. They were so big and ugly. None were slick blue-and-white. As she walked the rows in a state of confusion, trying to recall Arabic calligraphy painted on the tarmac, she stopped beside an F-14. She stood there, in the middle of the parking lot, then turned full circle, looking at size, not color.

She walked diagonally across two more rows and came to the last row, pacing off a slow, agonizing litany, a roll call of manufacturers by nation of origin. American, American, British, American, French, Italian, Italian, American.

Vixen.

She stopped before the cone and reached up to touch the sleek, wicked-looking nose. A humdinger of a needle point that swelled to curve wonderfully around the smooth bubble of fiberglass and molded smart glass that gave the pilot a full one-hundred-eighty-degree view of the sky. Vixen.

Not blue-and-white.

She touched the fender over the nose wheel, ran her hand under the fiberglass belly beneath the cockpit. She sniffed deeply, smelling oil and paint and high-octane petrol. Her beautiful blue-and-white Vixen was unrecognizable in morbid gray, mottled green and dirty tan.

Crossing under the plane's belly, Haley stumbled to the pilot's port. The door was locked. Digging inside the deep pocket of her trousers, she fumbled around her scant possessions for a small silver key.

She found it, opened the lock and scrambled upward, wiggling onto the fine-leather-upholstered contoured seat. It caressed the aches in her spine like a glove. A feeling of being home and safe at last washed over her at the oh, so familiar smells and surroundings. A minute courtesy light glowed on the instrument panel, illuminating the cockpit, which had not been altered in any way.

"Vixen."

Haley spread her hands on the butterfly wheel, sighed and pulled the door shut to extinguish the courtesy light. Setting the lock made noise. Shutting the door made noise. Haley sat in the dark, scanning the field of planes and held her breath. No one came, no alarm went up.

She dreaded what would happen when she started the engine and hijacked her own plane. She stared out the windscreen, making a mental map of the obstacles she would have to dodge to clear the parking lot and reach the tarmac.

What if something really big tried to land when she attempted an illegal takeoff? She could lose her licenses—all of them—forever. Somehow, that didn't seem important. If she got airborne, everything else would just have to work out whatever way it did.

But she didn't move. She sat there in the dark, staring with burning eyes at the field of planes, almost holding her breath. Still, no one came.

It was weird. Really weird. No soldiers moving around. No planes coming in. No runway lights. No lights in the tower. A ghost base. Empty. Quiet as a tomb. Except for her pounding heart and the odd way her breath rasped in her dried-out sinuses and parched lungs.

They must be on maneuvers or sleeping or maybe watching some entertainment, she thought. Maybe an Arab counterpart to Bob Hope was visiting the base. There was activity, but none of it was near this field of parked, idle planes. By degrees, she let her breath out and began to feel safe.

First, she had to empty her pockets. Deep in the trouser pockets under the long tunic shirt, under the heavy dolman robe, she carried her wallet, passport and all the vital papers for the plane. She pulled out the clumped handful of sticky dates that she had been determined to save until she was inside the Vixen, and one by one, ate the reward. She even licked her filthy hands, putting them inside her mouth to suck away the sticky sweetness that adhered to her grime-covered fingers.

Haley felt like crying. A sob escaped her throat, but no tears washed out of her eyes. She closed her eyes because they hurt. Her gritty contacts felt welded to her corneas. Even though she knew better, she rubbed them with the heels of her palms. Very soon she was going to have to take her contacts out and give those orbs a rest. But not now. Now she had to start the Vixen and coax the lady into the sky.

That was a tall order. Suddenly, all her courage seemed to have deserted her.

"This is not the place to fall apart, Haley Bennett," she told herself crossly. "So what if you've been to hell and back. So what if you've done the stupidest thing in the world, like falling for a man who will never love you back! In one second, no less! He damn sure doesn't give a fig about you. Get a grip!"

Her voice broke then and she shook her head violently.

"You just get down to business and do what you're supposed to. Get this plane started and fly to Kuwait. One hour, you can be in and out of that airport like a hawk. Five minutes on the ground to get Dad and Jack on this plane and you're out of there. That's what you're going to do. Now get a grip!"

# Chapter 10

Haley shook the emotional baggage from her mind, fumbled for the key in her lap and slotted it into the ignition. She turned the switch to On and leaned forward to the computer console. One beep sounded, signaling once the hard disk had booted. She slid the keyboard toward her, and typed ''Ali Baba'' on the blank screen.

The screen flashed white, then black, then lit up blue with a white border.

*Hello Haley Bennett.*

She typed *Hello Vixen,* and punched enter.

The screen responded, *Systems check in progress,* and a series of numbers flashed with accompanying beeps, signifying all functions were in order. Finally, the words *systems check complete, begin ignition sequence* appeared.

Haley sat back and punched one key, Enter. While the computer did all the work, she licked date residue from her left hand. A secondary screen provided her a report on the fuel mix. It was too rich, a higher octane than the plane was used to. Only two of the four petrol tanks were full. Did she want to cancel ignition and cap the tanks? the computer asked. Yes or no? *No.* Enter. The computer said impartially, *Fuel mix will decrease engine performance by .003 percent. Not critical. Enter flight plan now.*

Haley's fingers hovered over the QWERTY keyboard. The only destination she could think of was her bed at home. She tried to moisten her dry lips with a tongue that still felt swollen and numb. Home was twelve hours away. She didn't have it in her to push her body that far.

There was a bed on the Vixen, a wonderful fantasy bed, sheeted in designer silks. She could crawl back there, strip the bed and collapse on it. Sleep off her exhaustion. There was water in the storage tanks. She could strip down, clean up and try this later. And not fail at it when she had her wits back. Her strength back.

Sighing deeply because that was a solution she could live with, Haley let her fingers rest on the home keys then typed *Close systems, park head.* Enter.

The screen flashed, invalid code, retry, abort, fail.

Haley muttered a curse, and again typed *Park head.*

*Are you sure?*

"Listen, you stupid computer," Haley growled crankily, "don't get smart with me."

She typed *no* and went through her shut-down sequence again. It should have worked. It didn't. She was too tired to work her way through a systems glitch. The quickest way to shut down the computer was to turn the key, but that would subvert her lockouts. The plane would automatically go to manual ignition.

She went back to the beginning one more time, and hit the same snag. Reading the snotty *Are you sure?* question, Haley wanted to smash her fist through the blue screen.

She almost passed out when a long arm reached past the back of her seat and one finger punched the n key. Then those lean, tanned fingers pushed hers aside and typed *Forty Thieves,* then pushed Enter, and the Vixen shut down.

"Very clever." A forceful hand clamped down on Haley's right hand before she could snatch her key from the ignition. Haley's heart dropped all the way down to her proverbial socks. "Very predictable, yes, but very clever."

Zayn Haaris slid the key into a pocket of his fatigues, removed her passport, wallet and papers from the console and dropped them into another pocket.

"Get up. Let's go."

He pulled her hard in the direction he meant for her to go. Haley only half managed to get her feet under her before he had dragged her out of the cockpit.

Speechless, stunned because he'd appeared out of nowhere and had been there waiting for her to come stumbling into the trap he'd baited so carefully, she couldn't figure out if she wanted to kiss him or kill him. She made up her mind it was the latter when he shoved her toward the rear exit, his hand hard and fast on her upper arm.

Trying to jerk free, she voiced a complaint. "I don't need your assistance!" Even though her legs nearly collapsed underneath her.

At the closed door, Zayn hit his fist on the rosewood panel, twice. Immediately, the outer lock rotated and the hydraulic door slid sideways. A set of metal stairs stood in place and a whole platoon of soldiers waited to take her prisoner.

Trying once again to wrench her arm out of his grip, Haley said through clenched teeth. "You got what you wanted. Let me go!"

Zayn yanked her off-balance on the last step, dragging her against him. "Go ahead, provoke me!"

Haley couldn't muster a curse to hurl at him anywhere near vile enough. She had a vision of cool Haley Bennett dissolving in a screaming, horribly childish tantrum on a Saudi tarmac. That image prevented her from making a complete fool of herself.

She found her stiff upper lip as she was dragged to a jeep and tossed inside with the sheik, who crammed his too-big body next to hers. Some flunky drove without lights through clustered buildings half sunk underground. They stopped at one of the bunkers. The outer entry she was pulled through was pitch-dark. A steel door swung shut behind them, and they were inside a room, the lights blindingly bright.

Haley shielded her eyes with her free hand. Zayn gasped at what the lights revealed.

Several soldiers had told him what the blue-eyed urchin at the checkpoint looked like. The crew that found her wandering in the desert had also debriefed him. Hearing about her effective disguise was nothing compared to seeing it.

Not in a million chances would he ever have guessed the creature before him was a beautiful woman.

Filthy, she was dirtier than a mud logger on the most remote oil field. Zayn spun her to face him and yanked her plain *kuffiyah* off her head. If she'd cut that hair or ruined it, he was going to kill her. Roughly, he unwound the close binding of black cotton turbaned round her head.

"Ow!" Haley pushed his hands away, lurching back. She got a glimpse of the unchecked anger in his face. That made her wince more than having her hair pulled.

"Get in there," Zayn said through gritted teeth. "You are going to wash and scrub and scour this...this..."

Words failed Sheik Haji Haaris. In neither his language nor hers could he come up with a description foul enough to convey to her exactly what she looked like.

Haley jumped the second his hand shot out from his side. She wasn't quick enough to dodge the oncoming blow. But he didn't strike. Instead, his fist dug into her grime-covered clothes. She was jerked sideways and roughly shoved ahead of him through a door into another room.

Zayn hit a wall switch. An overhead light flooded the cubicle with harsh bright light. Haley found herself in a sterile, white-tiled bathroom. It was plain and simple—shower, toilet and wall-hung sink—and nowhere near big enough to contain a man in a rage and her, too.

Above the sink, screwed to the wall, was a mirror fit for little more than shaving and putting a part in hair. Flicking her eyes toward it, Haley glimpsed a horrible apparition next to the handsome Zayn Haji Haaris. He reached past the wraith, yanked the plastic shower curtain aside, twisted the knobs and a stream of water shot from the shower head.

"Get in there!"

Thinking she was going to be thrown in, anyway, Haley did exactly what he said and stepped inside the stream of water, clothes and all. There was an orange bar of soap on the sink. Zayn grabbed it and shoved it into Haley's hand.

"Scrub!"

A pair of pale blue eyes in a coal miner's face blinked at him. He couldn't begin to read her expression. She turned the bar over in her hands, rubbing it between blackened palms. A gray lather formed, but the grease on her skin only blackened the bar. The dirt wasn't affected at all.

Too angry to risk putting his thoughts into words, Zayn marched out of the bathroom, slamming every door he passed forcefully shut behind him.

He stood in the middle of his quarters and ran his fingers through his hair, looking around him like a crazy man. There wasn't enough soap in the world to get her clean.

He stalked to the supply room four buildings down and ordered a sergeant out of bed, made him open the store and issue him detergent, mechanic's cream, vegetable grease, pumice soap, everything and anything that could be used to cut through dirt. He carried a heavy carton in his hands when he walked back into the semi-underground housing.

Inside the shower stall, she had made little progress, though the bar of soap had whittled to almost nothing. Haley sat on the floor of the stall, stripped to tunic and cotton trousers, scrubbing a foot that was the color of a hot roofer's tar-soaked mop. She was white around her knees where the trousers were rolled back to dingy cuffs, smeary gray to the prominent anklebone and tar-black below.

"It won't come off," she said lamentably.

The sound of horror in her voice tore something loose inside Zayn's chest. He flipped the lid down on the toilet, dropped the carton onto it and knelt on the wet floor beside her. He shut off the water and grabbed a towel.

Haley took the cloth from him, patting it on her hands, on her feet, blotting her face. In the strong light, her face and neck were a funny ocher-brown. Nutmeg, Zayn finally defined it in his mind, the color of light crude spilling on the ground.

Without a word spoken, Zayn twisted the top off the waterless cleaner, picked up her right foot and laved a handful of the substance onto it.

Haley shivered a little, watching his hands move, massaging the white cream all over her foot, between her toes, up her ankle. He added more and rubbed more, the white stuff turned gray, dissolving. The white towel in her hands looked like something used to clean a crankcase.

"You're mad about the plane," she said.

"Do not speak to me."

"It's my plane. Now it's ugly."

"I'm not going to discuss it."

"Did you fly it?"

Zayn shot her a quelling look.

"You did, didn't you? You got your hacker baby brother to break into my program, didn't you?" Haley jerked forward, squishing water from her clothes, and dug her fingers into the can of cleaner. She worked on her hands. He scrubbed her ankle and the bottom of her leg. Every pore seemed embedded with dirt. Every crease filled.

"Why won't you discuss it?" Haley demanded as she wiped her hands on the towel and repeated the process. He started on her left foot.

Not until the third treatment with the waterless cleaner did the gunk begin to loosen. Zayn held her left foot in his hand and stared at it. The arch was never going to come clean. The goo between her toes belonged on a Cairo guttersnipe.

"I have never been so filthy in my life," Haley said. She didn't like the way his eyes shot daggers at her.

He opened another can of cleaner and pulled her forward, bringing a handful of white cream up to her face. Talking and seeing wasn't going to be allowed. She shut her mouth and closed her eyes. His fingers worked and worked, lathered and wiped, creamed her up again, and again and again.

He tore her collarless shirt halfway off her shoulders and he started rubbing handfuls of the stuff into her neck, up her throat, around her ears. Haley peeked open greasy eyes and didn't know she looked like a raccoon. At least she wasn't sunburned, except on her eyelids.

"I'm hungry."

Zayn sat back on his heels, dropping his hands from her neck and glared at her. "You're hungry?"

"And tired. And I don't want you to be mad at me."

He tossed the blackened towel at her. "Wipe off your face and neck and don't forget your ears, inside them."

He stood and left, slamming the door.

Wearily, Haley hoisted herself up from the floor of the shower. She looked inside the box, found soap powder and three gritty bars of soap. She stripped off her sodden clothes, turned the water back on, adjusted the temperature and began to scrub, determined to get herself clean.

*   *   *

Adjacent to the bathroom was a small closet. There, Haley found extra towels and a robe. Her skin was pretty funny-looking, but she'd had all the scrubbing she could stand. She couldn't work the fine-tooth comb in the medicine cabinet through her hair, so she wound it in a towel and tied the belt of the robe secure at her waist.

Nothing from her disguise could be salvaged. She bundled the ruined clothes and towels into the trash and padded into the next room.

It was a very small apartment. What passed for living space was postage stamp in size. It held a vinyl couch and a table with two chrome chairs. There wasn't room for anything else. A partition split off the minuscule kitchen and sitting room from the single bedroom, which contained a single bed and lone chest of drawers.

Zayn occupied the wedge of kitchen, overwhelming the space, rattling a frying pan over a gas burner. Eggshells were strewn about the dinky countertop next to a stainless-steel sink. He did not look up at her. He lifted the pan from the flame and slid the cooked contents onto two plates, dropped a fork onto each and picked them up.

"Sit, eat." He reached around her to put both plates on the table.

The food smelled very good, of green peppers and onions. There was sausage cut up into the eggs, as well, and tomatoes. Haley wanted to tell him how good the food smelled. Mouth watering, she sat down in silence and waited for him. He came with a carton of milk and two glasses.

"Eat," he said more forcefully when he'd sat down.

There was a good possibility that Haley wasn't going to be able to swallow a single bite, no matter how hungry she was.

He ate five or six bites then tore a hunk off a flat loaf of bread. Studying her gray face, he wondered if his sisters-in-law and their mothers could do anything to salvage her beautiful skin. He doubted it.

Haley forced herself to swallow everything she put in her mouth. She drank half her milk and thanked him when he topped up the glass. His silence was killing her.

"Can I tell you something, please?"

"You have nothing to say to me that I will listen to."

"Okay, fine." Haley compressed her mouth, hurting over his coldness. But she wasn't going to keep still and quiet, like some little kid being punished. He was going to hear her questions and she was going to have answers, one way or another.

She waited until he'd finished his food, then tried again.

"This morning, yesterday morning, whichever, a bus from Kuwait stopped at Al Auda. This one old man had all kinds of money with him. Bundles of it. He began to wave it around, trying to sell it, I think. No one would take it. Not even the soldiers. They all threw it away."

"Kuwaiti currency," Zayn said soberly.

"Has the whole economy crashed? Kuwait is the richest country in the world," Haley asked, shocked.

"Kuwait is an occupied territory. Worthless Iraqi money replaces the Kuwaiti dinar. My home is being systematically raped and plundered."

Haley stared for a long time at his fierce expression. Deep lines ravaged his features, lines that hadn't been there the first time she'd seen him. It wasn't only her foolish actions that had left their impact on his face. His troubles ran much deeper.

"How can Iraq do that? What will you do?"

"It is not your concern what we Arabs will do."

Haley dropped her gaze to her empty plate. Was his hostility to her based on the fact that she was non-Arab? She sensed something. He certainly had a dim view of American women . . . or maybe just her. Unable to sort that through, she shook her head slightly. She wanted to comfort him, but didn't know how or even where to begin. What could you tell someone whose country had been crushed? What words she thought of seemed hopelessly inadequate.

"Have you had any word from your father?" she asked. "Do you know if he is all right?"

"No. There has been no word. The last report only verified that he was seen at the airport by others on the morning of the invasion. A friend reported that a very tall red-haired American was with him. Your father is red-haired?"

"Yes." Haley nodded. "Is that all? Did your friend know anything else? Were they all right?"

Zayn took a deep breath and released it slowly. He wouldn't be the one to tell her that his contact saw bullets take down her father. "That information is now over a week old. There has been nothing more."

"It's not very reassuring," Haley admitted.

The silence lengthened between them, but it was no longer fraught with the tensions that had existed prior to their meal together.

Haley gathered the plates, glasses and debris from the meal and washed the dishes, dried and put them away. Zayn sat in stony silence staring at a wall embellished by one framed picture of the Prophet. When she was done, drying her hands on a cup towel, he said, "Go to bed, Haley Bennett."

She'd had a glimpse of the bed. This was not Anaiza. She asked cautiously, "Where do you sleep?"

He steepled his hands before his face and looked at her harshly. "That is not your concern."

Haley tossed the dish towel to the countertop.

"Fine, it's not my concern. Nothing is my concern. You won't discuss it. What does concern me, Sheik Haaris? Will you discuss what happens to me personally? Am I under arrest? Are you sending me to jail?"

Zayn drew a deliberately deep breath before rising to his feet. He would like to soften his expression for her, even draw her inside his arms and give her the comfort she was signaling that she so desperately needed. He could not. First, because he would not take such blatant advantage of her emotional turmoil. Second, because he could no longer trust himself if he came within one inch of her. For the time being, it was better that he remain aloof and remote and her tender feelings were the only thing endangered.

"If it is within my power, I will return you to Anaiza," Zayn answered. "Here, I can make no guarantees for your safety. The Republican Guard is massed on the border, poised to take control of the Saudi oil fields south of Kuwait. There is nothing in this world that can stop them. Saddam Hussein's formidable army will mow through this desert like locust devouring wheat. And you, my foolish American, are standing on the first target they will attack, this military base. Now, do you understand?"

Haley's teeth pressed deeply into her lower lip and she shook her head. "No. I don't."

Zayn closed the distance between them, grasped her shoulders and shook her. "What terms do you understand? Do you know what a red alert is? Can you comprehend that this base is now a closed fortress, sitting in the path of the biggest army my world has ever seen? Hussein wants the oil fields and he's going to have them, by whatever force necessary."

"Yes, I can understand that," Haley shouted back at him. "But it's not my fault. I didn't start a war. You've been treating me as if I'm your enemy, and I'm not."

"I'm yelling at you because your stupidity has landed you where no woman belongs! It isn't safe! I don't need the worry of keeping watch over some reckless, blundering American woman. I've got the lives and welfare of thousands of my people to look out after, and you keep preventing me from doing the job I must do."

Stung, Haley tilted her chin, showing injured pride. "Well, you don't have to worry about me anymore. I'll stay out of your way."

"It is too damn late for that!" His growl was so fierce it made the hair on her neck stand up. "You don't understand, do you?" he said.

"Understand what?"

"Do you have any idea of the hell you've put me through for the last twenty-four hours?"

"*You've* been through? Why, you arrogant, conceited oaf, I'm the one who's been suffering, wandering in your stupid desert, trying to get here. Just so I could take my plane to Kuwait, pick up my father and godfather and get the hell back home! You could have helped me, but no, you acted like a desert bandit and threw me inside your own private harem!"

"Forget it!" Then Zayn's voice dropped several octaves into a low, feral growl. "Americans never understand anything. You would have died in the desert. I diverted ten patrols from their necessary duties to search the desert for you. Can you understand that? It wasn't an accident those soldiers found you stumbling over your own feet! And you'd better thank God they did. A few more hours and you would have collapsed and been food for the scorpions."

The bald truth in his words made Haley shudder. She could think of nothing to say in her defense that would diminish his righteous temper. She folded her arms across her chest defensively and met the burning anger in his eyes.

"I'm sorry."

"Oh?" Zayn reared back, astonished. "You're sorry? Do you think that by saying that you make up for the agony of discovering you missing last night? The torture I've been through this whole day? Not knowing whether you were alive or dead or in some horrible trouble? Does that make everything all right again? Is that what works at home when you get in over your head? Do you bat your beautiful eyes and hang your head prettily and everything is like it was before? All is forgiven?"

Haley shook her head. "No. I had no idea... that you would... that I'd... Look, I am sorry. My running away was a stupid thing to do. I will admit that, now. I didn't know that when I started out. I'm a Texan. I live in the desert, too, sort of." She finished on a lame note, because beautiful green San Antonio was nothing like the stark Summan.

"I didn't do this to hurt you," she went on. "I did think it would be better if we didn't see each other again. I really thought I could just make it here quickly, get into the Vixen and leave. I know my father is alive. He's hurt, but he's okay. If I can just get to Kuwait, to the airport there, to our hangar, I can get Dad out before something terrible happens to him. And my godfather, too."

Zayn stared hard at her stubborn, determined, beautiful face. It didn't matter that her intentions were pure. She was a woman and she was more vulnerable than she realized. Nor would he admit how truly distraught her disappearance had made him feel. He'd torn a strip off Ali that wasn't likely to ever grow back, figuratively.

"I have only one question to that, Haley Bennett."

"What?" she asked, hoping he could see her reasons and understand her motivations.

"Suppose something horrible has happened to your father. Do you think he'd actually want you there with him?"

Haley thought back to the last words she'd heard her father shout at her over their radios. She flashed a look at Zayn Haaris's intense and beautiful eyes. Did she have to answer that? He knew the answer.

"No, he wouldn't."

Some of the tension in Zayn eased. "Thank you for an honest answer."

Haley's mouth dried. Yes, she'd given him honesty, but she saw immediately that he took more from it than she had intended. It reinforced his self-proclaimed right to act as her protector.

"Well, don't let it go to your head," Haley said. "I don't let my dad tell me what to do any more than I let my brothers treat me like a doormat. I have to do what I think is best. I'm not a coward. Maybe some women would take a back seat in the face of trouble, but I don't."

"Then you leave me no choice except to remove such decisions from your hands completely. You will remain inside the quarters until I can safely return you to Anaiza."

Haley glared at him. "Why don't you be honest and call a spade a spade. I'm under arrest, right?"

"You may consider it any damned thing you like."

"You self-righteous son of a bitch!" Haley stifled the urge to strike him. Instead, she turned on her bare heel and fled to the stark, plain bedroom.

Defeated, Zayn let her go. He'd put the truth baldly. Diplomacy wasn't his long suit; defense was. The Saudi military, the whole world, waited to discern the next move of Saddam Hussein.

Zayn's greatest fear was the Republican Guard. No military personnel could leave the base. For the moment, Zayn was as trapped as Haley.

# Chapter 11

Zayn was gone when Haley woke from her troubled sleep.

The door of the windowless apartment was locked from the outside. There was a tray of prepared food on the table, plain and ordinary. It was food. She ate it.

She spent her time working on her skin, cleaning fingernails, scraping cuticles clean, washing and rewashing and combing tangles out of her hair.

The housing was very quiet because it was partly underground. She slept during the hottest, stuffiest part of the day. When she awoke, there was another meal on the table, but no Zayn. No nothing.

If this was what prison was like, she wasn't going to enjoy it. Time ate at her. She marked its passage by the arrival of meals. The soldier that brought the meals was the antithesis of kind Ali. He had a rough, fear-inspiring scowl, burly arms and pock-marked skin. Haley stayed out of his way.

She drank gallons of water before her dry throat finally abated. Even when her third day of isolated confinement came, she still craved water continuously. One day in the desert had done that. It boggled her mind. How could the Arabs stand it?

The mirror told her when she had regained her natural complexion. She was sitting at the foot of the bed, all pink and clean, wrapped in the terry-cloth robe from another bath when Zayn finally returned. She didn't hear him come in, only saw him when he stood in the opening between sleeping and sitting rooms. He held a brown paper package in one hand, the other gripped the metal frame of the door.

"Hello." Haley's startled heart thumped in her chest. He looked so tired. His mouth was tight, grim, and gray shadows haunted his eyes. "You are well?"

"Oh?" Haley shrugged and pulled the knot on her robe tighter as she stood. She'd had fantasies in her boredom, all of them with him at the center. "Yes, I'm well. And you?"

"As can be expected. I have brought you clothes. Put them on."

He offered the package, which was tied up with string. Haley looked at it, wondered about it. For three days, there hadn't been so much as a sock added to her sole outfit of a toweling robe. She wasn't stupid. If he kept her naked, she couldn't go anywhere. Now he'd brought clothes.

The silence crackled between them as crisply as the paper wrapping when she took the bundle from his hand.

"Am I going somewhere?" Haley pulled the package to her chest and crossed her arms over it.

"Yes."

Studying his face, Haley held back a hundred questions. Maybe she'd learned something in the silence of the past few days. What she thought and had to say about things didn't make a whole lot of difference. She slipped the string off and opened the paper.

A shower of silk garments fell onto the smoothly made bed. She lifted the thin straps of a black slip. It was of the finest quality, lace formed its smooth bodice and the deep hem.

She turned to see if Zayn was still there, but he had left the doorway. Peeking, she saw him standing with his back to her, contemplating his Prophet.

Haley untied her robe and laid it on the bed. She drew the slip over her head and shivered as the silk touched her skin. It clung to her breasts, slithered like a Harlow gown over her hips and thighs, spread comfortably around her ankles. A deep slit from hem to knee allowed her to take a full stride in it.

There was more, an overdress, dark-colored and devoid of adornment. It was fitted at the waist and zipped up the back to a high neck. The sleeves were long enough for her arms, which surprised her. There were sheer stockings with snug elastic tops that reached to her midthigh, and simple leather flats from the best Italian shoemaker.

She removed the string at the end of her braid and combed her hair, sweeping it straight back from her face, letting it fall unbound down her back. She crumpled the paper and string into a ball and put them in the trash, hung the robe in the little closet and went to stand in the sitting room.

"I'm ready."

Zayn turned. What he saw shocked him more than the unholy apparition of slime several nights before. Haley was stunning. He remembered her skimpy, sexy black dinner dress; she looked like a kid in that costume compared to the woman she was now. She was elegant, a slender beauty. She had many, many facets, this unexpected American find of his.

Zayn motioned with his hand for her to come to him. From his pocket he withdrew a black silk scarf. Turning it with experienced hands, he brought it behind her head, drawing the narrow ends around her throat. It fit snugly across her forehead and temples, encircled the neck and fastened behind her head at her nape. Her hair was too long, too thick to be contained as it should have been. A sheet of burnished gold hung down her back to her hips. Touching it, he was assured by the soft silky feel of it, not a hair had been harmed by her filthy disguise.

He had laid the *abba* aside when he'd entered earlier. Now he picked the garment up and held it open for her like a coat. He circled her shoulders and fastened the frog at her throat, raised the hood over her head. A second frog at her breasts held the cloak further secure and closed, slits in the sides allowed her hands movement.

This curious, not so heavy outer garment was a hooded cape, Haley discovered. It was long enough to sweep the ground at her feet. She stretched her neck, easing the confinement beneath hood and scarf and looked up at Zayn.

All he could see now was her face. A pale, beautiful face with huge, imploring blue eyes and tempting, ruby red lips. He touched her chin, catching the point of it between his fingers. "Kiss me."

"Is this goodbye?" Haley frowned. Her eyes blurred with tears. She reached for him, catching hold of his arms.

Zayn shook his head, unable to manage any words of reassurance. What he was about to ask of her was beyond redemption. She had the right to refuse him, but he had prayed long and hard that she had the courage he thought she did.

She struggled with the tightening in her throat and the mist blurring her eyes. Then, holding his arms firmly, she leaned into him, putting her mouth to his. Haley vowed to savor the taste of him all her days, if this was the last moment she was to have with him.

Nearly overcome by the passion and promise of her kiss, Zayn had to grip her shoulders and set her away from him. He held her shoulders tight and looked somberly into her face. He could not bear to be separated from her again. He could not leave her behind. He could not go forward without her.

"Do you still want to go to Kuwait to look for your father?"

That question was the very last thing Haley had expected to hear from him. She blinked, twice, stunned. "You know I do."

"Are you certain of that? The desert was not kind to you. Would you risk it again?"

"I would risk anything to help my father. If it meant I had to walk through hell itself, I would do so to save him."

Zayn's expression was almost unreadable. "I thought as much. Many things have happened in the passing days. I have word from the resistance in Kuwait City that my father and yours may have escaped capture and arrest."

"Arrest?" Haley voiced alarm.

"Yes, arrest. All the Americans in the country are being taken to Baghdad to be used as bartering coins to keep your government from interfering. My hope is that I will be able to find our fathers and remove them in secret from the Republican Guard. I have other family members who are in danger, two very cherished sisters, mere babies of only eight years. There is a chance they can be rescued, that your plane at the airport will provide us the means to spirit all our loved ones out of danger. It will be dangerous, and I have no guarantee of success. Your Vixen could be my family's only salvation."

"The Vixen One?" Haley's eyes widened as she comprehended his plan.

"Yes. I need to know if the other plane has the same lockout device you had on the Vixen Two. Is it valid to assume your father would have disabled that jet the way you disabled yours?"

Haley's thoughts spiraled. "Yes, most definitely." She wanted to go with him and feared if she told him anything else, he would not take her.

"Would your father use the same password as you did?"

"No." Haley's forehead tightened. "The password isn't fixed. We had no idea in advance what code your pilots would prefer. He could have chosen anything, like I did."

Zayn studied her face so intently Haley feared he'd uncover her lie. She had to go with him. She had to. He took a breath, coming to a decision. "I was afraid of that." He looked defeated. "I have not the time to send for Quadir. You are my only hope."

"You want me to go with you, to break the code if there's one in place?" Haley held her breath, hoping.

"Yes."

She exhaled, relieved. "And what do I get out of this? Will you promise me that we won't leave Kuwait without my father or my uncle Jack?"

"If you will, but think for a moment, Haley Bennett, you will see that I also need the same assurances from you. We must leave Kuwait together, when all the vital people have been assembled."

"I can live with that," Haley answered. "Is there anything else I should know?"

At that question, Zayn's fingers tightened on her shoulders. "You have already proven to me that you have the courage to move amid my people without fearing the consequences. I must be brutally honest with you. You are going to have to go through customs to enter Kuwait. The only way I can protect you, to keep you from being taken prisoner for your citizenship, is by making you my wife."

"Say what?" Haley stiffened. Zayn's hands kept her from backing away.

"As the wife of a defender of the faith, a *haji*, an orthodox man, you do not have to answer any man's questions. You never have to speak for yourself, admit your nationality or show your face. You will be safe. It is the only way I can take you with me into Kuwait. Do you consent to the marriage?"

"I don't get it. What do you mean?"

"It is so basic and simple that your western mind will not believe it possible." Zayn's fingers tightened. "By the tenets of

Islam, if you become my wife, the wife of a sworn upholder of the faith, you become sequestered under the holy laws of purdah. No man other than I may look at your face. It is the easiest way to subvert the Iraqis. The Saudis have offered me diplomatic immunity in exchange for carrying certain documents to the ambassador. If you agree to marry me, you may go with me. I swear to you, I will protect your life with my own."

"You're not giving me much time to think about this," Haley whispered. She heard the urgency of his tone, the immediacy. "Can't we just pretend we're married and do the same thing?"

"No." Zayn's head moved in definite negation of that suggestion. "I am a man of my word, Haley. I cannot lie or practice the arts of deceit others do. It must be true, or I cannot take the risk of bringing you with me. I will arrange for you to be taken back to Anaiza."

"No." Haley clutched hold of his forearms.

"Haley." Zayn looked deeply into her questioning eyes. He had to convince her. It would be useless to go forward with such a reckless plan as the one he'd conceived and have the whole carefully constructed operation fail because one wickedly fast American jet wouldn't crank over because of a lockout. Eventually, he knew he could subvert the lockout, but the minute he began his assault on the hangar where resistance members had assured him the Bennett jet was housed, the Iraqis would be onto his desperate plot. He hated to admit it, but they had to move with the skill of Israeli commandos. They must be in and out of Al Kuwait International in the blink of a cat's eye.

"In the household of a *haj,* a woman is strictly protected. No Muslim dares question this. Our tenets are too ingrained. You will pass through customs under my wing, sheltered by the diplomatic immunity I am given, shielded by my faith. Behind a veil, you will be safe. It is the only way. Your only other avenue into Kuwait is to present your own documents. Please, Haley, believe me when I tell you this—one glimpse at your American passport would bring on your immediate arrest."

"Phew!" Haley's eyebrows rose appreciably. "Just like Beirut, huh?"

"Very close." Zayn would not tell her that it was already a hundred times worse than Beirut.

"All right." Haley made up her mind. Her father's life was at stake. "If it means I get into the Bennett hangar, I will do this any way you say will work."

Zayn's relief was so complete that his hands gentled on her shoulders and he drew her to him and kissed her lips. The deep hunger that woke all his sleeping demons of desire when he touched her was as strong now as it had ever been. She felt it, too, wrapping her arms tightly around his neck, returning his kiss with equal passion.

He forced himself to end the kiss and separate their yearning bodies, ordering his mind to bank the passions that flared so easily between them. He stroked one finger across her moist, trembling lower lip.

"You must not speak English to anyone once we leave this room."

"I understand."

"*Aeywah* is yes in Arabic, *lae* is no. Can you remember that?"

Haley nodded. He frowned, his mouth tightening as if some other worry greater than any he'd expressed to her preyed heavily on his mind.

"I cannot impress upon you how very important your silence will be. Swear to me, Haley. On your father's life, you will not speak to anyone. Your accent . . . it is a dead giveaway."

"I swear. I won't speak at all if my silence is so important."

"All right. I have your word. I shall have to trust you at the risk of my life and your own." His fingers strayed to her hand and stroked it tenderly. "Do not be afraid. Do not worry about the marriage. Divorce is easy to obtain under the laws of Islam."

"Meaning, we are marrying in name only?" Haley's words came out muffled. She couldn't allow herself the luxury of wondering if that fact pleased or displeased her.

"When we have returned safely to Anaiza and this is over," he told her, "I will not hold you bound to the words we speak before the *amman*. But until then, you will obey me in all things, Haley. That is the way it will have to be."

"What is an *amman*?" Haley asked.

"An Islamic holy man."

"A priest?"

"The equivalent in my religion. What is your answer?"

Haley's eyes closed briefly. God was God no matter the culture. Her own beliefs were very strong. It would be a valid marriage in her eyes. Even if she did not repeat the words *in sickness and in health, for richer or for poorer... till death do us part,* she would be thinking them.

She licked her lips and tucked her head down for a moment, composing herself. Zayn held her loosely, not making any demands. Her throat ran dry as her brother's cryptic words on the computer screen flashed through her head. *Goose gassed, Vix disabled.* Should she tell Zayn that there might not be a fast getaway jet ready to spirit his entrapped family out of the country? If she admitted that she had another plane, the DC-7, would he find he had no reason to take her with him? The goose had no sophisticated lockout capability.

Then she remembered the other disturbing words her brother had sent to her. *Dad poss. injury rt. leg, gunshot, Jack at hangar.* She had two people she loved depending on her to get them free of a war zone. She couldn't risk being left behind.

"All right." Haley straightened, withdrawing from the comfort his nearness provided. She'd feel better going along, anyway. In this crazy land, it hurt too much to be separated from Zayn for any reason. "I will marry you."

"And I, you," Zayn said solemnly. "The *amman* waits outside. I will bring him in now." Though she had time to ask about how the marriage would be dissolved, she did not. Nor did Zayn bring up the subject again.

The ceremony, which was simple in the extreme, was nonetheless binding for the solemnity of the Muslim priest that performed it. Two ranking Saudi officers stood by as somber, silent witnesses to its completion.

That done, Zayn Haaris moved with the pace of a desert whirlwind, sweeping Haley into the storm with him.

After sitting for days in silent, austere isolation, little more than an hour after she'd vowed her body and soul into Zayn's keeping, Haley stepped into hell on earth, Kuwait International Airport.

She was the lone woman accompanying twelve Saudi diplomats. As they disembarked from the plane, Zayn put a leash into Haley's hand. Caesar padded at Haley's side with regal indifference to the scene around him.

Zayn didn't explain the dog's mission. Haley didn't ask. She held the leash and followed, period.

Haley walked with Minister Jaleel, the head of the Saudi mission, at his sedate, unhurried pace. She twisted her head, scanning the destruction that surrounded them. The sheer black gauze of her veil colored her view but did not block it.

Zayn moved closer to her. She could not, it seemed, help being herself, observant, curious, questioning. Stepping up beside her, he clasped her arm and squeezed it. Before they reached the tarmac at the bottom of the plane's steps, he put his lips close to her ear and said sternly, "Put your head down. Do not look closely at things. The wife of a *haj* would never be so bold."

It wasn't mutiny in Haley's eyes behind the veil when she looked up at him. It was confusion. He offered no sympathy. There was no time. An Iraqi soldier waited to meet them at the bottom of the ramp.

*Maybe,* thought Haley, *when this is done, I will take great pleasure in killing him slowly.* Would she have given him carte blanche if she had known the full extent of what was coming? If he'd explained to her what had really happened in Kuwait?

Now, she saw the horror that had transpired. She was in danger. Each of these diplomats was in grave danger. Everyone in Kuwait was in great danger. In her ignorance, she had been ready to face anything to find her father. How could she ever find him in this sea of disaster. Not a building surrounding the airport was intact.

Artillery guns and the tanks of the rapidly deployed Republican Guard pointed their silent muzzles at their last targets—the commercial jets hooked up to the terminal's skyways. No one had bothered to remove the debris, whether it be strewn luggage or dead bodies.

If the airport could be so hideous, Haley dreaded what she would see inside the city.

The shattered terminal had the haunted appearance of a set constructed for a surrealistic movie. Carcasses and the guts of broken planes, burned-out service trucks and bullet-ridden limousines had been bulldozed into a pile off the tarmac. The control tower was a stump of concrete supporting a twisted tangle of iron and dangling aluminum.

Shattered glass lay everywhere. Bomb craters gouged out whole sections of sidewalk. The makeshift rough planks laid across them rattled shakily underfoot.

Inside, the half-gutted terminal was worse, far worse. The stench of death hung as heavily in the heated air as the rank odor of backed-up sewage and rotting food. A pestilence of black flies made Haley grateful for her veil. She was appalled to find that the terminal was now a prison for all the people who had been trapped inside it. The food-service staff, ticket sellers, travel agents, airline workers, mechanics, pilots and too many passengers who, like Haley, had picked the wrong day to travel.

Their escort of six Iraqi soldiers, seemingly oblivious to the indolent heat, swaggered ahead of the diplomats, clearing a way through the crowded concourse. They shouted at and shoved aside trapped travelers with the butts of their machine guns. Babies screamed, old ladies cried out and begged for help, clutching desperately at the diplomats' robes as the entourage passed.

Grown men of every nationality imaginable stood by, looking helpless, confused and dazed. Some sat on luggage and held their heads between their hands.

She came to a dead stop when a small Arab child threw herself into the path of the diplomats, her little arms reaching for Haley's skirt. An old woman quickly gathered the child back to her. She put a hand over the child's face to muffle her cry. "Momma" in any language sounded nearly the same to Haley's ears.

Not even the screaming child halted the diplomats on their sedate and stately walk to the only exit.

Shaken, with Zayn's hand firm at her elbow, Haley moved on. But this time as she looked into the groups of crowded, contained people, waiting for planes that were never going to come, Haley saw what was missing. The women.

There were girls of tender years of each nationality. Boys and youths, fathers, grandfathers, uncles and old women. All appeared worn-out, exhausted, hungry and stressed beyond belief. But the young women, the pretty mothers, the comely stewardesses were nowhere to be seen. Haley's blood ran cold imagining the horrifying fates of the young women who belonged with these terrorized folk.

Suddenly seething with fury unlike any she'd ever felt before, she turned to Zayn. His hand tightened on her upper arm. Did the arrogant fool truly expect her meek obedience as token for his protection in the face of this? Too furious for her own good, Haley yanked her arm free. She was crazy for having given him her word to stay silent. He was crazy for setting such an impossible condition upon his offer to bring her with him.

At least behind the veil, no one could see the grim set of her mouth or the gnashing of her teeth. Her unseen hands clenched against the urge to snatch an Uzi and turn it on the soldiers. Why the hell didn't the Saudis do something? Why didn't Zayn?

Concerned, Zayn returned his light grip on Haley's arm, determined to keep her moving. Minister Jaleel spoke easily to the Iraqi officer, deflecting his attention from the lone woman in their party.

Then they came to a huge gap in the building's wall. Haley stopped and openly looked for the orange-and-white hangar that housed Bennett Air. She had to know which of her company's major assets in Kuwait still existed.

She saw it. There at the far west corner of the runway, housed against a cluster of charter offices. The orange-and-white facade facing her was intact. Haley's study also located soldiers, tanks, artillery, barricades of wire and cross bars that quarantined that end of the airport. She couldn't hold back a groan.

Zayn tugged on her arm, bringing her attention back inside the terminal. Haley wished he'd left well enough alone and left her behind at the airfield.

The sun broiled through the busted plates of glass and illuminated the unswept residue on the terminal's floor. Untended garbage in the looted restaurants fouled the hot, still air. Every shop along the concourse was stripped bare, as though a rioting mob had pillaged all the goods. There was no order, rhyme or reason for what she saw. The damage conveyed a random maliciousness, making the sight all the more unnerving.

At the exit, their progress stopped. There, at a table, a more bombastic Iraqi controlled the gate and he took an immediate and keen interest in Haley. Lust blazed out of his black eyes and he licked his lips with obvious anticipation when he commanded the diplomats to present their credentials.

Minister Jaleel protested this. The soldier refused to relent on his new Iraqi rule, no woman could enter without being searched, photographed and identified.

As Minister Jaleel produced his papers, Haley started to shake. She had no identification. She had the clothes on her back and a dog on a leash, nothing else. Protesting in Arabic that this sort of demand was atrocious, Zayn slapped his diplomat's pass and passport into the hands of the beefy Iraqi soldier. Then Zayn took deferential hold of Haley's arm and drew her closer to him.

Haley didn't dare make a mistake now. The soldier flipped through Zayn's passport slowly. A portrait from Haley's wallet was affixed below Zayn's, with a Saudi seal embossing and blurring her face. The soldier insisted she remove her veil. The gleam in his eyes made Haley sweat. Caesar growled and inched closer to her.

Dropping his knuckles to the table, Zayn challenged the officer. "Dare you defy the commandments of Mohammed?" Haley blinked, not understanding the words, but getting his meaning nevertheless.

All twelve diplomats added their voices to the argument. They struck an impasse. Minister Jaleel demanded to see the officer in charge of the entire airport.

Just then, a higher-ranking Iraqi officer came out of an office nearby and intervened. "What is the problem?"

"Not a problem, I am certain," Minister Jaleel said, and smiled.

Zayn spoke from true outrage. "This infidel would demand the wife of a *haj* show her face in a public place when the law of Mohammed forbids it!"

Minister Jaleel placed himself bodily between Zayn and the Iraqis as he appealed to the newly arrived, older officer. "These young soldiers have been very zealous in the performance of their duty. That has troubled my young adjutant, whose devotion to Allah is the rule of his life. We seek assurances that they will not trouble the *haji's* wife. Can you give that, my friend?"

"The woman has no diplomatic status," the stubborn soldier argued. It was the leer from the men surrounding him that worried Haley.

"Where I go, my wife goes." Zayn stood on the tenets of his faith.

"Most certainly—" the older officer bowed his shoulders with respect to Zayn's status "—but we cannot let a woman pass into Iraq without being assured of her true identity. A protected woman, posing as the wife of a *haj,* could be a traitor. How are we to verify who she is if her face remains hidden?"

"You have my word, and by the Koran, that is enough."

The Iraqis were not following orders, but going beyond the bounds of them, refusing to honor beliefs as old as the Koran. Zayn knew what their purpose was. He swallowed his fury at the fate of the women taken forcibly from the airport. Over that, his hands were tied. Allah help him if these bastards tried to take Haley from him.

"Haale," Zayn called Haley to secure her attention. She was looking all around again. Even through the veil, her eyes looked overlarge and troubled. Zayn could see them so clearly, he feared every soldier could tell how blue they were.

She moved to his side like a soft current, drawing her *abba* close about her shoulders in a parody of modesty, which Zayn was positive she did not have.

"Do not shame me, we are in a public place." Zayn scolded harshly in Arabic. "This is not a place for a woman. They think you must be carrying some weapons. You will walk through the security device, the detectors, to prove that you have nothing to hide on your person."

Everything he said was Greek to her, except his tone. By it, Haley thought she'd blundered again. Very much afraid, Haley gripped his forearm, a wide gold wedding band on her ring finger. She shook her head, whispering, "*Lae,* Zayn."

"Don't be silly," he said in Arabic, patting her hand reassuringly. "I will go with you. Come, Caesar."

"There," Minister Jaleel said to the soldiers. "Does that not satisfy you? Now, let us pass. We are here at the invitation of your president and are under his protection."

Zayn took Haley's hand and led her to the tall metal detector. *Is this all that was about?* Haley thought. The dog went through, then she, then Zayn. No bells went off, no alarms sounded. They were in Kuwait.

As she sank into the back seat of a crowded Mercedes limousine, she let out a long sigh of relief. The three cars of the diplomats' convoy moved slowly through the city. That was a blur from where Haley sat, surrounded by men, with Caesar stretched uncomfortably in front of them.

She had an impression of barricades, soldiers and little else. The city streets were deserted. Not a single store was open for business. The wind off the gulf blew sand along sidewalks devoid of life, save for roaming, lost dogs. Al Kuwait was a ghost town populated only by Iraqi soldiers.

Without traffic to slow them, it wasn't long before the cars turned inside the walled gates of the Saudi embassy. This time, Saudi soldiers in familiar uniforms and with friendlier dispositions, went through the same precautions as the Iraqis, with one exception. They did not question Zayn Haji Haaris about his wife.

Once inside the high, secure walls of the compound, all semblance of a ghost town evaporated. The large embassy complex was jammed with people both inside and out, which slowed their progress on the walk from the cars to the embassy doors. Several dark men caught Zayn's attention immediately. They spoke with him in the same rapidly fired, excited manner Haley had observed the Saudis use in the desert. She watched Zayn's face for clues, since it was not possible for her to understand any of their words. His features never lightened from their look of grave seriousness.

Obviously there was no good news to report.

They were again held up on a long hallway where stairs converged from upper and lower floors at a side entry door to the embassy. That conversation ended abruptly. Zayn pulled Haley to the stairwell that descended into the basement. They went down two levels, to a subbasement with only two doors on opposite sides of the steps.

Zayn produced a key to one of the heavy steel doors, inserted it into the lock and swung the door inward.

He pulled her inside a cool, darkened room full of rows of desks and computer terminals. All of the machines were on. A few ever-moving antiburn screens of asteroid showers gave the subterranean room the appearance of a transplanted NASA control center. There was no one present to hear Zayn say in English, "Sit down at a terminal, please."

Haley was one step ahead of him mentally, already looking for the nearest familiar keyboard with a modem and an internet screen. She sat down, chewing a corner of her lip, not ask-

# Chapter 12

Zayn pointed to the console in front of her. "You know how to download files via the internet, correct?"

Haley shrugged, uncertain how much knowledge she wanted to reveal. "Yes. So?"

"So, I want you to access these numbers, open the files and copy everything you can to floppy disks."

Haley shifted uneasily. "Suppose the documents are protected?"

Zayn laid the little black book open on the desk with a page open to phone numbers and codes. "It's important, Haley. Just do it for me, please. I haven't got time to explain things. You have an hour...maybe."

"An hour till what?"

"Till the resistance sabotages the power plant. All electrical power in Kuwait will cease to exist. Hurry."

Caesar stretched and sank onto the floor at Haley's feet. Zayn left, locking her and the dog inside the abandoned room. Haley found a carton of formatted floppies and settled at the console, jumped to the previous menu and scanned it, deciding on her available alternate options. As her fingers flew across the keyboard typing Zayn's access numbers directly into the Ethernet, she told Caesar, "It's good I learned to type via touch, not hunt-and-peck."

Caesar yawned, clearly unimpressed. Haley typed in the file transfer protocol that followed Zayn's carefully printed numbers, accessing heaven only knew what. She was into somebody's mainframe and the Gopher began shuffling file after file, telling Haley when it was time to insert another disk into the A drive.

Every time the Gopher asked for a password, she put in the next code written in Zayn's black book. It gave her entry into each file. And she hadn't the foggiest idea what in the name of creation she was copying.

There were seven cryptic numbers on Zayn's list. It took fifteen disks to copy everything, fifteen more to make backups. According to the wall clock, she had thirty minutes. Staving off her own anxiety, she made copies of her copies, then sat thinking his hacker little brother could have done this from the office in Anaiza. But then again, maybe the kid couldn't if the international trunk lines weren't working.

When she finished, she packed each set in an empty box. Then she tried calling home. It was a futile effort. No matter what international code she dialed, the line cropped up dead. "Drat!"

Then she wondered if she could call anywhere in Kuwait. Slapping her forehead for her own stupidity, she searched the room for a telephone book. The city Yellow Pages gave her the number to the hangar.

Before she could get back to her seat and call Bennett Industries, Kuwait, the lights went out. The computer screens fritzed. The subbasement turned into a tomb. Caesar woofed. Haley stumbled over chairs and felt her way back to the dog. She collapsed onto the swivel chair, breathing hard, frustrated and angry. So much for bright ideas acted on too late!

Caesar complained noisily until Zayn opened the door and shone a bright flashlight into the gloom. Haley grabbed Caesar's leash, Zayn's black book and the disks, and hurried to him, anxious to get upstairs and into daylight.

In the soundproof basement, she hadn't heard the explosions. On the ground floor, she heard plenty of aftershocks and saw the effects. All the people in the embassy yards had rushed to the doors, trying to get inside. People inside were trying to get out.

It was bedlam. Harried staff members couldn't deal with the sudden surge of fear incited by the power failure. People upstairs flooded downstairs. The crush bordered on a stampede. Zayn passed through the crowd, calming people, telling everyone it was the resistance working. He never let go of Haley's hand.

She noticed Saudi women working alongside Saudi men at a frantic pace. None wore anything remotely resembling her *abba*. One harried female clerk regarded Haley with a longing look that could only be called envy. That floored Haley. What could there possibly be about this getup that caused any woman to feel envy for it? She felt like a nun, or worse, someone dressed for the final day of judgment.

Because she was dawdling, Zayn again noticed Haley's unchecked curiosity. This time, he barked an Arabic order that made the dog heel and look alert.

Haley had had just about enough of Zayn's behavior. They were safe in the embassy. She started to protest, then the Saudi ambassador burst out of his office, a stream of assistants in his wake. The mood in the embassy shifted dramatically.

The ambassador shouted for the newly arrived delegation. His mottled face regained some of its color when Minister Jaleel stepped forward. Spouting his news, he urged the diplomats into his office. Zayn hurried off with the delegation, deserting Haley.

The lights surged as emergency generators kicked into overdrive. An audible sigh of relief swept the reception room. The air conditioner resumed circulating air and the talking returned to its previous frantic pitch.

It took Haley several minutes to catch the gist of what had happened, which she gleaned from two businessmen who had cornered a frantic secretary and demanded an explanation.

"Hussein has annexed Kuwait. From this day hence, Kuwait no longer exists. We have twenty-four hours to empty our embassy. As of dawn tomorrow, all Iraqi borders will be closed. No one will leave the occupied territory. No one without diplomatic status will be allowed to enter. All Kuwaiti citizens must surrender their documents and be issued official residence documents of Iraqi Province 19."

This message spread like wildfire throughout the English-speaking part of the throng. Haley quirked her eyebrow, reconsidering the run on somebody's computer records she'd just made. Zayn must have known what was coming. Like any smart businessman, he was cutting his losses, salvaging what he could. She couldn't blame him. In his situation, she'd have done the same.

She wandered through the impossible crowd, as lost and disoriented as the next person. It amazed her that the Saudis had taken in so many people who weren't their fellow countrymen. A veritable United Nations was crammed within its protective walls. Every last soul had reached the point of panic, especially people with young families in tow.

"We are arranging for planes." She listened as an aide soothed a very worried Australian. "We are trying very hard, you understand."

"Surely something can be done more quickly," the man argued.

"It takes time to make travel arrangements."

"It's been days. Yesterday, Hussein was withdrawing. Today, he's annexing a country! How many lies do you expect us to swallow?"

"I am sorry you are upset. We are all upset. We are doing everything we can to evacuate all of you. Saudi commercial flights have been severely restricted. Kuwait Air has ceased to operate. The airport suffered great damage. My government is trying to arrange for additional airplanes. There is nothing more I can do. You must wait your turn."

"But they just announced that this embassy must shut down within twenty-four hours. Where will we go? The soldiers are arresting anyone on the streets."

Another man with a strong Canadian accent joined in, saying, "And shooting those who resist arrest like cattle."

"My dear sirs," the aide said patiently, "at this particular moment, all Kuwaiti citizens are being forced to surrender their birth certificates pending reissue of Iraqi citizenship papers. Those of us, you included, safe here inside this embassy, stand a much better chance of retaining our integrity as well as our nationality than the Kuwaiti. There are fifty-three children and twenty-one pregnant Saudi women who must be evacuated first. We are doing the best we can."

"Well, it is damn well not good enough." The Canadian expressed the frustration of all the waiting masses. "This embassy could afford to buy dozens of airplanes."

"No doubt Saudi Arabia can buy all the planes it desires," the aide snapped. "There are none for sale in Kuwait. Airplanes do us little good when every pilot with good sense has already departed the country. Best you start praying for buses."

The young Saudi aide ended the discussion on that chilling note. His *dishdasha* fluttered around his ankles as he stalked away. Haley hastened after the young man, catching him at the bottom of a wide stairway. She tugged on his sleeve, stopping him on the first riser.

"Excuse me." Haley spoke quietly. "I just heard what you said to those gentlemen. I am a pilot and I have a plane, a DC-7, at the airport. It can carry one hundred and five adults. I might possibly have one other smaller jet that will safely transport ten."

As the aide turned, his eyes widened in disbelief. By the expression on his face, he had just seen Lot's wife, unsalted, gifted with the power of speech.

Haley brought her fingers up to move the *abba* aside. She wasn't exposing any more than her forehead and her eyes, really. "While I cannot fly both planes at the same time, I know of two, possibly three other pilots who could assist moving these people to Saudi Arabia."

The man looked as if he was about to faint. *"Aesfae, issaeyaedea. Mae mea' nea haeazae?"*

"I'm afraid you will have to speak English." Haley pulled aside the corner of the veil that Zayn had tucked over her face. "I do not speak Arabic."

"You do not...?" The aide flushed as red as a rose. Haley couldn't see what his problem was. "Madam, you must cover your face! You are outside of the presence of your husband and his family."

Haley chose not to shake the pompous little jerk by the scruff of his neck. He couldn't have been a day over twenty-one, if that.

"I'm not..." Haley almost said "married," but corrected herself in the nick of time. She was married, technically, though that marriage wasn't three hours old. "I'm not about to be put off just because I am a woman, young man."

"You must cover your face, madam."

"Don't insult me. I am telling you that I own a plane capable of emptying this embassy over the next twenty-four hours. Now, do you want to go to your superiors with a solution that will earn you a commendation from King Fahd, or do you want me to report you to the nearest ranking official for being rude beyond redemption and insulting a princess?"

Haley wondered if she was pushing her luck with that last, very bold assumption. She didn't think so. Zayn was a prince. That made her titular princess in somebody's book.

"You are American?" the aide sputtered.

"Ah, you are quick," Haley said sharply. "Are you going to help find a solution to our mutual dilemma? Or will you continue to lecture me on the finer points of proper Muslim dress?"

"Come this way, please, but I beg you, cover your face. You will cause much trouble if you do not. Tempers are short today."

"You don't know the half of it," Haley muttered. She tucked the tail of black silk back in place under her eyes and followed the young man through the crowded lower rooms. "Can you find someone with the authority to get my plane cleared for takeoff with the Iraqi in charge of the airport?"

"Yes. It can be done. I will see to it immediately."

"Fine. Thank you." Haley's hand dropped to idly scratch the head of the loyal dog at her side. "While you do that, is there someplace I might get a cup of coffee?"

"This way. I will take you to the women's quarters."

"No, you won't." Haley had tucked her veil back over her face, but her eyes remained fastened on the young Saudi official in a dominating stare. "I will take my chances in the open. I trust you Saudis as far as I can throw you. You lock up a woman much too easily. Take me where I can discreetly observe those Englishmen."

"This is terribly improper." On the second floor overlooking the common hall, she was given a seat in an alcove abutting a small balcony. "How is it that you have access to a plane of your own, *lalla?*" the aide asked.

"Easily." Haley saw no reason not to answer the young man's question. "My father is president of Bennett Air. We keep a hangar in the Kuwait airport and have several permanent employees in the country."

"I see." The young man frowned. "Is your father in Kuwait?"

"Yes, though I haven't seen him for more than a week."

"I am sorry to hear that," he said with great sympathy. "May I assume that you have made this dangerous offer as a means to get him and yourself out of the country, as well?"

Wisely, Haley opted for diplomacy. "You may assume what you like. I am here because my husband brought me with him."

"Yes, I see. And these planes of your company, you have the authority to dispose of them?"

"In the present circumstances, my father will avidly support any decision I make that benefits the most people."

"The odds are, he has been taken hostage. Many Americans have."

Haley was certain a flash of angry pain must have crossed her eyes, for the young man issued a sincere apology and backed off. She glanced over the gallery railing at the milling throng.

Too many people, all trapped, and the borders closing in one day. It was too much to deal with effectively. No wonder there was panic.

She couldn't help being selfish, hoping to find a way to get to the airport and her father and Jack. She had better odds of getting into the Bennett hangar with Saudi influence and diplomatic immunity. That brought her back to Zayn. She had promised him an airplane—the Vixen One—to get his family out of the city. She had to do both.

"One more thing." She touched the aide's sleeve, detaining him. "I must get a message to my husband, Zayn Haaris. He is in a meeting with the ambassador."

All the color in the young man's face drained into his *dishdasha.* "You are the wife of Sheik Zayn Haji Haaris?"

What an odd reaction, Haley thought. She said, "Yes, I am. Does that make a difference?"

Apparently it did. The man pressed his palms together and half bowed to her, muttering in Arabic. "Sheik Haaris will have my head when he hears of this. I dare not risk angering him."

"Don't be an ass. Sheik Haaris knew what he bargained for when he married me," Haley said smartly.

"This is terrible, terrible," the Saudi exclaimed. He bowed. "Please, Issaeyaedea Haaris, forgive my impertinence. A servant will see to your comforts immediately."

"I won't be sequestered," Haley told him very firmly.

"No, no. Everything will be as you wish, *lalla.*"

*Lalla,* huh? Haley grinned under the veil. She rather liked the immediate deference being Zayn Haaris's wife afforded her. Had she known she'd have gotten that reaction, she'd have done some name dropping sooner.

A servant brought her coffee and cakes, small sandwiches and lemonade. Caesar snuffled inquiringly at the bounty of appealing food. As Haley fed him a finger sandwich, several children watched her from the doorway of a nearby room. They were a solemn lot for kindergartners. Huge fearful eyes and grim little mouths, they dared not step past the threshold where they were contained.

On the lower floor, oil company workers, technicians and laborers swarmed around the embassy staff like bees in an angry hive. Outdoors in neat gardens, more people milled about, restless, winding in a long twisting queue that eventually came inside the building.

Haley sat in her isolated domain in a crowd, the dog regally guarding her feet. Caesar surveyed everything, watching, alert and threatening in a rather mysterious way. When a servant came and cleared away the table, Haley silently nodded to his polite inquiries.

Shortly, the young Saudi aide returned with an older, more august-looking personage whose dark eyes were troubled and suspicious. A chair was brought forward for him to sit opposite her at the small table.

"Forgive the delay, Issaeyaedea Haaris. Hamid has explained to me your offer. You have a plane, do you?"

"Yes, I covered that with your assistant."

"Hamid gave the bare details, and I have taken the liberty of verifying what I could. Hence, my delay in coming to you to discuss this more thoroughly."

"Isn't time working against that? You have less than twenty-three hours to evacuate the embassy. Correct?"

"That is correct. I have just finished a telephone conference with the Iraqi military commander at the airport. He will allow the purchase of only one plane in the Bennett hangar, the DC-7. His price is high, but he has agreed that the plane may be loaded with the citizens we are sheltering within our walls. I need to know your company's value for that plane, Issaeyaedea Haaris.''

"You want to buy it?" Haley said in surprise.

"We must buy it. If it is not owned by the Saudi government, the Iraqis will not allow it to depart the airport. They have confiscated all personal and real property in Kuwait. Only diplomatic missions are excluded.''

"They can't do that." The secretary's statements had touched a raw nerve.

"What an occupying army can and cannot do is a moot point in our discussion, *issaeyaedea*.''

"Dammit, my company has a very heavy investment here," Haley grumbled. What next?

"There have been heavy financial losses incurred in recent days. It is my conservative opinion that there are more to come. Can you put a price on your company's DC-7?''

Haley's head moved in a negative motion. "No, not really. Where I come from, when someone wants to make a gift for a good cause, there are no strings attached. Nobody back home is going to argue the price if it means my father and godfather get out of this country. It is an old plane, still airworthy, but that's about the scope of it. Ten dollars will do, to my mind. You offer whatever you think the Iraqis will accept and I can live with that.''

Secretary Devir relaxed somewhat against the back of his chair, his eyes just a little less cold. "You do not wish to make a profit?''

Haley looked to the small, scared faces in the nearby doorway. "I wish to get those children out of here and I regret that I don't have something better to offer you than a battered old company workhorse to do it.''

The attaché followed her gaze and nodded in quiet agreement. "Issaeyaedea Haaris, if your plane will take these children to my country, it will be the finest plane Saudi Arabia has ever purchased. Now, I must go and interrupt the ambassador's meeting to speak with Sheik Haaris. I must have his permission, as well.''

That rang Haley's internal alarm. She leaned forward and put one hand on the crisp sleeve of the attaché's robe. "Don't do that," she said insistently.

"But I must, *issaeyaedea*. You cannot leave this embassy without your husband's written permission. Nor could we complete the sale without his consent. We will need you present when we enter the Bennett hangar. The adjutant at the airport informs me that the hangar is barricaded from the inside by your company's loyal workers. "With typical American defiance, they have refused to surrender to the occupation. There is apparently an old man within the building who, when threatened, has shouted several threats about remembering the Alamo."

Haley tightened all over with that bit of news. "Uncle Jack," she said quietly, almost to herself. "That's just like him. 'Remember the Alamo,' leave it to him to do such a thing." She addressed the attaché. "I can get us in. Set your mind to rest. As to telling my husband what I'm doing, he'll just look at you and wonder why you are being so provincial. We came here for the express purpose of getting as many people out of the war zone as possible. He is a Kuwaiti, you know, and much more liberal in his beliefs than you orthodox Saudis. I don't need his permission to do anything. You are only going to waste more precious time."

The man smiled then, for the first time. It wasn't a very big smile and it was about as wry as a smile could get and still be a smile, but it did lighten his grim expression some. "You have misunderstood the point, again, *issaeyaedea*. We are doing this the Saudi way. The Iraqi in charge would think it most suspicious if you did not have written permission from your husband in hand."

"Fine, that's not a problem. Give me a sheet of paper. I will write it myself."

"I cannot do that."

"You think the Iraqis know my husband's signature or his handwriting?"

"*Lalla*, it is not our custom to do things dishonestly."

"Oh, for pity's sake," Haley exclaimed in exasperation. "Zayn's meeting could last for hours. He'll be furious if I cause an interruption for such a trivial thing as a letter of permission. Frankly, sir, I don't take that lightly. He has a terrible temper when he is provoked. Your aide seems to know that.

"Why would you want to risk offending a powerful man when the options are so obvious," she continued. "The thugs at the airport probably cannot even read. Think of those children. My plane will only hold a hundred or so people. How many flights will it take to empty this building? Which of these people are you willing to sacrifice for want of a signature? Draw up the permission paper and sign it. Or ask someone else to scrawl a signature upon it. We are wasting time."

"The sheik's integrity will be at issue," the man insisted. "You do not understand these things, the complexity of them."

"I understand cowardice," Haley snapped. "Let us quit haggling and get with the program. Which one of those papers is a bill of sale? Give it to me and I will sign it now."

Haley put her hand out and received the bill of sale. She examined it and, borrowing the attaché's pen, hastily filled in the required blanks that concerned her company. She signed it as an officer of Bennett Industries, then shoved the document back to the diplomat.

Reluctantly, he took the pen and countersigned the document, calling his junior forward to act as witness. The young man gave him a large checkbook, from which he carefully wrote out a check and precisely separated the draft from the sheet.

Haley folded the check in half without even looking at it, and decided it would keep just fine in Zayn's little black book.

"Come, Caesar." Haley stood and walked determinedly into the children's room.

The little faces never brightened. Older brothers and sisters held little ones, comforting them. The babies seemed the most discontent. There were some women in the room, black-robed, veiled women who cared for the smallest, kept the littlest ones safe around the hems of their skirts. At the door, Haley turned and looked back at the official.

"Hurry," she quietly urged. "Every minute we delay risks many, many lives."

Secretary Devir rose, bowing to her. "As you wish, Issaeyaedea Haaris. I will bring your papers and the signature you need.

How ridiculous! Haley's mouth twisted wryly beneath the covering veil. It was ludicrous that a sane diplomat would purchase from her a plane, accept her signature on a contract of sale, but needed Zayn Haaris's signature to allow her to walk out the embassy doors.

She searched for a discarded shopping bag suitable for carrying her armful of disks. And what was she supposed to do with them and Zayn's wicked little black book? Take them with her, she supposed.

Shortly, the embassy employees began preparing the children for departure. Cars were brought through the crowded grounds to the doors of the building. Haley did not stay long watching. A young official escorted her to a private car and she was sent to the airport with three Saudi soldiers. The limousine went straight to the orange-and-white hangar, stopping very near the steel door on the side.

The driver climbed out and strode to the door with his rifle in hand. He knocked and waited. Haley watched, chewing on the corner of her lip. Caesar growled, putting his paws on the seat to lean his slobbery head to the closed window, watching. He quivered from one end to the other, whined and looked back at her, drooling on the fine leather upholstery. Haley took up the dangling lead.

Someone had come to the door and was arguing with the Saudi.

"I must get out."

Haley's announcement brought the rest of her guard and Captain Nassif to their feet at once. While one soldier opened her door, the other soldier and the captain formed a flank around her.

"Please, allow me." She moved the soldier aside, and pounded hard on the steel door. "Jack Winslow! Uncle Jack, are you there? It's me, Haley. Please, open the door."

"Haley? Haley, is that you?" a voice responded.

"Yes, Jack, it's me. Can you open the door for me?"

Almost immediately, the sound of barricades being pulled aside made Haley grin. Jack Winslow wasn't really her uncle. He was an old and dear friend of her father's. The title of uncle was honorary, but he was her godfather. When she'd been little, calling him godfather had been too much to say correctly. Uncle Jack had been easy and had stuck down through the years. She didn't have a true uncle she loved more dearly.

When he finally pulled open the heavy door he almost slammed it shut in her face. Haley didn't wonder why, not with her dressed in a Saudi shroud. She pushed forward immediately, only to be met by the barrel of a Colt revolver.

"What kind of trick is this?" Jack sputtered, outraged.

"For God's sake, don't shoot, Jack. It's no trick. It's really me." Haley yanked the veil aside. Caesar started barking.

Jack recognized her voice, all right, but he still blocked the entry and wagged his gun at the uniformed men. "Haley? What the hell is going on?"

"It's all right, Uncle Jack. The soldiers are Saudis. Let us in, please. Shut up, Caesar!" She tugged hard on the dog's collar to silence him.

Jack pulled the door back just enough for them to squeeze inside one by one. He didn't put away his pistol, either. "What in Sam Hill are you doing here with them?"

"It's a long story."

The hangar was dark and vast. The air hung stagnant, hot and close, laden with smells of fuel, oil and sweat. The hangar was small by company standards; four Vixens would fit comfortably. The goose ate up most of the space. Haley dropped the dog's leash. Caesar bolted, sniffing, growling, barking at shadows.

She turned to the soldiers and gave them orders to get the big overhead doors open. They eyed the rumpled old man who hadn't uncocked his pistol. Jack may have been outnumbered, but obviously, he wasn't placated yet.

"You sure these guys are Saudis?" He shut the door with his back and dropped an iron bar in place singlehandedly.

"I'm sure they're Saudis." Haley took time now to look at her godfather. Jack Winslow looked awful. A feral gleam haunted his eyes. She doubted he'd had a shave or a change of clothes in days. "Trust me, and fill me in on what's happened here."

When he didn't answer immediately, she said, "Jack, talk to me, dammit. Where the hell is Dad?"

Jack's eyes shied away from Haley's so fast it wasn't funny. He glared at the Saudis, instead, then looked back at her. "I've been holding down the fort for days. What are you doing here? Last I heard, your daddy told you to go home."

Something didn't jibe. The attaché had said the Iraqis reported resisters inside the hangar. One old man with a Colt 45 couldn't have held off the army on the tarmac. Maybe he didn't feel safe admitting anything. Haley gave him the benefit of the doubt.

She began to assess the damage. Two craters yawned in the steel roof on the back corner. Twisted steel girders and aluminum panels draped downward in a gruesome, Calder-like mobile. Empty boxes and crates were strewn across the concrete floor. The office was gutted. Not one piece of the state-of-the-art communications equipment remained. Lifting her hem to pick her way over the debris, Haley looked at Jack for some explanation.

"Them bastards took every damn thing that wasn't nailed down," Jack told her bitterly. Then he fell into step beside her and swung his arm around her shoulders and gave her a sly wink and a big hug. He jerked his grizzled chin at the DC-7.

Haley stopped at a pile of cardboard and foam-packing refuse and looked at the goose. It was smaller than she remembered . . . and older. "What about Dad? Where'd he go? I had word from Tommy he was hurt. Something about a gunshot. What gives?"

Jack's arm tightened on her shoulders. He said, "Kid, are you gonna make me tell you how they took him? Them damned Iraqis. They came here busting up everything. Your dad convinced them the goose wouldn't get airborne, so they left it once they'd stripped out the interior. They took everything else. And then when they had what they wanted, they took him as a hostage and left me here to make some kind of ransom deal with the company. I don't know where he is."

Nearly all the steel in Haley's shoulders left her then and she slumped and was caught in Jack's embrace. "I'm sorry, kid."

"It is against the law of the Koran for an infidel to touch the wife of a *haj*," a soldier said fiercely in English.

"So what?" Jack rounded on the man who had spoken. Then his arm tightened harder around Haley and he said, "Wife? What did he mean?"

"Jack." Haley laid her hand on his forearm, pushing the nose of the pistol down. "There have been some serious changes, Okay? Listen to me. What the soldier just said is true. He's only acting on his orders to protect me. These guys are my bodyguards—the dog, too. I've sort of made a deal with the Saudis. I sold them the goose to ferry all the people trapped in their embassy out of Kuwait. We haven't much time. The Iraqis are closing Kuwait's borders tomorrow morning. After that, no one gets out of the country. Nobody gets in. Is the goose still gassed up and ready to go?''

Jack stared at her as if she'd dropped in from another planet. ''You can't do that. How in the hell are you and me gonna get out of here?''

''We're flying the goose, Jack. That's how. You're my co-pilot. Come on, I'll explain everything in the air.''

''You better start explaining right now, 'cause I ain't liking this one bit . . . starting with this wild getup covering you from head to toe. Um, uh, if your sister Katie could see you now, she'd be boiling you in your own feminist oil.''

''Let's leave my sisters out of this, okay?'' Haley walked resolutely toward the goose. ''Get the doors open, guys, and the wheel chucks out from under the tires. I'll get the plane started.''

As she ducked under the goose's nose, she came to a dead stop, gaping at the empty concrete space that stretched as far as the hangar's wall.

''Where the hell is the Vixen One?''

## Chapter 13

"Baghdad, I reckon," Jack said. "Ain't you heard one damn thing I said, Haley? They took *everything.*"

"Oh, no." Haley howled. How many more shocks could she take? "What happened to it? Come on, Jack, give me some answers. Tommy told me the Vix was disabled. How could the Iraqis have taken it?"

"Hell, it was only scratched and nicked. I slapped some bondo on it right after me and your dad got it off the apron. Might have got it painted, too, if there had been enough time. There wasn't. Hell, there's a war going on here, Haley. We couldn't hold out against cannons and machine guns."

"You're telling me they just pirated the plane and took it? How the hell did they start it?"

"How do you think? Your dad started it for them. 'Course, it helped that one of them put a gun to my head."

"Oh, God, Jack, they didn't."

"For all the good I've done the company right now, they could have shot me and been done with it, but your dad thought otherwise."

"I guess so."

Haley shook her head. Suddenly, she jumped and grabbed the strap on the door of the cockpit, yanking hard as she dropped back to the ground. The inboard steps crashed onto the concrete beside her, inciting Caesar to bark and howl.

"Oh, shut up, dog!" Haley reached for his leash and yanked him back to her side. She waved the Saudis toward the big hangar doors, motioning that she needed them opened now.

A couple of scorch marks blurred the lettering under the goose's belly. On the ground two feet from the burn, a crater of powdered concrete marked where a shell had impacted the floor. Haley pointed at a new square of freshly welded metal on the plane's belly.

"What caused that?"

"Mortar fire." Jack said. "Took a couple of shots on the interior when your dad and I were getting the Vixen inside the hangar. Boy, that was a close one, I'll tell you. Damn glad you didn't land the other plane. We'd have lost that one, too, the way things turned out."

Haley moved to examine the rivets and the patch. It looked solid enough, the bead on the welding smooth. "Is the patch going to hold?"

"Now, what do you think? Have I ever had one come loose?" Jack scrambled up the steps and turned, offering her a hand.

Raising her skirt, Haley took his assistance for the steep climb. Caesar was a bit skittish, not liking climbing the steps one bit. She hauled him in, anyway, and shoved him into the cabin and closed the door, then opened it and looked back at the gutted cabin.

"Good God, nothing is sacred. What are they going to do with those old seats? I'm flying out babies and children and women first."

"You got me on the first question. As for passengers, I guess you're just gonna have to fly real steady and careful." Jack shrugged as she tossed the shopping bag containing the disks and Zayn's book under the console and dropped into the pilot's seat. Jack handed her a ring of company keys.

While she waited for the soldiers to open the hangar doors, Haley sat thinking. No Vixen. She closed her eyes, unable to confront the betrayal she'd dealt Zayn Haaris. "Is this damn crate gonna start?" she said finally.

"Yes, it's gonna start. The only thing wrong with this baby is its paint job and lack of creature comforts. She's raring to get us the hell out of here."

"She'd better." Haley reached for the ignition. One turn and lights came on.

Caesar clawed on the cockpit cargo-bay door, woofing.

"I gotta tell you something, Haley," Jack said as he sank onto the seat beside her. "This hasn't done a lot of good for my old ticker."

Just then, the hangar doors parted and a stream of bright sunlight slid into the cockpit, blinding them both. Ducking her head, Haley concentrated on the engines, listening as each started, idled and hummed with power. She couldn't look at Jack for a minute or so. When she did, she saw the pasty gray color of his skin, the pain showing around his eyes. Her mouth tightened grimly.

Not wanting to retire just because he'd had two heart attacks, Jack Winslow had opted to take this peaceful assignment in Kuwait, tending the telephones, minding the planes when they came in. It was supposed to be a vacation, at least, a rest from the frantic pace of work at home.

"Don't worry, Jack, I'll get you out of here. The Saudis have good doctors. I've even seen one, myself."

She didn't elaborate and Jack didn't probe. It took too much concentration to drive the goose out of the hangar safely and start maneuvering it around barricades, potholes and bomb craters. She waited while the soldiers shut the doors and boarded via the passenger door in the back. They came forward and Caesar bounded out of the cockpit the moment they opened the door.

"Issaeyaedea Haaris, there are no seats for the children," Captain Nassif said in English.

"I just found that out, captain. I guess it's the Iraqi military's idea of renovation. We'll just have to do the best we can to pillow the littlest ones, and I'll be very, very careful. I am sorry."

"We're damn lucky we've still got these seats to sit in," Jack grumbled. "But don't worry, Haley's gonna treat this old lady like she's made of blown glass. Nice and easy, right Haley-girl. Nice and easy."

Jack motioned to threatening muzzles of field artillery that had been aimed at the hangar. "That's what we were facing. And the main reason they got the Vixen One."

"Looks like they meant business," Haley admitted.

"That's putting it mildly." Jack pointed to a crater on the taxi lane she needed to avoid. "It sure wasn't any fancy tea-party reception your poor old man pulled up into, like it was gonna be. Sheik Haaris had even brought his wife and daughters. I dragged out the crystal punch bowl and had caterers all lined up for the party. Hmmph!"

That bit of news raised one of Haley's eyebrows. "I thought the planes were for his sons."

"Well, yeah, there were a passel of them hanging around, but them girls was real pretty things. Sweet, lordy, every one of them is a living doll."

It was Haley's turn to snort a hmmph and she did as she stopped the plane.

"What are you stopping here for?" Jack asked.

Haley pointed to the four jeeps and the Iraqi officers barring access to the runway. "The plane has to be inspected before we can load the children from the embassy."

"Don't tell me that. Oh, no."

"What do you mean, 'Don't tell me that' and 'oh, no'?"

"Park it, Haley, and you'd better come with me. Is that dog as mean as I think he is?"

"He's a cupcake."

"Well, kick him to make him madder n'hell."

"Jack!"

"Either that or you better have a hell of a lot of *mordida* to pay those vultures. They're bloodsucking thugs, ever-last one of 'em!"

Jack was out of the copilot's seat, reaching for Caesar's collar. The dog took instant offense and bared his teeth. "Well, that's just what we need. Who'd you get the dog from?"

"My husband, Zayn Haaris."

"The *Haj's* son? I'll be a monkey's uncle. I always knew you'd aim high, Haley-girl. Come on, there ain't no time to waste."

Haley clambered out of her seat and followed Jack. Something had Jack in a stir, another silent signal to her that things with the goose weren't what they seemed. She trotted down the steps on his heels, ducking under the tail. Jack stopped at the first cargo bay, unlocked it and swung it open.

Her Saudi guards wouldn't allow the Iraqis into the plane until Haley was off it. Nassif stuck to her side like glue. Caesar ran the point, barking and snapping at Jack's heels until the door of the first cargo bay was opened. Then Caesar went wild.

The huge dog bounded into the lowered bay and clambered all over the first aluminum storage container. Normally, the containers held luggage or goods to be shipped, but for this trip, Haley wasn't loading any luggage or cargo. All the weight she was taking on board would be human.

Still, the dog acted as if he'd found a live rabbit and sniffed the seams of the container, clawed at it and wagged his long scraggly tail excessively.

"Caesar!" Haley scrambled after the animal, grabbing his leash, dragging him down. "Heel!" she ordered. Immediately he crouched on all fours and turned appealing eyes up at her, thumped his tail and whined. "Stay," she commanded. To be certain he would stay on the floor, she knelt on the metal floor and tied his leash to a cleat. He bared his teeth and growled viciously when the Iraqi soldiers came near.

Afraid that the mean-looking soldier pointing a rifle at them might shoot the dog for the hell of it, Haley wrapped her arms around the animal's neck. The dog strained at his tether, barking ferociously at the soldier peering into the cargo bay.

"*Lae!*" Thank God for the Saudi who intervened with a heated, excited spate of Arabic on both Haley and Caesar's behalf. A vicious, fang-baring growl backed everyone away. Jack grinned broader than a Texas mile. The Iraqi snarled just as viciously, cocking his gun, as if he was about to put an end to the dog's challenge. Jack proffered a wad of American money, bargaining for the dog's life.

The soldier snapped a killing look at Caesar, added a dismissive, scornful one for Haley, then he took Jack's cash and sauntered down the tarmac, looking the old plane over, smacking the butt of his automatic rifle into the plane's riveted metal plates.

Exhaling with relief, Jack shut the cargo door. Caesar continued barking furiously. Jack hurried down to the next bay, thrusting it open, inviting the soldiers to inspect it. He banged on several shipping containers, proving they were hollow and empty.

The Iraqis' inspection was cursory, a lazy once-over. They spent more time in the cabin, searching cubbies and the galley, as if the empty refrigerators might contain food. Not until they were finished and off the plane did Haley's Saudi guard allow her to return to the cockpit.

Haley watched the ranking Saudi hand over to the Iraqi officer a payoff that was the equivalent of blood money. Only then did Nassif motion that she could return to the plane.

Haley's heart hammered hard as she sank into the pilot's chair. Jack muttered. "*Mordida*, what did I tell you? The damn vultures."

Haley nodded her head and looked under the console for the shopping bag she'd dropped there before starting the engines earlier. "Thank God, it's still here."

"What's that?" Jack's seat creaked as he leaned toward the shield, craning his neck to watch a convoy of Saudi embassy vehicles roll up the tarmac. Haley snatched open the bag to make certain the three boxes of disks and Zayn's book was still inside. They were.

"Nothing, just my stuff."

"Them kids are here. How many are we cramming into this crate?"

"I don't know. Nobody gave me a number." Haley looked out the window. Zayn emerged from the first sedan. "Hold on, Jack, there's trouble."

"Now what?"

Haley gulped and tried to hide behind the windscreen support. "My husband is here, Sheik Zayn Haaris."

"What?" Suddenly, Jack grabbed his chest; the shock of her words had obviously upset him. Haley panicked when she saw how pale his lips had gone.

"Where's your digitalis? Jack, please!"

"I got it, I got it," he said crankily, fumbling in his shirt pocket for the vial of medicine. His hands were trembling as he opened the lid and slid a pill under his tongue. He took several deep breaths before calming down. That very effectively kept Haley's attention riveted to him, not on the tall man escorting children from cars onto the gutted goose.

Jack finally caught his breath, then said painfully, "Haaris shouldn't be here. If the Iraqis recognize him, they'll mow him down and won't give a damn how many kids they shoot to death with him."

"Why would they shoot him?"

"Money, power, what else? The Haaris family is connected to the Bank of Kuwait. You got no idea what the assets of this country are. We're talking bucks, Haley-girl. On a scale little people like you and me can't even comprehend."

A fine sheen of sweat dotted Jack's upper lip. Haley reached across and smoothed his rumpled hair. "You okay?"

"I've been better." Jack leaned against the seat back, resting. "How much longer?"

Haley looked out the windshield. Zayn pulled her eyes like a beacon. She sighed, watching him lift a squalling child from the car and wait for an old woman to take his arm. He walked at her pace to the plane.

A queue had formed, herded by the Saudis, children of all ages and women whose expressions were hidden behind concealing veils. Conspicuously absent were the husbands, fathers and sons. There were no teenagers.

Haley willed Zayn onto the plane. Ten cars, one diplomat to each one, all returned to their vehicles. Everyone opened a door and sank into the air-conditioned sedans. Except for Zayn, who stood by the flags wagging in the wind on the fenders of the lead car. His military bearing was so obvious as he stood straight and tall, princely, in silent concerned study of the old Bennett workhorse.

"Jack," Haley whispered without taking her eyes off the man on the tarmac. "Tell me the truth. Is this plane in good enough shape to get these children across the border?"

"Mechanically, this old bird's a Rolls-Royce. Just 'cause she looks like a tramp doesn't mean she is."

"I just have to be sure," Haley told him. Besides her concern for the children's safety, she was also anxious about Zayn's opinion. If anything happened to these babies . . . well, that thought didn't merit completing. As for her private battles with the man in the sultan's robe, they had to wait till this war was over.

Apparently feeling steadier, Jack got up and looked into the cabin, making certain everyone was seated on the floor, holding on to something secure. He came back and closed the cockpit door softly, took his seat and let out a deep breath.

"I don't know, Haley-girl. All them babies got their eyes bigger than saucers. They ain't never seen no plane that looks like this one. I think you're going to have to forgo the barrel rolls this time.''

That was exactly the right touch Haley needed. With a last longing look at Zayn, she raised her hand in a salute and turned her attention to the task at hand.

Jack flipped switches, called off readings on the dials. He adjusted the pressure gauges and set the fans to cycle full blast. Back in the cabin, the Saudi guards led the children in a song, helping channel fears that at any minute could break into hysterics.

"Come on, Haley, do your stuff. Get this crate the hell out of Kuwait." It was what he didn't say that had her scared half to death. Those containers hadn't been empty. Caesar didn't go crazy without just cause.

"Okay, Jack, buckle up." Haley yanked the veil from her face, taking a deep cleansing breath. "Let's go."

The goose's engines accelerated, deafening her ears to the pounding of her heart. Haley cast one look back to the tarmac. The embassy cars rolled rapidly away.

Zayn Haaris remained in Kuwait.

The goose lumbered forward. Haley turned it square at the end of the runway. With a mile of cratered surface stretching before her, Haley wasn't as confident as she had been in the embassy. She brought the engines up to full power, looked to Jack for the go-ahead. There wasn't a controller on this decimated air field. Haley didn't see any Iraqi MiGs parked on the tarmac, which meant they weren't taking any chances bringing in their plane without radio communications.

"Don't worry about them craters," he told her. "You'll have this baby off the ground in five hundred meters. Go on, Haley, let her rip."

No radio, no control. They were on their own. The responsibility for the cabin full of children sat like a rock on Haley's soul. Her hands were slick with sweat.

"Go on, Haley," Jack urged.

"One question."

"Don't ask." Jack nodded his head in the direction of the field artillery pointing their deadly barrels straight at them. His eyes warned, *no questions.*

Grimly, Haley jerked her chin down once, released the brakes and tightened her grip on the wheel. The old plane lurched forward, its wheels bumping over pits, rocks and chunks of blasted concrete.

"Keep to the left," Jack cautioned.

"We better do this together."

"I'm right here with you." His hands were on the dual wheel, helping hold the critical front tire on course.

"I have one question," Haley said through her teeth, straining her shoulders to hold the front wheel bouncing through divot after divot. "Is my dog gonna be all right in that cargo bay?"

"Now, honey, do you think I'd risk a life if I hadn't already taken care of the pressure?"

"It's a dog, dammit," Haley snarled.

"That ain't all that's in there," Jack said so low she could barely hear him above the whine of the engines. "The man who signs my paycheck is cramped up in one of them crates."

"What?" Haley gasped. She froze, looking at him, her jaw sagging.

"Come on, Haley, get this sucker airborne, now!"

Swallowing a million questions, Haley hauled back on the throttle, shifting all her weight on the brakes until the engine whine was so shrill it could shatter glass. She released the brakes and the goose shot forward.

Old Jack was right about the pits in the runway. The goose was off the ground before the craters were under its wheels. "They ought to fix that."

"Keeps them from landing any MiGs the way it is," Jack muttered. He sat back against the seat, breathing harshly.

Airborne and climbing steadily over the Persian Gulf, Haley took it slow and easy as she banked south. Jack pulled on a headset and the minute they crossed the border he made contact with Saudi control at Dhahran and was given coordinates for their landing site.

"What the hell?" He jotted down numbers, grumbling. "The Saudis are sending us to the middle of the damn desert."

Haley nodded, looking at the coordinates he showed her. "Yeah, I'll bet I know exactly where we're going." To a spot in the desert she was already familiar with. She was right, too. They weren't airborne an hour.

Landing was a piece of cake compared to taking off. She set the goose down without a shudder and taxied over the now-familiar road to the stretch of under-the-sand-dune hangars. This time, a flagman brought her to a berth populated by Red Crescent vans and medical technicians as well as Saudi soldiers. Yellow school buses were lined up beside the taxiway to evacuate the children to safety.

The moment Haley brought the plane to a final stop, Jack was out of his harness, struggling to get to his feet. "Come on, girl." He was hurting now. Haley could see it. "Let's get that dog unpacked."

"I'm going back, Jack."

"What?" Jack turned in the narrow door to the cabin. "I said, I'm going back. There's a thousand more people where these kids came from. I've got about nineteen hours left before the Iraqis close the border."

"You can't go back. Kid, those Iraqis don't care who they shoot or rape. Dammit, Haley, your father's toting a bullet in his right leg. I gotta get him out of the cargo bin. I got Sheik Haaris there, too, his wife, a passel of his kids. They all need a doctor's care."

"What?" Haley shouted.

"I said, I've got the old sheik stuffed in one of those crates, too. His sons and daughters and his wife, too. Now, come on. I'm gonna need some help."

"Well, that tears it. Jack, why the hell didn't you tell me? We've been in the air an hour!"

"I wasn't risking their lives, not for nothing. You think them Iraqis wouldn't have blown us out of the air? They would have. Sheik Haaris is a marked man. They been trying to kill him from day one of the invasion."

"And you let me leave his eldest son standing out there in broad daylight on the runway like a sacrificial target? I'm going back, Jack. He's risking his life in Kuwait to find his dad and rescue his family. I've got to go back and tell him we just brought them here."

"You ain't going back, Haley. What about Jim?"

Torn, Haley didn't know what to decide, then she did. "How bad is Dad hurt?"

"Hell, we were both hurt worse in Vietnam, but we ain't as young as we used to be. Now, get up, you're going with me." Jack reached out a gnarled hand to take hold of her and pull her along if necessary.

"Nope." Haley dodged him, swinging down to snatch the shopping bag off the floor. She stuck that in his hand. "I'm not leaving this plane, Jack." Haley regained her seat and stubbornly fastened the harness over her chest. "You've got a job to do, Mr. Winslow. So do I. I'm the only pilot on this bird. You get Dad and Sheik Haaris and his family off this plane. Then you get them over to the doctors waiting down there. And you get in line to be seen and treated, too."

"Your daddy ain't gonna like this."

"My dad's incapacitated. That makes me the ranking officer in charge. Now get off this plane. That's an order!"

Jack's weather-wrinkled face reddened. "Ha!" he snorted. "That's mutiny, girl. I got a paper that says I'm CEO of Mideast operations and I can outorder you any day of the week."

"No, you can't, Jack," Haley said, softening her response.

"I'm not forgetting that you dusted my britches more times than I want to remember when I was a kid. But right now, I've got to do the most serious job I've ever been handed. You give that bag to Sheik Haaris and tell Dad not to worry about me. I'll be back in two hours with Zayn."

"You're as stubborn as that cantankerous old man of yours. Hell's bells, I've wasted enough breath arguing. You know the boss is gonna have my head for this."

"And a good slice out of my hide, too, but I'm in this too deep to chicken out now. Jack, don't forget to give the sheik that bag."

"What's in it?" Jack gripped the plastic sack.

"Floppy disks and his son's little black book."

"Ha! Ain't that a kicker."

"Just make sure the sheik gets it."

"I will. You be careful, y'hear."

"Yes, sir." Haley saluted smartly and grinned.

Jack was gone. Haley chewed on her thumbnail watching the children fan out toward the soldiers. On the other side of the plane, an attendant capped off the goose's tanks with fuel. The heavily accented voice of the controller chatted on the radio. Distracted, Haley heard the man tell her another pilot and a navigator were coming on board. Jack had help opening the cargo bays. Caesar jumped onto the ground, barking and leaping. Medics scrambled forward pulling stretchers.

Straining to see, Haley's heart lurched when she finally saw her father laid onto a white sheeted stretcher. He was alert, wincing in pain, his leg bandaged thickly around his thigh. He was still dressed in his blue-and-white flight suit. It was bloodstained clear down to his ankle.

She closed her eyes and bit on her lip, staying the sudden urge to jump ship. How she wanted to bury her head against her father's warm chest. She jerked her chin up and allowed herself to look her fill. Her heart was in Kuwait. She had to go back.

A dark-haired little girl clutched his hand, refusing to leave his side. Two boys who looked very much like Quadir Haaris helped a blond woman who was having trouble walking to the ground, then a silver-haired man. Caesar bolted for the older man, licking his hand, running circles around them all until one of the youths got hold of his leash and quieted him.

The older man spoke to Jim Bennett, then looked up at the plane and smiled. When he did that, Haley knew who he was. Sheik Wali Haj Haaris.

The doors were closed, the bays shut. The two-member Saudi flight crew joined her in the cabin. It was four-fifteen in the afternoon. There was time for eight, possibly nine round trips. Nine hundred people. It wasn't enough.

Going back seemed the most foolish thing she had done yet. Wanting to know what the news was, Haley asked for an update, then regretted it when she heard both Saudis' estimation of the crisis. On the brink of global war, and she had just taken off, flying back into the ignition box.

"Are the Russians involved?"

"Everyone is involved," said the older pilot who sat in her copilot's seat. His English was pretty good. He'd told her he'd done his flight training at Randolf Air Force Base.

Haley relinquished the pilot's seat right after they landed again in Al Kuwait. From her vantage point she could see an eleventh car had been added to the embassy's caravan, a beautiful white Rolls-Royce.

"Wow," she said admiringly. "Somebody with a lot of rank is in that one, right?"

The Saudi major grinned. "His highness, the ambassador."

"Bail-out time," Haley mumbled to herself, searching the emptying vehicles for the man she'd come to retrieve. He wasn't there. She double-checked, looking over each robed official wearing an embassy badge.

A knot of fear sickened her. What if Zayn had been taken prisoner? What if . . . a hundred possible reasons for his not being here rushed through her at once. If he wasn't here, he had to be back at the embassy. She had to know for certain.

She carefully shut down all the plane's vitals, going over the goose's temperament with the major. When she gathered up her discarded veils, Haley noticed how badly her hands were shaking. She swung the *abba* over her shoulders but almost didn't get the frogs fastened. Trying to calm herself, she twisted the plain band of gold circling her ring finger. She made up her mind quickly.

She smiled at the major and the navigator. "Now that you guys know where all the chug holes are, I'm giving this plane over to you. Just remember, throttle it hard at the start of the runway and get the engines up to maximum thrust before you release the brakes. And don't forget, this baby needs all the room she can get to stop."

The Saudi major studied her for a long moment. He didn't say she couldn't go, for which Haley silently blessed him.

"No problem. Good luck, lady."

"Lady, huh?" Haley shot him a grin and dropped the gauzy cloth over her face. She was beginning to like the Saudis. Smoothing down the material over her dress, she fussed with the garment for a moment. "Do you think I'll pass muster?"

"You already have, *issaeyaedea.*" The major gave her a sharp salute.

Squaring her shoulders, Haley marched through the empty cabin. No matter what, she was going to make certain Zayn Haji Haaris left Kuwait before the border closed.

She tried to imagine the look on Zayn's face when she told him how his family had been hidden at Bennett Air. They were now safe due to the crafty wiles of an old Texan. Her smile beneath her veil was brilliant. She waited with Nassif and the other Saudi guards for the door to open.

That smile vanished when an Iraqi soldier swung aside the hydraulic door. Panic swamped her. She had no way to explain who she was, why she was back. The man pointed his Uzi at her and Haley dropped her gaze, intimidated. Captain Nassif voiced a sharp complaint, gently moving her aside so that the Iraqi could see the plane contained no other occupants. Abruptly, the Iraqi signaled they could go down the steps.

Gripping her *abba* against the tug of the wind, Haley followed Captain Nassif on to the beastly hot tarmac. On the ground, she stood apart from the milling soldiers as they searched the plane, opening cargo bays, dragging out the empty aluminum containers. They checked every inch of the plane before signaling that the embassy cars could advance and unload.

Haley watched the performance with a jaded eye, knowing that this show was all for the ambassador's benefit, to impress him and milk the Saudi government for another exorbitant fee. It worked, too. Another briefcase full of cash was handed over to the high-ranking Iraqi. The thug was making a killing.

The ambassador boarded first, and Haley figured he was in for a rude surprise. The rest of the passengers hurried after him. Zayn was not among them. When all the cars had emptied, she walked to the flashy Rolls, looked inside and wondered what it would be like to ride in such a luxurious car. But she went past it, moving to the familiar sedan. That driver recognized her, jumped out to swing open a back door.

Settling back against the vinyl upholstery, Haley reminded herself she was a Ford, not a Rolls. The seat was hot. The air-conditioning didn't work. Her guards took the remaining seats in the same car.

Almost at once, all the drivers returned. Iraqi soldiers actually closed the doors all down the line of cars. No questions had been asked of Haley.

She scooted to the middle of the back seat. The convoy departed before the goose did.

There was no turning back.

# Chapter 14

The white Rolls led the way and was stopped at the first barricade outside the airport complex. Four soldiers harassed the lead driver, then without warning, the point of a machine gun was leveled in the driver's window. The chauffeur bolted out with his hands up, a very frightened look on his face.

As Haley watched, one soldier tossed his weapon into the Rolls and got inside. Nassif leaned out his passenger-side window, hollering at the ousted chauffeur. Then he jerked back in and threw open the car door, shouting and waving.

The dispossessed driver ran and threw himself into the front seat. Rivulets of sweat coursed down his face from his limp *kuffiyah*. Both chattered excitedly, moving their hands in frantic pumping motions that told Haley the Rolls driver wanted her driver to step on it.

With royal flags snapping, the white Rolls peeled out of the checkpoint, bounced over the median and sped off down the broad avenue. The hijacking floored Haley. Diplomatic status was sacrosanct the world over. Not in Kuwait, apparently.

Her driver wasted no time evacuating the scene of the crime. The small flags on the sedan's fenders didn't seem so inviolate to Haley anymore. Clearly, concessions from the Iraqis came from bribes, not international law.

She was relieved when they entered the Saudi embassy compound. The concrete walls and guarded entrance gave some protection against outright takeover from outside. But for how long? How many hours were left before the border shut and total anarchy reigned?

She found Zayn before her car stopped under the sally port. He was in the open yard, surrounded by a cluster of wild-looking men, volatile, untamed and well-armed. Their robes were not the refined garb of the Saudis. A few were bareheaded, but most wore *kuffiyahs* secured by black *'iquals*. Haley's eyebrow quirked. Bedouin bandits? Kuwait resistance? She didn't want to know. Maybe he sought word of his father.

She felt a flare of pride at the news she was bringing him. She felt he should know she was back. That he should sense her presence and be able to find her just as she was able to instantly locate him.

Her driver stopped under the ambassador's shaded entrance. Both drivers leaped out the sedan, shouting the news that the ambassador's Rolls had been stolen. That raised another growl of angry Arabic amid the citizenry.

Her driver turned back, opened her door with a flourish. Haley gathered her *abba* and emerged from the car. Because of the drivers' news, people had gathered closer, their chatter escalating.

She turned slowly, marking the size of the throng. The men she'd overheard speaking English earlier were in the next caravan. She could see that there were no women or children left to evacuate.

A strong gust of hot wind swept across the yard. It tugged at her *abba*, flattening the veil against her face and throat. The same gust of wind sent the tails of Zayn's *kuffiyah* flapping behind his shoulders. It did not blow the cloth away, but it did make him turn and look at the archway where Haley stood.

Concealed by a veil, she couldn't be certain that he could tell that her eyes were locked on his. But he stared hard at her, not moving his eyes while a man in shorts pleaded some case in his ear. His shoulders stiffened, and his eyebrow raised in a manner she knew was a characteristic of his. She wondered what he was thinking.

She inclined her head, acknowledging his regard, then turned to the door Nassif held open for her. This entrance opened to a stairwell that rose to the second floor only. On the landing, she passed the young aide she had first spoken to. Haley nodded to him, but passed him without speaking. His mouth sagged open in total shock.

A servant led her to the women's quarters. Here, in splendid privacy, the diplomats' wives and young children had been luxuriously housed, judging from the remaining buffet set out on a broad table. The spacious room was littered with personal items—forgotten toys, games, packages of diapers and luggage. It was all so sad, Haley thought.

Though it had large windows, the room was not brightly illuminated by natural light. Each pane of glass had an intricate, detailed screen fastened to it. She knew what kind of room it was, this secluded portion of the house. The harem.

Haley removed the *abba* and confining silk headpiece, kicked off her shoes and sat to strip her stockings from her legs. As she neatly folded the clothing, she considered her hunger. She was ravenous. She had to think when she had last eaten. A bite or two while she waited for the Saudi aide and attaché to make up their minds and accept her offer of the plane.

She fixed a plate of chicken salad. There were crisp round crackers, fruits, several casseroles, fool and mutton and various breads, as well as soft cheese, sharply flavored and tangy.

She made coffee and let herself sink onto the most comfortable-looking divan as she ate. When she finished the meal, she was a little on edge because Zayn had not come.

He had seen her, recognized her. What was the holdup? Was she going to have to hunt him down? Haley stood at the windows, watching another caravan return from the round trip to the airport.

Time was running out. People dolefully watched those given higher priority get in the cars to go to the airport. One lousy plane wasn't enough. They needed a fleet. She could see the Persian Gulf. See fires burning in the city. The glass and scrolled screen didn't keep out the sporadic sounds of gunfire.

The last car departed and the soldiers closed the gates. The embassy quieted more with each departure. Haley stayed by the window watching what she could, munching idly on a cracker now and then.

Finally, there was a soft rap on the door. The same servant that had led her to these quarters peeked in, searched the room for other occupants. Seeing none, he stood aside, holding the door wide open. Zayn nearly knocked the man down when he strode angrily inside the quarters. He came to a rest at the corner of an exquisite red, black and yellow Persian carpet. With one flick of his hand, the servant was dismissed.

Until the door was firmly closed, Zayn held himself rigid, glaring at her, not saying a word. Then his hands moved to his headpiece and he yanked it off, tossing both *'iqual* and *kuffi-yah* onto the nearest piece of furniture. The gesture said quite a lot to Haley. She grimaced and wiggled her bare toes against the carpet.

"Explain what you have been doing behind my back," he snapped.

No "Hello," no, "Gee, it's good to see you alive and well." Just his unreasonable fury. Haley faced him squarely, the ornate window at her back. Her head was bare, she had removed her robe and she felt a hundred degrees cooler wearing just the beautiful silk dress that swept down to her toes. A woman needed a suit of steel when confronting an arrogant pig like him.

"Do I have permission to speak?" She couldn't resist the gibe. She knew a touch of wickedness lit in her eyes, sending him a different message loud and clear.

"You spoke enough when you were forbidden to. Enough to have word spread like wildfire through the embassy of the *Amerikana woman* who can fly airplanes and would rescue all the Saudis. How stupid can you get? Don't you realize there are spies everywhere?"

"Which question do you want answered first? Obviously I am stupid enough to try to help you. Though why I bothered I'll never know."

"Heaven help me, I am going to strike her!" Zayn spun around, eyes and hands beseeching the powers above.

"You wouldn't dare." Haley retreated as he advanced, his gold-trimmed robe parting over his legs.

"Oh, wouldn't I?" Zayn snarled, pushed to the maximum.

"I haven't caused any trouble," Haley insisted. "I found a way to get people out of this country, which is something nobody else in this godforsaken place has managed to do in days. I cannot believe that people just stand around, wringing their hands, doing absolutely nothing, letting those goons with rifles take everything they have."

Zayn planted his fists at his sides. "You don't know what you're talking about."

"The hell I don't," Haley declared. "I'm mad as hell, and I refuse to act like a helpless twit. I refuse to passively wait for an ax to fall on my head. Nobody intimidates me."

"Oh, I understand now. You got a rush, didn't you? A great big ego boost to your head all because you flew a forty-year-old plane jammed with a hundred frightened children out of Kuwait. How fortunate we *third worlders* are to have Americans to our rescue!"

"You've no need to be sarcastic," Haley replied, stung.

"I want you to know, Issaeyaedea Haaris, that over ten thousand people, and more than half of those, very young children, have passed through this embassy in the past five days. All have been transported safely out of Kuwait and into Saudi Arabia without risking a single life."

"Oh?" That statement took Haley down a peg. She held the urge to ask for proof. He was livid enough already. "Well, sorry, it didn't look like that to me. According to the desperate Canadians and Australians downstairs, nobody was going anywhere."

"Canadians who gave up on their own diplomatic corps. Australians who heard a rumor that the Saudis were getting people out quickly and safely. You listened to gossip and came to your own conclusions."

"Okay, call me a bloody fool, so I did." Haley thought her admission ought to turn his anger aside. "I also did something you might have some appreciation for. I got into my company's hangar. You'll never guess who happened to be there. Jack, my dad and your father had turned it into a bunker."

"What?" Zayn's hands clamped onto her upper arms.

"They're all right," Haley said quickly. "Everybody. Jack Winslow hid them all in the shipping containers inside the DC-7. When the Iraqis came in to strip the place, he kept your family and my dad safe. I flew them all to Saudi Arabia in the goose. They are safe."

Zayn's hands dropped from her arms. "Do you truly expect me to believe that?"

"Yes, I do. You expect me to believe the Saudis are running an underground railroad that moves people out of here faster than the New York subway system. You better believe me, because they're out of here, gone like the wind."

"Damn you, it could have been anyone hidden in those containers. Did you see them? Describe them."

"I don't have to describe my own father, you damned fool. Oh, I could kick you, you make me so mad."

Hurt by his reaction, Haley turned her back on him and stalked toward the exit. "I'm leaving. I've come back and told you your family is safe. If you don't believe me, fine. Stay here! Get yourself shot. See if I care."

She ran to the door and almost succeeded in opening it wide enough to escape through, when his palm slammed into the wood and banged the door in her face. Haley spun around. His hands flattened against the door. His body trapped hers.

He growled in a harsh, menacing tone, "Answer me this, what the hell are you doing back here? All the women have been evacuated."

A moment passed as a host of smart answers fought to make the first score on her side. She kept her mouth shut, refusing to retaliate. There was enough fighting going on all around them. They had to try to get along.

Zayn's hands grasped her shoulders, shaking her harshly. Haley looked up at his burning eyes.

"Answer me, damn you."

He was worried about her, that was the problem. She squeezed her hands between their bodies and touched his face, stroking the sharp stubble of his shadowing beard. "I wasn't sure you would believe a message that came word of mouth, without proof, Sheik Haji Haaris."

Haley leaned into his hurting embrace and pressed her mouth to his.

"You decided!" Zayn growled fiercely against her yielding mouth. He pressed her painfully against the wall, his mouth slashing across hers in desperate hunger for something more. His hands shook as they moved up, grasping the sides of her head, imprisoning her.

"You decided!" He pulled his mouth away, his voice low thunder in her ears. "Woman, can you not understand the danger we are in?"

Haley's mouth burned. She tasted blood and fury.

"Damn you!" His fingers, knotted in her hair, held her still. His right hand dug into the fine silk clothing near her throat. Her bodice split with a harsh, loud rip down to her waist.

Haley gasped for a ragged breath of air, her heart pounded in her chest like a jackhammer on concrete. A second deliberate yank from his powerful hand and the dress gave way completely, pooling to a silken tumble at her feet. The room was private, but nowhere near private enough for what he had in mind.

"Zayn, Zayn, please, let me tell you . . ."

Her plea was cut off by his harsh mouth ruthlessly silencing her.

"No," he growled against her lips. His fingers gripped her jaw, holding her face still beneath his. The coldness of his eyes silenced her. "Did you like that?"

"No." Haley tried to shake her head, but his hand on her jaw kept her as still as a mouse in a sprung trap.

"Do you know what the Iraqis will do to a female spy? A beautiful woman with a body such as the one you have?"

Haley snapped open her eyes. "I don't want to know."

Zayn's fingers slid down her throat. The thin silk and lace of her slip was no protection. The ribbon straps tore loose with the slightest tug of his strong hand. She clutched at the bodice, vainly trying to hold the only garment she wore in place on her body.

"They will rape you. A hundred men will have you before one day in captivity has passed. You will be pawed at, held down, beaten and abused until madness is your only escape. That is what you have come back to, my stupid American woman."

"Stop it! Stop trying to frighten me!" Haley pushed his hand away.

They both froze, their breathing harsh and rapid. Two powerful tempers throbbing in the sultry air.

Her breasts heaved. Haley managed to keep them covered as she tossed her tangled hair off her shoulder. "I would kill myself before submitting to treatment like that."

"Do you think so?" Zayn shook his head. "The will to live even in such misery is stronger than you can imagine. Women submit and become their captors' whores. Would you like me to take you to the infirmary on the third floor, where there are a score of women who swore the very same thing you just did."

Haley stared hard at his dark, uncompromising eyes. "You don't mean it."

Though it took a great struggle to do so, Zayn drew in a controlling and temperate breath. "I do. You could have comforted some of those women. They are flight attendants who were kidnapped from the airport and taken to a hotel downtown and used brutally. Some of them might still harbor the love of flying that you have."

"Oh, God." Haley fought a well of tears rising in her eyes. "Why is this happening?"

"Because this is war."

A sob escaped behind her hand as she covered her mouth.

"Haley." Zayn reached for her. This time, his hands were very tender as he caught her shoulders and pulled her against his chest. He settled his arms around her as her head ducked under his chin. "You should not have come back. I was glad that you were gone."

She drew a deep, ragged breath and said, "I came back for you. I couldn't bear it if anything happened to you."

"Well, we are both in a fine mess, now, aren't we?" Zayn produced a handkerchief and handed it to her, watching as she mopped up her eyes. "I had begun to believe you had nerves of galvanized steel. You cry rather prettily when properly primed."

"If you think I'm mopping my face so you'll have sympathy for me, you'd better think again, Omar."

Zayn grunted. Her insult wasn't delivered with the same stinging heat of several days ago. He raised his head, spying the laden table. "Have you eaten?"

"I managed a salad and some crackers after I got here."

"I haven't eaten in ages. Come, sit with me."

Haley knotted the torn ribbon straps of her slip behind her neck. She reached down and caught up the fabulous dress, examining the damage done to it.

Zayn cocked his eyebrow at her. "I won't apologize. You needed the lesson. Be thankful it only cost you a dress."

"Oh, I'm thankful," Haley agreed. "I just want to know which door of Gucci's Al Kuwait is still open."

"I don't think I will have any trouble providing you with another garment."

Zayn's mood had changed. His rampant chauvinism was back. He gave her a cool, assessing look, which didn't do a thing for her frayed temper.

"I'm going to have to pound you if you keep this up."

"Then don't call me Omar, unless you change your mind and want to be treated like a concubine I have purchased."

"Point taken."

He moved to the table and fixed a plate, pausing over selecting slices of cold cuts and cheeses to look at her as she smoothed the slip across her hips. She looked up from adjusting the lacy bodice and found his eyes very heated and telling.

"Have I told you since marrying you, Issaeyaedea Haaris what a beautiful woman you are?"

"No. That inspiring bit of flattery has been lacking in your dialogue so far."

"Put a tape on the cassette player, would you, please? I can't help feeling that any embassy has ears in every corner. Shall I fix you a plate?"

"No, I had plenty earlier." Haley did as he asked, watching his eyes for approval of the volume as she adjusted it. He looked like a man who'd been to hell and back. Obviously, their frequent battles weren't helping him.

She got a cup of coffee and joined him at a table placed near a silent, dark television. She watched him eat. He was as picky as she was; it appeared he ate out of necessity and not pleasure in these stressful times.

"Where are the disks?" Zayn asked after he'd finished most of the pita sandwich piled with olives and tomatoes.

"I handed them to Jack Winslow. He'll get them to your father. They are safe."

"Was anyone hurt?"

Haley's forehead knitted. "My dad looked pretty grim. The boys and the two little girls looked in great shape. Your father was very straight and upright, just like you. There was a woman with very blond hair who seemed to have a great deal of trouble moving, but I do not know if she was injured or ill."

"Quadir's mother, Karen."

"She isn't an Arab, is she?"

"Scandinavian."

"Oh, really?" Haley's eyebrow shot upward then and she stared at Zayn. "It's true, then."

"What is true?"

"That oil princes have a thing for blond women."

He popped the last bite of sandwich into his mouth and munched it thoughtfully. "Are you asking my own preference?"

"Possibly."

"I have never thought of myself as being different from any other educated man. I like a woman with hair that I can touch. The color has never been important until recently."

"Oh?" Haley decided not to pursue that line of conversation. She propped her chin on her fist and changed the subject. "There is little time left before the borders are closed. How are we going to get out of here?"

"Now you want to talk straight talk, hmm? You have come into a trap. My exalted, protected diplomatic status has been revoked. When you opened your lovely mouth and identified your husband as a Kuwaiti sheik using falsified Saudi documents, you added another price to my head. The Iraqis are not pleased. I am labeled a spy and a traitor. When I set foot outside these walls, I will be arrested and executed. And you, my dear, will submit to the fate I have just explained at length to you."

Horror had increased in Haley's heart with every word Zayn had so calmly said. "You've got to be kidding."

"Oh, no. I am most certainly not." Zayn lifted his shoulders in a mocking shrug. "Thus far, the Iraqis haven't shown any compassion. If we are caught, we will both die—for spying, for subversion, for defying the Iraqi will. What does it matter the charge? Certain people have been marked for death from the onset. I am one of them."

"Great," Haley grumbled. "What's that got to do with me? I haven't done anything to the Iraqis."

"Ah, but you have. Those disks are vital, and you know where they are. This is not a game, Haley." Zayn didn't stop there, speaking so softly she could barely hear his accusations, but she did. "Had you not opened your mouth and given away your identity, the spies in this embassy wouldn't have learned of my identity. Now, it is too late. Everyone knows you are the wife of the Haji Haaris."

This was not good news. Haley raised anguished eyes, searching his. "Zayn, I couldn't stand back doing nothing with all those children looking so frightened. What were the options? Weren't their lives worth it?''

''Certainly.'' He exhaled. ''But they would have been moved within a few hours, regardless of your interference.''

Was it worth it? Had she done the right thing in the long run? She had to think of the men, women and children who were now safe because of the Bennett DC-7. Her own father's life was definitely worth it to her.

For a second or two, her mouth worked up and down with several unspoken rejoinders.

Zayn's eyes bored into hers. His answer was both condemning and damning. ''You could have waited until I was summoned from the ambassador's office. Had you done so, I would have managed an explanation for the Iraqis that would not have compromised our identities.''

He was right. Haley wilted against the back of her chair, rubbing aching temples with both hands. ''I swear, I only wanted to help,'' she said in a raw voice.

''And so you did,'' Zayn concluded. ''The sentiment of your actions has not escaped me. You have made your decision to stand by your Arab husband. Now you will live with the consequences of that decision.''

Zayn left the table. He had to figure out how to rescue her. He went to the divan to stretch out, tired, weary from days of running and maneuvering and doing. Haley watched him, confused by her crazy urge to comfort him. She couldn't get anything right.

She eased round the divan and knelt on the floor, leaning over to massage his neck and shoulders. ''You look so tired. You haven't slept in days, have you?''

''No.'' Zayn opened his eyes and caught both her hands, holding them away from his head. ''Don't mother me.''

Her slip gaped. His eyes raked her breasts. Haley worried the corner of her lip, expecting another explosion of temper.

''The minute I saw you, I knew you were dangerous.''

''Oh, really?'' She wiggled her hands free of his and began rubbing his shoulders, anyway. ''What makes little ol' me so dangerous?''

''You have a ready answer for everything. My country is dissolving before my very eyes. There are more people who must be evacuated before I can think about myself.''

"All right, I'll buy that," Haley said as she worked at the tense muscles at the back of his neck. "So how are we going to accomplish this evacuation?"

"I do not recall using the word *we*."

Haley looked at the clock, biting her tongue so she wouldn't argue. "In eleven more hours the border closes."

"*You think I don't know that!*" Zayn shot to his feet so quickly Haley didn't have a chance to back out of range. "Don't press me and don't argue with me!"

The great Oz had spoken. He'd just drawn the proverbial line in the sand and dared her not to cross it. Haley rose, feeling the balance of power waver between them.

It was now or never to play any trump card she held. She could bluff. Let Zayn take his anger out on her, tomorrow. She would survive. More important, if her bluff was successful, so would he. Fair or foul, she determined she had the right to get him on the goose and out of Kuwait, alive.

"The Vixen One is gassed and ready to go," she lied. "I checked it out when we went into the hangar. It had some damage done to its body when my dad landed in the middle of the invasion, but Jack repaired it."

"You did what?" All color ran from Zayn's face. He came around the divan and his hands locked onto her wrists.

Undaunted, Haley thrust out her chin at him in a direct challenge. "It's not what I did. It's what I want to do. Get the hell out of here! The Vixen will carry ten easy, more if there is no luggage."

"Answer my question. Did you start that plane while there were Iraqi soldiers watching every move made inside that hangar?"

God forgive her, but Haley wasn't going back on her lie. "I didn't start it. I said I checked it out. That means I ran a systems check on the computer, that's all. All you have to do is let your people in the resistance know what time to be at the airport."

"Oh, Haley, Haley," Zayn said in an exhausted voice. "You really think things are that simple." Abruptly, he released her and turned away, pacing, more agitated than ever.

"We have to get in the next caravan and go to the airport. That's all. We can be out in an hour's time."

"Do you really think you can just march into that hangar, start the Vixen and fly off into the sky? Are you that blind...that naive? Can't you see that there is a war going on here? My country is being annihilated. I can't just fly off into the sunset without ever looking back."

Haley sighed. She had to convince him. "Yes, you can, Zayn. You can and you must. You haven't any other choice."

# Chapter 15

When her earnest, heartfelt words failed to sway him, Haley changed tactics. She could act hard and tough, too. "As to flying off into the so-called sunset, that is essentially what I did with the DC-7. The people who get out of here won't be silent, Zayn. The world will know the truth about the Iraqi invasion. The only way to fight this is to get out of here alive, so that you can come back in a position of strength. You're one man, one leader. Stay here and you become a martyr, that's all. Come with me to the airport and I'll get you safely away in the Vixen One."

"In case you haven't been paying attention, Haley Bennett, it took a hell of a lot more pull than your sweet blue eyes to get that DC-7 airborne. All property in Kuwait has been confiscated. The Vixen One belongs to Iraq."

"The hell it does!" He'd hit the nail on the head with that last statement, but Haley would go to her grave denying that at this moment. Not when there was one-millionth of a chance she might convince him to go along with her.

"Arguing with you is pointless." Zayn plowed his fingers through his hair.

"Zayn, please, listen to me. Even if the state has taken over everything, the commander at the airport will do anything for a price. All it takes is money. You've got my wallet. I've cash and traveler's checks, maybe we can buy the Vixen's way out of here.''

"The Vixen!" he retorted hotly. "That plane couldn't get a rat out of this country in one piece now. Didn't you listen to a word I said?"

Haley moved defensively away from the undertow of his mounting temper.

"You haven't the slightest concept of what is going on here," he declared with absolute finality.

"Zayn, we can argue about it later. Let's just go, please. Let's go downstairs and get a place in the next caravan. Time is running—"

"Yes!" he cut her off forcefully. "I know what time it is! As if I didn't have enough to deal with, now I'm stuck finding a safe way out of Kuwait for you."

That hurt. Slapped in the face by his attitude, Haley turned mutinous. "Well, you don't have to bother, Mr. Haaris. The American Embassy is just down the street. They'll get me home just fine."

"And you're going to call a taxi and hop over there?" Zayn snapped his fingers. "Just like that, huh?"

Haley glared at him, ignoring the damage his sharp words did to her dignity. Where he was concerned she didn't have any, only pride. "I doubt if I need to prove to you how well I can manage. You can take my word for it. If I say I'm going there, I'll get there, somehow."

"The hell you will. You are going to sit right here, in this room, under guard if necessary, until I arrange a suitable means to get you out of the country."

"I don't think I qualify as one of those individuals vital to the survival of Kuwait. Quit wasting your time with me. I can take care of myself."

"Allah deliver me from independent American women!" Zayn marched to the door. His eyes were cold and hard as he took up his *kuffiyah* and *'iqual* from the table where he'd tossed it. "Fortunately, there is only one door granting access from the harem, Issaeyaedea Haaris. You will remained sequestered until I have made arrangements for you."

"Dammit, Zayn," Haley protested in growing panic. "This is an embassy. They can issue papers in any name they want, can't they? We can have new documents made. Assume different identities."

"My Saudi friends are not in the business of forging documents."

"The hell they aren't. I came in here on a forged document."

"No, Issaeyaedea Haaris, you entered Iraqi Province 19 under the diplomatic passport of your Arab husband. And now you will learn the first lesson of an Arab wife. Obedience. Make no mistake, this door will be guarded from here on."

He grabbed up the remnants of her torn dress, *abba* and veil then spun on his heel, stalking out, the door slamming violently in his wake.

"Dammit, Zayn!" she repeated. "Don't lock me in here!"

Stunned, Haley stood there like a rock as the bolt in the lock shot home.

"Zayn, wait, I've got something important to tell you!" The man was the stubbornest, most infuriating, mule-headed jackass she'd ever met in her life!

Too angry for words, Haley kicked a cushion clear across the room. Lord, how would he react if she went at him with the truth? Reversed the whole crazy tale she'd just told him about the Vixen. Could she get him to leave Kuwait then? No! Of course not! He had a mission to save the world!

Haley found no rest in the growing silence that engulfed the embassy. She held her own until an explosion went off so close by, it shattered one of the heavy glass panes on the outer side of the filigree screens.

Shaken, Haley picked herself up off the floor and felt a rush of heat push into the room. Noise from the city did, too. Where the embassy's air-conditioning, thick walls and heavy glass had muffled what went on outside before, now the sounds of war and the stench of Kuwait burning couldn't be ignored.

That rattled her.

"I'm getting out of here!" Haley announced to no one. That blast settled it for her. She began rifling through the abandoned luggage, forcing locks with a table knife. The first one contained useless designer gowns. Another yielded Pakistani blouses, ankle-length skirts, sashes, cotton cloths that were so long they could only be saris.

The harem had the required opulent bath, which she needed to investigate. It, too, was littered with discards—cosmetics, perfume, toiletries, oils, creams, even a jar of henna skin paint and fine-pointed sable brushes. Haley brushed and parted her hair and worked handfuls of baby oil into it at her scalp. Wet with oil, her hair was not so blond. She plaited it tight and wound the two braids close to her head, pinning them secure.

The result was frightening. Her slicked-back hair was dull and lifeless. That only made her skin look paler. What good was a tan, anyway, when her eyes were as blue as a summer sky?

For the time being, she left her contacts soaking and sorted through the clothes she'd brought into the bath. A couple of layers seemed to be the best arrangement of clashing colors and patterns. She practiced winding the sari, then inspected her efforts. Sloppy. She took it off.

"Haley!" Zayn called her name the moment he stepped inside the harem.

"I'm in the bathroom," Haley answered grumpily. *Now you come back,* she thought mutinously. *I'll be damned if I'll tell you a thing! Stupid arrogant man!*

Zayn caught her in the act of stepping into a pair of black trousers.

"What the..." Zayn's question died on his lips. Haley turned to face him, sliding the pants over her slender hips to fasten them at her waist. She was nude and too beautiful for words. "What have you done to your hair?"

"Don't growl at me!" Haley snapped as she reached for a shirt and dragged it on. "It's baby oil. It'll wash out when I get home, providing I've still got a head on my shoulders. How are we getting out of here? I'm leaving Kuwait, even if I have to walk to the border. I won't stay."

"You aren't walking. I've made other arrangements. Before we discuss that, you will wash your hair and let it down."

Haley whipped around and faced him, her fingers at the buttons of the blouse, fastening it closed. "And if I refuse, do you plan to bully me into obeying?"

"What do you think?" Zayn quietly closed the bathroom door behind his back. Haley stood very still, concentrating on his expression. She'd seen that look before, just prior to being dragged into the smallest bathroom she'd ever visited in her life.

"Fine!" Haley ripped open the shirt, showering him with a hail of button fire. She tossed it to the floor, realizing she was getting rather inured to stripping before him. It seemed to happen every time they met. Snatching a jar of shampoo from the counter, she stalked to the shower. A flick of her wrist sent a gush of spraying water splashing at the tiled floor. "Forget the fact that I'm a blonde. Forget that I'm trying to make myself look more normal for this part of the world!"

She angrily dropped her trousers and stepped naked into the shower, slamming the glass door behind her. The glass was clear, no impediment to Zayn's view. Even so, he crossed to the door, pulled it open and propped his shoulder against the frame.

"What are you trying to look like?"

"Like anything, anyone, no one. Especially not some smart-mouthed, got-it-all American girl, which is all you seem to think I am. Okay?"

"Okay." Zayn reached past her to turn the shower head so that water did not splash on his clothes. She was spoiling for a fight. Angry hands pulled at pins and yanked at bands. She poured a huge glob of shampoo in her palm then attacked her scalp until it fairly foamed, folding up long wads of hair, scrubbing with adept practiced hands.

Not until she had rinsed with her back to the spray of water and wiped soap out of her eyes did she realize he was still standing in the open door watching her.

"What are you doing? Get out of here!" Haley yelled. Her lashes spiked with water and she squinted to see him. "Damn you, Zayn, leave!"

"Be quiet." He admired her breasts, unable to stop himself from reaching out and touching her slick skin, wet with shampoo trails. He found a deep satisfying pleasure at discovering that her hair coloring was natural, proved so by the teasing display of curls at the joining of her thighs. "Enjoy the water. You will not see much of it for some time."

"Why?"

"Finish washing your hair. It still smells like a newborn's nursery in here."

"Don't laugh at me. And get out of here. I have no intention of playing games with you."

Haley dumped more shampoo on her head, scrubbing with a vengeance. But every time she opened her eyes, he was still there, leering at her. Rinsing the soap away again, she realized she'd had enough. "For heaven's sake, we're in a Saudi embassy. They've probably got a camera in the shower head! I'll get arrested and sent to jail!''

"You are my wife, Issaeyaedea Haaris."

"In name only."

"You think so?" Zayn's right hand reached out to cup her breast.

"Zayn!" Haley gasped, sinking back into the splash of water. It blinded her and sent scrubbed hair and shampoo foaming across her face and shoulders. Zayn caught her wrist as she reached up to shove the tangle of hair away, and pulled her to him.

He gripped her waist firmly, one hand free to stroke her breast, the other holding her wet body against his own. "I have earned the right to admire my beautiful wife as she bathes."

"Zayn." Haley shook her hair free of her eyes and grasped his shoulders tightly. His broad hands dropped to her waist, lifting her off her feet. "What are you doing?"

His grip tightened, pressing her higher, above his head. Turning, Zayn dropped her belly on his shoulder, wrapped both his arms around her struggling thighs. "I am going to make love to you until you beg for mercy."

"For pity's sake, we haven't got time for this. They are going to close the border in a couple of hours!"

"Exactly so," Zayn answered, marching into the salon with her half slung and dripping on his shoulder. "And it will be well after that before we make any attempt to leave the serenity of this secure and very private chamber. We will sleep and eat and indulge in the one pastime we should have engaged in at first meeting."

Haley bounced on the wide divan as he dropped her. She scrambled half-upright, arms and legs splaying, only to be caught by the downward drop of his determined body onto hers. She struggled for a moment, then realized he definitely had the advantage. She was naked and wet and spread-eagle beneath him, his hips crushing against hers, his hands gripping her wrists, holding them still.

"You don't want me. You just want to punish me for getting in your way, or else you want to make me submit to your will."

"Oh, I want you." Zayn's head dipped and his mouth touched her breast, tasting it at long last. "I have wanted this for quite some time now . . . so have you."

"That's not true." Haley gasped and squirmed. His tongue touched the sensitive peak of her nipple, sent a shudder whipping through her. "Oh, Zayn." Haley shivered.

His mouth opened, taking the whole rosy aureola inside the heated cavity of his mouth. Squirming against the unbelievable pleasure of his tongue and teeth stroking her, Haley tried again to dissuade him before it was too late.

"I will scream."

"Scream all you like." Zayn kissed her breast and raised his head, smiling wickedly at her. "This embassy is empty. There are ten men left inside its secure walls. They await my command. Not a one cares for interior comforts and would never interfere between a husband and his wife."

"Zayn, please don't do this," Haley implored him. "Not in anger, please."

"I am not angry, Haley. I am aroused. I'm tormented beyond my strength. You have won the battle between us. I cannot turn my back on you and walk away. I am in this with you until it is finished."

"Pardon me if I don't exactly take that as a promise of undying true love."

"I did not promise you my undying love. I gave you my name, my arm raised forever in protection of you, my wealth and my soul. What more do you want?"

"You promised me all of that? When?" Haley asked.

"Before the *amman*."

She hadn't known what the words spoken before the Muslim holy man had been, nor what she was saying by repeating certain words. "What did I promise?"

Zayn smiled and kissed her mouth, savoring the taste of her lips. "To honor me, to obey me and to give me sons of your body."

Haley wound her arms around his neck and drew his shoulders down to her. Outside, another bomb exploded and the building reverberated. The residue of desert heat washed into the lounge through the broken windows. She disregarded it all, pulling Zayn's head closer to her own.

"I don't think either of us will have the time for sons."

"We have time for ourselves—nothing else should matter," Zayn intoned reverently and dipped his head to capture her mouth. They had this moment for the rest of the vow. "I swore to myself days ago that when I made love to you, it would not be in a blind rush. I will be at my leisure, with all the time in the world to devote to worshiping every inch of you. I assure you, you will be satisfied completely, Issaeyaedea Haaris.''

Haley gasped and tightened her grip upon his shoulders, tormented by the truth that he always had her at her most vulnerable, while she never had but a scrap of his skin to touch and caress.

Another explosion sounded in the near distance. The embassy generator died and the lights flickered twice then went out altogether. Haley jerked her head sideways, looking to the heavy grillwork that protected the room. Zayn caught her jaw and pulled her face back to his.

"That was the resistance. They will be busy throughout the night."

Haley shivered. She pressed her forehead against his rough cheek. "That's a reassuring thought."

"You've no need to be frightened. I'll be with you. I will protect you with my life."

"Who protects you?"

"Allah and the good will of my people."

"I hate to be the dumb schmuck telling the emperor he's wearing no clothes, but judging by the way you treat—"

Zayn laid a restraining finger across her lips. "Don't," he suggested.

Haley tucked her finger inside the high collar of his *dishdasha* and deliberately snapped the top button. "All right. I won't say it. Let's talk about clothes. I'm not wearing any. Why is it you Arab men like this kind of garment? Guys back home would have their libidos all bent out of shape if they were wearing a robe. It certainly doesn't seem to affect yours."

Zayn laughed as he propped his elbow on the divan and gave her access to all his *dishdasha's* buttons if she liked. Her other hand dropped from his shoulder to speed up the process of disrobing him.

"Perhaps the answer to your question lies in the fact that an Arab doesn't flaunt his masculinity the way American men do."

"Now, that's a crock." Haley's mouth pulled to one side in wry disagreement. She kept her eyes on the buttons, opening one after another with suddenly clumsy fingers. An inefficient way to uncover his chest, but well worth the effort when she reached the last one and spread open the cotton cloth with slow, deliberate movements. "Oh, my."

"Hmm?" Zayn dropped his head, seeking the curve of her ear. "So you like my chest, do you?"

"I'd like it better if you would take this off," Haley suggested as she pushed material down his shoulders.

"Not yet." Zayn lowered his body slowly, feeling the heat of her breasts against his skin for the first time. He let his tongue trace the sensitive outline of her ear, then kissed her throat. Kiss by kiss he came back to her mouth.

Her lips were moist and parted, trembling as he covered them. She threaded her fingers through his chest hair, stroking and teasing, moving downward to touch his belly. He was glad the restraint of his own clothes slowed them down. He wanted to savor every sweet, delicious inch of her.

He drew her tongue inside his mouth, holding it, toying with it, then delved deep within her. She exhaled a muffled little groan of need and arched against him. Knowing what she wanted, he moved his hand to her woman's core. Her curls were tight and springy, damp against his fingertips. He cupped her, feeling her heat. It almost drove him over the brink.

A warm, delicious shiver made Haley gasp out loud. She pulled back from Zayn's kiss, a little alarmed. She hadn't ever let a man touch her as he was touching her.

He dropped a soft, reassuring kiss on the nearly invisible tremble of her full lips.

"In the desert, water is a most precious commodity," he told her. "Rain comes only a few times in a season. When the water flows, everything blooms. Flowers open overnight, fruit and leaves appear. All life is renewed. A woman is very like the desert. Here, where I am touching you, lies the well of eternity. A man lucky enough to hold and truly cherish this, life's sweetest well, in the palm of his hand is blessed many, many times. He will be loved and give love in return. He will have children born of the woman he cherishes, Allah willing. I would have that solace from you, Haale. Can you feel how your body flows like spring water rushing into a dry wadi for me?"

Haley felt the building turbulent sensations and closed her eyes, marveling at the gentle awakening of desire his hand coaxed from her as he parted and touched the soft inner folds. She could die from the pleasure of it. She nuzzled against his cheek, hearing the scratching of his unshaven jaw, touching her lips to his ear. "I feel as if I am melting, turning to liquid fire."

His touch became bolder, more aggressive, exploring. She tightened as his finger dipped inside her. There was a moment of small, burning pain that faded when he withdrew.

Shifting his weight, Zayn turned her face and kissed her deeply. She had brought him a gift he had not expected. Virginity. That pleased him more than he could ever say, but he regretted that their first joining would be accompanied by pain for her.

"Is something wrong? Why did you stop?" Haley asked.

"Shh." Zayn sat up, pulling the long tunic off, tossing it behind the divan.

"Oh." Haley closed her mouth, realizing that he'd stopped to take off his clothes. She pressed up on her elbows, squinting to make out his movements in the dark.

Boots dropped to the floor. Socks plopped over them. The zip of his trousers scraped. The springs in the divan groaned, accepting his weight once again.

He drew her against the length of his body, knees touching, thighs meeting, fingers entwined as palms meshed. His body was rough and hard, bristled with hair, scented of coffee and musk.

She closed her eyes as his lips touched hers and their kiss became one of merging desire and hunger. Words were no longer necessary. Haley welcomed him into her arms, waiting to learn secrets only he would teach her.

Under the press of her fingers, she discovered the steady hammering of his heart, the cadence becoming more familiar by the moment.

Her own heart heaved almost painfully in the tightness of her chest. Touching and being touched was so exquisite. She tasted the salty tang of his forehead, the warm sweetness of his mouth and ran her fingertips across his hair-covered chest. She loved the wonderful slickness of his upper arms, firm and hard with well-used muscle beneath taut skin. His throat was as rough as his unshaven cheeks against the caress of her lips. She couldn't help wondering how handsome he would be when his beard was full-grown.

He caught her hand, pulling it away from the curls on his chest and kissed her palm.

"Touch me, Haale."

He showed her how, holding her hand against his thickened shaft. Staring wild-eyed, Haley thanked the Lord for the darkness and the power failure. She swallowed a little convulsively, pressing her fingers around the throbbing, pulsing evidence of his desire for her. He was hard, the skin taut with tension.

"I want you very, very much." Zayn kissed her hungrily, turning her onto her back.

Haley opened her legs to him, trembling as he moved between her thighs, positioning himself. He looked down to where their bodies would merge and his fingers found that so-sensitive nub, stroking it with slow, agonizing sensuous rhythm. She arched upward against him, feeling the throb of his shaft at the edge of her.

Then he braced his hands on the divan, grasped her shoulders and began moving inside her, one slow stroke at a time.

The heat and pressure had built within her to a level of impossible-to-deny need. She felt the stretching of her body, his intrusion, coming so slowly, so steadily, until he filled her.

Haley did not realize she held on to his wrists and dug her fingernails into his veins. With one more bold and determined thrust, Zayn plunged into her, seated to the hilt. He dropped over her, drawing her into his embrace, kissing her deeply, his tongue dancing in rhythm, teaching her the pulse of lovemaking one beat at a time.

It was madness. Haley thought it would go on forever and ever, like a slow undulating dance. She was virgin by choice, but not ignorant of the ways of love. Nothing she'd ever imagined or heard of had prepared her for the reality of orgasm's building urges and pressing demanding need to reach completion.

She felt as if she were preparing to sky-dive, marking the target on the ground beneath her and stepping up to the edge of the door. There, the wind blasted at her, pushing her back and sucking her forward. She stood on the brink of the earth, caught and held off center, time and again, until finally she begged for release and let go of all restraints that kept her from plunging down from the heights.

Then she went over the edge.

Zayn caught her screams in his mouth. His body strained with the need to release, yet he held back deliberately, withholding his own pleasure for the joy of tasting hers. Then at last, her muscles tightened around him as fiercely as her long legs locked onto his hips. She drew him inside her, pulling and pulling, pleasing him like no other woman ever had.

Then he went rigid with explosion, his seed rushing inside her. His heart hammered erratically. He dropped his head to her shoulder, gasping for air, his sweat mingling with hers, pooling on their joined bellies.

"Oh, my," Haley whispered. "Momma never told me it would be like this."

# Chapter 16

Officially, the Saudi embassy closed at midnight, well within the deadline imposed upon all diplomatic missions by Iraq. Unofficially... according to Zayn's sources in the underground Kuwaiti resistance... most of the embassies continued operations covertly, resisting the occupation forces. Most notably the American charge d'affaire was barricaded behind their walls with a bunker mentality, deliberately holding out against the invasion forces.

The few Iraqi patrols that came near the Saudi embassy decided that the Bedouins camped in the embassy's outer courtyard could stay for a while. They had better pickings in other parts of the city, and while they were occupied with looting Kuwait's well-established businesses and harassing the American holdouts, the Saudi embassy remained a safe haven for those hidden behind its walls.

Several nights after the closing of the borders, Zayn and Haley moved to the subbasement of an upscale apartment complex that overlooked Kuwait's bay.

The Iraqis at that point had begun a systematic, street by street search for all things of value. Military trucks backed up to loading docks and stripped away each building's furnishings, including faucets, toilets and doorknobs. The building they moved into had already been looted, hence it was declared safe by the resistance.

With the whole city without electricity, telephones, gas and water, Haley wasn't very fond of the limitations placed upon normal living in the days that followed the closing of the borders. Modern buildings turned to furnaces in the relentless sun without air-conditioning. It wasn't all that much cooler in the subbasement. They did have water because the Iraqis had broken the pipes when they'd stripped the building, flooding part of the basement. As to how potable that water was, Haley didn't ask. No one left in Kuwait could afford to be picky.

Although she tried to sleep by the day, Haley found it impossible to really rest. It was too hot, too close, too dusty. And it seemed as if every time she did drop off, machine-gun fire jolted her awake. She would jerk upright, searching for Zayn in the dim shadows. Usually, she found him close by, in conversation with his allies.

She was jittery, with an ear always cocked to the roar of military vehicles on the streets. She couldn't ignore the sounds of strife that marred every hour of the day in Al Kuwait City. The longer they delayed, the more anxious Haley became. Conversely, the less she could fathom Zayn's stubborn refusal to make a move out of their safe hideaway.

Then she finally understood what he was waiting for when he led her out of the subbasement.

Zayn had waited for a *kaus,* a dust storm. It began in the late afternoon when the August heat was at its worst . . . a broiling 122 degrees. The hot wind blew off the desert and red sand obliterated the sky.

Stinging sand gusts roared through the canyonlike gorges of the empty, gutted modern buildings above them with galelike force. It drove the roaming patrols of Iraqi soldiers into shelters and blinded those who had to remain at their posts, guarding checkpoints on the main roads out of the city.

When dusk came, Zayn and Haley made their flight across Al Kuwait City's deserted streets on foot.

They were guided by two armed and cloaked members of the Kuwaiti resistance who knew which of the intersections manned by Iraqi soldiers had to be most avoided.

The city was really weird that night, unlike any city Haley had ever experienced. The *kaus* had a howl to it and showed no mercy to anything in its path. The force of the stinging sand could strip the paint from a new car. Haley didn't like what it did to human skin and eyes. She lost her contacts to the *kaus*. She couldn't get another pair until they reached Riyadh. If they ever did.

She judged the loss to the *kaus* a worthy cause. The sandstorm enabled Zayn to pass Iraqi checkpoints undetected.

At Al Jahrah they met back up with the Bedouins. Haley thought she recognized one or two of them from the embassy, but without her contacts, she wasn't certain. Besides, she was under the same stricture in departure, as she had been during their arrival...Zayn had forbidden her to speak—to anyone this time.

As jumpy as she was by then, she was obeying that edict to the letter.

Zayn blended right into the lean pack of swarthy mustachioed Bedouins. All claimed to be his cousin. The tribe's elders, his uncles, refused to give up their nomadic life. They had acquired a baby named Kasim at a hospital inside the city. Haley was given to understand that the baby's parents had been shot dead trying to escape the city on the day of the invasion. He was a grandson of one of the Saudi princes.

They held over at Al Jahrah until the storm died late in the night. The Bedouins acquired a Nissan truck. Haley didn't ask how. It didn't have any tags or inspection stickers and looked as if it had just come off a showroom floor.

The twelve of them, thirteen including Kasim, piled into the little truck and struck out across the oil fields northwest of Al Kuwait. Kasim squalled at every loud noise and rooted at Haley's breast relentlessly. She was the only woman on the truck. Haley prayed for milk she could never produce. The old driver, Uncle Haasan, nudged her ribs, dragged a bottle from a pack beneath his feet and flashed his gold-tooth at her.

Lost without language, Haley had fed the baby, rocked it in her arms and held her breath when they came upon an Iraqi checkpoint. It was daylight then. All roads to the south and west of Al Kuwait swelled with desperate people trying to escape the country.

It seemed as if a million people were moving west on foot. Foreign workers whose jobs ended when their employers, Kuwaiti citizens, were killed, arrested or taken hostage to Iraq, sought the faraway safe border of Jordan.

The soldiers manning the checkpoint couldn't begin to handle all the people that swarmed around them. They checked papers randomly. When one looked inside the cab of the Nissan, Haasan began a long harangue, complaining that the soldiers in the city had blown up his truck and injured three of his sons.

The soldier cast a skeptical look in the back of the pickup, but the bandaged Bedouins and their bloody clothes apparently convinced him that Haasan was telling the truth. He told the old Bedouin to drive west across the desert through Iraq. That was the quickest way around the crowded road to Basra.

Haasan turned onto the packed desert. He had no trouble finding his own way through the sand dunes.

Before nightfall they reached his main camp in the shadow of an oil field. The field had been commandeered by a squad of hungry Iraqi soldiers. They bartered for fresh mutton and asked for women to entertain them, offering liquor and boxes of stolen computers as payment. Some kind of deal had been reached. Haley didn't know the details. The old sheik had four computer monitors and one keyboard the next morning when camp was broken and the tribe packed up and moved on.

Six weeks later Haley was an old hand at desert living, having easily adapted to the simple, nomadic lifestyle of the Bedouins from waterhole to waterhole. Only a trickle of water flowed out of the rocks at their most recent campsite, but it was a steady flow down the uneven slope to the wadi. There it formed a shallow pool.

Haley sat on a red sandstone ledge bathing Kasim in the cool springwater as the sun sank into Iraq. Zayn's people scattered across the floor of the desert. The Bedouin men wore rifles slung across their shoulders and the women could sling a heavy roll of canvas from the bed of a truck or off a camel's back just as easily as they hoisted an infant into their arms.

A thousand sheep milled restlessly round the camp and the drying wadi. A troop of camels moaned and complained and refused to get onto their feet and out of the way of the thirsty horses.

Kasim's tiny face screwed up into a scowl and he bellowed with outrage as Haley doused his head with handfuls of cool water.

"Shh, shh," Haley crooned to him soothingly. She held his small body securely, soaping his feisty arms and legs. The whole procedure left her about as wet as the four-month-old infant. She sat back against a rock, pillowing the wet baby against her upraised knees. Picking up a corner of her long shawl, she used the soft cloth to blot the moisture from the baby's skin. In the dry heat of the desert, it was almost unnecessary to pat off anything but the creases of skin. Kasim hated having his face washed the most. His outrageous howl reminded her of that fact.

"Quiet him," a stern voice ordered in Arabic from high on the rocks.

"*Aeywah,*" Haley responded without looking back, and bent her head, crooning softly to the baby once more, receiving a toothless smile for her efforts.

Her command of his language improved daily. Zayn grinned proudly, taking his possessive gaze from the idyllic scene at the pool to the crevices in the rocks and shifting sands in the next valley. His eyes narrowed against the glare of the sunset, and remembering his purpose for standing guard, his expression hardened.

Haley slanted her eyes at Zayn with unveiled admiration. He looked as comfortable standing guard on the rocks with a rifle propped loosely against his hip as he had looked sauntering across the tarmac to her the first time she'd laid eyes on him. She liked it when he watched her.

Kasim tumbled his body forward against Haley's damp blouse and nuzzled for a breast. She patted the baby's head and offered him a bottle of goat's milk to drink. Even those small, insignificant motions drew Zayn's attention back to her. His woman was the worst distraction he had ever encountered. He turned his head until he could no longer see so much as a glimpse of her colorful skirt or golden hair. Maybe that would help him keep his mind on scouting.

"Kasim has grown nicely, don't you think?" Haley observed.

"*Aeywah,*" Zayn answered.

Haley pivoted, squinting in the softening light. The setting sun tinted the rocks red and gold. The finest part of the day had come. She strained her eyes to make out details of Zayn's form, the ever-present rifle, the long drape of his dusty burnoose. She ascertained his gaze upon her by the tightness of her breasts and the simmering heat centered in her belly. Her damp cottons clung to her.

Wetting one hand, she smoothed back her hair. It shone like a river of pure gold down her back. Zayn grunted softly, shifting uncomfortably as desire hardened him. He had consented to letting her come to his guard post because she had wanted to bathe herself and the baby before the night's march began.

"Are you...sulking because of last night?" Haley spoke haltingly, having to search for the correct words.

"If my honored uncle raises his offer to thirty camels and one stallion, he may have you," he said bluntly, and followed that with an explicit and testy curse.

"You *are* sulking." Haley laughed very softly. "Kasim is only a baby. He can't help waking up when strange noises disturb his sleep."

"In my next life I will beg for a wife who knows the value of expressing her pleasure in silence. It was not I who woke Kasim."

"But you were the one who knocked down the center support of the tent," Haley reminded him.

"I will forget the stallion and the camels. Haasan can have you for ten goats."

"Hmmph!" Haley fastened Kasim's diaper and stood up, deftly winding her shawl round her head and shoulders, completely covering all traces of her identity. With the long shawl the baby was securely fastened to her body and she had one arm free to use for other duties.

A hot breeze stirred her layered skirts around her bare feet. They were as tanned and brown as her hands and face. Zayn grinned because she fully comprehended his taunt.

"You can sleep with the camels tonight."

She turned to leave him, picking her way down the stony path. Zayn's boots scattered rocks as he bounded off his perch, following her. She was a fast learner in all things. From behind, there was no way of knowing she was not born to a nomadic tribe. Her walk was easy-gaited, her feet as sure as a goat's, her modest attention to customary dress as practiced as a woman born in Arabia. There the similarities ended.

The deep tan only enhanced her beauty. The sun had lightened her hair and her eyebrows. Her blue eyes were exotic. Every man in the tribe wanted her, every woman envied her. Yet they had accepted her. It was her adoring, unselfish care for the orphaned infant that earned her the Bedouins grudging respect.

Zayn drew abreast of Haley. The baby grinned at him. Haley bowed her head and kissed the child's soft cheek. ''Do not get so attached to the boy,'' Zayn cautioned. ''He is Arab and belongs to the desert.''

Zayn's words cut like a knife. Haley glared at him, a sharp retort springing to mind, but the effort to translate something cutting and deliberately nasty tied her tongue in a knot. Zayn walked past her, a shower of stones preceding his feet. She resorted to hissing in forbidden English, ''You're acting like a jealous pig! Kasim is only a baby!''

Zayn spun round, his dark face intimidating. He took the baby from her makeshift sling. He spoke clearly and slowly, to make certain she understood. ''I refuse to fight with you over someone else's baby. Go down to the camp and see to packing my belongings. Make yourself useful.''

Kasim howled, wailing for Haley's softer arms. Zayn tucked the boy firmly under his arm. Haley clamped her mouth shut, ground her teeth and fled down the hill of sand and rocks. He took the crying infant to Yamilla, his cousin with the toddling daughter. Kasim quieted once he was presented with a full breast to feast upon.

Zayn's feisty old uncle Haasan chuckled from his comfortable seat on a rug outside his tent. He never missed a thing that happened in his camp. Watching a woman run rings around his powerful nephew was the finest show he'd seen in years.

Haley paused a moment at the edge of the man's carpet to bow a polite, respectful greeting, then she ducked inside the darkness of the goat- and camel-skin tent.

Haley stomped her bare feet on a carpet and let out a curse. It wasn't her fault Kasim took exception to having Zayn make love to her. She hadn't been the one to wake the sleeping baby. Well, she wouldn't have if Zayn wasn't so impossibly thorough in his lovemaking.

She'd never thought she would complain about that. Though when they had first joined his uncle's tribe, she had been appalled at the idea of making love in a tent where someone else slept beyond a carpet or flap of camel skin.

Haley soon discovered that one became very accustomed to differentiating sounds in the desert at night. There might be the comforting crackle of a fire burning out or the significant snore from old Haasan. Even the animals had patterns to their nighttime calls and movements.

At first, she simply wouldn't consider making love at all, but gradually she became so relaxed that the lack of privacy no longer mattered. The Bedouins were very respectful of one's privacy. They treated all necessary bodily functions as a natural course of life itself. People regularly sneezed and passed wind and coughed, and no one paid it any attention. Judging from the varying ages of the children of the tribe, they had intercourse just as frequently.

Haley gathered shirts and washed trousers, packing hers and Zayn's few clothes into several secure rolls. She found her sandals and sat to fasten them on her callused feet.

A corner of the dividing flap lifted, and Kabira al-Sabah grinned at Haley.

"Do you need help?" Kabira asked. The camp was nearly packed. Only Haasan's tent needed to be dismantled. Kasim howled from nearby. His crying grated on Haley's nerves.

*"Lae."* Haley shook her head, gathering up a lone sock and Zayn's extra boots from under their carpet to tuck in the last pack. Kabira helped her lift her bundles and take them outside to a kneeling camel. Haley stood well away from the vicious biter's head, until it came her turn to tie up her packs.

The tribe's youngsters herded the sheep together, starting them on the southward trek across the desert. Haley knew they were deep in what was called the Neutral Zone, a no-man's land of scattered oil fields and red sand desert.

Water holes, such as the clear pool they'd come across yesterday, came few and far between. The stock was well rested, hence they would push deeper into the Summan for the next several days.

As the last tent was brought down, Haley listened to the commotion the men made, cursing a worn-out truck that wouldn't crank over. She could tell the truck needed new points and plugs, but trying to tell a Bedouin anything about their trucks was like trying to reason with a camel. It couldn't be done. Not if the one trying to use reason was a woman.

Haley really liked the Bedouins. They were a curious mixture of old and new. A 1990 Ford truck augmented the tribe's camels and horses. A late-model Nissan with four-wheel drive ran shotgun when they moved, but their workhorse was the ancient Mercedes that carried most of their tents and heavier possessions on its flatbed. Other than their ofttimes temperamental automobiles, their life-style was amazingly simple and uncomplicated.

They kept hours with the sun, rising early, resting when the heat was at its worst. Meals were important, communal and enjoyable, though cooking was very plain and the range of food limited. The majority of any day's work involved caring for the animals. Their nomadic philosophy was very basic. When one source of water began to dry up, they moved to another, herding sheep and goats across the desert.

When they camped, out came frames and dyed yarn. In the evenings, half the tribe sat to work on the most wonderful rugs Haley had ever seen. The other half tripped the light fantastic playing flutes and reeds and battered drums. The young women were wild sprites who lived each night to dance round a flickering fire.

Judging from the way the unmarried girls jangled their bracelets and coin-edged belts at her husband, Haley thought a few had a yen to be wife number two or three or four to Sheik Haji Haaris. Zayn had a very easy way of dealing with their flirtatious behavior. He laughed and joked with them and reminded them they were cousins. He bedded Haley.

Once, Yamilla had laughingly attempted to pull Haley into dancing with the women. Zayn had instantly laid his hand on her forearm and said only, *lae*. No.

Haley hadn't the foggiest idea what day of the week it was, though she did realize they were now in the month of October. Sometimes that bothered her greatly, especially when she thought about how worried her parents must be. It certainly didn't do her any good to fret about things she couldn't alter. The thing was, she felt very safe with Zayn's Bedouins, and she was very happy with Zayn.

* * *

Yamilla finished tying up her bundles and called to Haley to tie up her packs. Haley turned away from the noisy argument of the men over the ailing Mercedes truck. Minding the snapping teeth of the camel, Haley tied her and Zayn's bundled clothes secure. Her sandals slapped against her heels as she edged closer to the ailing truck.

Sheik Haasan threw up his hands, announcing they would have to leave the truck. His sons and nephews groaned, concurring, some cursing, others saying the vehicle had given many years and miles of service.

"So be it," Said, the sheik's eldest son, declared. He was guilty of flooding it. He climbed out of the battered, rickety interior.

"I can fix it." Haley tugged at Zayn's rolled-up sleeve as he tinkered under the hood. He glanced at her briefly.

"Go with the women."

The boys not herding the sheep and goats clambered onto the truck and began tossing down the packs and tents stacked on the flatbed. Youths brought up more camels. Haley got out of their way. The work of packing continued.

Zayn stood back, wiping his dirty hands on a rag and talking to Uncle Haasan before he reached up to take a bundle of tenting from three boys. Haley tugged on Zayn's sleeve again. Damn, but she hated the way women were brushed aside or blatantly ignored.

This time he turned around, his biceps bulging with the weight of the tenting. He snapped, "Haale, get out of the way!"

"Your wife has a habit of not obeying you," Said al-Sabah observed over the swaying neck of a camel.

"That's because she is an Americana *sheikka*," piped up ten-year-old Labid, moving a canvas pack as big as he was.

"I am not a *sheikka*," Haley corrected the boy. "I am an ordinary woman, no different from any others from my country. In America, women and men are equal. In Arabia, the only woman a man will listen to is a *sheikka*. But even then, I doubt it happens." She spoke the Arabic words correctly, not stumbling over any of them. Still the men all laughed, including Sheik Haasan.

"I can fix the truck," she repeated.

Zayn heaved his burden onto Said's camel. Said began lashing the bundle to a wooden frame.

"See. She never obeys you." Said spoke rather too disparagingly, from Haley's point of view. She shot the cousin a quelling look, not that it did much good.

"Give me your quirt," Zayn requested of Said.

Said laughed bluntly, "What for? You will not use it."

"You will whip her?" Labid popped up from the back of the camel, ropes dangling from his teeth. Said pulled out his quirt and handed it to his younger cousin. Haley stood her ground, her pointed gaze on Zayn.

Zayn grinned as he turned around to face her, the whip in his hand. He motioned to the southward-moving assortment of animals, people and vehicles, not lowering himself to repeat his command verbally.

Haley knew what he meant, but the truck was valuable. He knew that she knew there was no reason to leave it. He was smiling, which she knew meant he was not angry. Not like last night when the baby had caused such a ruckus the whole camp had woken. Haley turned to Sheik Haasan.

"Uncle Haasan, in Anaiza my husband has great need of a fine truck such as this one. He is much too proud to tell you that. Would you give it to him if I can start it?"

Old Haasan cackled. "No, I would not. It is much too valuable to me, and he is rich enough to buy fifty trucks better than it."

"Is it worth thirty camels and a fine Arabian stallion?"

"More than that, you foolish child."

"If it is worth so much, why would you leave it here? I can make it run like new."

"You, my child, make an old man wish he could run like new. But a truck..." His words dissolved into a crackly old man's laugh. "Do as you have been told, *lalla,* I hear your young one squalling. Stay here and defy your husband and you will wish he had left you behind in Al Kuwait."

Haley turned back to Zayn, "I can fix it."

"You have till the sunlight is gone to try," Zayn answered her. Which wasn't very damn long at all, Haley concluded. She kicked up her hem and clambered up on the truck's high bumper, reached inside the hood and began unscrewing the top of the air filter to get access to the carburetor. Labid scrambled up beside her and sat on the fender peering into the mass of greasy wires.

"Can you really fix it, *lalla?*" he asked incredulously.

"Of course." Haley grinned, inhaling the scent of gas and oil as if it was an old familiar friend. She handed the boy the filthy filter. "Go and bang all the dirt out of this, will you please, Labid?"

"Sure!" He was glad to help. Another set of shoulders joined her. Zayn's. He folded his arms, leaning forward, blocking her light.

"I don't care whether you make this truck run or not, my American princess. You go too far. You make me look a fool."

"No, I don't." Haley paused in scraping oily gummed sand out of the carburetor to look up at Zayn and read his expression. Daylight was rapidly fading. Contacts or no contacts, she could read his face just fine. His mouth was set, firm and unyielding. "I don't mean to."

Zayn reached a hand back to rub the muscles in his neck. "I know that. You are what you are. An adorably interfering American who has a solution for everything. It is part of your charm and your appeal to me. But to my cousins, you are a disobedient wife who needs to be disciplined. I do not like being put in the position of having to dispense desert justice. And with the troubles and worries that keep disturbing my thoughts regarding my country, I wish you would not provoke my temper."

"Saving face is that important to the Bedouins?"

"What do you think?" Zayn refolded his arms and watched what she did inside the engine.

Haley gave a negligent shrug, but she vowed to be more careful in the future. Even in the desert, one must keep up appearances.

She poked in the air baffle, knocking off the crust of carbon and said, "Once this truck is running, everyone will forget that I did not obey you when you told me to go join the women."

"To the Bedouin, fixing an engine is a man's job."

"Would you prefer it if I stand aside and tell you what to do?" She scraped the blade of a knife around the intake valve, freeing years of carbon buildup and gunk from inside it. "Do you know how to take out spark plugs and gap them?"

"No." Zayn's answer was bland.

"It is useful information. Want to learn?"

"No."

"Oh." Haley drew the sound out as she lifted the distributor cap and removed the rotor. She reached in a pocket and produced a nail nipper, opened it jackknife-fashion and used the tiny file to scrape the contact points. "What do you do when your car breaks down on some busy street in London?"

"Call for a wrecker, I suppose. My cars do not break down. Each of my chauffeurs are qualified mechanics and keep my vehicles in tip-top shape."

"It doesn't bother you to depend on other people?"

"I have better things to do with my time when I am in England and France than to tinker with engines."

"Such as?"

"I had a board seat on a corporation that managed a great deal of Kuwait's international assets."

Haley heard the ambiguity of his past-tense reference. Did that mean he thought his job was gone? She wondered what losses Bennett Industries had suffered. They were a drop in the bucket compared to the devastation of Kuwait.

She regretted the inability to communicate with the outside world. It must have been all of six or seven weeks since she had flown the goose back into Kuwait. Her father's injuries would be healed and he'd be back at work. Her mother would be worried sick about her. But Haley personally didn't have to worry about her job. It would always be there. She didn't have to worry about her home. She'd never lived anywhere except with her parents.

She decided it would be better if she tried to turn Zayn's thoughts away from his weightier troubles.

"So, you're really an accountant, eh?" Haley teased, looking for a lighter note. "Ah, exciting stuff, huh? I'm more of a hands-on person." Haley dropped the rotor back in its sleeve. "This truck needs a really good tune-up. It misfires badly. I can set the timing faster. That will help. Tell your cousin that it will lurch badly if he gives it too much gas. He has a heavy foot on the accelerator."

Labid popped up beside Zayn with the air filter. "Is this clean enough?"

"Excellent, Labid," Haley said. "You are the best air-filter cleaner I have ever met. Thank you." She banged it a couple of times against the fender. Very little sand fell out of it. "With care, even in the desert, a truck could last twenty, thirty years, but not a filter. Remember that, Labid."

She dropped the part into place and checked all the connections. "You can crank it up now," she told Zayn.

"No, not me. You may have the honor."

"No, I can't. I have to stay right here and adjust the choke. Labid, will you start the truck?"

"Can I?"

"No!" Zayn refused. "Nor will you remain here, leaning inside this blasted machine when it lurches into gear. The hood will crash down and break your spine."

"It's perfectly safe."

"No."

"You are the most obstinate man I have ever known."

"That is right, I am. Come, my darling. We have a date with destiny."

"Fine." Haley leaned against him and put a kiss on his lips. "I would very much like to have you all to myself for a while. Can we let the others go ahead of us and catch up later? I will scrub your back at the pool," she suggested.

Distracted by her quick, promising kiss, Zayn was tempted. "Regrettably, no. We're on hostile land. There is safety in numbers."

"Ah, well, I tried." Haley picked up the few tools, released the support on the hood and let it drop with a loud clank. She dropped the tools on the floor of the truck, under the pedals. "Before I face another camel ride, I'm going to start this truck."

Zayn passed more tools to Labid, then gestured graciously to Haley to take a seat inside the cab. "Be my guest. If you ask me nicely, I will put cushions on your saddle. You will need them when I am done."

"Promises, promises." Haley climbed into the cab. The cracked upholstery scratched. The springs complained. The clutch needed a power lifter to push it to the floor. It took the force of both her arms to press the stick shift to neutral. Undaunted, Haley smiled, accomplishing what no man present thought she could. Zayn leaned one foot against the running board, grinning.

"What will you give me if it works?" Haley teased.

"I will up my price for you to fifty camels."

"Fifty?" Haley considered that a definite improvement over his last claim of ten goats. She wasn't as insulted now as she had been the first time Haasan had offered Zayn twenty of the nasty creatures for her. "Just for the record, if one of these men decides to match your price, will you take it?"

"What do you think?"

# Chapter 17

Haley laughed. "I think all your bantering is just a tradition you men enjoy because it's more interesting to talk about horses and camels. After all, now you've got oil."

The corners of Zayn's mouth quirked. "The daylight is gone. Start your engine, Haale." Her name had a different sound on his lips and in his language.

Haley stood on the clutch, held her hip against the gearshift and cranked the starter. The engine fired and backfired. She pulled the choke, biting worriedly on her lip until the engine rumbled.

Delighted, Haley pumped the gas hard. The engine roared with sheer power firing. It was a triumphant sound that thrilled Haley all the way to her bones. How long had it been since she had felt the hum of an engine under her touch? Too long, too long, indeed.

Dancing across the flatbed, Labid yelled shrilly, "*Lalla* did it!"

Haley shoved the gearshift into first and let up on the clutch.

"Hang on," Haley warned, savoring the moment while she could. "We're going for a ride!"

Said al-Sabah leaped onto the opposite running board.

"*Lae!* I said no!" Zayn shouted. The truck lunged over its level sandbar, spewing rocks at the camels.

"Dammit Haale! I said start it, not drive it!" Zayn ran alongside. He jumped onto the running board. The open door swung at him, tumbling him gracelessly onto the stony desert. Labid howled with laughter. Camels lurched to their feet, bolting.

Said hollered, "*Lalla, lae!* You can't drive this old truck. Stop!"

"Oh, yes I can!" Haley shouted back. Cramming in the clutch, Haley fought for second gear, then gathered speed. The truck bolted into third gear on a fast roll down a bumpy hill, chasing goats and sheep.

"You did it, you did it!" Labid chanted.

"I sure did!" Haley gasped on the bouncy ride across the desert floor, plowing over boulders and bouncing into gullies.

It took the arms of an Olympic heavyweight wrestler to keep the jerky steering wheel on track. Said clung on, hauling himself hand over hand inside the cab. His huge hand shot out, grabbing the wheel, yanking it hard right.

The truck spun into a skidding, dust-spewing, rock-throwing, one-eighty turn. More sheep jumped and bleated and scattered. More camels howled and bolted, dragging tents and bundles in their wake.

"Step on the brake!" Said shouted.

Haley hammered in the horrible clutch, downshifting. A lamb cut across her path, chased by a small boy. She stood on both brake and clutch, fighting Said for control of the wheel, barely missing the child. The truck rumbled up a low embankment, sheep fleeing its bumper.

Then the wheels went over the revetment's top and slid through the sand hill, stopping in a billowing cloud of dust. Said shoved the gearshift into neutral, and the engine idled.

Haley sat back, weak and out of breath, the fun of the wild ride gone in what might have come to a tragedy. She put on the headlights. They gleamed into a melee.

A hundred sheep were stampeding away from the light's beam. Several floundered, tangling in the low desert brush. Then the oddest thing happened. One lamb flew skyward, spinning head over tail across the headlight's twin beam. Then another flew.

Said reached out and caught Haley's head, yanking her roughly downward onto the seat. He didn't move quite quickly enough. She saw the muzzle of the cannon move and the brush over it wasn't brush at all. It was camouflage netting.

"Get down!" Said shoved her to the floor.

Zayn caught up with the stalled truck, jumping onto the running board, grabbing the rocking door as he scrambled into the driver's seat.

"Labid, get in here," Said ordered his son. The boy instantly dropped inside the cab through the missing back window.

"Haley, get as far under the seat as you can," Zayn hissed in English, then in Arabic, "Cover her hair with something."

Haley didn't need to be told twice. She pressed herself under the seat as far as she could go, grabbed her hair and pulled it out of sight beneath Zayn's legs. She felt something heavy drop over her and the adjustment of three pair of legs as the men tried to hide her.

"Hello, my brothers." One Iraqi soldier sauntered out from under the netting. Perhaps a dozen more were busy chasing sheep out of their net-covered bunker. "Welcome to Little Baghdad."

Zayn cursed. He should have detected this nest of vipers when he'd stood watch. Said pulled his rifle from his shoulder and passed it to Zayn.

"Allah be with you." Zayn gave the usual greeting, hating having to use his hands for anything except getting his fingers on the rifle's trigger.

"What has happened to your truck?"

"It is most temperamental," Zayn explained. Labid pulled the camel skin over the stock, hiding it. The boy scooted to the edge of the seat, peering out the window, to see his first Iraqi tank. The great muzzle of the tank's gun was pointed right at them.

Just then, Sheik Haasan came riding his camel over the ridge and discovered Judgment Day. He fired his rifle into the air and trilled the tribe's war cry.

More Iraqis emerged from their underground bunker. Zayn could see their smiles gleaming in the headlights. They turned their machine guns skyward and fired a round. Then one trained his gun toward the ground and slaughtered the confused sheep with a blast of bullets.

"Be still," Said reassured his son, his hand firmly on the boy's trembling shoulder.

"How many are you?" The soldier at the window of the truck peered inside, fanning Zayn with sour, whiskey-laden breath.

"Five families, a thousand animals," Zayn replied. "Less now."

"Ah." The Iraqi shouted to his comrades to cease their firing. "We have need of fresh meat. They will not go to waste. Do you have cigarettes?"

"It is forbidden," Zayn answered.

He swung the muzzle of his gun at Zayn's face and casually leaned one arm on the door, looking hard at Zayn, studying him. "You are Sunni?"

"*Lae*, Shiite."

"Ah, so was I until I joined the army." The soldier slapped his chest, laughing at his joke. "It's desolate out here, far from Baghdad. There are no entertainments. We wait for days and do nothing but fill bags with sand. You will come and join us. We will roast the dead animals. Smoke and gamble. We have plenty of liquor, though if you are a religious man, you will not touch it, eh? Perhaps your boy will."

The barrel of his machine gun pointed ominously at Labid's handsome face. "What tribe are you from, boy?"

"He is—"

"Let the boy answer!"

"I am al-Sabah," Labid declared with innate nobility.

"Ah-ha! What direction have you come from?"

"East, behind the sand hills." Zayn pointed back to where they had been camped, within two kilometers of this outpost. His throat ran dry.

"Where are your women?"

Haley pressed her cheek against the floorboard. Her fingers clutched an adjustable spanner, gripping it so tightly her knuckles hurt. She had followed some of the discussion because the Iraqi spoke very loud. Zayn's increasing tension flowed through her. It was hard to hear his answers because the truck's engine hummed evenly now, warmed up and ready to run several hundred miles. Although she did hear Zayn's clipped response about the Bedouin women, "With the caravan."

"I think you will get out now, my Bedouin friend. You and the boy. You—" He nodded his head, indicating Said "—you will go and bring us five, six women, as many as you have that are young and beautiful. If you like, you may leave any *ferengi* women you have boldly tried to rescue from Al Kuwait."

"We have no foreign women. Our women are our mothers, wives and sisters."

"Now, why is it I do not believe you, Bedouin?" He jammed the barrel of his gun into the soft tissue under Zayn's jaw and lazily reached forward, picking one long golden hair from the shoulder of his burnoose. "This is not fiber from a lamb or a camel, Bedouin."

"You are correct," Zayn relented. "It is from the tail of my Arabian. Walk to the ridge and you will see we have many white horses with us."

"I don't want a horse. I want a woman. Now, do as I said. Get out of the truck, now! Take the boy with you. Do not bring any old crones whose bellies have stretched and breasts hang to their knees. Tell your old sheik that if he values his son and grandson to do as we say. You may camp five kilometers west of here. When we are done with your women, we will send them to you."

Haley raised her head, bumping Zayn's leg. The door of the truck jerked open. "Get out, or I'll shoot the boy," the soldier said.

"The truck will stall if I release the clutch," Zayn told him. He forced the stick shift forward. The gears ground terribly.

Haley turned her head, twisting her arm free, the wrench a ready weapon in her hand.

"I said, get out. To the devil with your truck." The Iraqi fired his weapon, splaying bullets into the truck bed. They thudded into the sand, ricocheted off the steel and burst the tires. The truck lurched sideways. The door swung wide open.

Zayn dropped his hand from the gearshift, his fingers finding the trigger of his gun. Haley slammed the wrench as hard as she could into the soldier's crotch. It was the best target she had. His burping gun went silent.

One more bullet exploded with deafening force inside the truck as Zayn shot the soldier.

"Get out!" Zayn tossed the smoking rifle back to Said.

The Bedouin caught the gun and grabbed his son, leaping clear of the truck in one mighty jump. Zayn was out of the truck, catching Haley's shoulders and hauling her roughly from the floor.

"Run!" he ordered, pushing her over the body of the writhing Iraqi.

Behind them the truck lights blinded the Iraqis.

There were shouts and confusion. Zayn pushed Haley over the revetment of sand, shoving her forward as a line of machine-gun fire hit the sand.

She fell, rolling, Zayn's body slamming into hers. They tumbled over and over to the bottom of the small hill, then Zayn covered her.

The cannon exploded. A mortar shell fired with deadly accuracy at short range, blew the truck to kingdom come. A huge fireball filled the sky. Bullets whistled through the dune, sending a small avalanche of sand down on top of them.

Camel and sheep screamed. The single clap of Bedouin rifles returning fire echoed nearby. A hail of raining parts and burning shrapnel pounded into the sand all around Zayn and Haley. She saw something strike him. Elsewhere, someone else screamed, wounded.

"Come on." Zayn commanded in Haley's ear, hauling her onto her shaking legs. The glow of the fire consuming the truck was behind them. Ahead, the desert was pitch black.

But it wasn't silent. The Bedouins had taken positions and fired single rounds, accurate and deadly, into the heart of the Iraqi bunker.

They ran, Zayn dragging and pushing Haley ahead of him.

One of his cousins boldly crept up the backside of the revetment. The Iraqis were busy firing their machine guns at the darkness beyond the burning truck. He struck the flint of a disposable lighter and lit the swatch of cotton hanging from a bottle of gasoline. Then he bravely stood on the rise behind them and tossed the Molotov cocktail into the cab of the tank.

The explosion and fire turned men into screaming torches, rolling and jumping in the sand. Others fled the fire in their bunker, only to find their own ridge lined with rifles poking over the sand. They were shot down one by one.

The stench of burning flesh and bloody wool filled the bowl of earth. There was no more movement.

Sheik Haasan stood and motioned his sons and nephews to remain where they were. A suffering Iraqi turned his hairless, melted head and face toward the old Bedouin. His bloody hands begged for mercy. Haasan raised his rifle stock to his shoulder, his gnarled finger pulled the trigger.

"An eye for an eye." he intoned solemnly. "Allah curse your soul for eternity."

"For al-Sabah!" Ten voices chanted from the dune.

The last bullet echoed across the desert. Zayn's legs buckled under him. Haley tumbled to the earth with him. Her chest labored, burning in agony. Her legs screamed with pain. Zayn's body nearly crushed hers. A cough choked with dust racked her.

"Haley." Zayn's fingers dug into her flesh, tugging on cloth. "I can't get up."

"You're hurt," she managed to say those words. Nothing else. She coughed again, three short bursts to clear her aching lungs. She had never run like that in her life.

Digging her fingers into the sand, she pushed to raise herself. His weight pinned her legs. His head drooped across her belly.

Haley put her hand on him and felt something warm and sticky soaking his back. "Zayn!"

"It's all right." He clutched her waist, holding on to her. The pain subsided a little. He inched his body up hers, pressing her down into the sand.

"Zayn." Haley wrapped her arms around his shoulders, holding him tight. "Let me get up. Let me help you. Oh, God, oh, God, you're bleeding."

"Hush, shh, shh. Haasan will find us. Be quiet." His fingers stroked her face. He laid his cheek against hers.

"For the love of God, you'll bleed to death!"

"Shh! It's all right...a flesh wound. Nothing more. Kiss me." His lips pressed against her mouth.

Haley grasped his head between her fingers and kissed him with all the hungering, desperate, grateful love she held for him in her heart.

"Slowly, my love," Zayn cautioned, smiling at her. "Remember, I told you, we have all the time in the world."

Haley wasn't exactly of the same opinion, even if she wished it were true. She accepted his kiss and kissed him in return. But not much time passed before Uncle Haasan found them. Zayn was lifted onto the bed of the little pickup for some impromptu surgery.

Five pieces of shrapnel were picked out of his back, most of which were embedded in his right shoulder and hip. The wounds were carefully cleaned, stitched and dressed by Yamilla. The communal medicine chest was well supplied with antibiotics and sterile bandages.

Less than an hour later, they were on the move south once more. Sheik Haasan very much wanted to put good distance between his tribe and the burned-out Iraqi bunker.

So did Haley.

# Chapter 18

No one told Haley she was in Saudi Arabia. After meeting the Iraqis, they moved steadily due south for three days, stopping only to rest the animals. No tents had been set up. Sheik Haasan wouldn't risk making camp for longer than it took to make meal cakes on a griddle.

A painful stitch tugged at Haley's side, a cramp from the sling that kept Kasim anchored to her. She needed her hands to beat the stick on the ground that kept the sheep moving. Labid was her shepherd partner for this section of the flock.

She wanted to sit down and rest and wait for Zayn. The sheep wanted water and something to eat. So she and Labid kept moving, dutifully herding the animals across the barren land.

"Don't worry, *lalla*. There is water up ahead," Labid reminded her. "A smaller oasis than the last one, but it is not far now."

Which Haley told herself could be another march of twenty or thirty miles. How could she know? She couldn't see date palms in the dark. Even if she'd known where to look, without her contacts, she couldn't see clearly past the reach of her own arm.

"You don't think I would get us lost, do you?"

Glancing back, Haley was comforted by the nearby presence of other bleating sheep. She could make out the silhouettes of camel riders against the pearly glow of the rising moon and hear the putter of the Nissan's engine bringing up the rear. "No, we are fine," she said.

At their last resting place, the tribe had taken some time to reorganize, tightening up the spread of camels, horses and sheep. Zayn and four of his cousins had ridden out on horseback to scout the western stretch of desert. There had been more precautions taken since their deadly meeting with the Iraqis.

The stars came out and the moon rose, a wonderful moon, full and bright. There were no lights from civilization to dull them, nor clouds or pollution to haze. The temperature dropped rapidly. Inside the coil of her shawl, Kasim cuddled warm and secure against Haley's body. Acclimatized now to the desert's dramatic changes, she realized that she liked the strange, austere landscape.

Camels grunted, moving in a surefooted line parallel to her. A large cloud of rising dust showed her where the main herd was. She cocked her ear to sounds beyond the bleating noise of her sheep.

"*Lalla,* the sheik is coming," Labid said.

Haley squinted at the distance. "Is it your grandfather?"

"No, *lalla.* It is Sheik Haaris."

"Oh." Haley proudly squared her shoulders. "Yes, I hear his horse, too. Let's keep moving, shall we?"

"Maybe we'd better wait," Labid said carefully.

"Don't be silly, they are catching up."

"My father will whip me for going so far from the tribe."

"I will tell him how well you protect me."

"It will not help. I know my duty. My father knows it, too. I don't think he has forgiven me for the truck. He said that I am at fault for encouraging you in your wildness. I am sorry if I caused you to be beaten."

"By whom? I haven't been touched."

"Sheik Zayn did not beat you for driving the truck into the nest of Iraqis?" Labid said incredulously.

Haley wanted to say that Zayn was in no condition to beat anyone after having five pieces of shrapnel picked from his back. That wouldn't do any good for his esteem among the

Bedouins. Haley raised her chin proudly. "He thanked me for taking him where he had the chance to kill his enemies."

"Ahh," Labid responded. "I understand."

The boy understood that his way of life demanded retaliation in kind. Haley sighed, she couldn't argue with that rationale in these circumstances. Her own horror had certainly tempered to justice at the sight of Zayn's bloody back.

"Oh, Labid, I hope someday you understand that all people must be free to choose their own way, even ladies who like to drive trucks. Come, let us go a little farther. Sheik Haaris will reach us soon enough."

Haley whistled at the sheep and snapped her stick upon the ground. She was good at this job; even blind as a bat, she could find white woolly creatures and keep them together. They trotted along, ambling, then suddenly the leading pair went tumbling over a ditch in the sand.

"What the hell!" someone shouted. Then more lambs tumbled. Another curse rent the air. A man stood buried to his hips, gripping a wiggling lamb.

Stick raised to clobber a predator, Haley screamed as she recognized the man as a soldier standing upright in a foxhole.

"Halt!" he ordered. He threw the lamb aside to snatch up his rifle and point it at Haley. "Who goes there?"

"*Lalla!*" Labid broke into a run through the milling sheep.

"What are you doing here?" Haley shouted. "You scared me half to death!"

"Me! What are *you* doing here?"

Labid cut loose with an ear-splitting Bedouin war cry and hurled his body between Haley and the soldier, ready to do battle with a stick. "Run to the women, *lalla!*"

The sheep bleated and ran. Across the desert floor shots fired. Haley snatched the boy off his feet, pulling him away from the armed marine.

"Don't shoot!" she ordered. "We're friendly. What in the name of heaven are you doing here?"

Just as thoroughly surprised, the solder shouted back, "I'm stationed here, lady. Are you an American?"

"*Lalla,* run, I will save you!"

"I'm more than American." Haley declared. "I'm Texan!"

"I'll be damned, lady, so am I. Welcome home."

"Haley!" Zayn thundered, emerging from the blanket of darkness on a charging Arabian horse. It skidded to a halt between her and the soldier. Under her heavy shawl, Kasim cut loose with an angry disturbed howl.

"Zayn, it's the U.S. Marines. The marines are here! What are they doing here?" She lifted the baby out of confinement and settled him on her shoulder, patting him reassuringly.

A radio crackled and a voice demanded to know what was happening. "Sarge, it's me, Woodie, point 7-57-Alpha. I've got a woman and a screaming kid, about ten thousand sheep and a tribe of Bedouins coming across the border."

"Haley, go back to the women," Zayn said as he dropped from his tasseled saddle.

"He's a marine, Zayn." Haley exclaimed again. "We're safe. We made it!"

"Are you refugees from Kuwait?" The soldier's backup came forward, rifle ready, but asking questions first.

"You bet we are," Haley declared.

Zayn stepped between her and the marine, pointing to the shadowy distance where there was safety in the tribe. Needing to calm and change Kasim, Haley hurried back to the caravan with news that would probably make old Haasan's *kuffiyah* spin.

Labid turned the sheep and trotted up beside her.

"Who are they? They are not Saudi soldiers."

"No, no, they aren't," Haley answered the boy. "They are my people, marines."

"Americans? Marines? Why are they here?" The boy's curiosity was clearly too great to tolerate being left out of the men's business. He charged back to Zayn and procured a job, holding the horse.

Haley was torn, not knowing which way to go, back to the security of the Bedouins, or toward the protection of American marines. Which way was safety?

Then the horror of the truth sunk in. Marines in the Saudi desert meant only one thing. War.

Tears formed in her eyes, and this time Haley made no effort to staunch them. She sought the security of the women. There she cuddled Kasim and cried as he clutched his fat little arms around her neck. She knelt on the ground, rocking back and forth, crooning soft words to him, soothing him with kisses and warm hands.

Dear God, how would she part with this baby she had grown to love so much? After this time in the desert, she felt like his mother. Being a mother was a very nice feeling.

Women and children settled around her, a wall of security and protection while the men gravitated to the discussion at the foxhole. Before long, a jeep-like armored vehicle rolled out of the distant darkness, two others racing after it. More American soldiers joined the Bedouins.

The crackle and pop of radios mixed with sounds of desert creatures scuttling across the sand hunting for food. Before she shifted any part of her body, Haley carefully looked around for scorpions or centipedes searching for scarabs to eat.

Kabira tried to interest Haley in some coffee and a few biscuits. "I can't eat," Haley admitted to Said al-Sabah's wife. "I'm too tied up in knots."

"They are your people, Haale?" the Bedouin woman asked. All the women had donned their veils. Haley didn't have a veil, but she drew her shawl over her head, tucking part of it over her face. Kabira's dark eyes assessed the young marines with interest. "Now I understand why you are so tall and handsome."

Yamilla shifted her sleeping daughter in her arms and turned to look at the American soldiers.

"They are not my family," Haley explained. "They are countrymen. Not all of them are tall and blond. There are all kinds of people in America, from every country in the world."

Yamilla shook her head solemnly. "I do not understand. Clans must stay together, united against others. You will know what I mean by that when you meet Sheik Haaris's wife. She is very beautiful, but she rules with a fierce and jealous hand. Her sons are treated differently than any others have been. It is not easy to be a second or third wife. You will see."

"What?" Haley swallowed. "The sheik has other wives?"

"Of course," Yamilla said expressively. "Four wives are a tradition with the al-Haaris clan. That is why they are blessed with many, many sons and much power."

This was the first that Haley had heard of that. She paled behind the cotton head covering. Her mind and her thoughts were a complete blur. Before she'd gotten herself into this mess, had she asked if Zayn was married? Good Lord, she couldn't remember. What she did remember was that he had assured her their marriage need not be binding to either of them. It was expedient at the time, the most necessary course of action.

She wondered what arrangements Zayn was making. Would he just turn her over to the Americans? Would he return to Kuwait and join the resistance?

"You should try to sleep a while. I will hold Kasim if you like." Kabira broke into Haley's tumultuous thoughts.

"No, he is fine." Haley vowed not to release the baby one minute before she had to.

Soon, much, much too soon, there were bright lights in the sky and lots of noise—helicopters sweeping northward. The first machine that landed created a sandstorm below it; it bore the symbol of America, stars and stripes.

The helicopter was American, marine issue, but the officers climbing out of it were Saudis. They were there to pick up Zayn.

He angled his way through the tribe, clasping arms, saying his words of thanks until he came to the women surrounding Haley. He did not step into the group, nor did he speak to any except his elder uncle. Kasim slept with his thumb in his mouth. Kabira pressed a bottle of fresh goat's milk into Haley's hand and whispered to her, "The sheik waits for you. Go now."

Labid tugged on Haley's arm. "*Lalla*, I am sorry I did not have to protect you. If you come back, maybe I will have another chance. I like it when you drive the truck. That was more fun than when my poppa drives it."

"Thank you, Labid." Haley kissed the young boy's cheek. "I will try my best to come back and see you again. I am honored that you are my friend."

"Come, Haley." Zayn took hold of her arm, drawing her away, into the helicopter.

The Blackhawk's blades circled, kicking up swirls of dirt. Kasim didn't like the wind and screamed, but no one could hear his crying except Haley.

At King Khalid Military City, a squadron of Kuwaiti and Saudi soldiers mustered out in the dead of night to greet their general. Zayn leaped out of the helicopter into a welcome of joyous shouts. He waved a hand to the men beyond the sweep of the chopper's blades and reached back to help Haley to the ground.

Haley saw him wince as he flexed his shoulders. "We made it!" he shouted triumphantly.

She nodded, her throat too constricted to speak. He put his arm around her waist and they both ran, ducking instinctively lower until they cleared the sweep of the chopper's rotating blades.

He was joined by wildly jubilant Kuwaiti soldiers and Saudi comrades who had been informed he was safely returning from the occupied territory. The Saudis rolled out their best military red carpet to welcome him as a returning hero. They had thought him dead, lost forever.

There were so few Kuwaiti soldiers and they knew each other well. Beneath the celebration was sadness born of grief and loss. A month ago, they had been countrymen. Now they were homeless refugees, men without a country.

A Saudi doctor came and took Kasim from Haley. A translator informed Haley that Kasim was a prince and very, very much wanted by his grandfather. She should have felt relieved, but letting go of the baby was the hardest thing she'd ever had to do. She stroked Kasim's shock of dark hair, kissed him one last time and let him go.

Haley pulled away from the happy Arab crowd, a lone woman, out of place and hurting more than she ever believed possible.

It was over.

She walked out of the hangar into the desert night. Beyond the celebration of Zayn's return there was quiet. The American crew of the Blackhawk lingered beside it, drinking coffee from disposable cups. The pilot and copilot looked at her. One laughed and said, "That's the first woman I've seen since coming to Saudi. Will they all be dressed like that?"

The other chuckled, muttering a response too low for Haley to hear. Neither realized that she could understand them. She didn't know who to turn to. She wasn't Arab, Saudi or Kuwaiti, but she had lost something of what it meant to be American. Where did she belong now?

Was the Vixen still here? She could go home this very moment if it was.

Haley sighed. Zayn was in his element, bustling about giving orders that people would jump to obey. After a while, he came out, looking for her, puzzled by her disappearance. He was clearly relieved when he found her.

He drew her to him, dislodging the covering of her shawl, kissing her, his arms tight around her. The kiss surprised Haley. The color of her hair glowing in the moonlight surprised all of the lounging marines.

Haley shivered, knowing the Saudis didn't tolerate outrageous displays of affection, even from a sheik.

"Why are you so moody?" Zayn asked. "We are safe now. We must hurry. I have made arrangements for us to go to Anaiza."

Haley resisted being swept away by his elation. He didn't even realize Kasim was gone. "What about your shoulder?"

"That is nothing. I want to go home. A doctor can see me there." Zayn gripped her arms with both his forceful hands. "What is the matter, Haley?"

"You wouldn't understand in a million years!"

His hands dropped. They faced one another, practically on the same ground where they had faced off the very first time. This time the battle lines were obscure. Zayn's natural arrogance and fierce Arab pride made him tower over her. Haley knew why. An Arab wife did not argue with her husband in public.

"We are going to Anaiza. End of discussion."

"Have you consulted me about that? I think you have assumed a great deal, Sheik Zayn Haaris." Haley turned away, stomping past the conclave of soldiers. Their argument had pinned the ears back of every Arab and brought looks of genuine interest from the Americans.

Fine, she thought rebelliously. He hadn't consulted her for one damned minute before he'd radioed ahead to Kasim's family and made arrangements for him. Well, she wasn't a helpless infant, needing someone to speak on her behalf. She had a voice of her own, opinions that mattered. Dammit, she loved him. Couldn't he think of how she felt being left out of every important decision? No, he couldn't. Arab men weren't programmed to think like that.

Her long-legged, angry stride ate up the concrete. Some distance from the open hangar, a jeep scooted to a slow roll, keeping pace with her determined stalk. Zayn leaped out of the moving vehicle. Haley shouted at him and his driver. "Go away!"

"I have chased you for the last time." He bounded across the paving and blocked her path. "Get in the jeep."

"You'll be very sorry if you touch me," Haley warned him. "I'm very, very angry and I'm hurt and I want to be alone."

Zayn cast an exasperated look at his driver, motioning him to wait. He dropped his hands to his sides, useless appendages at the moment. "Why are you angry? What has hurt you? Haley, I will move the sands from here to the sea to fix it, if you will just tell me what is wrong."

Haley's angry face screwed up in conflicting knots. "Kasim." She blurted out the baby's name. She held another more painful hurt inside, the revelation that she was not Zayn's only wife. She couldn't live with that. Not ever.

"Kasim?" Zayn stared down at her, at that bulky shawl she'd worn for ages inside of which there had always seemed to be a grinning, drooling infant anytime he'd wanted to touch her. "Where is he?"

"Gone." Haley burst into tears. "A doctor from Riyadh rushed here immediately to get him. He took him. I didn't even have a chance to properly say goodbye. I wanted to write his grandparents a letter about how well he took the journey and send it with him. There is no time for anything that really matters."

"Haley, let's go someplace private to sort this out."

"No. Don't touch me. You had no right to take Kasim like that! You could have given me time. Given the baby time. I love him!"

"I did not take Kasim away from you."

He took hold of her shoulders carefully and drew her against his body.

"Yes, you did!" Haley pounded a very weak, exhausted fist against his chest. "No one gave us any time. He cried! For the love of God, he's just a little baby!"

Zayn wrapped her in his arms, hugging her tightly. "Haley, I only asked the pilot to radio ahead to his grandfather that the boy was safe. You must know by now that an Arab will move heaven and earth to protect his children."

Haley sniffed and pushed herself away from his embrace.

"Where do you think you are going?" Zayn caught her arm, preventing her from walking away.

"I don't know. I don't belong here." She wagged her hand at the base, the buildings surrounding them.

"Then will you please get in the jeep and let me take you away from here?"

"No. I don't want to go inside any building with you. You always lock me up."

"Haley, I am going to take you to Anaiza."

She stared at him, feeling all the hurts and pain moving like a flood of water inside of her. "Zayn, I think I really want to go home right now. I don't know. Maybe it was finally hearing my own language spoken. I'm homesick. I need to go home."

"Fine. You want to go home. Please get in the jeep so that we can get some rest sometime tonight. I want a bath, a hot meal and a decent bed under my back. I don't want to stand out here arguing until dawn."

"You will take me to the airport at Riyadh? Now?"

Zayn took a deep breath. What good would it do him to lie to her? Then she would only add another sin to his mounting list of errors against her. "No. I will not take you to Riyadh now. I just told you exactly the order of what I am willing to do this night. A bath, a hot meal and a decent bed. Get in the jeep."

"All right." She circled around him. It was the fourth time he'd made the order and twice he'd said please. She was counting things like that. It was important to her. When they first met, he'd declared himself a man who never repeated a command twice. He had changed, as far as she was concerned.

Inside the jeep, Haley leaned her cheek against Zayn's shoulder, accepting the comfort of his left arm wrapped around her.

The vehicle zipped past three blocks and a runway that was lit up like a county park on the Fourth of July. She would swear she saw C-5's being unloaded, those huge lumbering cargo ships that flew in and out of Kelly Air Force Base back home.

Then, she really didn't know what she was seeing. Her eyes hurt from the constant strain of overusing them. It wasn't tears, she told herself. The jeep stopped beside a helicopter. It was manned by a three-man crew, the rotors already spinning.

"We aren't going to spend the night here?" Haley asked. He had that tiny apartment.

"No. There is no room for us here. There are close to a hundred thousand soldiers here. We are going to Anaiza, now."

"I am not going to Anaiza. Give me the key to my Vixen and I'll go home tonight."

"No, Haley. Stop pushing me."

"Quit bullying me!" Haley resisted being pulled out of the jeep.

"Then do as I ask."

"I can't go to Anaiza looking like this. I'm filthy. Your...your servants . . . your family will think badly of me."

Zayn snapped. He dropped his hands to the side of the jeep and leaned menacingly over her, his face black as thunder. The private at the wheel stared rigidly ahead into the black night. "Get out of this jeep and get on that helicopter. Fasten your seat belt and don't say another word."

Haley started to balk, but then she decided she'd said enough. She cast a backward fulminating glare at him as she hiked up her skirt and climbed onto the helicopter. Zayn was right behind her. The rotors hit high whine. She dropped onto the hard bench, snapped her seat belt in place and glared to the empty rear of the chopper.

Zayn left her alone. She tried to figure out how she was going to face the pain that would come with eventual separation from him. That would hurt even worse than letting go of Kasim. Not that she came up with any plausible means to lessen the hurt. She wanted the parting over and done with. A clean break. She couldn't think of any possible reason for her to meet his family. They weren't going to approve of her.

It would have been better all the way around if they had just parted at the base. Haley slumped against the wall and closed her eyes. Her arms, so accustomed to a baby's weight, felt empty. What would she do without Kasim? Without Zayn?

The flight went on, endlessly. Sleep evaded her. The closer they came to Anaiza, the more she tensed.

# Chapter 19

There were very few lights in the compound and less in the little town in the valley below it, Haley noticed as the chopper lowered onto the landing pad at Anaiza. Men from the house bounded up the outer steps to welcome Zayn. Haley recognized only Ali. Two other men whooped a warm greeting to Zayn, clasping him warmly, kissing both his cheeks.

Within the great hall, Haley had ample light to see details of the two new men. One was introduced to her as Saul, the second, Daud Haj Haaris. Saul sported a bushy mustache. Daud wore glasses like Quadir. Haley was briefly introduced as Zayn's wife. Their reactions were stiff and formal. They welcomed her into their family, but no one pressed for details. She knew they didn't like her.

The servant, Ali, bowed to her and detained her hand with reserve. "You caused us many worried moments, Issaeyaedea Haaris. I have promised my sheik that will never happen again. Your safety and well-being is our greatest concern. Welcome home."

A sleeping quiet reigned inside the palace. The three brothers exchanged limited information. Haley waited for the bomb to fall . . . for the brothers to tell Zayn his Kuwaiti wife and children resided safe and sound within, but no one said that. Haley's knees quaked visibly when Zayn grasped her hand, wished his brothers an abrupt good-night and hauled her along in his wake to another wing.

Even if she'd tried, Haley couldn't have broken his grip upon her wrist. She tripped along behind him, clutching her skirts and dragging the shawl, running to keep up. They came to a gallery, bounded by gardens on one side and swimming pool on the other. Then all at once, they were in a private master bedroom whose proportions could only be termed gigantic.

Zayn closed the door firmly, dropped her hand and pointed to an opening on the right wall. "The bathroom is over there. You've got five minutes if you want to shower alone."

Before Haley had walked ten paces to that door, a servant emerged from another door, welcoming the sheik, asking how he could be of service. Haley ducked inside the bath. She'd played racquetball in smaller places.

The servant brought her heated towels and a robe, and turned on the water in the shower. It flowed from spigots on three walls. There wasn't a door for privacy. Haley made certain the man departed before undressing. She managed a desultory scrub, nothing more.

"Time's up," Zayn announced. He strolled in, a towel wrapped around his hips.

Haley relinquished the shower to him. Not that there wasn't room enough for both of them. If he decided to collect a harem of fifty, he could invite them all in for a shower together. She pulled the toweling robe over her wet body and sat on a bench, watching him, trying to get her nerve up to ask him for the truth. The real truth, starting with how much she loved him. On second thought, maybe ending with that might be better.

"You are really done in," she heard him say.

She jerked her head up to find that he was out of the shower, the water had been turned off and he was back in that sexy little towel skirting his hips.

"Come on." He offered her his hand, and Haley took it.

She wasn't positive how it happened, but the next thing she was absolutely certain of was his hot and hard body pressing her down into the soft, silken comfort of his expansive bed.

There weren't any rocks poking through the carpets at her back. There wasn't a sleeping baby tucked into the nearby corner. His lips were moist and soothing as they touched her skin.

Her limbs were leaden but malleable. She had no resistance; she wanted and needed him desperately.

He kissed her belly and opened her thighs and told her she would feel much, much better afterward. Then he kissed her where he'd never kissed her before, his mouth hot and famished, a torment to her tired, guilty soul. It was absolutely more than Haley could bear.

He wasn't supposed to give to her when she was such a brat, such a horrible, selfish fool who could not share the most wonderful man in the world with another woman. It hurt her to the depths of her soul to think that he might have been this intimate with another.

She tried to stop him, tried to pull his head up, but his strength remained intact, enough of it that her weak protests made no difference. His tongue stroked and tormented and teased her until she screamed with need, begging him to plunge inside her and satisfy the horrible ache he'd ignited. But he didn't stop. He wouldn't give her that filling release.

Zayn shook away her grasping hands and took his time, deliberately. He had learned her body slowly and carefully since he had first tasted it in Kuwait. Zayn had waited a long, long time to have her in his own private and secure apartment. Where lights blazed brightly. Where she could scream and beg and moan or threaten or cry. He savored every orgasm she experienced, every nuance of bringing her to the utmost limit of her senses.

He wasn't going to wait for her to wake up refreshed and restored and fighting mad, demanding to be on the first westbound plane out of Riyadh, tomorrow. Because after what she'd been through, she felt just as he did: she wanted home. So he took advantage of her weakness now and seduced her thoroughly.

Haley's breath shortened into gasping sobs when he planted himself within her tight swollen sheath. Her breasts hardened with passion, full and tight and aching from his delirious suckling. He kissed her deeply. His tongue dueled with hers as his shaft matched the ritual dance within her throbbing, contracting womb.

He was giving her his soul and his son, God willing.

The tension and heat mounted between them and he rode hard. The lesson was hers to learn. He wasn't ever letting her go. She did not realize that, yet.

The time would come when she did.

Haley screamed when his seed flooded hot within her. Zayn fell upon her, cradled in her arms, pillowed by her welcoming hips. Her body trembled, her inner thighs shaking with contractions that soothed and softened him. Her hands stroked across knotted muscles of his back, banking the fires for the night.

Zayn kissed her swollen mouth and smoothed back her damp tangled hair. He settled her to his side, cradled in the curve of his arm, patted her hip reassuringly. "Sleep well, Issaeyaedea Haaris."

Haley drew in a ragged breath. "Zayn, there is something—"

One finger of his right hand pressed over her lips, a gesture asking for silence.

"Not now," he commanded softly. "We have all the time in the world for questions, tomorrow."

He felt her tongue moisten her lips and touch his finger in doing so. She quieted. Shortly, she slept deeply, her body open and vulnerable to his touch and his curious gaze.

Though he felt as if he'd known this woman forever, seeing her naked on his bed was a new experience. Zayn's chest swelled with the tightness of possession. She was a unique and exotic jewel, more precious to him than any person he'd ever known.

He sat up, leaning across her hips, his hand propped against the firm mattress beside her. He watched her face, soft and beautiful and angelic in sleep. Her golden hair tangled and spilled around her, a cloud of silken softness unmatchable by anything man could make. He bent his head and kissed the sweet rosy peak of her breast.

Her skin felt cool to his touch. Zayn rose and caught the sheet, spreading it out across her. He went about the room, switching off the lights one by one. Last, he knelt briefly on his rug facing Mecca and thanked Allah for giving him safe passage, for blessing his days, for giving him light at Anaiza and granting him forty days in the desert with Haley Bennett.

Ravenous with hunger, Zayn rang for Ali and ordered a meal to be served him in his study. At his desk he sat and sorted his mail, setting the most important aside. He picked up the phone and began to make the round of telephone calls, to New York, London, Paris, Athens, contacting his brothers and a daunting number of uncles the world over.

From his top drawer he removed the file he'd composed when he'd last sat at this chair to tally who was missing, known dead, captured. It was detailed, family first, then friends, neighbors, working associates, servants.

To his great relief, his secretary had annotated his list and logged all the data into his computer. Also attached to the file was a personal letter from the exiled Kuwaiti minister of statistics, thanking Zayn for his courageous effort in bringing out of their besieged country the master lists of all public records regarding Kuwait citizenship.

Zayn smiled wryly as he laid aside his file. It wasn't he who had so courageously raided the mainframe at the ministry of statistics. Haley had copied all of that so vital for reconstruction information. Zayn simply hadn't had the time. If the day came that Kuwait was ever autonomous again, it would be Haley who deserved his government's gratitude.

It was 8:00 a.m., when Ali came with the meal and served him. "I have taken the liberty of summoning your secretary, my sheik."

Ali opened a steaming lid and placed a gold-edged plate piled with sausages and a spicy omelet before Zayn. "Your father bids me tell you that he will most graciously wait until you have eaten before he will see you."

"Thank you, Ali, I am famished. You should have told my father to come and join me." Zayn relaxed as Ali filled his cup with fragrant coffee. "Make certain you have a pot of coffee taken to Haley when she wakes up."

"Issaeyaedea Haaris has already risen, my sheik. She asked for breakfast early and requested a car and driver. She apprised me that she was most concerned regarding her clothing and does not want to meet your family in the dirty garments of the desert."

The coffee cup in Zayn's hand dropped with a clank onto the saucer. "What did you say?"

Ali raised alarmed eyes, instantly taking a cloth to mop up the spill before the hot liquid could touch the sheik's white robe, and repeated his words.

"Ali, you gave that woman access to an automobile?" Zayn bounded to his feet.

"I do not see what the problem is, my sheik." Ali's dark face paled. Zayn swore vehemently, knocking his chair aside as he moved away from the table.

"My sheik, what about your meal?"

"Take it away," he answered, running blindly through the rooms, leaping over small obstacles. He threw open both doors to his bedroom, sending them crashing resoundingly against the walls. *She couldn't have left him!*

There were no lights on. The sun flooded in through the east-facing windows. The bed was rumpled and empty. The glass doors stood open, the morning wind rifling the sheers.

"Haley!"

Zayn's voice echoed emptily against the walls, resounding in the deserted bath, filtering down the courtyard and past the garages. He bolted, running out the open glass partitions. Inside the garage, all the stalls were full except one. His Mercedes sedan was missing. The overhead doors behind it were wide open. She was gone.

# Chapter 20

*November 17, 1990*

"You think Matt's gonna limp forever?" Katie Bennett asked her younger sister as Matt loomed into view in the glass windows outside the company lunchroom.

"Naw, he hobbles to get sympathy," the oldest of the three Bennett sisters, Margie, yawned. "Doesn't want Dad's bullet to get all the glory."

"I know." Haley picked up a chip from the square of waxed paper between them, then put it back. It may have been lunchtime, but she had no appetite. "Doc Tipton say's he'll get over it."

"But cranky, boy howdy!" Katie complained. "If he doesn't get off my back, I'm going to take another two weeks of vacation. So, Haley, how did you get out of Saudi Arabia?"

"Well..." Haley demurred. Her natural drawl was back in place, but that was the only thing about her that hadn't seemed to have changed completely. "You know, I've only been over this a hundred and fifty times. I should have taped it."

"Or Katie should have canceled her vacation and been home to meet you," Margie chided Katie for not being home.

"I couldn't get a flight out of the Virgin Islands," Katie tried to justify her absence at Haley's homecoming. "It's not like I didn't try. Do you have any idea what it's like to exchange tickets on a package tour? I was so desperate, I asked Dad to send a plane after me. You should have heard what he said about that." Katie dropped her voice several octaves. "'You've got to be kidding. All my pilots are grounded.' So, tell me. How did you escape?"

Haley sighed. She didn't fault Katie for not being home. She understood how difficulties came up when one went traveling abroad. That didn't mean she wanted to go back over all the minute details of her adventure one more time. It was just too painful to keep opening the wound. But when Katie just sat there with an expectant look on her freckled face, waiting for some kind of answer, Haley said, "I borrowed Sheik Haaris' Mercedes and drove to Riyadh."

"Alone?"

"Sort of. Actually, I found a kindred soul in a little village on the way to the capital. A widow who ran her own clothing shop and longed to be liberated. She volunteered her son to drive me the rest of the way to the airport and escort me to the plane. I had to have an *abba*—you know, that black cape Saudi women wear over their clothes. Things just sort of escalated from there."

"You are so resourceful," Margie admitted. "I would never have thought of doing that. I've only got one question. How long are you going to wait before you tell Mom and Dad the real truth?"

Katie's green eyes widened. Her tousled red head bobbed forward in interest. "What *real truth?*"

"Thanks, Margie. Start an uproar, why don't you?"

"*Me* start an uproar? Kid, you've cornered the market on it. Dad's right. You've got to settle down."

"Well, I like that," Haley said with not as much good-natured grace as she had exhibited in the past. Her sisters' ribbing too often came too close to exposing the raw hurts Haley kept well hidden from her parents.

The door of the lunchroom burst open. "Haley!" Tommy Bennett bellowed to the rafters. "Get downstairs! You're wanted in Dad's office PDQ."

All three sisters exchanged looks.

Haley shrugged, rising from her seat, explaining the unasked question between them. "I'm pretty sure I'm all caught up with work. I even got that mess with the three crop dusters straightened out."

"Hurry up, will ya!" Tommy barked. "We can't get anything done with you around here."

Haley gritted her teeth, withholding comment. In this domain of Bennetts, she existed at the bottom of the pecking order. She hurried downstairs, passing through the crush of ongoing projects, technicians and scattered tools. Jane, her dad's secretary, didn't even look up when Haley entered.

"Go on in. He's waiting."

"Thanks." Haley pushed open the door to the inner sanctum. Her dad's office was four times the size of her cramped, crowded and cluttered space. But she was her father's daughter through and through. He had as much junk piled up waiting for his attention as she did. Busy meant clutter. Haley was glad to be busy. It kept her from hovering in front of CNN, breathlessly waiting the next broadcast from the Mideast.

"Sit down, kid." Jim Bennett had an ear to the phone. Haley moved his three-toed yellow cat and sat down. The cat padded out the door.

At intervals, her dad said, "Yeah, yeah, I got it. Right. Yeah. Okay, I'll get back to you as soon as I've got an answer." Then he hung up the phone.

Haley straightened a bit in her seat, smiling, accepting his rather confused stare. Since no words were forthcoming, she prompted, "Tommy said you wanted to see me."

"Yeah." Jim Bennett cocked his head to the side, studying her some more.

"Well?"

"Yeah, well, I guess I'm kind of confused."

"Confused about what?"

"Confused about why you hadn't told your mother and I what went on in Kuwait and Saudi Arabia."

"I did tell you."

Jim paused, rubbing broad red fingers across his chin, his jaw tugging his mouth sideways. "Everything?"

"Most of it. What I remember."

"Selective memory, huh?"

"Dad, come on. It's over. What's the problem?"

"Well," he drawled, shifting through the stacks of papers piled so high Haley couldn't see his phone or the keyboard of his computer. "I've got a letter here, somewhere, telling me some strange things."

"What things?"

"I've got a bill here for a forty-thousand-dollar Mercedes...a warrant for your arrest for two counts of auto theft...two misdemeanor felonies for traveling cross-country without permission...an extradition order for leaving Saudi Arabia without your husband's permission... That's right...it says *husband*. Ah...you want to clue me in on this?" Jim's bland tone vanished and he shouted. "What the hell is going on?"

Haley flinched. "You're kidding me."

"Do I look like I'm kidding you?"

"No."

Jim said nothing. He stared at his daughter, then dropped his hand on his desk, exasperated. "You know what, kid?"

"No."

"You're fired. You can take the rest of the day off. Go home. Sit down at the damned kitchen table and tell your mother what the hell is going on with you so that when I get home she can explain to me how in Sam Hill the mind of a twenty-four-year-old female works."

"Am I really fired?"

"Until I get some kind of explanation that makes sense, you damn sure are. Let the door hit you where the good Lord split you."

"Well, that's gratitude for you. After I did all of Margie's work and my own and got Matt's overload caught up, too. I've been working like a dog the whole damn month since I've been home. Fat lot you care."

"Yeah, well, you had three months' playtime in the desert before that, remember. Get gone!"

"I'm outta here!" Haley snapped right back.

"You better go straight home if you know what's good for you."

Haley stalked out of her dad's office. Jane's usually bent head was up as Haley passed the secretary's desk. Uncle Jack was lounging against the doorframe, blocking it.

"What are you doing here, Uncle Jack?"

"Oh, I'm riding shotgun. Got orders to take you home."

Haley swung around, searching the anteroom. Her dad leaned out his door looking like thunder had already struck him. "Well, let's go then. Take me home."

Riding passenger in the company truck, Haley didn't have a good word to say. Jack asked a few questions, but got no answers. He pulled up the curved driveway of the big hacienda-style house on Contour Drive, idling under the shade of a live oak. "Tell your mother howdy."

"Will do." Haley pushed open the door. She paused, letting the November heat rush at her face, and met Jack's questioning gaze. "What?"

"I didn't say nothing, Haley girl," he said. "That don't mean I don't think you ought to come clean and tell everybody what you did."

"I didn't do anything wrong, Jack."

"Well, I don't know. You married a man and you left him. That ain't exactly nothing, Haley. Judging from what I'm hearing round the plant...sounds to me like there's a kid on the way, too. You're gonna have to do some explaining sometime."

Haley shrugged as if she didn't care. "It happens. Getting pregnant's no big shotgun deal anymore."

"You know that for a fact?"

Haley looked away, remembering the last time Zayn had made love to her. She didn't want that memory dragged out again either. She took a deep breath and said in a civil voice, "See ya tomorrow, Jack."

She walked up the wide, terraced path to the house, swinging open the front door. As always, the house was dark and cool inside, the thick stucco walls a natural barrier to Texas heat. Haley kicked off her shoes and plodded barefoot down the polished tile floor.

"Mom, I'm home."

"Is that you, Haley? Your dad called and told me you were coming." Emma Bennett's voice drifted from the direction of the kitchen. "I'm on the sun porch having coffee. Come join me."

Haley paused at the dining-room table to look through the day's mail, grumbling because there weren't any letters from halfway across the world for her. But her dad could get arrest warrants and bills for Mercedeses that were sitting in airport parking lots! She resumed walking, tugging her shirt out of the waist of her jeans, pulling the rubber band from the back of her head as she entered the kitchen. She stopped at the refrigerator and opened it, the light illuminating a loaded interior with absolutely nothing she wanted to eat. She pulled a handful of washed grapes from a bowl.

"Dad's on a tear," she called as she approached the sun-room by way of explaining her earlier-than-normal return home. "He fired me," she said as she entered the room.

"Again? Well, I can't say I'm surprised." Emma smiled and looked at the man seated beside her. "I believe no introductions are necessary. Haley, I am very disappointed that you did not tell me you married this fine young man."

Haley gasped. "Zayn? What are you doing here?"

Emma remained seated as Zayn rose to his feet.

Haley swallowed, staring hard at the tall man, unable to believe her eyes. Zayn was here…in her mother's sun-room…the wild, natural garden blooming with late crape myrtles and calla lilies at his back. She couldn't fault his suit or the immaculate shirt. His eyes held hers fixed. But he didn't say anything.

Awkwardly, she dropped the grapes onto the table.

"Why?"

Zayn took a deep breath. "That is my question, Haley."

Emma cleared her throat and rose from her cushioned seat. "You will have to forgive me, both of you. I sense you need to talk. I'll tend my roses."

Emma excused herself, taking up sun hat, gardening gloves and pruning sheers, and retreated to her sun-dappled garden.

Deserted, except for Zayn's overpowering presence, Haley felt as gauche as a kid. She didn't know what to do with her hands and was at a complete loss for what to say. The distance between them was only a few feet, but it was the most formidable chasm she'd ever faced. Remembering her manners at last, she waved to the chair he'd vacated.

"Please, sit down. Make yourself comfortable."

"Am I welcome here?" Zayn asked.

"Of course, of course you are. I…I…I just never expected you would come here." She folded her arms together, gripping her elbows, to stop herself from throwing her arms around him.

"It is not so far away. You have a beautiful home and a gracious mother," Zayn replied. He took a second deep breath. "Do you want me to leave?"

Haley's hands dropped to her sides. "Oh, no, no. Please don't. Just let me look at you. You look so...so fine, so beautiful and strong. Just the way I remember."

"I, too, have been haunted by memories, Haale.' Have you no better greeting for me? Will you not come to me and give me a kiss of welcome?"

Haley moistened her dry, nervous lips, helplessly shaking her head. "I don't know if I should. Terrible things come over me when I am in your arms. I knew from the start that we were poorly matched, but I couldn't refuse you a kiss, or anything else you ever wanted from me."

A wry smile turned the corners of Zayn's mouth. He had seen her maneuver through the same reluctance before, repeat almost the same words in trying to deny her attraction to him. It troubled him to have come this great distance to see her and she couldn't or wouldn't bridge the final gap between them. "I have asked for a lot from you, Haley Bennett, but I want much, much more."

His hands opened at his sides. "Come. Do not be afraid of the love I bring to you."

"What?" Haley's knees buckled. She caught hold of the edge of the table, her knuckles turning white with pressure as she gripped it. "What did you say?"

"I asked that you not be afraid of the love I bring you."

A tremor rocked up her spine, causing her head to wobble slightly. The declaration of love almost sent her rushing into his arms. But she stopped herself, holding back. Her voice was a choking whisper when she spoke. "What about your... other...women, wives? Zayn, I love you so much I cannot share you with someone else. I could take anything else, most of it, but I cannot share you with other women."

"Is that why you left me, Haley?" He pushed the chair he'd been sitting in back under the table, removing its obstruction from his path. Slowly, he walked toward her.

Haley backed up.

"Answer me, Haley Bennett. It is very important that I know the reason you left me. Was it because you thought I had other wives?"

"Don't you? I was told that I should consider myself fortunate." Haley realized he was not waiting for her to come to him. He was prepared to come all the way to her. She stopped retreating and said, "Do you have other wives?"

"No." Zayn stopped when the tips of his polished shoes braced the edge of her bare feet. "I have never taken a wife until I asked you to marry me."

Haley stared into his obsidian eyes. "Never?"

"Never," he repeated somberly. "You are the first and only wife I shall ever have, Haale. There is no room in my heart or my life for another. Is that why you left me, Haley?"

She felt the terrible weight that had rested on her heart for so long lift as she nodded her head and whispered, "Yes, that is one reason why I left you."

"What were the others?" he asked calmly.

"Because the adventure was over. When you asked to marry me, you said it was not for keeps. I didn't want to become a burden to you or keep you from doing what you needed to do."

Zayn reached forward, taking a loose hold of the waist of her jeans, grazing his thumbs on the cotton-covered skin above her belt line.

"At the time I asked you to marry me, I believed it was a dire necessity that I take you with me. I thought my reasons were for the sake of my family and my country, but that was not true. I couldn't bear to be parted from you. I wanted you and was afraid that if I did not keep you with me at all times, I would lose you forever."

His hands tightened at her waist, but the gap between their bodies remained the same.

"I have waited patiently all my life for you, Haley Bennett. Once Allah put you into my hands, I could wait no longer. Forgive me."

"Oh, Zayn, you'll never know how glad I am that you have come for me at last." Haley burst forward, into his arms, desperate for the healing feel of his strength surrounding her. She caught his face with trembling hands and kissed with all the hunger that had tormented her every lonely day at home.

Zayn's grip was equally fierce, possessive, holding her tall, slender body tight against his own, feeling how perfectly she matched him, vowing to never let her go again. The searing heat of their mouths joining drove him wild. He had to catch her face and set her back slightly to maintain his control. There were tears in Haley's eyes.

"I did not think you would want me back once it was over," she said. "I was so selfish, from the very first day to the last, thinking only of myself and my needs. I was a terrible, spoiled brat. I was ashamed of all the trouble I had caused you. Even when I had to give Kasim back to his family, I wanted to keep him because I wanted to go on loving him. I was a coward. Afraid your family would hate me. Afraid that I would have to compete against other women who would know you better. I'm sorry if I hurt you."

"Haley, you were brave and courageous. You were never without nerve or willingness to go on against all odds. I was proud of you."

"But I made you suffer unnecessarily. I could never be honest and tell you that I loved you because I feared you would laugh at me . . . And I have another confession."

"I will understand if you tell me you do not want an Arab husband." Zayn held her firmly by the waist, steeling himself for the final blow. He had come to her, seen her, assured himself that she was safe and well. She was loved and adored by her family. He could be satisfied with that if he had to be.

"No, no, it isn't that." Haley's head moved back and forth denying his words. "I love you with all my heart. I was more afraid of that than anything I have ever experienced in my life. My heart will break if you tell me you do not want to take me back with you."

"I will take you anywhere in the world that you want to live. Lisbon, London, Athens, New York, even here if that is your desire."

"Anaiza?" Haley asked.

"We will always have Anaiza, Haley. It is my winter home. But I am not a man who is limited anywhere and so long as there are planes to fly . . . the sky is my Summan . . ." His voice trailed off as his lips sought hers more tenderly.

"Oh!" Haley sighed.

One long, lingering kiss later, Zayn set her firmly back from him and took her left hand in his. From his pocket he withdrew the gold band she had left on his vanity. His eyes met hers, boring into the depths of her soul. "From this moment forward, I give you my name, my honor, my wealth, my soul, all my worldly goods and my love within my heart. Do you freely accept all that I am, Haley Bennett?''

"I do accept you, Zayn Haaris.''

"Forsaking all others?''

"Yes.''

"Will you live with me, go where I go, follow my nomadic life through change and sometimes turmoil?''

"Yes.''

"Will you give me children?''

At that question, Haley stiffened, her eyes widening. "I—I didn't tell you,'' Haley stammered. "I think . . . I am pregnant already.''

Zayn's face flushed, then he took a deep breath and said. "*Inshallah.* May we have all the children God will grant us.''

"Amen.'' Haley grinned.

"Then I can ask for nothing more. I am honored to take you to wife, Haley Jane Bennett.''

Haley was dazed for a moment, her gaze captured by the gold band circling her finger once again. Then she raised her chin and looked into the dark pools of Zayn's eyes. She knew she would never, ever be happier than she was that moment. He proved her wrong a moment later when he kissed her and unleashed the full force of his devastating power, to ignite all her senses at once.

It might have gone on forever until they abandoned all good sense and made love on the floor, except a rough voice cleared itself loudly and shattered Zayn's concentration.

"I hate to break up this here party of two, but is it possible, Haji Haaris, that you could let go of my daughter for ten minutes' time and explain to me just what the hell is going on here in my sun-room?''

Haley was oblivious to most of her father's speech, until he got to the point where he was shouting about what the hell was going on. She bounded out of Zayn's arms, her face coloring, not even able to remember how they'd gotten so deeply entwined. Zayn needed a moment to compose himself before facing Jim Bennett.

"In all honesty,'' Zayn said, tucking Haley's trembling hand into the crook of his arm, "I am in the process of seducing my wife once again. I hope that meets with your approval, Mr. Bennett.''

"Well, I'll be damned," Jim drawled. "Wait till I tell Jack this news."

As abruptly as he'd arrived, Jim Bennett about-faced and left them. Haley slapped a hand over her mouth to suppress a giggle.

"What's that laugh about?"

"Jack already knows," Haley replied.

"You explained what I am to you to another man, but not to your mother and father?"

"Well," Haley drawled, "I told my sisters all about you, and my mother all the censored parts. You know, if I'd told my brothers or my dad that you'd broken my heart, you'd have had to marry me Texas-style."

"And what is marriage Texas-style?"

"With a rifle in your back."

Zayn gave a loud whoop as he caught Haley up in his arms and twirled her around. "That is a custom stolen from the Bedouin."

Haley wrapped her arms around his shoulders and bent her head to kiss him. The spinning stopped the moment her lips touched his. Zayn slowly let her slide down his body so that their kiss could deepen naturally. His odyssey to find his vixen was over. Haley Bennett was now truly his. No matter what the future held, so long as his Haley loved him, life would be very, very good. No man on earth could ask for more.

\* \* \* \* \*

Author's note: This is a work of fiction.

# As seen on TV!
## *Free Gift Offer*

With a Free Gift proof-of-purchase from any Silhouette® book,
you can receive a beautiful cubic zirconia pendant.

This gorgeous marquise-shaped stone is a genuine cubic
zirconia—accented by an 18" gold tone necklace.

(Approximate retail value $19.95)

## Send for yours today…
## compliments of ▼ *Silhouette*®
<sub>TM</sub>

To receive your free gift, a cubic zirconia pendant, send us one original proof-of-
purchase, photocopies not accepted, from the back of any Silhouette Romance™,
Silhouette Desire®, Silhouette Special Edition®, Silhouette Intimate Moments®
or Silhouette Yours Truly™ title available in August, September, October, November and
December at your favorite retail outlet, together with the Free Gift Certificate, plus a
check or money order for $1.65 U.S./$2.15 CAN. (do not send cash) to cover postage and
handling, payable to Silhouette Free Gift Offer. We will send you the specified gift. Allow
6 to 8 weeks for delivery. Offer good until December 31, 1996 or while quantities last.
Offer valid in the U.S. and Canada only.

## *Free Gift Certificate*

Name: _____

Address: _____

City: _____ State/Province: _____ Zip/Postal Code: _____

Mail this certificate, one proof-of-purchase and a check or money order for postage
and handling to: SILHOUETTE FREE GIFT OFFER 1996. In the U.S.: 3010 Walden
Avenue, P.O. Box 9077, Buffalo NY 14269-9077. In Canada: P.O. Box 613, Fort Erie,
Ontario L2Z 5X3.

---

### FREE GIFT OFFER                                084-KMD
ONE PROOF-OF-PURCHASE
To collect your fabulous FREE GIFT, a cubic zirconia pendant, you must include this
original proof-of-purchase for each gift with the properly completed Free Gift Certificate.

---

084-KMD-R

## FAST CASH 4031 DRAW RULES
## NO PURCHASE OR OBLIGATION NECESSARY

Fifty prizes of $50 each will be awarded in random drawings to be conducted no later than 3/28/97 from amongst all eligible responses to this prize offer received as of 2/14/97. To enter, follow directions, affix 1st-class postage and mail OR write Fast Cash 4031 on a 3" x 5" card along with your name and address and mail that card to: Harlequin's Fast Cash 4031 Draw, P.O. Box 1395, Buffalo, NY 14240-1395 OR P.O. Box 618, Fort Erie, Ontario L2A 5X3. (Limit: one entry per outer envelope; all entries must be sent via 1st-class mail.) Limit: one prize per household. Odds of winning are determined by the number of eligible responses received. Offer is open only to residents of the U.S. (except Puerto Rico) and Canada and is void wherever prohibited by law. All applicable laws and regulations apply. Any litigation within the province of Quebec respecting the conduct and awarding of a prize in this sweepstakes maybe submitted to the Régie des alcools, des courses et des jeux. In order for a Canadian resident to win a prize, that person will be required to correctly answer a time-limited arithmetical skill-testing question to be administered by mail. Names of winners available after 4/28/97 by sending a self-addressed, stamped envelope to: Fast Cash 4031 Draw Winners, P.O. Box 4200, Blair, NE 68009-4200.

## OFFICIAL RULES
## MILLION DOLLAR SWEEPSTAKES
## NO PURCHASE NECESSARY TO ENTER

1.  To enter, follow the directions published. Method of entry may vary. For eligibility, entries must be received no later than March 31, 1998. No liability is assumed for printing errors, lost, late, non-delivered or misdirected entries.

    To determine winners, the sweepstakes numbers assigned to submitted entries will be compared against a list of randomly pre-selected prize winning numbers. In the event all prizes are not claimed via the return of prize winning numbers, random drawings will be held from among all other entries received to award unclaimed prizes.

2.  Prize winners will be determined no later than June 30, 1998. Selection of winning numbers and random drawings are under the supervision of D. L. Blair, Inc., an independent judging organization whose decisions are final. Limit: one prize to a family or organization. No substitution will be made for any prize, except as offered. Taxes and duties on all prizes are the sole responsibility of winners. Winners will be notified by mail. Odds of winning are determined by the number of eligible entries distributed and received.

3.  Sweepstakes open to residents of the U.S. (except Puerto Rico), Canada and Europe who are 18 years of age or older, except employees and immediate family members of Torstar Corp., D. L. Blair, Inc., their affiliates, subsidiaries, and all other agencies, entities, and persons connected with the use, marketing or conduct of this sweepstakes. All applicable laws and regulations apply. Sweepstakes offer void wherever prohibited by law. Any litigation within the province of Quebec respecting the conduct and awarding of a prize in this sweepstakes must be submitted to the Régie des alcools, des courses et des jeux. In order to win a prize, residents of Canada will be required to correctly answer a time-limited arithmetical skill-testing question to be administered by mail.

4.  Winners of major prizes (Grand through Fourth) will be obligated to sign and return an Affidavit of Eligibility and Release of Liability within 30 days of notification. In the event of non-compliance within this time period or if a prize is returned as undeliverable, D. L. Blair, Inc. may at its sole discretion award that prize to an alternate winner. By acceptance of their prize, winners consent to use of their names, photographs or other likeness for purposes of advertising, trade and promotion on behalf of Torstar Corp., its affiliates and subsidiaries, without further compensation unless prohibited by law. Torstar Corp. and D. L. Blair, Inc., their affiliates and subsidiaries are not responsible for errors in printing of sweepstakes and prizewinning numbers. In the event a duplication of a prizewinning number occurs, a random drawing will be held from among all entries received with that prizewinning number to award that prize.

SWP-S12ZD1

5. This sweepstakes is presented by Torstar Corp., its subsidiaries and affiliates in conjunction with book, merchandise and/or product offerings. The number of prizes to be awarded and their value are as follows: Grand Prize — $1,000,000 (payable at $33,333.33 a year for 30 years); First Prize — $50,000; Second Prize — $10,000; Third Prize — $5,000; 3 Fourth Prizes — $1,000 each; 10 Fifth Prizes — $250 each; 1,000 Sixth Prizes — $10 each. Values of all prizes are in U.S. currency. Prizes in each level will be presented in different creative executions, including various currencies, vehicles, merchandise and travel. Any presentation of a prize level in a currency other than U.S. currency represents an approximate equivalent to the U.S. currency prize for that level, at that time. Prize winners will have the opportunity of selecting any prize offered for that level; however, the actual non U.S. currency equivalent prize, if offered and selected, shall be awarded at the exchange rate existing at 3:00 P.M. New York time on March 31, 1998. A travel prize option, if offered and selected by winner, must be completed within 12 months of selection and is subject to: traveling companion(s) completing and returning a Release of Liability prior to travel; and hotel and flight accommodations availability. For a current list of all prize options offered within prize levels, send a self-addressed, stamped envelope (WA residents need not affix postage) to: MILLION DOLLAR SWEEPSTAKES Prize Options, P.O. Box 4456, Blair, NE 68009-4456, USA.

6. For a list of prize winners (available after July 31, 1998) send a separate, stamped, self-addressed envelope to: MILLION DOLLAR SWEEPSTAKES Winners, P.O. Box 4459, Blair, NE 68009-4459, USA.

### EXTRA BONUS PRIZE DRAWING
### NO PURCHASE OR OBLIGATION NECESSARY TO ENTER

7. The Extra Bonus Prize will be awarded in a random drawing to be conducted no later than 5/30/98 from among all entries received. To qualify, entries must be received by 3/31/98 and comply with published directions. Prize ($50,000) is valued in U.S. currency. Prize will be presented in different creative expressions, including various currencies, vehicles, merchandise and travel. Any presentation in a currency other than U.S. currency represents an approximate equivalent to the U.S. currency value at that time. Prize winner will have the opportunity of selecting any prize offered in any presentation of the Extra Bonus Prize Drawing; however, the actual non U.S. currency equivalent prize, if offered and selected by winner, shall be awarded at the exchange rate existing at 3:00 P.M. New York time on March 31, 1998. For a current list of prize options offered, send a self-addressed, stamped envelope (WA residents need not affix postage) to: Extra Bonus Prize Options, P.O. Box 4462, Blair, NE 68009-4462, USA. All eligibility requirements and restrictions of the MILLION DOLLAR SWEEPSTAKES apply. Odds of winning are dependent upon number of eligible entries received. No substitution for prize except as offered. For the name of winner (available after 7/31/98), send a self-addressed, stamped envelope to: Extra Bonus Prize Winner, P.O. Box 4463, Blair, NE 68009-4463, USA.

SWP-S12ZD2

# COMING NEXT MONTH